**Praise for *New York Times* bestselling author
Heather Graham**

"An incredible storyteller."

—*Los Angeles Daily News*

"[Heather] Graham has the uncanny ability to
bring her books to life, using exceptionally vivid
details to add depth to all the people and places."
—*RT Book Reviews*, Top Pick, on *Waking the Dead*

"Once again, Heather Graham has outdone
herself… This chilling novel has everything:
suspense, romance, intrigue and an ending that
takes your breath away."

—*Suspense Magazine* on *The Betrayed*

**Praise for *USA TODAY* bestselling author
Tara Taylor Quinn**

"[Tara Taylor] Quinn writes touching stories
about real people that transcend plot type or
genre."

—*All About Romance*

"Readers will enjoy Quinn's easy-to-love
characters, mysterious plot and sweet romance as
they quickly turn the pages."
—*RT Book Reviews* on *Once Upon a Friendship*

New York Times and *USA TODAY* bestselling author **Heather Graham** has written more than a hundred novels, many of which have been featured by the Doubleday Book Club and the Literary Guild. An avid scuba diver, ballroom dancer and mother of five, she still enjoys her south Florida home, but loves to travel, as well, from locations such as Cairo, Egypt, to her own backyard, the Florida Keys. Reading, however, is the pastime she still loves best, and she is a member of many writing groups. She's the winner of a Romance Writers of America Lifetime Achievement Award and a Thriller Writers' Silver Bullet. She is an active member of International Thriller Writers and Mystery Writers of America, and also the founder of The Slush Pile Players, an author band and theatrical group. Heather hosts the annual Writers for New Orleans conference to benefit both the city, which is near and dear to her heart, and various other causes, and she hosts a ball each year at the RT Booklovers Convention to benefit pediatric AIDS foundations.

For more information, check out her website, www.theoriginalheathergraham.com. You can also find Heather on Facebook.

An author of more than seventy novels, **Tara Taylor Quinn** is a *USA TODAY* bestselling author with more than seven million copies sold. She is known for delivering emotional and psychologically astute novels of suspense and romance. Tara is a past president of Romance Writers of America. She has won a Readers' Choice Award and is a five-time finalist for an RWA RITA® Award, a finalist for a Reviewers' Choice Award and a Booksellers' Best Award. She has also appeared on TV across the country, including *CBS Sunday Morning*. She supports the National Domestic Violence Hotline. If you or someone you know might be a victim of domestic violence in the United States, please contact 1-800-799-7233.

New York Times Bestselling Author

HEATHER GRAHAM

STRANGERS IN PARADISE

HARLEQUIN®BESTSELLING AUTHOR COLLECTION

ISBN-13: 978-0-373-01038-7

Strangers in Paradise

Copyright © 2016 by Harlequin Books S.A.

The publisher acknowledges the copyright holders
of the individual works as follows:

Strangers in Paradise
Copyright © 1988 by Heather Graham Pozzessere

Sheltered in His Arms
Copyright © 2001 by Tara Taylor Quinn

Recycling programs
for this product may
not exist in your area.

Printed in U.S.A.

CONTENTS

Also by HEATHER GRAHAM

* * * * *

Look for Heather Graham's next novel
HAUNTED DESTINY
available now from MIRA Books

STRANGERS IN PARADISE

Heather Graham

Prologue

June 2, 1863
Fernandina Beach, Florida

"Miz Eugenia! Miz Eugenia! Look!"

Eugenia straightened, easing the pain in her back, and stared out through the long trail of pines to the distant beach, where Mary's call directed her. Her sewing fell unheeded to her feet; she rose, her heart pounding, her soul soaring, dizzy with incredulity and relief.

A man was alighting from a small skiff. The waves on the beach pounded against his high black cavalry boots as he splashed through the water. From a distance, he was beautiful and perfect.

"Pierre!" Upon the porch of the old house, Eugenia whispered his name, afraid to voice it too loudly lest he disappear. She wanted so badly for him to be real and not a fantasy created by the summer's heat, by the shimmering waves of sun pounding against the scrub and sand.

"Pierre!"

He was real. Tall and regal in his handsome uniform of butternut and gray, with his medals reflecting the sun. He was far away, but Eugenia was certain that he saw her, certain that his blue hawk's eyes had met her own and that the love they shared sang and soared likewise in his soul.

He started to run down the sand path, which was carpeted in pine needles and shaded by branches. Sun and shadow, shadow and sun—she could no longer see his face clearly, but she gave a glad cry and leaped down the steps, clutching her heavy spill of skirts in her hand so that she could run, too—run to meet her beautiful man in his butternut and gray and hurl herself into his arms.

Sunlight continued to glitter through the trees, golden as it fell upon her love. She felt the carpet of sand and pine under her feet, and the great rush of her breath. She could see the fine planes and lines of his features, the intelligence and tenderness in his eyes. She could see the strain in his face as he, too, ran, and she could see the love he bore for her, the need to touch.

"Pierre…"

"Eugenia!" He nearly wept her name. She flew the last few steps, those steps that brought her into his arms. He lifted her high and swirled her beneath the sun. He stared into her face, trembling, cherishing the mere fact that he could look upon her, and she was beautiful.

Eugenia saw that in truth he was not perfect. His butternut and gray were tattered and worn, there were slashes in his handsome boots, and his medals were rusted and dark.

"Oh, Pierre!" Eugenia cried, not so much from his uniform as from the strain that lined his handsome face. "Tell me! What has happened? Pierre, why are you here? Is something wrong?"

"Are you not glad to see your husband?" he charged her.

"Ever so glad! But—"

"No, Eugenia! No buts, no words. Just hold me. And I'll hold you, tenderly, this night. Tenderly, with all my love."

He carried her back along that path of softest pine and gentle sand. His eyes held hers, drinking in the sight of her so desperately. And she, in turn, could not take her gaze from him, her cavalier. Pierre, handsome, magnificent, tender Pierre, with his fine eyes and clear-cut features and beautiful golden hair. Pierre, scarred and hard and wounded and sometimes bitter, but ever gentle to her, his bride.

They reached the house. Mary mumbled something in welcome, and Pierre gave her a dazzling smile. He paused to give her a hug, to ask after his infant son, who was asleep in Mary's old, gnarled arms. Tears came to Mary's eyes, but she winked back as Pierre winked at her and asked if they might have dinner a wee bit late that night.

Eugenia was still in his arms as he kicked open the screen door with his foot. He knew the house by heart, for it was his house; he had built it. He did not need to look for the stairs; he walked to them easily, his eyes, with all their adoration, still boring into those of his wife. He climbed the stairs and took her to their room, and although they were the only ones on the barren peninsula, he locked the door.

And then he made love to her.

Desperately, Eugenia thought. So hungry, so hard, so fevered. She could not hold him tightly enough, she could not give enough, she could not sate him. He was a soldier, she reminded herself. A soldier, long gone from home, barely back from battle. But he touched her again and again, and he kissed her with a fascinated hunger, as if he had never known the taste of her lips before. He entwined his limbs with hers and held her, as if he could not bear to part.

"My love, my love," she whispered to him. She adored him in turn; sensed his needs, and she gave in to them, all. Stars lit the heavens again and again for her, and when he whispered apologies, thinking himself too rough, she hushed him and whispered in turn that he was the only lover she could ever want.

Dinner was very late. Pierre dandled his son on his knee while Mary served, and Mary and Eugenia did their best to speak lightly, to laugh, to entertain their soldier home from the war. Dinner was wonderful— broiled grouper in Mary's old Louisiana creole sauce, but Pierre had noted that fish was the diet because the domestic fowl were gone, and when Mary took their little boy up to bed, Eugenia was forced to admit that, yes, the Yankees had come again, and they had taken the chickens and the pigs and even old Gretchen, the mule. Pierre swore in fury, and then he stared at Eugenia with panic and accusation. She went to him, swearing that the Yanks had been gentlemen plunderers—none had shown her anything but respect.

She hesitated. "They'll not come here again. Even as they waltz in and out of Jacksonville. They won't come because—"

"Because of your father," Pierre supplied bitterly, referring to Eugenia's father, General George Drew of Baltimore. His home was being spared by the Yanks because his wife was one.

"Dammit," Pierre said simply. He sank back into his chair. With a cry of distress, Eugenia came to him, knelt at his feet and gripped his hands.

"I love you, Pierre. I love you so much!"

"You should go back to him."

"I will never leave you."

He lifted her onto his lap and cradled her there, holding her tight against the pulse of his heart. "I have to leave," he said softly. "The Old Man—General Lee—is determined to make a thrust northward. I have to be back in Richmond in forty-eight hours."

"Pierre, no! You've just—"

"I have to go back."

"You sound so…strange, Pierre." She tightened her arms around him.

"I'm frightened, my Genie, and I can't even describe why," he told her. "Not frightened of battle anymore, for I've been there too many times. I'm frightened…for the future."

"We shall win!"

He smiled, for his Northern-born belle had one loyalty: to his cause, whatever it should be.

An ocean breeze swept by him, drawing goose pimples to his flesh, and he knew. They would not win.

He buried his face against his wife's slender throat, inhaling her scent, feeling already the pain of parting. He held her fiercely. "You need not fear, Eugenia. I will provide for you—always. I've been careful. The money is in the house."

He whispered to her, though they were alone.

"Yes, yes, I will be fine—but I will not need anything. When this is over, we will be together, love."

"Yes, together, my love."

Eugenia loved him too well to tell him that she knew the South was dead. She did not tell him that the money he had hidden in the house, his Confederate currency, was as useless as the paper it had been printed on. He was her man, her provider. She would not tell him that he had provided her with ashes.

And he did not tell her that he felt a cold breeze, a cold, icy wind that whistled plaintively, like a ghost moaning and crying. Warning, foreboding. Whispering that death was ever near.

He took her in his arms and carried her up the stairs once again. Their eyes met.

They smiled, so tenderly, so lovingly.

"We're having another baby, Pierre."

"What?"

His arms tightened. She smiled sweetly, happy, pleased, smug.

"A baby, Pierre."

"My love!"

He kissed her reverently.

All through the night, he loved her reverently.

Pierre woke before Eugenia. Restless, he wrapped a sheet around himself and checked his hiding place, pulling the brick from the wall in silence.

A beautiful glitter greeted him. He inhaled and exhaled.

He had to go back to the war. He wanted to take his pregnant wife and his young son and disappear forever. But he was a soldier; he could not forsake his duty. He could assure himself, though, that whatever came, Eugenia would not want for anything.

He replaced the brick.

No, Eugenia would not want for anything.

Chapter 1

The fear she felt was terrible. It tore into her heart and her mind, and even into her soul. It paralyzed and mesmerized. With swift and stunning ease, it stole Alexi's breath, and as in a nightmare, she could not scream, for the sound would not come. She knew only that something touched her. Something had her.

And that it was flesh.

Flesh touched her, warm and vibrant. Flesh…that seemed to cover steel. Fingers that were long and compelled by some superhuman strength.

Flesh…

For what seemed like aeons, Alexi could do nothing but let the fact that she had been accosted sweep into her consciousness. It was so dark—she had never known a darkness so total as this night. No stars, no moon, no streetlights—she might have fallen off into a deep pit of eternal space, rather than onto the dusty floorboards of the decaying, historic house. She might be encountering anyone or anything, and all she recognized was...

Flesh. Searing and warm and frightfully powerful against her own. It had come so quickly. She had crawled through the window and the arms had swept around her, and she had been down and breathless and now, as fear curled into her like an evil, living thing, she could begin to feel the body and the muscle.

And she still couldn't scream. She couldn't bear force. She had known it before, and she had come here to escape the threat of it.

She tried for sound, desperately. A gasped whimper escaped from her—she knew that she was being subdued by a man. Even in the darkness, she knew instinctively that he was lean but wiry, that he was lithe and powerful. Her position was becoming ever more precarious. Her wrist was suddenly jerked and she was rolled, and there was more warmth, warmth and power all around her as she was suddenly laid flat, her back to the floor.

A thigh straddled roughly over her; she was suffocating.

Good God, fight!

She tried to emerge from the terror that encompassed her. Again she could feel heat and strength and tremendous, taut vitality. In the darkness she felt it— the fingers groping to find her other hand, to secure it so she would be powerless in the horrible darkness.

At last the paralysis broke. Sound burst from her, and she screamed. She could fight; she had learned to fight. Panic surged through her, and she twisted

and writhed, ferocious and desperate in her attempt
to escape.

She tried to kick, to wrench, to roll, to flail at the
body attacking her. Her voice rose hysterically, totally
incoherent. And she punched with all her strength, trying to slap, scratch, gouge—cause some injury. She
caught him hard in the chin.

He swore hoarsely. Belatedly she wondered if she
shouldn't have remained still. Who was he? What was
he doing in the house? She hadn't heard a thing, hadn't
seen a thing, and he had suddenly come down on top
of her. He was a thief, a robber...or a rapist or a murderer. And screaming probably wouldn't help her; here
she was, out in this godforsaken peninsula of blackness, yelling when there was no help to be had, struggling when she was bound to lose.

She screamed again anyway. And fought. He was
breathing harder; she knew it despite her own ragged
gulps for air. She could feel his breath against her
cheek, warm and scented with mint. She could feel
more of his body, hard against hers, as he silently and
competently worked to subdue her.

Flesh...

She felt more flesh against her wrists, and then he
had her again in a vise. She felt her hands dragged
swiftly and relentlessly high over her head, and she
knew that she was at the mercy of the dark entity in
the night.

No...

Tears stung her eyes. She had run too far for it to
come to this! With an incredible burst of energy, she
wrenched one hand free and sent it flying out full

force. She struck him, and she heard him grunt. And she heard his startled "Dammit!"

His arm snaked out in the blackness to catch and secure her wrist once again.

And then all she knew was the sound of breathing.

His, mildly labored, so close it touched her cheeks and her chin. Hers, maddened, ragged, racing gulps. Fear was a living thing. Parasitic, it raged inside of her, tore at her heart and her soul, and she couldn't do anything but lie there, imprisoned, thinking.

This was it. Death was near. She'd been desperate to run away, and now, for all her determination, she was going to die. She didn't know how yet. He might strangle her. Wind one hand around her throat and squeeze...

"Stop it! I don't want to hurt you! All right, now, don't move. Don't even think about moving. Do you understand?"

It was a husky voice. Harsh and coolly grating.

I don't want to hurt you. The words echoed in her mind, and she tried to comprehend them; she longed to trust him.

The darkness was so strange. She couldn't see, but she felt so acutely. She sensed, she felt, as he released her, as he balanced on his feet above her.

She was still shivering, still yearning to give way again to panic and strike out at him and run. She was dazed and she needed to think, desperately needed to be clever, and she could not come up with one rational thought. She could smell him so keenly in the black void of this world of fear, and that made her panic further, for his scent was pleasant, subtle, clean, like the salt breeze that came in from the ocean. She was so well-known for her reserve, for her cool thinking under pressure, and here she was, in stark, painful panic, when she most desperately needed a calculating mind. But how could she have imagined this situation? So close to that which she had run from, taking her so swiftly by surprise, stripping away all veneers and making her pathetically vulnerable.

Fight! she warned herself. Don't give up....

"Please..." She could barely form the whisper.

But then, quite suddenly, there was light. Brilliant and blinding and flooding over her features. She blinked against it, trying to see. She raised her arm to shield her eyes from the brutal radiance.

"Who are you?" the voice demanded.

Dear God, she wasn't *just* being attacked; she was being attacked by a thief or a murderer who asked questions. One of them was mad. She had every right to be! She was going to be living here. He had been prowling around in the darkness. He must have waited while she had fumbled with the door; he had stalked her in silence, watching while she came to the window and broke it to tumble inside—and into his ruthless hold.

She couldn't speak; she started to tremble.

"Who are you?" he raged again.

Harsh, stark, male, deliberate, demanding. She lost all sense of reason. Her arms were free. He had even moved back a little; his weight rested on his haunches rather than full against her hips.

"Arrgh!" Another sound escaped her, shrill with effort. He swore, but did not lose his balance. Alexi managed to do more than twist her skirt higher upon her hips and bring him harder against her as he struggled to maintain his new hold on both her wrists with one hand and keep the flashlight harsh against her face with the other.

She wanted to think; she kept shaking, and her words tore from her in gasping spurts. "Don't kill me. Please don't kill me."

"Kill you?"

"I'm worth money. Alive, I mean. Not dead. I'm really not worth a single red cent dead. My insurance isn't paid up. But I swear, if you'll just leave me—alive—I can make it worth your while. I—"

"Dammit, I'm not going to kill you. I'm trying very hard not to hurt you!"

She didn't dare feel relief. Still, sweeping sensations that left her weak coursed through her, and to her amazement, she heard her own voice again. "Who are you?"

"I asked first. And..." She could have sworn there was a touch of amusement in his voice. "And *you're* the one asking the favors."

She swallowed, stretching out her fingers. If he'd only move that horrible flashlight! Then she could think, could muster up a semblance of dignity and courage.

"Who the hell are you? I want an answer now," he demanded.

His fingers were so tight in their grip around her wrists. She clenched her teeth in sudden pain, aware of the fearsome power that held her.

"Alexi Jordan."

"You're not."

He had stated it so flatly that for a moment she herself wondered who else she might be.

"I am!"

He moved. The heat, the tight, vibrantly muscled hold he had on her body was gone; he was on his feet and was dragging her along with him.

"Ms. Jordan isn't due until tomorrow. Who are you? Speak up, now, or I'll call the police."

"The police?"

"Of course. You're trespassing."

"*You're* trespassing!"

"Let's call the police and find out."

"Yes! Let's do that!"

He was walking next, pulling her along. Alexi was blinded all over again when the light left her face to flash over the floor. She tried to wrench her hand away as the light played eerily over the spiderweb-dusted living room, with its shrouded sofa and chairs.

He wrenched her hand and she choked, then spewed forth a long series of oaths. She was close to sobs, ready to laugh and to cry. She should have been handling it all so much better.

"You'll go to jail for this!" she threatened.

"Really? Weren't you just asking me nicely not to kill you?"

She fell silent, jerked back against him, this unknown man, this stranger in the darkness. Her heart was pounding at a rapid, fluttering speed; she could feel its fevered pulse against the slower throb of his own, so close had he brought her to himself.

And she still didn't know his face—whether he was young or old, whether his eyes were blue or gray. She would never forget his voice or mistake it for another, she knew. The low, husky quality to the sure baritone. Cool and quiet and commanding...

And he had just said "kill." She was at his mercy and she had forgotten and lashed out in fury and now…

"What do you want?" she whispered, licking her lips.

She gasped as he lifted her; she landed upon the dusty sofa before she could protest again. He fell into the chair opposite her; she heard the movement, heard the old chair creak. The small splay of illumination from the flashlight fell upon her purse, which was in the hands that had so easily subdued her. She thought about bolting—but she could never make an escape. She could see the outline of his body. He was casually sprawled in the chair as he delved into her bag. She was still certain that he could move like the wind if she made any attempt to rise.

Alexi cleared her throat. It was only her purse, not her body. Despite that, despite her fear, she felt violated. "You don't—you can't…"

Her voice faded away, she could feel his eyes on her. She couldn't see him, but she could feel his eyes—compelling, scornful…amused?

"Five lipsticks? Brush, comb, pencil, pad, more lipstick, compact, keys, more lipstick, tissue, more lipstick—aha! At last, a wallet. And you are *really*… Alexi Jordan."

The light zoomed back to her face. Alexi bit her lip, reddening, and she didn't know why. If he was going to kill her, she didn't need to blush for her own murderer. But he had said something about calling the police. He had said that he didn't want to hurt her.

"Please…" she said.

He was silent. The light continued to play mercilessly over her features.

She was something out of a fairy tale, Rex decided, staring at her in the flood of light. Surely she was legendary. He barely noted that her eyes were still filled with terror; they were so incredibly green and wide. Tendrils of hair were escaping from a once-neat knot—hair caught by the light, hair that burned within that light like true spun gold. It wasn't pale, and it wasn't tawny; it was gold. It framed a face with the most perfect classical features he had ever seen. High, elegant cheekbones; small, straight nose; fine, determined chin; arching, honeyed brows. Even in total dishevelment, she was stunning. Her beauty was breathtaking. Stealing the heart, the senses, the mind...

He realized he was still standing there, thoughtlessly leveling the light into her eyes. At last he saw how badly she was shaking.

She was Alexi Jordan. Gene's granddaughter. Hell, he'd supposedly been guarding the place. He'd attacked her. He hadn't wanted her here—he hadn't wanted anyone here. But he sure as hell hadn't meant to battle it out with her. He opened his mouth to say something. Then he knew that it wouldn't be enough. He had to go to her, touch her. She was still so afraid.

Alexi gasped as fear again curled through her. The man was coming toward her. She cringed; he leaned over her, touched her cheek, then took her hand.

"My God, you're shaking like a leaf!"

"You, you—"

"I'm not going to hurt you!"

"You attacked me!"

"I had to know who you were. I thought you were a thief, coming in that window the way that you did. You're all right now."

No, she wasn't. She was sitting in complete darkness with a man who had attacked her, and she couldn't stop trembling. He sat beside her, and she wasn't sure what he was saying, only that his words were soft and reassuring. Then, to her horror, she was half sobbing and half laughing and he was sitting beside her, and in that awful darkness she was in his arms as he stroked her hair—and she still didn't have any idea who he was or even what he looked like.

"Shush, it's all right now. It's all right." The same hands that had held her with such cold, brutal strength were capable of an uncanny tenderness. He held her as if she were a frightened child, easing his fingertips under her chin to lift her face. "It's all right. My God, I'm sorry. I didn't know."

She knew his voice, knew his scent. She knew the harshness and the tenderness of his arms, but she didn't know his name or the color of his eyes. She stiffened, her tremors beginning to fade at last with the reassurance of his words and the new security of his form.

"I'm, uh, sorry." She pushed away from him, feeling a furious rush of embarrassment. She was apologizing, and he was in *her* house. Gene's house. A total stranger. "Who are you?"

He stood. She instantly felt the distance between them. It was over—whatever it had been. The violence, and the tenderness.

"Rex Morrow."

Rex Morrow. Her mind moved quickly now. Rex

Morrow. He wasn't going to kill her. Rex murdered people—yes, by the dozens—but only in print. Alexi had decided long before this miserable meeting between them that his work was the result of a dark and macabre mind.

She sprang to her feet, desperate for light. Rex Morrow. Gene had warned her. He had told her that he shared the peninsula with only one other man: the writer Rex Morrow. And that Rex was keeping an eye on the place.

He had promised that the electricity was on, too. She fumbled her way toward what she hoped was a wall, anxious to find a switch. She bit her lip, fighting emotion. Emotion was dangerous. Maybe she was better off with the lights off. She'd panicked at his assault; she'd fallen hysterically into his arms with relief. She'd screamed, she'd cried—she, who prided herself on having learned to be calm and reserved, if nothing else, in life.

The flashlight arced and flared abruptly, its glare of light showing her plainly where the switch was. She came to it and quickly hit it, swiveling abruptly to lean against the wall and stare at the man who already knew her weaknesses too well. Perhaps light would wash away the absurd intimacy; perhaps it could even give her back some sense of dignity.

He was dark, and disturbingly young. For some reason she'd been convinced that he had to have lived through World War II to have written some of the books he had on espionage during the period. He couldn't have been older than thirty-five. Equally disturbing, he was attractive. His jeans were worn, and his shirt was a black knit that seemed almost a match for the ebony of his hair. His eyes, too, were dark, the deepest brown she had ever seen. He was tanned and handsome, with high, rugged cheekbones, a long, straight nose—somewhat prominent, she determined—and a full mouth that was both sensual and cynical. He didn't seem to resent her full, appraising stare, but then he was returning it, and she was alarmed to discover herself wondering what he was seeing in her.

Dishevelment, she decided wearily. It would be difficult for anyone to break into a house through a window and be attacked and wrestled down and still appear well-groomed.

"Alexi Jordan—in the flesh," he murmured. His tone was cool, as if everything that had happened in the darkness was an embarrassment to him, too. He shook his head as if to clear it, strode toward Alexi and then right past her in the archway by the light switch, apparently very familiar with the house. She watched him, frowning, then followed him.

He went through the big, once-beautiful hallway and disappeared through a swinging door.

The door nearly caught her in the face, fueling her anger and irritation—residues of drastic fear. She was the one with the right to be here—and he had assaulted her and mauled her, and had not even offered an apology.

Light—blessed light! She felt so much more competent and able now, more like the woman she had carefully and painstakingly developed. She paused, reddening at the thought of how she had whimpered in fear, reddening further when she recalled how easily she had cried in his arms when he had simply told her that he wasn't going to kill her. She should call the police. She had every right to be furious.

She slammed against the door to open it and entered the kitchen.

He'd helped himself to a beer. The rest of the house might be a decaying, musty, dusty mess, but someone had kept up the kitchen—and had apparently seen fit to stock the refrigerator with beer.

"Have a beer," Alexi invited him caustically.

He raised the one he had already taken and threw his head back to take a long swallow. He lowered the bottle and pulled out one of the heavy oak chairs at the the butcher-block table.

"Alexi Jordan in the flesh."

What had he heard about her? she wondered. It didn't matter. She had come here to be alone—not to form friendships. She smiled without emotion and replied in kind. "The one and only Rex Morrow."

He arched a dark brow. "I take it your grandfather told you that I lived out here."

"Great-grandfather," Alexi corrected him. "Yes, of course. How else would I know you?" She should have known right away. Gene had told her that Rex Morrow was the only inhabitant of the peninsula. She had just been too immersed in her own thoughts at the time to pay proper attention. Thinking back, she should also have known that Gene might have him watching the place. She'd heard that Morrow had tried to buy the house so that he could own the entire strip of land. But, though Gene seemed fond of his neighbor, he would never sell the Brandywine house.

"My picture is on my book jackets," Rex told her.

"I certainly wouldn't buy your books in hardcover, Mr. Morrow."

He smiled. "You don't care for my writing, I take it?"

"Product of a dark mind," she said. Actually, she admired him. She couldn't read his books easily, though. They were frightening and very realistic—and tore into the human psyche. They could make her afraid of the dark—and afraid to live alone. She didn't need to be afraid of imaginary things.

And his characters stayed with the reader long after the story had been read, long after it should have been forgotten.

Besides she felt defensive. She'd known him a few minutes; because of the circumstances, he had seen far too deeply into her fears and emotions. And he'd attacked her. He still hadn't apologized. In fact, it seemed as if he was annoyed with her.

"Would you like a beer, Ms. Jordan?"

"No. I'd like you out of my house. I'd like you to apologize for accosting me on my own property."

He gazed down, then looked up again with a smile, but there was a good deal of hostility in that smile.

"Ms. Jordan, it isn't your house. It's Gene's house. And I don't owe you any apology. I promised Gene I'd watch out for the place. You weren't due until tomorrow—and who the hell would have expected you out here, alone, in the pitch darkness, breaking into the house through a window?"

"I wasn't expecting anyone to be inside."

"I wasn't expecting anyone to break in. We're even."

"Far from even."

As he watched her, she had no idea of what he was thinking; she felt that his assessment found her wanting.

"You won't be staying," he said at last with a shrug and a smile.

"Won't I?"

She liked his smile even less when it deepened and his gaze scanned her from head to toe once again.

"No. You won't be here long." He stood again and walked toward her. His strides were slow, and didn't come all the way to her. Just close enough to look down. She estimated that he was six-three or six-four, and she was barely five-six. She silently gritted her teeth. She wasn't going to let him intimidate her now. He had already done so, and quite well. There was light now, and he wasn't touching her. She could bring back the reserve that had stood her so well against so much.

"This is a quiet place, Ms. Jordan. Very quiet. The biggest excitement in these parts is when Joe Lacey pinches the waitresses in the downtown café. There are only two houses out here on the peninsula— Gene's here, and mine. I get the impression that you need a certain amount of society. But you've only got one neighbor, lady, and that neighbor is me. And I'm not the sociable type."

"How interesting." Alexi crossed her arms over her chest and leaned back against the wall. "Well, then, why don't you take your beer out of my refrigerator and then get your gruesome soul out of my house, Mr. Morrow?"

He took a long moment to answer; his expression in that time gave away nothing of his emotions.

"You can keep the beer. You're going to need it."

"Why is that?"

"This place is falling apart."

"Yes, it is, isn't it?" she returned pleasantly.

"And you're going to handle it all?"

"Yes, I am. Now, if you'll please—"

"I don't want company, Ms. Jordan."

"You keep saying that—and you're standing in my house!"

He hesitated, taking a long, deep breath, as if he were very carefully going to try to explain something to a child.

"Let me be blunt, Ms. Jordan—"

"You haven't been so yet? Please, don't be at all polite or courteous on my account," she told him with caustic sweetness.

"I don't want you here. I value my privacy."

"I'm really sorry, Mr. Morrow. I think I did read somewhere that you were a total eccentric, moody and miserable, but there are property laws in the good ol' U.S. of A. And this is not your property. You do not own the whole peninsula! Now, this house has been in my family for over a hundred years—"

"It's supposed to be haunted, you know," he interrupted her, as if it might have been a sudden inspiration, an if-you-can't-bully-her-out-scare-her-out technique.

She smiled.

"As long as the ghosts will leave me alone, I'll be just fine with them," she told him.

He threw up his hands. "You can't possibly mean to stay out here by yourself."

"But I do."

"Ah...you're running away."

She was—exactly. And the old Brandywine house had seemed like the ideal place. Gene had been pleading with someone in the family to come home. To this home. Admittedly, she'd humored him at first, as had her cousins. But then the disaster with John had occurred, and...yes, she was running away.

"Let me be blunt, Mr. Morrow," Alexi said. "I'm staying."

He stared at her steadily a long while. Then he took in her stature from head to toe once again and started to laugh.

"I'll lay odds you don't make a week," he said.

"I'll last."

He made a sound that was like a derisive snort and walked past her again. "We'll see, won't we?"

"Is that some kind of a threat?" Alexi followed him down the beautiful old hallway toward the front door. The light was low once again, filtering into the hallway from the living room and the kitchen. His dark good looks were a bit sinister in that shadowed realm. He really was striking, she thought. His features were both beautifully chiseled and masculine, and his eyes were so very dark.

Mesmerizing, one might have said.

"I wouldn't dream of threatening you," he told her after perusing her once again. "I'd thought you would be even taller," he said abruptly.

It had taken him a long, long time to realize that he had seen her before this night. That he should have known Alexi Jordan for being more than Gene Brandywine's expected relation. He had seen her in a different way, of course. In a classic, flowing Grecian gown. With the wind in her hair. He had seen her on the silver screen, seen her in fantasy.

Her classical features had been put to good use.

Despite herself, Alexi flushed. "You recognized me."

"'The Face That Launched a Thousand Ships,'" he quoted from her last ad campaign for Helen of Troy products.

"Well, you son of a—!" she said suddenly, her temper soaring. "You kept denying that I was Alexi Jordan when you must have known—"

"No, I didn't know then. I didn't really recognize you from the ad until we were in the kitchen." He was irritated; she really irritated him. She made him feel defensive. She made it sound as if he had enjoyed scaring her.

And, somewhere deep inside, she scared him in return. Why? he wondered, puzzled. And then, of course, he knew. Maybe part of it had been the way that they had met. Part of it had been the terror in her eyes, the fear he had so desperately needed to assuage.

And part of it was simply that she was so achingly beautiful. So gloriously feminine. She made him wish that he had known her forever and forever, that he could reach out and pull her into his arms. To know her—as a lover.

He didn't mind wanting a woman. He just feared needing her. And she was the type of lover a man could come to need.

"You don't resemble the glamorous Helen in the least at the moment, you know," he told her bluntly. It was a lie. Her face could have launched a thousand ships had it been covered in mud.

"And whose fault is that?"

He shrugged. Despite herself, Alexi tried to repin some of the hair that was falling in tangles from her once neat and elegant knot.

He laughed. "I should have known from all the lipstick."

"Go home, Mr. Morrow, please. I'm looking for privacy, too."

His laughter faded. He studied her once again, and again, despite herself, she felt as if she was growing warm. As if there was something special about his eyes, about the way they fell over her and entered into her.

"Go—" She broke off, startled, as a shrill sound erupted in the night. She was so surprised that she nearly screamed. Then she was heartily glad that she had not, for it was only the phone.

"Oh," she murmured. Then she sighed with resignation, looking at him. "All right, where is it?"

"Parlor."

"Living room?"

"That living room is called a parlor."

She stiffened her shoulders and started for the parlor. She caught the phone on the fifth ring. It was Gene. Her great-grandfather had turned ninety-five last Christmas and could have passed for sixty. Alexi was ridiculously proud of him, but then she felt that she had a right to be. He was lean, but as straight as an arrow and as determined and sly as an old fox. He seldom ailed, and Alexi thought that she knew his secret. He'd never—through a long life of trials and tribulations—taken the time to feel sorry for himself, he had never ceased to love life, and he had never apologized for an absolute fascination with people. Everything and everyone interested Gene.

But he was too old, he had assured Alexi, to start the massive project of refurbishing his historical inheritance, the Brandywine house outside Fernandina Beach.

He had known she needed a place. A place to hide, to nurse her wounds. She had never explained everything to him; the bitter truth had been too hurtful and humiliating to admit, even to Gene.

Gene's voice came to her gruffly. "Thank God you're there. I tried the hotel in town, and the receptionist told me you had never checked in."

"Gene! Yes, I—"

"Young woman, where is your sense?"

At that moment, Alexi wanted to rap her beloved relative on the knuckles. His voice was so clear that she was sure Rex Morrow, who had followed her back into the parlor, was hearing every word.

"Gene, I really didn't want to stay in town. I made it into the city by six—"

"It's pitch-dark out there!"

"Well, yes—"

"Alexi, there are dangerous people in this world, even in a small place—maybe especially in a small place. You could have been attacked or assaulted or—"

There *are* dangerous people out here, and I *was* assaulted! Alexi almost snapped. Rex Morrow was watching her, smiling. He could hear every word.

He took the phone out of her hand.

"What are you—"

"Shh," he told her, sitting on the back of the Victorian sofa and casually dangling a leg. He smiled with a great deal of warmth when he spoke to Gene.

"Gene, Rex here."

"Rex, thank God. I'm glad I asked you to watch the place!"

"Gene, there's really not much going on out here, you know. No real danger, though Alexi might tell you differently. We had a bit of a run-in. Why didn't you give her the key?"

Alexi snatched the phone from him, reddening again. "He did give me the key."

"What? What?" They could both hear Gene's voice. "Key? I did give Alexi the key."

Rex arched a brow. "Why didn't you…use it?" he asked her slowly, once again as if he were speaking with a child who had proved to have little adult comprehension. "Or do you prefer breaking in the window over walking through the front door?"

"You broke a window?" Gene was shouting. For such an incredibly old man, he could shout incredibly loudly, Alexi thought.

"The key doesn't work!" Alexi shouted back.

There was a long sigh on the other end. "The key works, Alexi. You have to twist it in the lock. It's old. Old things have to be worked as carefully as old people. They're temperamental."

Rex Morrow stretched out a hand to her, palm up. "Give me the key."

"You go find it!" she hissed. "It's in my purse that you were tearing up!"

"Now what's going on?" Gene asked.

"Your wonder boy is going to go check it," Alexi said sweetly.

"Well, it works—you'll see," Gene said, mollified. "Now, you get someone in there right away to fix that window. You hear me?"

"First thing tomorrow, Gene," Alexi promised. "Hey!" she protested. Rex had dumped the contents of her purse onto the sofa to find the single key.

"Found it," he assured her.

"Oh, Lord," she groaned.

"What's wrong now?" Gene demanded.

"Nothing. Everything is wonderful. Just super," she muttered.

Rex Morrow was on his way back to the hallway and the front door. "Really, Gene. I'm here and I'm fine, and you just take care of yourself, okay?"

"Maybe you should get a dog, Alexi. A great big German shepherd or a Doberman. I'd feel better—"

"Gene, why ever would I need a dog when you left me a prowling cat?" she asked innocently.

Her great-grandfather started to say something, but he paused instead. She could see him in her mind's eye, scratching his white head in consternation.

"I'll keep in touch," Alexi promised hastily. "I'm excited to be here; it's a wonderful old place. I promise I'll fix it up with lots of love and tenderness. Love you. Bye!"

She hung up before he could say anything else. Then she stared at the phone for a moment, a nostalgic smile on her lips. She adored him. She was very lucky to have him, she knew. In the midst of pain, chaos and loneliness, he had always been there for her.

"The key works fine," Rex announced.

He was back in the room, extending the key to

her. She took it in silence, compressing her lips as he stared at her.

"You have to pull the door while you turn it," he said. "Want to try it while I'm still here?"

"No. Oh, all right—yes. Thank you."

Stiffly she preceded him down the hallway to the door. She thought that maybe she'd rather lock herself out and use the window again than falter in front of him, but really, why should she care?

She opened the door and threw the bolt from the inside. She slid the key in and twisted it, and it worked like a dream. Disgusted, Alexi thought it was a sad day when one couldn't even trust a piece of metal.

"I guess I've got it," she murmured.

Arms crossed over his chest, he shook his head. "Step outside and lock the door and try it. That's when you have the problem."

She stepped outside, but before she closed the door she asked him, "How did you get in?"

"I have my own key." He closed the door for her.

Alexi slipped her key into the lock. With the door closed, it was frightfully dark again. She could barely find the hole, and then she couldn't begin to get the damn thing to twist.

"Pull! Pull on the knob!"

She did. After a few more fumbles she got the key to twist, and the door opened.

She walked in, a smile of satisfaction brightening her eyes.

"Got it." She gritted her teeth. "Thank you."

"I wouldn't be quite so pleased. It took you long enough." Arms still casually crossed, he stared down at her, shaking his head. "And you're going to take on the task of reconstruction?"

"I'm a whiz at electricity."

"Are you?"

"Will you please go home?"

He smiled at her. "Your face is smudged."

"Is it?" She smiled serenely. She was sure it was. Her stockings were torn, her skirt was probably beyond repair, and she undoubtedly resembled a used mop.

He came a step nearer to her, raising a hand to her cheek. She remembered the tenderness with which he had held her when she was trembling and shaking in fear. When she had been vulnerable and weak.

She felt that same tenderness come from him now and the sensual draw of the rueful curl of his mouth. She should have stepped back. She didn't. She felt the brush of his thumb against her flesh and caught her breath. He didn't want her there; he had said so. And she wanted to be alone.

She didn't move, however. Except for the trembling that started up, inside of her this time. She just felt that touch.

"Good night, Ms. Jordan," he said softly.

He was out the door, warning her to bolt it, before she thought to reply.

Chapter 2

Alexi rinsed her face at the sink and dried it with paper towels. She had showered in the powder room beneath the stairs, but that was as far as she had ventured in her new realm—which wasn't really new at all. Twenty years before, she had spent a summer here with Gene. But twenty years was a long time, and the house was truly a disaster since Gene had left it so many months ago.

She sat at the butcher-block table to do her makeup, thinking that she didn't look much better than she had the night before. She had slept poorly. Sleeping on the kitchen floor hadn't helped, but strangely, once Rex Morrow had left, she had been really uneasy—too frightened to explore any further. But when she had slept, nightmares had awakened her again and again. Nightmares of John combining with the horrid fear that had assailed her with Rex's first touch last night. Naturally, perhaps. She'd been attacked. But then her dreams had become even more disconcerting. She'd dreamed of Rex Morrow in a far gentler way, of his eyes on her, of his touch, of his smile. Dreamed of the assurance in his voice. All night the visions had filtered through her mind. Violence, tenderness—both had stolen from her any hope of a good night's sleep.

She felt better once her makeup was on. Even before she had left home on her own—before John—she had learned that with makeup she could pretend that she was wearing a mask and that she could hide all expression and emotion behind it. That wasn't true, of course. But as she had aged, she had learned to create masks with her features, and the more years slipped by her, the greater comfort she took in concealing her feelings.

Rex Morrow had seen her feelings, she reminded herself. But it had proved as uncomfortable for him as it had for her. He wanted her gone, right? He valued his privacy; he wanted the land all to himself.

"Sorry, Mr. Morrow," she murmured out loud. "I'm not quite as pathetic as I appeared last night. And I'm staying."

She took a sip of coffee, then bit her lower lip. She wished she could forget how his eyes had moved over her, how his thumb had felt when he'd smoothed away the smudge on her cheek.

And she wished that she would get up and start cleaning.

But she decided that she wasn't going to plunge right in. Chicken? she challenged herself. Maybe. After last night, she deserved to take her time. She'd explore later. She was simply feeling lethargic. Today she'd go into town and find a rental car. Today, she reminded herself, was half over. It had been almost twelve when she had risen, because it had been at least six when she had finally slept.

It was three in the afternoon when she requested a taxi at last. She'd called Gene to assure him that her first night had gone well and that she was happy at the house. She told him the truth about what had happened with Rex when she had arrived, but she didn't tell him how frightened she had been or how she had collapsed in tears into a total stranger's arms. She laughed, making light of the incident. Anyone would have been terrified, she assured herself. But Gene was astute. She was afraid he might have learned more about her past from the incident than she wanted.

By four-thirty she had rented a little sedan. She had made friends with the taxi driver and the rental car clerk—everyone knew Gene, it seemed. They were glad to meet his great-granddaughter and fascinated to discover that she was the Helen of Troy lady. Alexi was a bit uneasy to find that she was so recognizable—she would have preferred anonymity. She convinced herself that it would be okay, then decided that she was going to like small-town living. The people were warm—if just a little bit nosy.

"You just be careful out there," the old gentleman at the agency warned her. "That peninsula can be a mighty scary place."

"Why?" Alexi asked. But he had already turned to help the businessman in line behind her. She shrugged and left for her car. Once inside, she tapped idly against the steering wheel. She should get going on her shop-

ping. There was nothing in the house. And whether
she had a professional cleaner or not, she needed all
kinds of detergents. And bug sprays. She was sure that
except for the kitchen the place was crawling.

But she wasn't really ready for work yet. And she
decided she would drive back to the peninsula. It
would be dark before long, and she wanted to see the
little spit of land in its entirety.

Alexi started the car, then froze. She stared at the
blond head and broad shoulders of a man slipping into
a rented Mustang next to her car. For a moment, her
stomach and heart careened; panic set in. Then he
turned. It wasn't John. She exhaled, shaking.

He couldn't have followed her here, she promised
herself. She had finished up with the Helen of Troy
campaign—and then she had run. He couldn't know
where. And no one would tell him.

She took several deep breaths and eased out of the
parking lot. She got lost only once, and then she was
on the one road that led to Gene's house. It was a horrible road, she quickly discovered. The town didn't
own it, Gene had told her once; he and Rex Morrow
owned it jointly. And apparently, Alexi thought with
a smile, neither of them had been very interested in
keeping it up. There were potholes everywhere.

She slowed to accommodate the bumps and juts,
but apparently she did so just a moment too late. The
car suddenly sputtered and died, spewing up a froth
of steam from the front. Alexi stared at it in disbelief
for a moment, then swore at herself and crawled out
of the driver's seat.

For fifteen minutes she tried to figure out how to
open the hood; once it was open, she wondered why

she had bothered. Steam was still spewing out, and she didn't have the faintest idea of what to do. She looked around, wondering how long a walk it was to the house. The peninsula was only about four miles long and one across, but both houses were at the far end of it.

Alexi swore and kicked a tire. She decided that people lied when they said that doing such things couldn't help—she felt ten times better for having kicked the car. She was annoyed that she didn't know what to do, but then she had never kept a car. She just hadn't needed one in New York.

It was getting dark, she perceived suddenly. And if she hadn't been stuck here, she would have thought that it was beautiful. The sky was burnt orange and pink, a lovely background for the pines and shrubs that littered the sandy ground. She had no idea how quickly the darkness fell there.

Alexi gave the car a withering stare, then decided she had best start walking toward the house. She could phone the rental agency, and they could call a mechanic and get the car out to the house for her.

Swinging her bag over her shoulder, Alexi started to walk. It really was beautiful, she assured herself. The sandy road at sunset, everything around it silent, the smell of the ocean heavy on the air. A breeze lifted her hair and touched her cheeks. She could imagine having a horse out here; it would be a beautiful place to ride. All the wonderful pines and palms and the endless sand, and beyond the trees, the endless ocean.

The sunset coloring around her slipped; the sky became gray. Alexi was glad that the house was on a peninsula; she knew she was walking in the right direction. There were no lights out here; she remembered the horrid blackness of the night before.

Suddenly she became aware of a sound behind her, following her. She stopped; the sound stopped. It was her imagination, she told herself. Darkness and solitude could do things like that. Who was she kidding? She was frightened. And she had a right to be. After last night...

Last night, Rex had pounced upon her right away. She had crawled through the window, and he had quickly grabbed her. This sound behind her was... stealthy. She was being stalked.

No. Her fears were getting out of hand. Rex had had an explanation. He'd thought that she was breaking into the house. But John couldn't have followed her—and John was a memory of misery, not terror. And this...this was a feeling that something evil was breathing down her spine. That some real injury was intended for her.

She inhaled—and then she started to run. Maybe her parents, in their distant wisdom, had been right. Maybe she shouldn't have come here, where there was no help, where there was nothing but darkness and the whisper of the breeze and if she screamed forever, no one would hear her.

She was breathless; she was certain that she heard soft footfalls on the sand behind her. She turned around to look and then screamed with total abandon as she ran smack into something hard.

She swung around again, looking up in amazement. She was about to fall when arms steadied her.

"Rex!"

"What in God's name are you doing, running like that?"

"Someone was following me."

She saw the doubt in his eyes and turned around again. Naturally, no one was there. Rex's hands were still on her arms. She looked up at him again, cleared her throat and stepped back. "I'm telling you the truth."

He walked around her and picked up her purse, which she hadn't realized she had dropped. He handed it to her. "We're the only inhabitants out here," he said lightly. She could still see doubt in his eyes.

"I didn't imagine you last night," she said angrily. His eyes seemed to darken as he studied her more intently, and for some reason she flushed uneasily. "I don't imagine things."

"I'm sure you don't."

He didn't believe her; she could hear it in his tone.

"I'm telling you—"

"What are you doing walking out here, anyway?"

"I was driving. The stupid rental car blew."

"Blew what?"

"Something."

He nodded. "Come on. We'll go back for it."

They didn't speak during the walk; he strode quickly and Alexi had enough to do to keep up. She was panting when they reached the car.

The steam had stopped. Rex took a look under the hood, then walked around to the driver's seat, arching a brow at Alexi as he took the keys from the ignition. He opened the trunk, found a container of water and filled something in the front. He slid into the driver's seat, turned the motor over—and it caught. He opened the passenger door.

"You blew a hose, that's all. I can pick one up for you in the morning. Come on, get in. I'll get you home. It'll go that far."

Alexi crawled in beside him and leaned against the seat.

"Thank you." She didn't look at him; she could feel his gaze slide her way as he drove. She wondered uneasily what he was thinking.

Rex drove the car up to the house. When they got out, he tossed her the keys, pointing to the house. "Glad you left a night-light on."

"I didn't know I had," she murmured.

"What?"

"Nothing, nothing," she said quickly. But she'd be damned if she could remember leaving lights on. She hadn't even explored the house yet—all she had really seen was the kitchen.

Rex automatically walked with her up the path to the front door. He frowned, when he saw the window that she had broken.

"You didn't get that fixed today. You should have."

"I will." She wondered why she had said it so quickly, so defensively. She didn't owe him any explanations.

She managed to open the door on the first try, and that was a nice boost to her ego. She turned and smiled at Rex, laughing. "I did it."

"Yes, you did."

She hesitated, wondering if she should invite him in. But then, he didn't want her anywhere near him, and she'd had a miserable night on his account. Still…

She trembled suddenly, looking down. He was a very attractive man. Tall, dark and—masculine. They were far from friends, yet in their first meeting they had taken a forbidden step toward intimacy. She had taken a step…and she wanted to retreat from it. He was rugged and blunt—a loner. They both wanted privacy.

"Thank you," she murmured.

"You're welcome," he said, staring at her as she went into the house. "I'll pick up that hose for you tomorrow."

"I should make the rental agency do it."

"It's no big thing."

She nodded, then realized that she was returning his stare. His eyes were so dark in the night. He was wearing jeans again, and a navy polo shirt. His arms, which were mostly bare, were tanned and nicely muscled.

She wanted to ask him in. Of all the things that had happened the night before, she remembered the tenderness in his voice and the feeling of his arms as he'd held her. Something warm inside her stirred, something she quickly fought.

She wasn't ready for a relationship. She might never be ready again in her life.

She knew he didn't want her here on the peninsula. He had warned her to go—he had even laid odds against her staying. Still, she wanted to see him smile, to hear him laugh. She wanted to know what lay in his past that he would crave this solitude, that could have made him so ruthless when he had first touched her, so gentle when he had realized how terrified she had been.

"Good night, then. Sleep well, Alexi."

"Good night, and thanks again."

Alexi stepped into the house, frowning as she looked around the lighted hallway.

But then, even as she stared, she heard a little noise—and the house was plunged into total darkness.

She didn't scream at first. Her heart shuddered instinctively, but she wasn't really afraid. The Brandywine house had been built in 1859, there could easily be problems with such things as electricity.

But then she heard the footsteps, loud and clear. They came crashing down the stairway. She could feel the wind.... The stairway was at the other end of the hall, and she was very aware that someone was close—very close—to her.

And it certainly wasn't Rex Morrow—not tonight. He had just gone out the front door.

She did scream then, just like a banshee. Someone had been upstairs. In the house.

"Alexi!"

There was a fierce pounding on the front door, and she knew the voice shouting her name belonged to Rex.

She turned around, groping madly in the darkness and found the lock. The stubborn thing refused to give at first. Where was the person who had made the sound of footsteps? Her scream had cut off all other sound, and now she didn't know if someone was still coming for her in the darkness or if that same someone had bolted on past.

"Please, please...!" she whispered to the ancient lock, and then, as if it were a cantankerous old man who needed to be politely placated, it groaned and gave.

She threw the door open. In the darkness she could just barely make out Rex Morrow's starkly handsome features. She nearly pitched herself against him, but then she remembered that the man was basically a hostile stranger, even though she knew Gene held him in the highest regard—and even though she had already clung to him once before.

She stepped back.

"Why did you scream?"

"The lights went out and—"

"I thought you were a whiz with electricity."

"I lied—but that's not why I screamed. Someone came running down the stairway."

"What?"

He looked at her so sharply that even in the darkness she felt his probing stare. Did he think that she was lying—or did he believe her all too easily?

"I told you—"

"Come on."

He took her hand, his fingers twining tightly around hers, and, with the ease of a cat in the dark, strode toward the parlor. He found the flashlight and cast its beam around. No intruder was there.

"Where did the…footsteps go?" he whispered huskily.

"I—I don't know. I screamed and… I don't know."

He brought her back into the hallway and stopped dead. Alexi crashed into his back, banging her nose. She rubbed it, thinking that the man had a nice scent. She remembered it; she would have known him anywhere by it. It was not so much that of an after-shave as that of the simple cleanliness of soap and the sea and the air. He might be hostile, but at least he was clean.

There was only so much one could expect from neighbors, she decided nervously.

He walked through the hall to the stairway, paused, then went into the kitchen. The rear door was still tightly locked.

"Well, your intruder didn't leave that way, and he didn't exit by the front door," Rex said. His tone was bland, but she could read his thoughts. He had decided that she was a neurotic who imagined things.

"I tell you—" she began irately.

"Right. You heard footsteps. We'll check the house."

"You think he's still in the house?"

"No, but we'll check."

Alexi knew he didn't believe anyone had been there to begin with. "Rex—"

"All right, all right. I said we'll search. If anyone is here, we'll find him. Or her. Or it."

He released her hand. Alexi didn't know how nervous she was until she realized that her fingers were still clinging to his. She flushed and turned away from him.

"Why did the lights go, then?" she demanded.

"Probably a fuse. Here, hold the flashlight and hang on a second."

She turned back around to take the flashlight from him. He went straight to the small drawer by the refrigerator, then went toward the pantry.

"I need more light."

Alexi followed him and let the beam play on the fuse box. A moment later, the kitchen light came on.

He looked at her. "Stay here. I'll check out the library and the ballroom and upstairs."

"Wait a minute!" Alexi protested, shivering.

"What?"

Impatiently he stopped at the kitchen door, his hand resting casually against the frame.

She swallowed and straightened with dignity and tried to walk slowly over to join him.

"I do read your books," she admitted. "And it's always the hapless idiot left alone while the other goes off to search who winds up...winds up with her throat slit!"

"Alexi..." he murmured slowly.

"Don't patronize me!" she commanded him.

He sighed, looked at her for a moment with a certain incredulity and then started to laugh.

"Okay. We'll search together. And I'm sorry. I'm not patronizing you. It's just usually so quiet out here that it's hard to imagine..." His voice trailed away, and he shrugged again. "Come on, then."

Smiling, he offered her his hand. She hesitated, then took it.

They returned to the hallway. Alexi nervously played the flashlight beam up the stairway. Rex grinned again and went to the wall, flicking a switch that lit the entire stairway.

"Gene did have a few things done," he told her.

There were only two other rooms on the ground floor—except for the little powder room beneath the stairway, which proved to be empty. To the right, behind the parlor, was the library, filled with ancient volumes and wall shelves and even an old running oak ladder reaching to the top shelves. Upon a dais with a wonderful old Persian carpet was a massive desk with a few overstuffed Eastleg chairs around it. Apart from that, the room was empty.

They crossed behind the stairway to the last room—the "ballroom," as Rex called it. It was big, with a dining set at one end with beautiful old hutches flanking it, and a baby grand across the room, toward the rear wall. Two huge paintings hung above the fireplace, one of a handsome blond man in full Confederate dress uniform, the other of a lovely woman in radiant white antebellum costume.

Forgetting the intruder for a moment, Alexi dropped Rex's hand and walked toward the paintings for a better look.

"Lieutenant General P. T. Brandywine and Eugenia," Rex said quietly.

"Yes, I know," Alexi murmured. She felt a bit awed; she hadn't been in the house since she'd been a small child, but she remembered the paintings, and she felt again the little thrill of looking at people from another day who were her direct antecedents.

"They say that he's the one who buried the Confederate treasure."

"What?" Alexi, forgetting her distant relatives, turned around and frowned at Rex.

He laughed. "You mean you never heard the story?"

She shook her head. "No. I mean, I've heard of Pierre and Eugenia. Pierre built the house. But I never heard anything about his treasure."

He smiled, locking his hands behind his back and casually sauntering into the room to look at the paintings.

"This area went back and forth during the Civil War like a Ping-Pong ball. The rebels held it one month; the Yankees took it the next. Pierre was one hell of a rebel—but it seems the last time he came home, he knew he wasn't going to make it back again. Somewhere in the house he buried a treasure. He was killed at Gettysburg in '63, and Eugenia never did return here. She went back to her father's house in Baltimore, and her children didn't come back here until the 1880s. Local legend has it that Pierre haunts the place to guard his stash, and the locals on the mainland all swear that it does exist."

"Why didn't Eugenia come back?"

Rex shrugged. "He was a rebel. At the end of the war, Confederate currency wasn't worth the paper it had been printed on. There was no real treasure. Maybe that's the reason that Pierre had to come back to haunt the place."

Alexi stared at him for a long moment. There seemed to be a glitter of mischief in his eyes. A slow, simmering anger burned inside her, along with a sudden suspicion. "Sure. Those footsteps belonged to my great-great-great-grandfather. You will not scare me out of this house!"

"What—?" He broke off with a furious scowl. "You foolish little brat. I'm not trying to scare you."

"The hell you're not! You want me out of here— God knows why. You don't have to see me, you know."

His eyes narrowed. "Maybe I should leave now."

She lifted her chin. She wanted him to stay. She wasn't afraid of ghosts, but someone alive had been in the house. Someone who had come here in stealth. Even if Rex didn't believe her.

She swung around. "This is ridiculous! I came to my old family home on what is supposed to be a deserted, desolate peninsula, and it's more like Grand Central Station!"

"Alexi—"

"Just go, if you want to!"

Rex watched her, his mouth tight and grim, then swung around. "I'll check the upstairs. If someone tries to slit your throat, just scream."

He was gone. Alexi stared after him, shivering, hating herself for being afraid. She hadn't been afraid to come—she'd been eager. She'd desperately wanted to be alone. Where there were no crowds, where people didn't recognize her. But she'd just barely gotten there, and already the darkness and the isolation were proving threatening.

Nothing was going to happen, she assured herself. But she wrapped her arms nervously about herself and returned to stare up at the paintings. Perhaps some kids believed in the legend about the gold. High school kids. They didn't want to harm her; they just wanted to find a treasure—a treasure that didn't really exist.

She smiled slowly. They were really marvelous-looking people; Pierre was striking, and his Eugenia was beautiful.

"Even if you could come back as a ghost," she said to Pierre's likeness with a wry grin, "you certainly wouldn't haunt me—I'm your own flesh and blood."

"Do you often talk to paintings?"

Startled, she swung around. Rex Morrow was leaning casually against the doorframe, watching her.

"Only now and then."

"Oh." He waited a moment. "Upstairs is clear. If anyone was in the house, he or she is definitely gone now."

"Good."

"Want me to call the police?"

"Think I should?" She realized that he still didn't believe her. Or maybe he didn't think she was lying—just that she was neurotic. Paranoid. And maybe he even felt a little guilty about her state of mind, since he had attacked her last night.

He paused, then shrugged at last. "Whoever it was is gone. Probably some kid from the town looking for Pierre's treasure. He probably left by that broken window. You *must* get it fixed."

"I will—tomorrow. First thing. And maybe it was someone looking for Pierre's treasure. Numismatically or historically, maybe those Confederate bills are worth something."

"Maybe."

"They could be collectible!"

"Sure. Confederate money is collectible. It's just not usually worth…"

"Worth what?"

"Only rare bills from certain banks are worth much. But who knows?" he offered.

They stood there for several moments, looking at each other across the ballroom.

"Well," he murmured.

"Well…" she echoed. Her gaze fell from his, and once again she wasn't at all sure what she wanted. He'd checked the place for her; she was sure now that it was empty.

He didn't want her on the peninsula. He had said so himself. It was certainly time that he left—and she should be happy for that, since he was such a doubting Thomas. But she couldn't help feeling uneasy. She didn't want him to go.

Fool! she told herself. Tell him "Thank you very

much," then let him go. A curious warmth was spreading through her. If he left now, they could remain casual acquaintances. But if she encouraged him to stay...

It was more than fear, more than uneasiness. She wanted him to stay. She wanted to know more about him. She wanted to watch him smile.

A slight tremor shook her; the warmth flooding her increased. She had the feeling that if she had him stay now, she would never be able to turn her back on him again. She was still staring at him and he was still watching her and no words were being spoken, but tension, real and tangible, seemed to be filling the air. Alexi inhaled deeply; she cleared her throat.

"I think I'll have one of your beers," she said. "Since they *are* in my refrigerator."

"Help yourself."

She hesitated. Then she spoke. "Want one?"

He, too, hesitated. It was as if he, too, sensed some form of commitment in the moment. Then he shrugged, and a slow smile that was rueful and sexy and insinuating curled the corners of his lip.

"Sure," he told her. "Sure. Why not?"

Chapter 3

Alexi passed him quickly and hurried on into the kitchen. She dug into the refrigerator for two beers.

"Are you the one who has kept the kitchen clean?" she asked casually. It was spotless; Alexi imagined that one could have eaten off the floor and not have worried about dirt or germs. The rest of the place was a dust bowl.

"In a manner of speaking. A woman comes out twice a week to do my place. She spends an hour or so here."

Alexi nodded and handed him a beer. She walked past him, somehow determined to sit in the parlor, even though the kitchen was by far the cleaner place.

Maybe it was the only way she could get herself to go back into the room.

She knew he was behind her. Once she reached

the parlor she sank heavily into the Victorian sofa, discovering that she was exhausted. Rex Morrow sat across from her, straddling a straight-backed chair. Cool Hand Luke in a contemporary dark knit.

He smiled again, and she realized he knew she was staring at him and wondering about him. And of course, at the same time, she realized that he was watching her speculatively.

"You're staring," he said.

"So are you."

He shrugged. "I'm curious."

"About what?"

He laughed, and it was an easy sound, surprisingly pleasant. "Well, you are Alexi Jordan."

She lifted her hands, eyeing him warily in return. "And you are Rex Morrow."

"Hardly worthy of the gossip columns."

"That's because writers get to keep their privacy."

"Only if they hole out in places like this."

She didn't say anything; she took a long sip of her beer, wrinkling her nose. She really didn't like the brand; its taste was too bitter for her.

It was better than nothing.

"Well?" he said insinuatingly, arching a dark brow.

"Well, what?"

"Want to tell me about it?"

"About what?"

"The rich, lusty scandal involving the one and only Alexi Jordan."

Only a writer could make it all sound so sordid, Alexi decided. But she couldn't deny the scandal. "Why on earth should I?" she countered smoothly.

He lifted his hands, grinning. "Well, because I'm curious, I suppose."

"Wonderful," she said, nodding gravely. "I should spill my guts to a novelist. Great idea."

He laughed. "I write horror and suspense, not soap operas. You're safe with me."

"Haven't you read all about it in the rags?"

"I only read the front pages of those things when I'm waiting in line at the grocery store. One of them said you left him for another man. Another said John Vinto left you for another woman. Some say you hate each other. That there are deep, dark secrets hidden away in it all. Some claim that the world-famous photographer and his world-famous wife are still on good terms. The best of friends. So, what's the real story?"

Alexi leaned back on the couch, closing her eyes. She was so tired of the whole thing, of being pursued. She still felt some of the pain—it was like being punch-drunk. The divorce had actually gone through almost a year ago.

"Who knows what is truth?" she said, not opening her eyes. She didn't know why she should tell Rex Morrow—of all people—anything. But an intimacy had formed between them. Strange. They were both hostile; neither of them seemed to be overladen with trust for the opposite sex. Still, though he was blunt about wanting the peninsula to himself, she felt that she could trust him. With things that were personal— with things she might not say to anyone else.

"We're definitely not friends," she blurted out.

"Hurt to talk?" he asked quietly. She felt his voice, felt it wash over her, and she was surprised at the sensitivity in his tone.

She opened her eyes. A wary smile came to her lips. "I can't tell you about it."

"No?"

"No." She kicked off her shoes and curled her stockinged toes under her, taking another long sip of the beer. She hadn't eaten all day, and the few sips of the alcohol she had taken warmed her and eased her humor. "Suffice it to say that it was all over a long time ago. It wasn't one woman—it was many. And it was more than that. John never felt that he had taken a wife; he considered himself to have acquired property. It doesn't matter at all anymore."

"You're afraid of him." It was a statement, not a question.

"No! No! How did—?" She stopped herself. She didn't want to admit anything about her relationship with John.

"You are," he said softly. "And I've hit a sore spot. I'm sorry."

"Don't be. I'm not. Really."

"You're a liar, but we'll let it go at that for the time being."

"I'm not—"

"You are. Something happened that was a rough deal."

"Ahh…" she murmured uneasily. "The plot thickens."

He smiled at her. She felt the cadence of his voice wash over her, and it didn't seem so terrible that he knew that much.

"You don't need to be afraid now," he said softly.

"Oh?"

She liked his smile. She liked the confidence in it.

She even liked his macho masculine arrogance as he stated, "I'm very particular about the peninsula. You don't want him around, he won't be."

Alexi laughed, honestly at first, then with a trace of unease. John could be dangerous when he chose.

"So that's it!" Rex said suddenly.

"What?"

He watched her, nodding like a sage with a new piece of wisdom that helped explain the world. "Someone running after you on the sand, footsteps on the stairway, your blind panic last night. You think your ex is after you."

"No! I really heard footsteps!"

"All right. You heard them."

"You still don't believe me!"

He sighed, and she realized that she was never going to convince him that the footsteps had been real. "You seem to have had it rough," he said simply.

She wasn't going to win an argument. And at the moment she was feeling a bit too languorous to care.

"Talk about rough!" Alexi laughed. She glanced at her beer bottle. "This thing is empty. Feel like getting me another? For a person who doesn't like people, you certainly are curious—and good at making those people you don't like talk."

He stood up and took the bottle. "I never said that I don't like people."

She closed her eyes again and leaned back as he left her. She had to be insane. She was sitting here drinking beer and enjoying his company and nearly spilling out far too much truth about herself. Or was she spilling it out? He sensed too much. After one bottle of beer, she was smiling too easily. Trusting too quickly. If he did delve into all her secrets, it would serve her right if he displayed them to the world in print. He would change the names of the innocent or the not-so-innocent.

But, of course, everyone always knew who the real culprit was.

Something cold touched her hand. He was standing over her with another beer. She smiled. She was tired and lethargic enough to do so.

"My turn," she murmured huskily.

"Uh-uh. We're not finished with you."

He didn't move, though. He was staring down at her head. If she'd had any energy left, she would have flinched when he touched her hair. "That's the closest shade I've seen to real gold. How on earth do you do it?"

She knew she should be offended, but she laughed. "I grow it, idiot!"

"Oh, yeah?"

"Oh, yeah. How do you get that color? Shoe polish?"

"No, idiot," he said in turn, grinning. "I grow it."

He returned to his chair and cast his leg easily over it to straddle it once again. "So let's go on here. Why are you so afraid of John Vinto? What happened?"

"Nothing happened. We hit the finale. That was it."

"That wasn't it at all. You married him…what? About four years ago or so?"

"Yes."

"You've been divorced almost a year?"

"Yes," Alexi said warily. "He, uh, was the photographer on some of the Helen of Troy stills," she said after a moment. She shrugged. "The campaign ended—publicity about the breakup would have created havoc on the set."

"You worked with him after."

"Yes."

"And you spent that year working—and being afraid of him."

She lowered her head quickly. She hadn't been afraid of him when there had been plenty of other people around. She'd taken great pains never to be alone with him after he...

She sighed softly. "No more, Mr. Morrow. Not tonight. Your turn." She took a sip of her new beer. The second didn't taste half as bitter as the first, and it was ice-cold and delicious. She mused that it was the first time she had let down her guard in—

Since John. She shivered at the thought and then opened her eyes wide, aware that Rex had seen her shiver. Something warned her that he missed little.

"You shouldn't have to fear anyone, Alexi," he told her softly.

"Really..." She suddenly sat bolt upright. "Rex, I don't talk about this—no one knows anything at all."

"I don't really know anything," he reminded her with a smile. There was a rueful, sensual curve to the corner of his lip that touched her heart and stirred some physical response in the pit of her abdomen.

"No one will ever know what I do know now," he said. "On my honor, Ms. Jordan."

"Thanks," she murmured uneasily. "If we're playing *This Is Your Life*, then you've got to give something."

He shrugged, lifting his hands. "I married the girl next door. I tried to write at night while I edited the obituaries during the day for a small paper. You know the story—trial and error and rejections, and the girl next door left me. She didn't sue for divorce, though—she waited until some of the money came in, created one of the finest performances I have ever seen in court and walked away with most of it. She was only allowed to live off me for seven years. I bought an old house in Temple Terrace that used to belong to a famous stripper. I raised horses and planted orange groves—and then went nuts because my address got out and every weirdo in the country would come by to look me up. They stole all the oranges—and one jerk even shot a horse for a souvenir. That's when I moved out here. The sheriff up on the mainland is great, and it's like a wonderful little conspiracy—the townspeople keep me safe, and I contribute heavily to all the community committees. Gene—when he was still here—was a neighbor I could abide. Then he decided he needed to be in a retirement cooperative. I tried to buy the house from him; he wasn't ready to let go." He stopped speaking, frowning as he looked at her.

"Have you eaten anything?"

"What? Uh, no. How—why did you ask that?"

He chuckled softly. "Because your eyes are rimmed with red, and it makes you look tired and hungry.

"Want me to call for a pizza?"

"You must be kidding. You can get a pizza all the way out here?"

"I have connections," he promised her gravely. "What do you want on it?"

"Anything."

Alexi leaned her head against the sofa again. She heard him stand and walk around to the phone and order a large pizza with peppers, onions, mushrooms and pepperoni from a man named Joe, with whom he chatted casually, saying that he was over at the Brandywine house and, yes, Gene's great-granddaughter was in and, yes, she was fine—just hungry.

He hung up at last.

"So Joe will send a pizza?"

"Yep."

"That's wonderful."

"Hmm."

She sat up, curling her toes beneath her again and smoothing her skirt.

"Hold still," he commanded her suddenly.

Startled, she looked at him, amazed at the tension in his features. He moved toward her, and she almost jumped, but he spoke again, quietly but with an authority that made her catch her breath.

"Hold still!"

A second later he swept something off her shoulder, dashed it to the ground and stomped upon it.

Alexi felt a bit ill. She jumped to her feet, shaking out her hair. "What was it?"

"A brown widow."

"A what?"

"A brown widow. A spider. It wouldn't have killed you, but they hurt like hell and can make you sick."

"Oh, God!"

"Hey—there are spiderwebs all over this place. You know that."

Alexi stood still and swallowed. She lifted her hands calmly. "I can—I can handle spiders."

"You can."

"Certainly. Spiders and bugs and—even mice. And rats! I can handle it, really I can. Just so long as—"

"So long as what?"

She lowered her head and shook it, concealing her eyes from him. "Nothing." Snakes. She hated snakes. She simply wasn't about to tell him. "I'll be okay."

"Then why don't you sit again?"

"Because the pizza is coming. And because we really should eat in the kitchen. Don't you think?"

He grinned, his head slightly cocked, as he studied her. "Sure."

They moved back to the kitchen. The light there seemed very bright and cheerful, and Alexi had the wonderful feeling that no spider or other creature would dare show its face in this scrubbed and scoured spot.

"Why didn't you have the rest of the place kept up?" Alexi complained, sliding into a chair at the butcher-block table.

He sat across from her, arching a brow. "Excuse me. I kept just the kitchen up because Gene asked me to keep an eye on the place—and I'm not fond of sitting around with crawling creatures. If I'd known that the delicate face that launched ships would be appearing, I would have given more thought to the niceties."

"Very funny. I am tough, you know," she said indignantly.

"Sure."

"Oh, lock yourself in a closet."

"Such vile language!"

He was laughing at her, she knew. Tired as she was, Alexi was back on her feet, totally aggravated. "Trust me, Mr. Morrow—I can get to it! And I will do it. I'll make it here. You can warn me and threaten me, but I'm not leaving."

He lowered his head and idly rubbed his temple with his fingertips. She realized that he was laughing at her again. "I will, and you'll see."

"Listen, the closest you've probably been to a spider before is watching Spiderman on the Saturday-morning cartoons. You grew up with maids and gardeners and—"

"I see. You toiled and starved all those years to make your own money, so you know all about being rough and tough and surviving. You couldn't have starved too damn long. You're what—? All of thirty-five now? They made a movie out of *Cat in the Night* ten years ago, so you weren't eating rice and potatoes all that long! And for your information, having money does not equate to sloth or stupidity or—"

"I never implied that you were stupid—"

"Or incapable or inept! I've damn well seen spiders before, and roaches and rats and—"

"Hey!" He came to his feet before her. A pity, she thought—it had been easier to rant and rave righteously when he had been sitting and she had been able to look down her nose at him. But now his hands were on her shoulders and he was smiling as he stared down at her and she knew that he was silently laughing again.

"No one likes things crawling on her—or him. And let's face it—you can't be accustomed to such shabby conditions," he said.

His smile faded suddenly.

"Or," he added softly, "a different kind of creepy-crawly. Intruders in the place."

"Oh!" She had forgotten all about the footsteps. Forgotten that someone had been in the house. That he or she or they had escaped when the lights had gone out and blackness had descended.

She backed away from Rex. "What…what do you think was…going on?"

Rex shrugged and grimaced. "Alexi, if—and I'm sorry, I do mean if—someone was in the house, I don't know. A tramp, a derelict, a burglar—"

"All the way out here?"

"Hey, they deliver pizza, don't they?"

"Do they? The pizza hasn't even gotten here yet!"

"Well, I'm sorry! It is a drive for the delivery man, you know. He isn't a block away on Madison Avenue."

"Oh, would you please stop it? We are not in the Amazon wilds."

"No, but close enough," Rex promised her good-naturedly. She stared at him with a good dose of malice. Then she nearly jumped, and she did let out a gasp, because the night was suddenly filled with an obnoxious sound, loud and blaring.

"Joe's boy's horn." Rex lifted his hands palm up. "It plays Dixie."

It did, indeed. Loudly.

"I'll get the pizza," he told her.

Still smiling—with his annoying superiority—Rex went out. Alexi followed him.

Joe's boy drove a large pickup. He was a cute, long-haired kid, tall and lanky. By the time Alexi came down the walkway, Rex was already holding the pizza and involved in a casual conversation.

"Oh, here she is."

"Wow!" the boy said. He straightened, pushed back

his long blond hair and put out his hand to shake her hand soundly. "The Helen of Troy lady! Boy, oh, boy, ma'am, when I see that ad with your hair all wild and your eyes all sexy and your arms going out while you're smiling that smile, I just get...well, I get—"

"Um, thanks," Alexi said dryly. She felt Rex staring at her. Maybe he had expected her to be like the woman in the ad. He was probably disappointed to discover she was quite ordinary. "The magic of cameras," she murmured.

"Oh, no, ma'am, you're better in the flesh!" He blushed furiously. "Well, I didn't mean flesh—" he stammered.

"I don't think she took any offense, Dusty," Rex drawled. "Well, thanks again for coming out. Oh, Alexi, Dusty wants your autograph."

"Mine?"

He lifted his hands innocently. "He already has mine."

She gave Dusty a brilliant smile—with only a hint of malice toward Rex.

"Dusty, if you don't mind waiting a day or two, I'll get my agent to send down some pictures and I'll autograph one to you."

"Would you? Wow. Oh, wow. Could you write something...kind of personal on it? The guys would sure be impressed!"

"With pleasure," she promised sweetly.

"Wow. Oh, wow."

Dusty kept repeating those words as he climbed into the cab of his truck. Alexi cheerfully waved until the truck disappeared into the night. She felt Rex staring at her again, and she turned to him, a cool question in her eyes.

"Well," he said smoothly, "you've certainly wired up that poor boy's libido."

"Have I? Shall I take the pizza?"

"No, my dear little heartbreaker. I can handle it."

He started back toward the house. Alexi followed him. To her surprise, she discovered herself suddenly enjoying the night. She felt revived and ready for battle.

But there was to be no battle—not that night.

Rex went through the hall to the kitchen and put the pizza box on the table. "There's a bolt on the wood door to the parlor. If you just slide it, you can be sure that no one will come in by way of the window you broke. It was probably just some vagrant who thought the house was unoccupied, but I'd bolt that door anyway. You can get the window fixed in the morning. You should have done it today."

"You're leaving?"

He nodded and walked to where she stood by the door, pausing just short of touching her. He placed a hand against the doorframe and leaned toward her, a wry grin set in the full, sensual contours of his mouth.

"You're playing a bit of havoc with my libido, too." He pushed away from the wall. "If you should need me, the number is in the book by the phone. Good night."

For some reason, she couldn't respond. She felt as if he had touched her...as if some intimacy had passed between them.

Nothing had happened at all.

By the time she could move, he was gone. She heard the front door quietly closing.

She hurried to it, biting her lower lip as she prepared to lock the door for the night. She was still so uneasy. Rex's being there had given her a certain courage. She knew that someone had been in the house. Had he really left? Was there, perhaps, some nook or cranny where the intruder could be hiding?

She gasped. There was another tapping at the door. Her fingers froze; she couldn't bring herself to answer it.

"Alexi?"

It was Rex. She threw the door open and prayed that he wouldn't hear the pounding of her heart.

"Rex," she murmured. She lowered her face quickly, trying to hide her relief, trying not to show the sheer joy she felt at seeing him again. "Um, did you forget something?"

"Yes."

He leaned against the doorframe, his hands in the pockets of his jeans. He studied her for the longest time, and then he sighed.

"You're making me absolutely insane, you know."

"I beg your pardon," she murmured.

He shook his head ruefully, then straightened. He placed his hands on her shoulders and pushed her into the hallway to allow himself room to enter. Wide-eyed, Alexi stared up at him.

"I'm staying!" he seemed to growl.

"You're what?" she whispered.

"I'll stay."

"You—you don't need to."

He shook his head impatiently. "I'll curl up in the

parlor. Since you haven't gotten the guest rooms prepared yet," he added dryly.

"Rex...you don't have to."

"Yes, I have to." He started for the parlor.

"You should at least have some pizza!"

"No. No, thanks. I should lie down and go to sleep as quickly as possible."

"Rex—"

"Alexi—dammit! I—" He cut himself off, his jaw twisting into a rigid line. He shook his head again and walked into the parlor. She heard the door slam. Hard.

Alexi retreated to the kitchen. She leaned against the door and breathed deeply. He was going to sleep in her house. She shouldn't make him do it. She shouldn't allow him to do it.

She trembled. She couldn't help it. She was very, very glad that he was just a few feet away.

Chapter 4

Even though she knew Rex was in the house—or perhaps because she knew Rex was in the house—Alexi spent a miserable night.

The kitchen floor was still a horrible bed; she swore to herself that she would get going on the house. When she first dozed off she nearly screamed herself awake, dreaming of a giant brown widow. She hadn't even known that "widows" came in "brown"—but she didn't want to meet another one.

Having woken herself up, she ate some of the pizza. Rex, bleary-eyed and rumpled, stumbled in, and at last they shared some of the pizza. When he returned to the parlor, she determined to settle down to sleep again. More dreams and nightmares plagued her. Disconcerting, disconnected nightmares in which men and women in antebellum dress swirled through the ballroom, laughing, chatting, talking. Beautiful people in silks and satins and velvets—but the dancers were transparent and the ballroom retained its dust and webbed decay. The only man with substance in her dreams was Rex Morrow—darkly handsome and somewhat diabolical, but totally compelling as he grinned wickedly and pointed in silence to the portraits of Pierre and Eugenia on the wall. She kept trying to reach him through the translucent dancers. She didn't know why, only that she needed to, and the more time that passed, the more desperate she became. Then, at the end, a giant brown spider with John's face pounced down between them and Alexi gasped and sprang up—and came awake, swearing softly as she realized a warm sun was spilling brilliantly through the windows.

She put coffee on and went in search of Rex, only to find the sofa empty, with a note where his body should have lain.

Gone home to bathe, shave and work. Checked on you—you were sleeping like a little lamb. Well, a sexy little lamb. Libido, you know. It's light and all seems well. Fix the window today, dammit! If you need anything, give me a ring. I'll be here.

So he was gone. Funny…she had been looking forward to seeing him. To sharing coffee. To laughing at her fears by the morning's light. She smiled, remembering how they had shared cold pizza. Neither of them had really been awake. She could barely remember anything they had said. She'd liked his cheeks looking a little scruffy; she'd liked all that dark hair of his in a mess over his forehead.

Well, Rex probably wouldn't be the same by daylight, either. He'd be hostile, annoyed, superior, doing that eccentric artist bit all over again. She swore that the next time she saw him she'd be in control. Competent, able—fearless.

Oh, yeah! But she had to get started.

Definitely. She had to do something here, she warned herself. When her dreams began to include shades of *The Fly*, she was falling into the realm of serious trouble.

By morning's light she was able to roam around the lower level of the house. The place appeared even shabbier.

"Steam cleaners will make a world of difference," she promised herself out loud.

Still hesitant of the creepy-crawly possibilities, she kept her suitcase in the kitchen. When the coffee had perked, she poured herself a cup and sipped it while she opened her suitcase. The coffee tasted good. Delicious. But not even the dose of caffeine really helped her mood. Her extended-wear contact lenses weren't "extending" very well—her vision was all blurry, and she swore softly again, wishing she could wear them with comfort and ease. She peered at her watch. It was only eight. She'd take a long shower, then remove her contacts, clean them and put them back in.

Alexi found her white terry robe, finished her coffee and considered exploring the upstairs for a bedroom and bath. Then, deciding that she would tackle the upstairs after she was dressed, she called and asked the steam cleaners in town to come out. Once they were finished, she would start vacuuming and sweeping and choose a room for herself. She really wasn't afraid of a few spiders and bugs—she just wanted to be a bit more fortified to deal with them.

So, determined, she grabbed her robe and headed for the little powder room beneath the stairs. She had noticed the night before that it did have a small shower stall. In fact, the little bathroom was really quite nice. Gene must have had it updated fairly recently.

Alexi turned on the light and grimaced at her reflection in the mirror over the sink. There were purple shadows beneath her red-rimmed eyes. She certainly didn't look one bit like the Helen of Troy lady. She was pale and drawn and resembled a wide-eyed, frightened child. She pinched her cheeks, then laughed, because she hadn't given them any color at all. She reflected a bit wryly that the only real beauty to her face lay in its shape; it was what was called a classical oval, with nice high cheekbones. John had told her once that a myriad of sins could be forgiven if one's cheekbones were good.

She laughed suddenly; she looked like hell, cheekbones or no.

"Tonight," she promised her reflection out loud, "I am going to sleep!"

Sobering, she turned away from her image and stripped off her clothing; there were a million things she wanted to do that day. Clean, clean, clean. And Rex was supposed to be bringing a new hose for the car. She also wanted a sound system and a television— modern amenities that had never interested Gene.

Alexi stepped into the little shower stall, surprised and pleased to see the modern shower-massage fixtures. She fiddled with the faucets, gasped as the water streamed out stone-cold, swore softly—then breathed a sigh of relief as heat came into the water. For several long, delighted moments she just stood there, feeling the delicious little needles of wet heat sear her skin. Steam rose all around her, and she closed her eyes, enjoying it. The shower felt so good, in fact, that everything began to look better. The Brandywine house was beautiful. A little elbow grease and she could make it into a showplace again. Gene had really done quite a bit already; the kitchen was warm and nice, and this little bathroom was just fine. Of course, she could see all sorts of possibilities. The kitchen could use a window seat, a big one, with plump, comfortable cushions. Some copper implements, some plants. It was a huge room and could be made into an exquisite family center.

Alexi reached for the shampoo, scrubbed it into her hair and rinsed it. She paused then, reflecting that she really did mean to get things together.

She couldn't wait to ask Rex in for a drink or a cup of coffee once she had things straightened out. I wonder why, she thought as the water beat against her face. Because, she reasoned, everything had gone wrong every time she'd seen him. She just wanted something to go right.

As she stood there, a little curl, warm and shimmering, began to wind in her stomach. She inhaled and exhaled quickly, alarmed at the realization that she wanted to see him again...just because she wanted to see him again. She was eager to hear the tone of his voice; she felt secure and comfortable when he was near.

It was a foolish feeling. She didn't want any entanglements; she didn't think she was really even *capable* of an entanglement. But the feeling was there, an ache, a nostalgia, poignant and sweet. She wanted to see him. No...he didn't even want her in the house. He wanted the land all to himself. He saw her as an intrusion on his privacy. But she couldn't help it; she found herself wondering about his relationships with other women. He had been blunt about his divorce, more cold than bitter. Yet she knew that his marriage had left a taste of ash in his mouth. Still, having met him...having experienced that strange feeling of intimacy on the first night, she started to shiver again.

She couldn't imagine him being alone, either. He was a man who liked women, who would attract them easily—with or without fame and fortune. But once burned... She knew the feeling well. He was quiet in his way; he spoke plainly but gave away very little emotion.

Maybe it wasn't there to give.

But she had been determined to come into the shower and scrub her hair and herself and be as... perfect as she could be. For when she saw him again. She didn't want to be breaking in; she didn't want to be running because she'd blown a hose in the car. She wanted to be composed and poised. Perhaps even cool...cool enough to regain the control that seemed to be slipping from her.

Alexi sighed and turned off the shower. She had steamed herself until the water had gone cold as she'd thought about Rex Morrow. If she could put that much concentration into the house, she'd have it a showplace in no time.

Alexi opened the shower door and groped for her towel. She found it and patted her face, blinking to clear her eyes. The mist from the shower should have cleaned her lenses somewhat, but they felt grittier than ever. It must have been all the dust from last night, she reasoned.

She started to step out of the stall, then noticed a curious dark line on the floor. A wire? She blinked, wishing again that she had better luck with her lenses. There shouldn't be a wire on the floor.

Nor did wires move by themselves.

Alexi gasped, hypnotized at first. There was something on the floor about a foot long and as thick as a telephone wire. Except that the top of this wire was rising and moving, and it had a little red ribbon of color right under the...

The head!

"Oh, my God!" she breathed aloud.

It was a snake—a small one, but a snake nonetheless, slithering, slinking across the bathroom floor.

Her throat constricted; she didn't move. She didn't know whether the snake was poisonous or not, and at that point it didn't really matter. She hated snakes; they scared her to death.

The creature paused, raised its head again, then started slithering toward the toilet bowl.

She swallowed. She had to move.

Trembling, Alexi reached out for her robe. Soaking wet, she slipped into it and belted it, still standing in the shower stall—and barely blinking as she kept her eyes trained on the snake. In desperation she looked around the little bathroom. A little tile side pocket in the wall held a magazine. Alexi grabbed it and rolled it up.

Panicked thoughts whirled through her mind. If she didn't kill it on the first swipe, would it bite her? She could just run....

No. Because if it slithered out of sight, she would never, never be able to sleep in the house again.

She stepped from the shower stall with her rolled-up weapon. She inhaled sharply, then smacked the snake. She jumped back, screaming. The blow hadn't stopped the creature in the least. It was just writhing and slinking more wildly now.

She attacked again—and again. Somewhere in her mind she realized that paper would not kill the serpent. It might not be big, but it had a tough hide.

Finally, though, the thing stopped. Or almost stopped. She had most of the body smashed against the base of the toilet. Only the head wavered a bit.

She swallowed sickly. What was the damn thing doing in her house? She felt like a torturer—but she was terrified.

Alexi dropped the paper. She had to get something. A spade—something with which she could scoop the creature up and out.

And kill it. It wasn't dead—and even though it was a snake, she hated to think of herself torturing the thing.

She backed away, then ran—into the kitchen and into the pantry. She wasn't sure what lay in the bottom shelves, but she had seen a number of tools there.

She found a heavy spade. Armed with it, Alexi made her way back to the bathroom, where she stopped dead still. The snake had disappeared.

"It couldn't have, it couldn't have," she whispered aloud, leaning against the wall. But it had.

She searched the bathroom, the floor, the shower stall. But there was no snake. She began to wonder if she had imagined the creature. Had the night been so bad that she had gone a little crazy? She didn't like spiders and bugs, but she could tolerate them. She was terrified of snakes, though. She had almost told Rex Morrow so last night after he had killed the spider.

Calm yourself, calm yourself. She tried to think rationally. She had seen the creature. And now it was gone. She drew in a deep breath. Had it been poisonous? What had it looked like? She was going to have to find out. She'd have to ask. She'd have to...

"Argh!" A gasping, desperate sound escaped her as she felt something slither over her foot. She looked down in terror. It was the snake.

She had her spade. She screamed, jumped—and slammed it down.

She dropped the spade, leaving the snake pinned beneath it, and backed away. Nearing the kitchen door, she turned.

Only to see another of the foot-long blackish creatures.

Sweat broke out all over her. Shaking, Alexi wrenched open the kitchen door and ran to the pantry again. She found a pipe wrench and raced back into the hallway. She swung the wrench down with force, careless of what she might do to the fine wooden floor.

She wasn't about to pick up the spade or the pipe wrench. She burst into the parlor instead. With trembling fingers she found Rex Morrow's phone number and dialed it.

"C'mon, c'mon, c'mon, c'mon…!" she muttered as the phone rang. When she heard Rex's voice on the other end, she started to speak, then realized it was an answering machine. He didn't identify himself by name; in a deep, pleasant voice said merely, "I can't get to the phone right now, but if you'll leave your name and number at the sound of the beep, I'll get back to you as soon as possible."

Alexi waited for the beep. "Rex, it's Alexi. Rex—" Her eyes widened, and she broke off with a long scream. There was another one! Another one, coming into the parlor!

She dropped the phone and raced to the fireplace. Grabbing the poker, she went for the snake.

She got it. Or at least got it pinned beneath the poker.

She had to get out. Just for a minute; just to breathe. Her hair was soaking wet, she was barefoot, and her robe was hardly even belted, but she had to get out.

Tears stinging her eyes, she raced for the front door. By the time she got the stubborn bolt to work, she was crying in great, gulping sobs.

She flung the door open and went running out and down the path, right into a pair of strong arms.

"Alexi!"

She screamed in panic at the feel of the strong fingers tight around her shoulders. Everything that touched her had become a snake, and she couldn't see anything, as her face was crunched to his chest.

"Alexi! What is it? Oh, my God, what happened? Is someone in there? Did someone hurt you? Alexi!"

Somehow the fact that it was Rex filtered into her mind.

"Oh, Rex!" She grabbed his shirt, her fingers like talons as they dug in. She moved even closer to him, trembling.

He shook her gently.

"Dammit, Alexi, what the hell happened? Did someone attack you?"

She shook her head, unable to talk.

"Alexi!"

He caught her hands and gently unwound her fingers from their death clutch upon him. He held them between his own, then slipped his hand beneath her chin to raise her eyes to his. She saw the concern in them, the raw anxiety in the hardened twist of his jaw.

"I tried to call you—" she gasped out.

"I know, dammit, I know! I was there! I heard you scream, and I ran here as fast as I could. Alexi, what—"

"Oh, it was horrible, Rex!"

"What, Alexi, for God's sake! What?"

Her eyes were glazed, her lips were trembling, her whole body was shaking. She was deathly pale, terrified.

And she was beautiful. Not even his confusion and fear for her could block that fact. She was scrubbed and damp, and her hair was soaked, but she was beautiful. Her eyes were huge and as green as emeralds with their glazing of moisture. She was pure and glorious beneath the sun. Her scent was soft and dazzling, as soft as the pressure of her body against his. She was a barefoot waif in a white robe, and he was painfully aware that she wore nothing beneath it.

And she called on everything primitive within him. He wanted to go out and do battle for her. He wanted to sweep her into his arms, hold her to his heart and swear that things would be okay. And he wanted, with a throbbing intensity, to take her away with him, away from any horror, and make love to her. To tear away that slim barrier of terry and drown in the soft, feminine scent of her.

"Alexi!"

He shook himself, mentally, physically. There could be some horrible, stark danger at hand, and he was nearly as mesmerized as she, shuddering with the hot pulse that rent a savage path throughout his body.

"Rex! Rex! They—they…"

"They—who?" he shouted.

"Sna—" She had to pause to wet her lips. "Snakes!"

"Snakes?" he queried skeptically, looking at her as if she had lost her mind.

His tone returned some of her sanity to her. "Snakes!" she yelled back. "Slithery, slimy, creeping creatures! Snakes."

"Where?"

"In the house!"

She was still trembling, but much less. He himself was shaking now, with emotion and with a growing anger. He'd half killed himself to reach her, terrified that a murder was afoot, and she was babbling along about snakes.

The glaze was gone from her eyes. They were still a deep emerald green, but she was angry, too. He set her from himself and strode quickly up the path to the house.

Well, Rex quickly discovered, she hadn't been lying. The house looked like a scene from a macabre murder mystery. Pipe wrench, spade, fire poker. A smile curving his lips, Rex walked up to the first of the victims in the hallway.

It was just a little ringneck, not even a foot long. It was still wobbling pathetically. Rex picked it up carefully and decided the creature still had a chance. He returned to the doorway and tossed the snake into a row of crotons that rimmed the front porch. Alexi, standing further down the path, stared at him incredulously.

"Alexi, it's just a ringneck."

"It's a snake!"

Rex frowned. "You shouldn't have tried to kill it; you should have just swept it out."

"It! There's a litter in there!"

He laughed. "Them."

"Don't you dare make fun of me! They could have been poisonous, and I wouldn't have known one way or the other. You do have poisonous snakes in the state, I take it?"

"Yes, we do have poisonous snakes. And I'm sorry. You're right; you wouldn't know. But these guys are harmless. They're actually good. They eat bugs. They till the soil. You should have just swept them all out."

"Fine!" she retorted. "They're welcome to be in the soil! But not in the house!" She was still shaking, he noted. "I'm not going back in! There are more, Rex! I have to get an exterminator. Today!"

He couldn't help it; he started laughing. She drew herself very, very straight and stared at him coldly. He raised his hands in the air.

"All right, all right. I'll see if I can rescue any of your other victims, then we'll go over to my house. It might be a good idea to get an exterminator."

Rex went back into the house, shaking his head at each "scene of the crime." The snakes were still alive—they were tough little creatures. He collected them in the spade and dropped them into the bushes. Alexi was still standing on the path. His brow arched, he waved to her, then went back inside and searched. He couldn't find any more of the ringnecks.

After putting her murder weapons away in the pantry, he paused, noting that her suitcase was on the kitchen table. He probably should take it for her, he thought.

He smiled slowly thinking, Uh-uh. After all, she had probably taken ten years off his life when she had screamed like that over the phone and then dropped the damn thing! He'd had horrible visions of a man's hands around her throat—and it had all been over a few harmless garden snakes!

Uh-uh. She was coming to his house now—because she was scared. With a streak of mischief, Rex determined that this was going to be a come-as-you-are party.

Still smiling, he closed the kitchen door. He had his own key to lock up the front.

He walked down the path, not sure if he wanted to strangle her himself...or take the chance of touching her again. He did neither; he walked past her a few feet, realized that she wasn't following him and turned back impatiently.

"Are you coming?"

She looked from him to the house. It irritated him a bit that she made it seem like a choice between two terrible evils. But then, he'd been irritated since he had met her. He'd thought that she was a sneak thief at

first. Then she'd been so indignant. Aloof, remote—
and condemning. Then she'd turned on the charm for
the poor kid with the pizza, and he'd felt the allure of
it sweep over him, a draw like a potent elixir. And
then he'd felt such acute terror...

Then such acute desire. Feeling her nearly naked,
crawling against him, almost a part of him. He wondered vaguely if she had any idea just what she had
done to him. She was so sensual, his reaction was instant. And he didn't like it. Dammit, he was a cynic.
He deserved to be. His marriage had taught him a
good lesson.

Especially when the female in question was Alexi
Jordan. "Alexi," he began crossly, wishing Gene's
great-granddaughter could have been someone else.
"You can always just go back in and—"

"No!" Ashen, she ran to catch up with him. Gasping
a little, she tugged at her loosening belt. Rex turned
forward, a slightly malicious grin tugging at the corners of his mouth. But it was also a wry smile. He
wasn't sure whom he was tormenting in his subtle
way: her—or himself. He should have been cool; he
shouldn't have cared. Life ought to have taught him a
few good lessons. But she got to him. She had crawled
instantly into his system and more slowly into his soul,
and he felt damned already.

"Where is your house?" she asked him.

"Just ahead," he replied curtly. He realized that she
was panting in her effort to keep up with him, but he
didn't slow down. "This isn't a big spit of land. Your
house... Gene's house," he said, correcting himself,
"is first. Mine is just past the bend."

Alexi looked around. By daylight, it seemed very

wild and primitive to her, barren in its way. Right around the house, plants grew beautifully. There were tall oaks and pines, the colorful crotons and a spray of begonias. Out on the road, though, the terrain became sandy; there was scrub grass and an occasional pine. In the distance, toward the water, sea grapes covered the horizon.

They made a left turn. There was only one other man-made structure on the peninsula. Rex's house. Like hers, it was Victorian. The porch that ran around the upper level was decorated with gingerbread. The house was freshly painted in a muted peach shade and seemed a serene part of the landscape. Also like her house, it seemed to sit up a bit from the low, sandy turf that surrounded it. Right beyond it, she knew, was the Atlantic. She could hear the surf even as they approached it. There was a draw, warm and inviting, to the sound of the waves, she mused. Alexi bit her lip, thinking that she was crazy, that she wanted to be anywhere but here. But then again, there was no way she was going to go back into a house with snakes.

A sudden stab of sharp pain seared into her foot. She swore and stopped. Trying to balance on her right foot to see the left one, she started to keel over.

Rex caught her arm, steadying her. "What did you do?" he asked.

"I don't know..." she began, but then she saw the trail of blood streaming from her sole.

"Must have been a broken shell," he said, in a voice that seemed just a bit apologetic. As if he had just realized that he had been moving as if in a marathon race while she had been barefoot, Alexi thought.

"It's all right," she murmured. "I can manage."

"Don't be absurd," he said impatiently. "You get too much sand in it and you'll have a real infection."

Before she could protest, he swept her into his arms. Out of a will to survive the rest of his breakneck-speed walk, she slipped her arms around his neck, flushing. "Really, I..."

"Oh, for Pete's sake."

Alexi fell silent. Maybe she would have been better off with the snakes after all. The sun was beating down on them both, but she wasn't at all convinced it was the sun that was warming her. He was hot, like molten steel. His chest was hard and fascinating; the feel of his arms about her was electric. She could feel his breathing, as well as each little ripple and nuance of his muscles, hard and trim, but living and mobile, too. She swallowed, because the temptation to touch was great. It was pure instinct, and she fought it. In fact, she hated instinct. He was probably annoyed that she might be thinking that being in his arms was more than it was....

And she couldn't quite fight that damned instinct, that feeling that he was everything wonderful and good about the male of the species, that the sun was warm, the surf inviting. That she wanted to touch all that taut muscle and flesh and that it might well be the most natural thing in the world to lie with him in the sand.

So much for being perfect! So much for being cool and aloof and completely in control! She thought of when she had been in the shower, where she'd dreamed of her next meeting with him. And here she was— cool, remote and dignified. Hah! She looked like hell again. Barefoot, with not a shred of makeup, her hair soaking wet, and dressed in nothing but a robe. And it wasn't just the miserable indignity of how she looked. She'd been hysterical at first, and she wasn't doing much better now. No wonder he wanted her out; she was nothing but trouble to him. Of course, he had been there when she'd needed him. And sometimes, when he looked at her, he was so very masculine and sexual that she was certain she must appeal to him in some sense. He was rude, but he could also be kind.

He had been very frank in saying that he wanted the house, that he wanted her out—but he had still helped her. Of course, he had tried to scare her last night, too. All that ridiculous bit about ghosts.

She paled in his arms, feeling ill. He'd brushed the spider off her and killed it. And she had almost told him how frightened she was of snakes. She had almost said the word. He had pressed her.

He had known. Known that she didn't like the bugs, but that she could bear them. He was intuitive; he was quick. He wanted her out...

She gasped suddenly, released her hold about his neck and slammed a tight fist against his chest.

"Hey—" Startled and furious, he stared down at her.

"You bastard!"

"What?"

"You did it! You knew I was terrified of snakes! You put them in there. Here I thought that you were being decent. You did it! You put me down, you—"

She didn't go any further, because he did put her down. In fact, he almost dropped her, then stood above her with a dark scowl knit into his features, his hands locked aggressively on his hips.

"I did no such damn thing!"

"You knew—"

"I didn't know anything, Ms. Jordan. And trust me, lady, I don't have the time to go digging up a pack of harmless little ringnecks just to get to you. You don't need help to blow it—I'm sure you'll manage on your own."

"Oh! You stupid—" She had tried to rise, but the weight on her foot was an agonizing pain. She broke off, gasping against the pain, teetering dangerously. He stretched an arm out; she tried to push him away, but as she started to fall she grabbed at him desperately.

Rex, unprepared, lost his balance, too. They crashed down into the sand together.

In a most compromising position. He was nearly stretched on top of her. And her robe…

Was nearly pushed to her waist.

And they were both aware of the position. Very painfully aware. Alexi couldn't think of a word to say; she couldn't move. She could only stare, stunned and miserable, into the hard, dark eyes above her. It seemed like an eternity in which she felt her naked body pressed to him, an eternity in which she felt all his muscles contract and harden.

An eternity…while she wished that she could be swallowed up by the sand.

Abruptly he pushed himself away from her. With supple agility, he landed on the balls of his feet. Blushing furiously, Alexi pushed her robe down.

"Damn you!" he said angrily. "Now, this time you just keep quiet! Throw out your accusations once we're there."

His arms streaked out for her so fast that she almost shrieked, afraid for a second that he meant violence. He picked her up again, his arms as rigid as pokers, shaking with anger. He started off again, his pace faster than ever.

He walked her up the steps to the porch, threw open the screen door and carried her inside. He turned almost instantly to the left, to the parlor. Seconds later she was deposited roughly upon a couch that was covered in soft beige leather. She scrambled to right herself, to pull her robe down around her knees.

"Don't move!" he warned her sharply. She tried miserably to relax. She made herself breathe slowly in and out as she looked at her surroundings. It was a nice room. Contemporary. The soft leather sofa sat across from two armchairs, all on warm earthen tile. A wall of arched windows looked out on the sea below. Her house and his were similar in construction, but here two rooms had been combined to make one huge one. To the rear, bookshelves lined the walls, and there were two long oak desks angled together with a computer-and-printer setup. She imagined that Rex must like his view of the sea very much. He could work, then stop and walk to the windows to watch the endless surf and the way the sun played over the water.

She tried not to imagine Rex at all.

And then he was back.

He had a bowl of water and a little box, and he sat by her on the sofa without a word, pulling her foot up onto his lap. His dark hair fell over his forehead; she couldn't see his eyes.

He moved quickly and competently, not apologizing or saying a word when she winced as he washed off her foot.

"Shell…it was still there," he said at last. She didn't reply, but bit her lip. He wasn't big on TLC, she mused wryly.

He opened the little box and sprayed something on her foot, then wrapped it in a gauze bandage. He moved back, dumping her foot less than graciously on the sofa. He stood, picked up the bowl and the box and disappeared again. The pain, which had been sharp, began to fade, and she wondered distractedly what he had sprayed on it. She felt like a fool. She realized that he most probably had not dug around in the ground to find a pack of snakes to set loose in her bathroom. Snakes. It was just the damn snakes. Anything else she could surely have dealt with….

She'd been half-naked. He'd known it; she'd known it. And they'd both felt the hard, erotic flow of heat. Where was he? She had to get out of here. Her palms began to sweat. She couldn't go back if there were more snakes. But she couldn't stay away forever. She couldn't stay on his couch, barely dressed….

Then he was back. He set a steaming mug on a small side table beside her, then walked across to sit in one of the chairs, staring at her. With hostility, she was certain. He had his own mug of steaming liquid, and sipped it broodingly.

Alexi tried to sit properly. She had to moisten her lips to speak. "Rex, I'm sorry. Perhaps—"

"Drink the coffee. It's spiked. It will help."

"I doubt it—"

"It's sure as hell helping me."

She didn't know why; she picked up the coffee cup.

She didn't know what it was laced with, but it was good, and it was strong. It warmed her hands and her throat, and it did help.

"I—" she began.

"The exterminators don't really do snakes," he told her dryly, "but they're coming out. I talked to a guy who said that they were probably just washed up by the rain and came through the broken window. When they finish, you won't have anything else. No spiders, no bugs. And a friend of mine from Ace GlassWorks will be out this afternoon to fix that window. His sister manages a cleaning outfit, and they'll be out, too. They do the works—sweep, wash and steam-clean. You should be in business then."

"Rex, thank you, but really—"

"You've got objections?"

"No, dammit, but really, it's my responsibility—" She broke off, frowning. She could hear the front door opening. Rex heard it, too. His brow knit, and he started to rise. Then he sat back.

"Who is that?" Alexi asked.

But by that time the woman was already in. "Rex?" She came into the parlor, carrying a bag of groceries. Trim and pretty, she looked to Alexi to be approximately fifty. There was an immense German shepherd at her heels; the dog instantly rushed to Rex, barking, greeting him.

The woman stared uncomfortably at Alexi, who sat there in a robe and nothing else, curled on the couch, the coffee cup in her hands.

The woman blushed.

Rex smiled. "Emily, hi. I forgot you were coming

this morning." He stood. The dog sat by his chair, panting, and woofing at Alexi.

"Shush, Samson. That's Alexi. She's a...friend. Alexi, this is Emily Rider. Emily, Alexi Jordan. Emily keeps everything in order for me."

"How do you do," Alexi said, wishing she could scratch Rex's eyes out. "I—I cut my foot."

"Oh," Emily said in disbelief. She smiled awkwardly, then gasped. "*The* Alexi Jordan?"

"There's only one," Rex said. "I hope."

"It's—it's a pleasure," Emily murmured. "I didn't mean to interrupt."

"There's nothing to interrupt!" Alexi said quickly—too quickly, she realized, for a woman who was sitting in her robe on a man's couch.

"Ah, well...have you had breakfast? I make wonderful omelets, Ms. Jordan."

"Really," Alexi protested. "Please don't go to any trouble—"

"No trouble at all!" Emily insisted. It was obvious to Alexi that the woman was dying to escape.

"Thanks, Emily," Rex called. Samson whined. Rex sat again, watching Alexi as he scratched the dog's head. "That is a most glorious shade of red," he told Alexi.

"What?"

"Your skin."

She whispered an oath to him.

He stood, still smiling. Samson trailed along with him, loyal and loving.

"Emily might need some help," he said.

Alexi rose carefully on one foot, using the couch for balance.

"Tell her the truth! She thinks that..."

"That what?"

"That I—that we—that we were sleeping together!"

"I suppose she does."

"Well, set her straight! Do you want her to think that?"

Rex chuckled softly. He cupped her cheek for an instant; the warmth of his breath feathered over her flesh. "Why not?"

"Why not?" Alexi echoed furiously.

"Doesn't every man fantasize about sleeping with the face that launched a thousand ships?" His brow was arched; he was mocking her, she was certain.

"Rex, damn you—"

"Of course, Alexi, there's much, much more to you than a beautiful face—isn't there?"

Samson barked; Rex walked out. Alexi, trembling, wanted to scream at him.

But she didn't want to scream with Emily there, so she sank weakly back to the sofa.

Chapter 5

Emily was busy cracking eggs when Rex came into the kitchen. He walked over to the refrigerator and pulled out the milk for her, smiling as he set it on the counter. He had seen her watching him covertly as she pretended great interest in the eggs.

"She's cute, huh," he commented, stealing a strip of green pepper and leaning against the counter.

Emily arched a brow. "Alexi Jordan? All you have to say about her is 'cute'?"

"Real cute?"

Emily sniffed. "She's probably the most glamorous woman in the world—"

Rex broke in on her with soft laughter. "Emily! Glamorous? You just saw her with wet hair in a worn terry robe!"

"She's still glamorous."

"She's flesh and blood," Rex said irritably, wondering at the bitterness in his own tone. He wanted her to be real, an ordinary woman, he thought dismally.

"Nice flesh," Emily commented dryly, pouring the eggs into the frying pan.

"Very nice." He grinned.

"When did you meet?"

"A few nights ago."

"Oh."

Her lips were pursed in silent disapproval, and Rex couldn't help but laugh again and give her a quick hug. "There's nothing going on, Emily. Alas, and woe is me—but that's the truth. She called over here this morning because her house was suddenly infested with snakes."

"Snakes?"

"Just some harmless ringnecks."

"How many?"

"Five."

Emily shuddered. "That poor creature! Well, you were right to bring her over here. I wonder if she should stay the night."

"I'd just love it," Rex told her wickedly.

"I'll stay, too, Casanova," Emily warned him. When she saw that he was about to take another pepper, she rapped him on the hand with her wooden spoon.

"Emily...you're showing no respect to me at all."

She sniffed again. Emily had a great talent for sniffing, he thought with a smile.

"Well, Mr. Popularity, maybe this is just what you need. The lady is far more renowned than you."

"Oh, really?"

"She's glamorous. You're merely...notorious."

Rex laughed good-naturedly.

"And you're usually rude to women," she went on.

"I am not."

"You are. You had a bad break with your wife, and you think they're all after something. So you figure you'll just use people first—and not get hurt in the end."

He was grateful that Emily didn't see that his features had gone taut; she was busy adding ingredients to her omelet. She wouldn't have cared anyway; she loved him like a son and had no qualms about treating him like one.

"Emily, Emily, you should be opening an office instead of cooking and cleaning for me," he said coolly.

"Well, it's true," Emily murmured. "I've seen you do it a million times. Some sexy thing moves in and you're all charm. Then you get what you want—and you're bored silly when the chase is over. But you always win. You've got the looks; you've got the way with women." She turned, pointing her spoon at him. "But maybe you are in trouble this time. She has tons and tons of her own money, and…" Emily paused to grin. "She's prettier than you are, too."

"Thank you, doctor!" Rex retorted. "What makes you think I'm after her?"

"You're not?"

"I'm not half as black as you paint me," Rex said flatly. "I only deal with ladies who know the game—and are willing to play. By my rules."

"The rule being fun only."

"Emily, come on! Fine, I've been around; they've been around. What's so wrong?"

"What's wrong is that you're lacking caring and commitment, growing together—love!"

"Love is a four-letter word," Rex told her flatly. Then he paused, swinging around. He could have sworn he'd heard movement by the kitchen door. He strode toward it and got there just in time to see the figure clad in white hobbling across the hall toward the parlor. He followed, angry. He didn't like being spied upon.

She had almost reached the couch. He didn't let her make it; he caught her elbow. "Can't I help you, Ms. Jordan?"

She spun to look at him, her cheeks flaming. "I—"

"You were spying on me!"

"Don't be absurd! You're not worth spying on! I was trying to see if I could do something, but I realized that I had stumbled on a personal conversation and I didn't want to hear it!" She jerked her elbow away from him, lost her balance and crashed down onto the couch.

Rex didn't know why he was so enraged at her. He didn't move to help her; he just stared at her. "The thing to do would have been to make your presence known!"

"This is ridiculous!"

Her eyes really were emerald, he mused, especially when they glittered with righteous anger.

She squared her shoulders, undaunted by his wrath or his form, which was rather solidly before her. She managed to stand, shoving by him, limping out of his way. "This whole thing is ridiculous! Thank you—I really do thank you for picking up the snakes. But I think I'll go home now. The snakes, at least, have better manners!"

She really was going to try to stumble home by herself. She was already heading toward the door.

"Alexi!"

She just kept going.

"Alexi, dammit—" He came after her, caught an arm and swung her around. He knew she would have to clutch at him to maintain her balance. She did; she curled her fingers around his arms and swore softly under her breath, tossing back her head to stare at him. Her hair was drying and it was wild, he saw, a beautiful, disheveled golden mane to frame her exquisite eyes and perfect features. He inhaled sharply, remembering what it was like to feel her body. Fool, he chided himself. He knew why he was so angry. She had heard everything that Emily had said to him. Every damning thing.

And he wanted her. Really wanted her, as he had never wanted anything in his life.

"Alexi... I'm sorry." Apologies weren't easy for him. They never had been.

"And I'm leaving," she said.

He smiled. "Back to the snakes?"

She looked down fleetingly. "There are all kinds of snakes, aren't there, Mr. Morrow?"

He laughed. She had heard everything. "Look, Ms. Jordan, I really am sorry. Be forgiving. After all, you cost me ten years of life with that scream this morning. Stay...please."

She lowered her head. "I feel—ridiculous. Your housekeeper must think that I'm—that I'm worse than what the tabloids say. And I can't wear a robe all day..."

"You can take it off," Rex said innocently, which immediately drew a scathing glance from her.

He shook his head ruefully. "No...you can't take it off. Look, sit down with Emily and have some breakfast. I'll go back over for your things. Maybe the exterminators will be there by now and I can get them started."

"You don't need to—"

"I want to. Relax. Enjoy Emily's company." He stepped away from her and whistled. "Samson!" The German shepherd came bounding in. He was huge, and when he swept by Alexi, she teetered dangerously, trying to catch her balance again. "Samson!" Rex chastised him, stepping forward quickly to catch Alexi. He smelled the soft, alluring scent of her hair as he caught her; he felt its velvet texture graze his cheek. He wanted to swear all over again.

"You'd better stay seated," he muttered, lifting her swiftly and depositing her upon the couch. Another mistake. He felt too much of her body. Too much smoothness beneath the terry. Smoothness that reminded him that there was nothing beneath it.

"I'll be back with your things," he said brusquely, then strode out, the shepherd obediently at his heels.

He was barely gone before Emily came to the doorway, smoothing her hands over her apron. She smiled shyly at Alexi. "I have everything ready." She frowned. "Where's Rex?"

"He—he went back over to my house. To Gene's house," Alexi said apologetically. She flushed again, wondering what the woman must think of her. Rex

Morrow—he was like a cyclone in her life. She never knew what to think. One moment she was fascinated; the next second she wanted to carve notches in his flesh...slowly. He was dangerous to her. To any woman, she thought, flushing all over again at the pieces of conversation she had heard. Oh, she couldn't be so foolish as to imagine having an affair with him. He was striking, sensual and sexual—and she was still reeling from the impact of her marriage. If there was anything she didn't need, it was an affair with someone like him.

Emily smiled at her suddenly; the smile was warm, shy, only slightly awkward.

"You really are beet red. I apologize if I gave you the idea that I was thinking...something...that I shouldn't have been thinking," she added hastily. "Rex told me about the snakes." She shuddered. "Ugh. I *know* they're harmless snakes—and I would have been in a tizzy, too, I assure you."

"Thanks," Alexi said, a little huskily. And before she really thought she murmured, "Rex told you—the truth?"

"Oh, he can be a pill, can't he?" She shook her head, but then it was clear to Alexi that Emily's affection for him rose to the fore. "But he's really very ethical." Emily laughed. "Honestly. He can be hard—but he does play up-front, and he's a strangely principled man. For this day and age, anyway," she added with a soft sigh. "Oh, here I am, going on and on, when your food is nice and hot. I'll bring it out—"

"Oh, no, please don't bother! I can get to the kitchen with no problem, really. I have to start walking. I have a lot of things to do."

"Let me help you."

Alexi protested; Emily insisted. They walked back to the kitchen, Alexi learning to put a little more weight on her foot with each movement.

Emily sat down with her, sharing the omelet that Rex had left behind. Alexi found out that Emily was a widow with four grown children. She also learned that Emily counted Rex as an adopted fifth child—and adored him with a fierce loyalty.

There was something about Emily, she reflected. The woman was warm and open and giving, and Alexi found herself trying to explain what she wanted to do. It began when Emily asked her why on earth she would want to leave modeling.

Alexi smiled, then laughed. "It's a miserable profession, that's why. People poke at you and prod at you for hours for a 'perfect' look. It's hour after hour under hot lights doing the same thing over and over again. But still, it isn't really that I'm trying to leave modeling." She hesitated, smiled ruefully, and stumbled into a lengthier explanation. "It's strange; I did come from money. But there's always been a golden rule in the family: everyone goes to work. Gene, my great-grandfather, owns a number of businesses, and everyone does something. We aren't expected to go into a family business, but there can be no freeloaders. My older brother is a lawyer; my cousins went into the business side of things. But then, suddenly, when I came along, no one thought that... I don't know; they didn't seem to think I was capable of anything! I went to college and studied interior design, and they all thought, Well, great, she can marry the right boy and be a perfect wife, mother and hostess. It was serious to me." She sighed. "Anyway, I walked out in a huff one night and wound up in New York City. Broke. And I wasn't about to call home. None of the design studios wanted much to do with a beginner—and I didn't have the time to wait for a job. Out of desperation I walked into one of the modeling agencies. And I was lucky. I did get work."

"But you want to be a designer?"

Alexi chewed on her omelet, thought a minute, then shrugged. "I don't know anymore. I lost a lot of confidence somewhere. But…" She paused, a grin curling her lip. "Gene is great. He has always been willing to take a chance. He was desperate for someone to come take care of the house—he doesn't want it out of the family after all of these years. And he believes in me. So I want to do the house for him, and I want to do it right."

Emily nodded as if she understood perfectly. "And you will do it!" she said firmly.

Alexi laughed dryly. "I'm not so sure. Last night I couldn't get the old key to work in the lock. This morning I ran in terror from garden snakes. I'm not proving very much, am I? And now Rex is out there with the exterminators and cleaners."

Emily smiled and put her hand over Alexi's. "Young lady, that doesn't mean a thing. That's one of the problems with people today—men and women! All this role business! Alexi, you'll do just fine. So what if you don't handle snakes well? That does not take anything away from your competence. We all need help now and then, and if people could just learn not only to give it but to accept it, the world would be a better place. And the divorce rate would be lower!"

"I don't know," Alexi said, chuckling. "I feel like an idiot right now. But maybe things will improve." She cut off another piece of her omelet, feeling that maybe she had blurted out too much to a stranger, no matter how nice that stranger was.

"Emily, where did Samson come from? Is he Rex's dog or yours?"

"Oh, no! That beast belongs to Rex. Body and soul." She went on to tell Alexi about Samson as a little puppy, and Alexi relaxed, feeling that the conversation had taken on a much more casual tone.

Tony Martelli, from Bugs, Incorporated, was just driving up to the Brandywine house when Rex reached it. He gave Rex a wave and hopped out of his truck, smiling. Rex waved back, smiling in turn. He liked Tony. He was a live-and-let-live kind of a guy. The man had a tendency to chew on a toothpick or a piece of grass and to listen much more than he talked. He gave Rex's house monthly service and was one of the few people Rex had invited to wander his beach when he had the chance.

"Snakes, huh?"

Rex laughed. "And everything else under the sun."

Tony squinted beneath the glare of the sun. "Well, we'll spray, but snakes… Well, you kind of have to find the little guys and put them out." He scratched his head. "It rained last night, but it wasn't really a flood. Wonder how they got in."

"There was a broken window."

"Maybe." Tony shrugged. "It wouldn't be unheard-of, but I find it kind of strange."

Rex frowned, remembering how Alexi had accused

him of putting the snakes into the house himself to
scare her out. She was convinced that someone had
been in the house last night. Maybe that same person
had come back in after he had left early this morning.

He walked up the path with Tony and opened the
door. Tony whistled. "How long has Gene been out
of here?"

"Awhile. Nine months, maybe."

"Nine months of breeding bugs. Well, I'll spray her
real good. And I'll look out for a nest of ringnecks. I
just doubt it, though, you know? If they were in the
house, Miz Jordan should have noticed them when
she came in, not this morning." He laughed suddenly,
"I've heard of ghosts in this place, but not snakes."

"Yeah." Rex laughed with Tony, but he wasn't
amused. Tony went out for his equipment. Rex went on
into the parlor and called the sheriff's office. A friend
of his—a budding story-teller named Mark Eliot—was
on the desk. Rex listened patiently to Mark's newest
plot line, then told him that he was pretty sure someone was sneaking around the Brandywine house.

"Anything broken into?" Mark asked.

"Well...only by the rightful tenant. She couldn't
get her key to work," Rex explained. Then he told
Mark about Alexi's hearing footsteps racing down the
stairs—and about the snakes. He was annoyed when
Mark chuckled.

"Snakes? You think somebody snuck in to leave a
pack of ringnecks?"

"Never mind..."

"Sorry, Rex, sorry," Mark apologized quickly.
"Want me to come out?"

"No, there's nothing you can do now. Maybe someone could make an extra patrol at night and keep an eye on things."

"Sure thing, Rex. Will do."

Rex hung up, wondering why he still didn't feel right about things. He heard a whining sound and felt a cold nose against his hand. He patted the dog absently; he had forgotten that Samson was with him. "You should have been here last night, monster," he told the dog affectionately. "You might have caught whoever ran. If there was a 'whoever.' Come on, boy. Let's get Alexi's stuff, huh?"

That didn't even seem to be such a good idea. In the kitchen, Rex began to close the open suitcase on the table; he hesitated. Everything of hers had a wonderful scent. Her clothes...

He picked up the soft silk blouse on top and brought it to his face. It seemed to whisper of her essence. He dropped it back into the suitcase and slammed the suitcase shut.

Samson stood by him, thumping his tail against the floor. "This is getting serious, Samson. Frightening. I barely know her."

How well did someone need to know a face that could launch a thousand ships?

He groaned out loud at the thought and picked up the suitcase. He found her purse in the parlor, called out to Tony that he would be right back and left the house. Ten minutes of brisk walking brought him back to his own.

To his own amazement, he didn't go in. He set Alexi's suitcase and purse inside the screen door, called out that he was dropping them off and turned around to walk back, Samson still at his heels.

His fingers were clenched into fists, braced behind his back. He knew he wouldn't go back that night. He'd give Emily a call and tell her that he would just stay at Gene's—making sure no more snakes appeared— and that he'd be back in the morning.

He just couldn't see Alexi Jordan again right away. It was still true that he barely knew her, and it was damned true that she was having an extraordinary effect on him. Unsettling. Insane.

The exterminator was just finishing up when Rex returned, and when Tony pulled out with his van, the cleaners were pulling in with theirs. Rex let them in with all their heavy-duty equipment, then went into the kitchen and heated up the remainder of the pizza, which he found in the refrigerator. He had it with a beer, reflecting that everything had suddenly turned into a sad state of affairs. He should have been working, and instead he was over here, hiding out from a blonde.

"Well, she is damned good-looking," he told Samson, stretching his legs out under the table. "The type that can seduce a guy and steal his soul, you say, Samson, boy? I agree, a hundred percent. I should stay away, huh? Hmm. Those eyes. With my luck, I'd be dumb enough to fall in love again. And she'd stay around for a month, then take off for the big city and her glamorous career. Aha!" He was silent for a minute, staring at the bottle. "I'll go nuts if I don't give it some good, sturdy effort." He sipped his beer reflectively. "But not until tomorrow. I'm not so sure I could take seeing her again today—take it and behave civilly. Okay, Samson, so I haven't been so civil so far.

I'm supposed to be a rude eccentric. I have my reputation to live up to, you know."

Just then the phone started to ring. It was Emily, worried. He assured her things were going fine. "Just tell Alexi to stay there tonight and I'll stay here. The cleaners seem to be doing just fine; Tony sprayed, and I can still smell the stuff all over. It will be much better by tomorrow.... Okay, take care."

He hung up, and walked into the hall, his hands in his pockets. The cleaning crew consisted of four men. They all knew what they were doing; they moved economically and efficiently. The house already looked better, and they hadn't even started with the steaming. He wandered back to the kitchen, restless. This was rough. He didn't know what to do. He didn't really know how to be idle.

He stared out the window over the sink for a moment, then smiled. In the drawer was a legal pad. He drew it out and sat at the table again. He could make this work.

He sketched out a rough story line about a wealthy family with a suddenly deceased patriarch. A family that began to die off rather quickly. He used Gene's house, and his victims fell as the snakes had, by the same weapons Alexi had utilized.

Within ten minutes, his fingers were flying over the page. A studious frown knitted his brow, and time became meaningless. His concentration was complete.

But then he realized that his heroine looked exactly like Alexi.

And his hero was strangely similar to himself.

He sat back, then forward again.

Well, what the hell, he thought. Who was he to argue with creative forces?

He was planning an awful lot of sex scenes for a murder mystery, though, he reflected. He paused, then laughed dryly.

What the hell...

Alexi stared up at the sun through the swaying fronds of a huge palm. She closed her eyes, the sun was so bright. But the warmth felt good against her flesh.

She rolled on her beach sheet and stared out at the water. The surf curled in softly, then ebbed in near silence. It was beautiful. Exquisitely beautiful. From here, the Atlantic seemed to stretch away forever. The sky tenderly kissed the water. It was peaceful and private. The sand was fine and white; the palms gave lovely shade.

She lay on her stomach, her chin cupped in her hands. She could even understand why Rex had seemed so aggrieved to discover that she was taking over the house. This was a paradise. Remote and exotic. Who would want intrusion?

She stretched and rolled onto her side again, idly drawing patterns in the sand.

Then, despite herself, she began to wonder if he came here often. Of course he did. Who wouldn't? The beach belonged to him. Not to both houses—to him.

He loved it, surely. His windows looked out over it. He probably walked over the sand all the time, possibly at sunset. At sunset, it would probably be even more beautiful. So very private.

And if he had a date...

He probably took her here. At sunset. He would
hold hands with her, and they would walk along the
sand. And maybe they would play where the water
washed over the sand in a soft gurgle. Maybe she
would laugh and spray him with water, and maybe
he would retaliate and they would fall to the sand.
They would make love with the water sliding over
them, warm and exciting. Their clothing would lie
strewn on the beach, but they really wouldn't need
to worry; it was so private here. What would he look
like...nude? Beautiful, she decided. He was so tall,
broad-shouldered, lean where he should be, bronzed
and so nicely, tightly sinewed.

"Hello."

Alexi gasped and whirled around. Instantly fire-
red coloring flushed her cheeks.

It was Rex. Of course it was Rex—it was his beach.
But she hadn't expected him here. She hadn't seen him
since he'd dropped her suitcase on his hallway floor.
That was almost two days ago. She still hadn't been
back into her house; she'd been in his, and he in hers.
Impatience had brought her to the beach. Impatience
and frustration. The cleaners had stayed so late on
Monday that she hadn't gone back, and on Tuesday he
had told Emily that the fumes were still too strong for
Alexi to be able to do anything worthwhile.

Alexi had been determined to go back anyway.
Emily had convinced her to stay, telling her that she
would do much better for herself in the next few days
if she allowed her foot to heal properly. And, Emily
had told her with a wink, Rex was working—he was
too immersed to notice the fumes.

"I said 'Hello,' not 'Take your clothes off, please.' Do you have to look so horrified to see me?"

"I'm not," she said quickly. She was. She looked down to the sand, not sure how to explain that he had interrupted her when she was imagining *him* without his clothes.

Not that he was wearing much. He was in a pair of cutoffs—and what she could see was very near what she had imagined. His flesh was very bronze, very sleek. His shoulders and chest were hard and sinewed; his legs were long and his thighs powerful. Dark hair grew on his chest in a swirl that tapered into a soft line down to the waistband of his shorts. He wore a gold St. Christopher medal and a black-banded sports watch.

He sank down beside her. She felt his gaze move over her, and it touched her with greater warmth than the sun. Actually, she wasn't exactly cocooned in clothing herself. Her bathing suit was one-piece, but it had no back, and the cut was very high on the thighs. To her horror, she felt her heartbeat quicken. Surely he could see the throb of her pulse in a dozen different places.

"Must you?" she demanded huskily.

"Must I what?"

"Come out with all those things."

"What things?"

"About clothing. Or lack of them. Or sleeping with the Helen of Troy lady."

He was silent for a moment, looking out to sea. He shrugged, then stared at her again. It took a lot of effort, but she finally lifted her eyes to his—and watched him as coolly as she could.

He smiled slowly, the curl of his lip very deliberate and sensual. "You were blushing before I opened my mouth."

"The sun—"

"Hah!"

Alexi threw her hands up. "Mr. Morrow, meet Ms. Jordan. How do you do? How do you do? Pleasant weather, isn't it? Lovely weather, really lovely. That, Mr. Morrow, is the type of conversation that people who have just met exchange!"

He laughed, leaning back on an elbow. "You're forgetting the way that we met."

"You mauled me."

"And I loved every minute of it."

"Would you stop?"

"If you want me to stop," he said evenly, "why are you out here on my beach in that bathing suit?"

"It *is* a beach! People wear bathing suits on beaches."

"Mmm. But not people who look like you, in bathing suits like that."

"I'll wear my long johns next time."

He laughed softly, then suddenly reached out for her shoulder and toppled her down beside him. She gasped, ready to protest, but then the smile left his face and he stared down at her so intently that all words fled from her mind. There was something about him. His eyes were so sharp they were almost pained; his features were taut and haggard.

He drew a finger down her cheek very slowly, barely touching her. Then he breezed that same finger over her lower lip, very slowly, never losing the sharp, hungry tension of his gaze upon her.

For the life of her, she couldn't move. She could

only imagine him as she had before: with a nameless woman on the beach—naked.

He was Rex Morrow, the famous, talented recluse, who used women—and the world couldn't possibly know that she was incredibly naive and pathetically vulnerable. Well, she had some pride, and she couldn't be used!

"Rex—"

"It's going to happen, you know."

"What?"

"Us. You and me. We're going to make love. Maybe right here, right where we are now."

"You're incredibly arrogant."

"I'm honest. Which you aren't at the moment."

"Someone should really slap you—hard," she told him disdainfully, though with some difficulty. He was still halfway over her. She could feel his body, so warm from the sun beating down upon it. So close. And both of them so…barren of substantial clothing. Her pulse was beating furiously again. And she wanted to touch him. She had never before known such temptation—a desire that defied good sense and pride and reason.

"Is that someone going to be you?" he said slyly.

"If you don't watch it," she warned.

"Can't you feel it?" he asked her lazily. "The sun-baked sand, the whisper of the waves, rising, ebbing… rising. Can't you feel the heat from the sun, from the earth, becoming a part of us?"

He touched the rampant pulse at the base of her throat.

"Can't you feel the rhythm…throbbing?"

"You're an arrogant SOB—that's what I can feel," she said coolly.

He laughed. The tension was gone; the hardened hunger of his gaze. He pushed himself up and landed on his feet with the grace of a great cat. He offered a hand to her. "Come on. I've got a present for you."

She stared warily at his hand, causing him to chuckle again.

"Nervous, Alexi? Think I'm going to toss you to the sand and maul you?" Impatiently he grabbed her hand and pulled her to her feet.

And then against his body. He arched a brow wickedly. "Don't worry. When we get to it, you'll be breathlessly eager."

Alexi coolly took a step backward, raising her chin, smiling as sweetly as she could.

"I hardly think so, Mr. Morrow."

He laughed, slipped an arm around her waist and started back toward the house. When they were nearly there, he lowered his head and murmured near her ear, "Liar."

"Ohh…" she groaned. *Really.* What incredible insolence, she thought. She stepped ahead of him again and turned around to face him challengingly. "You really like the suit, huh?"

"I like what's in it."

Alexi groaned. "Eat your heart out, then!" she teased.

Rex laughed. But when he caught up with her again and whispered what he did intend to do, it was so insinuative that the sensations that ripped through her, jagged and molten, felt dangerously as if he had followed through.

Chapter 6

At the path to the house, Rex suddenly stood still, crossing his arms over his chest. He nodded toward the front door.

"You first, Ms. Jordan."

She arched a brow, then shrugged, heading down the path. At the door she paused. "I don't have a key with me."

"It isn't locked."

She raised her brow more. "I'm having problems with people and footsteps, and you left the door open?"

"Samson is inside. I assure you—no one is in there with him."

"Oh." Alexi pushed open the door. Rex had been telling the truth; Samson was sitting in the hallway, just like a sentinel. He barked and thumped his tail against the floor. He was standing behind a large wicker basket with a red-white-and-blue checked cotton cloth extended beneath the handle.

"Good boy, Samson, but what is this?" Alexi said, then turned to look at Rex again.

"It's your present," he told her.

He smiled—a little awkwardly, she thought—and she lowered her head quickly, wondering if she was blushing again. There had been a nice touch to that smile. Endearing...frightening. She barely knew him, really. One minute he was making sexual innuendos, the next he was avoiding her—and then the next he was doing wonderful things for her.

"Well, open it up," Rex urged her.

Alexi knelt down and gingerly lifted up a piece of the cotton cloth. She saw movement first, and then she gasped, reaching into the basket. There were two of them—two little balls of silver fur. The one she held mewed, sticking out a tiny paw at her.

"Oh!" It was adorable. The cutest kitten she had ever seen. It was all that soft, wonderful silver color, except for its feet and its nose, which were black. Its hair was long and fluffy—and made it look much bigger than it was.

Samson barked excitedly. Alexi reflected that the giant shepherd could consume the kitten in one mouthful, but he didn't seem the least bit interested in trying. He barked again, watching Alexi as if he had planned it himself or as if he was very aware that he and Rex were handing out a present.

"Oh!" Alexi repeated, stroking the kitten. The second ball was crawling out of the basket, and she laughed, scooping that one up, too. "You're adorable. You're the cutest little things...."

She gazed up at Rex at last, aware that she was starting to gush. But they were a wonderful present. She was also certain that they were silver Persians—and that they had cost him a fair amount of money.

"Rex—"

He stooped down beside her, idly patting the dog. "I don't want Samson here getting jealous," he said lightly. "Do you like them…really?"

He gazed at her—somewhat anxiously, she thought—and she felt that the hall had suddenly become small. The two of them were very close and very scantily dressed, and yet it wasn't that at all, really; it was that expression in his eyes.

"They're darling. But, Rex, I—I can't accept them."

"Why?"

"They're Persians, right? They must have cost a mint."

"What?" He threw back his head and laughed, relieved. "I was afraid that you were allergic to them or something. Yes, they're Persians. They're three months old, but the breeder assured me they'd be perfect."

"Perfect?"

He grinned, a little wickedly now. "Mousers—except that I don't think you have any mice. You could, though—mice are rather universal. 'Snakers,' I guess you could call them. Cats are simply great to have for anything that creeps and crawls around."

"Oh! Oh, Rex, how thoughtful! Thank you, really. But again, how can I accept them?"

He shrugged. "You did me a great favor."

Alexi laughed. "I did you a favor? I haven't done a thing for you."

He grinned. "Want to pay me in trade?"

"Ha-ha. No."

"Ah, well." He shrugged. "I didn't think so. But, honest, you did me a favor."

"What?"

"I have my best plot in ages going now—thanks to your little murder victims all over the house."

"What?"

"The snakes," he explained. "I turned them into people. All murdered. One with the spade, one with the pipe wrench, and so on. I added some family greed and passion and jealousy, etcetera. It's going great."

"Oh!"

"See what I mean? You did me the favor."

"Oh. Oh…" Alexi stood up, cradling the kittens to her. She looked down the hallway. There wasn't a speck of dust. She hurried to the parlor door and threw it open. The window she had broken on her first night had been repaired; the room had been cleaned. The whole place smelled faintly and wonderfully of fresh pine. There couldn't possibly be a living bug in it, it was so spotless.

Rex stayed in the hallway, leaning idly against the doorframe. Alexi glanced at him, then brushed past him, hurrying to inspect the rest of the house. The ballroom had been scrubbed from ceiling to floor; the library, too, was devoid of a hint of dirt. The drapes and furniture even seemed to be different colors—lighter, more beautiful.

And there wasn't a trace of a snake—or of any of the weapons she had left lying around.

Rex was by the stairway, watching her. She maintained a certain distance from him as she rubbed her cheek against the kitten's soft fur.

"It's fabulous," she murmured. "Rex, thank you."

"Want to see upstairs?"

She nodded. He didn't move; he waited for her to precede him up the stairs. Samson rushed by, though, barking, and she nearly tripped over him.

She couldn't remember climbing the stairs as a child, so she didn't really have any comparisons to make. But it was wonderful. The subtle, clean scent of pine was everywhere; the windows were all open, and sunlight was streaming in. The house, which had always been fascinating, although a bit depressing in its dirt and darkness, now seemed warm and welcoming and bright. The runners over the hard wood were cream, with flower patterns in bright shades of maroon and pink and green. The hallway draperies were a cream tapestry, and the eight-paned windows were crystal clear.

Alexi switched both protesting kittens to one arm and began to throw doors open. There were four of them, two on either side of the landing. To her left was the master bedroom, a man's room with heavy oak furniture. She found the mistress's bedroom next, all done more delicately than Pierre's. The molded plaster showed beautifully on the clean ceilings. The wood was shining; the beds were immaculate.

Alexi stopped by Rex in the hallway and shoved the kittens into his arms, startling him so that he had to straighten and abandon his lazy lean against the banister.

"It's wonderful," she said.

"Thank you. Well, I didn't do it. The company did—and they'll bill you, you know."

"Oh, I know, but…" Her voice trailed away, and she walked down the hall to the next doors.

One of the rooms was a nursery. A shiny wooden cradle rocked slightly with the breeze coming in through an open window. The closet stretched wall-to-wall, and there was an old rocking horse, a twin bed and a cane bassinet. How darling! Alexi thought, and she hurried on out, eager to finish exploring.

The last room was a guest room—a genderless room, comfortable and quaint. The headboard was elaborately carved and went on to stretch the distance of the wall on either side of the bed to create great bookcases. The opposite wall was covered with a tapestry of a biblical scene. There was a fine brocaded Victorian love seat and another rocker; both faced the window, a little whatnot table between them.

Alexi loved it. She determined right away that this would be her room. She'd fill the cases with her TV and books. She could modernize for convenience without really changing anything.

She started to turn, only to collide with Rex. All of him. He must have set the kittens down somewhere, because she hit solid chest. Solid, masculine, hairy chest. Coarse dark hair teased too much of her own bare skin, and she stepped back.

"It's spotless. It's wonderful. They did a great job," she told him quickly.

He nodded. "They've got a good reputation."

Alexi stepped around him. The day wasn't hot; it was perfect, with a nice cooling breeze. But she was suddenly warm. Hot flashes soared through her, and now she was very determined not to be alone with him. Her imagination had come vividly alive, all in an

instant, living color. Perhaps it was more than imagination. Maybe it was the feel of the heat in the room, of
the tension…of his nearness. She could visualize him
sweeping her into his arms and falling with her upon
the antique bed. They really shouldn't have been past
the "How do you do, lovely weather" stage, and she
wanted to reach out and stroke the planes of his cheek.
Intimacy had never been that easy for her; making love
had taken time, and it had come far from naturally. It
was, by its nature, something that should come after
knowing a man deeply and well.

But this one…she wanted simply by virtue of
something that lived and stirred inside her, an aching, a wanting. And, though she was certain she could
never instigate anything, he surely could. But to him
it wouldn't mean anything; to her it would.

Alexi hurried into the hallway. Her heart was thun-
dering; her palms were damp. She didn't want him to
see her eyes, knowing they could bare her soul, tell
him everything she'd been thinking. One thing she
had decided about Rex Morrow—it would not pay for
him to be aware of all her weaknesses.

He was following her; she could feel him. She hurried on down the stairs, talking.

"Rex, it's all wonderful. No spiderwebs, no dirt,
no creeping, crawling creatures. Thank you. Thank
you so much. And you went to just the right degree…
I mean, thank you, but if you'd gone any further, it
wouldn't have been good. Do you know what I mean?
I'm trying to prove that I can do it. No, I don't have
to prove anything. Well, that's not the truth, really. I
suppose that I am trying to prove—"

"You're babbling—that's what you're doing."

She'd reached the landing; he spoke from behind her—close. A tingling crept along her spine, she was so aware of him. I'm confused! she wanted to scream. She'd never had feelings like this, and she didn't know what to do with them—but she did know that she should take things slowly and carefully.

"Am I?" she said, but she didn't turn around. She started walking again, pushing through the kitchen doorway. She let the door fall back, aware that he had plenty of time to catch it. She went straight to the refrigerator. "I'm dying of thirst. Don't you want something? The sun is murderous out on the beach. Hmm. I don't even know what's in here. I'm going to have to get out to the store today."

He curled his fingers gently around her arm and pulled her head out of the refrigerator and her body around so that she faced him. He wore a quizzical expression that was handsome against the fine, strong lines of his face. "What is wrong with you?"

"Nothing." She was breathless. "What do you want?"

He smiled slowly. "You."

"To drink."

"Are you afraid of me?" he asked.

"Not in the least."

"Good. I'll have a beer. And I'll get it myself, thanks. Want one? That is all you've got in the refrigerator."

"I shouldn't—"

"Why?"

He brought two out. Alexi nervously sat at the table. He sat across from her, and their knees brushed.

"Ah…" he murmured, and she saw that a secret smile had curved into his lips. "You *are* afraid."

"Of what? That you're going to attack me in my house? You've already done that, right? The first night."

"There's attack, and then there's attack...."

"Whatever." She waved a hand dismissively in the air. He reached across the table and opened her beer. Damn him! She took a long sip, and he was still smiling, fully aware that she was drinking the beer as if reaching for a lifeline.

He lifted his bottle to her.

"Me and thee and Eden."

"Do you try to pick up every woman over eighteen and under fifty?"

"No. Actually, I don't." He took a long swallow from his bottle, watching her. "Alexi...you have to know that you're beautiful. A woman who does Helen of Troy commercials has to be aware that she—"

He broke off abruptly. Alexi's eyes widened, wondering what he had been about to say that would have offended her.

"That she's what?" she demanded.

"Beautiful," he said with a shrug.

"That's not what you were going to say."

"All right." He sounded angry, she thought. "Sexy. Sensual, sexual. Is that what you want to hear?"

"No! No—no, it's not!"

"Well, then, why the hell push the point?"

"Could you go home, please?" She realized that she was sitting very straight, very primly, and that, in the bathing suit, she wasn't dressed for dignity. Nor did the beer bottle she was clutching do much for a feeling of aloofness, either.

"Yeah," he said thickly, rising. "Yeah, maybe I

should do just that. 'Cause you know what, lady? You scare the hell out of me, too."

"What?" she demanded, startled. No one could scare him; it had to be a line. But she felt bad—no, she felt guilty as hell. He had done everything for her. And somehow he seemed to understand her. She didn't want anyone in the family to know that she was anything but entirely competent; Rex didn't think that she wasn't competent, just because the snakes had nearly paralyzed her. He'd had the cleaners in; he hadn't really changed anything. He'd known instinctively just how far to go. He'd given her his own home; he'd spent time here—and he was a busy man. He'd bought her the beautiful kittens, just so that she would feel that she had some protection against things that slithered and crawled.

Rex reached across the table and gently cupped her cheek in his hand, stroking her flesh lightly with his thumb. "I said you're kind of scary yourself, my sweet. You own and you possess and you steal into a soul…without a touch."

Into a soul… She couldn't look away from his eyes. Dark and fascinating. All of him. She remembered spilling out everything on their first meeting, remembered thinking of him on the beach, aware that he was there, strong and masculine, and wishing that she could curl against him and laugh, because he seemed to understand so easily the things she needed.

She lowered her head; his hand fell away. She wondered if it wasn't time for a little more honesty, and she was amazed that she could bluntly say what she intended. "You'd find me atrociously disappointing," she said. Her voice was low, even weary. But she looked up and met his eyes again and felt the warmth suffuse her. "Looks can be deceiving. What you see isn't the real me."

"I see fire and warmth and beauty."

"It—it isn't there."

"It needs only to be awakened."

"And you're the one to do it, I take it."

"I think I already have."

"I think you have tremendous nerve."

He laughed suddenly. "Probably. But then, like I said, you do things to the psyche and the body...." His voice trailed away, and he shrugged. He had a bunch of papers on the counter, and he turned away, shuffling them together.

"Don't forget to feed the kittens."

"You're leaving?"

"You told me to."

"Well, I didn't mean it. I'm sorry. All right, well, I meant it when I said it, but only because—"

"Because I was hitting on you?" He was amused, she thought. She cast him an acid gaze, and he laughed again. "Well, I can't promise to quit, especially when you're half-naked."

"You're more naked than I am."

He smiled. "I suppose I should be glad that you noticed. Aha! That's it."

"What's it?"

He thumped an elbow onto the table, then leaned forward. "You're more afraid of yourself than you are of me."

"Don't be absurd."

"You are. You don't want me asking, because you're willing to give."

Alexi groaned, wishing she weren't trembling inside. "You win; I give up. Go home."

"For now," he promised, straightening and going for his papers once again. "But you know how it is. A man, a woman, an island—"

"This isn't an island."

"Close enough. But for now, goodbye, my love."

Alexi stood and followed him out to the hallway. He whistled, and Samson came bounding out from the parlor. The kittens followed after him. Poor Samson had a tortured look about him. It seemed that the kittens hadn't recognized the fact that the shepherd was a hundred times their size; they had adopted him as a surrogate parent.

"Henpecked by a couple of kittens, huh, boy?" Rex said, laughing.

"His master would never be henpecked, I take it?" Alexi queried, crossing her arms over her chest.

He looked at her across their menagerie. He took a long moment to answer, and when he did, his tone was careful, measured.

"No. His master would never be henpecked. Nor would he peck in return. Any relationship only works with give-and-take."

Alexi lowered her head suddenly, feeling a little dizzy. There were things she liked about him so much. He'd been amazed that she had been somewhat insane over a nest of little snakes, but he hadn't played upon that fear. She realized suddenly that he was blunt because he was honest, but that he would never gain his own strength from the weakness of another.

He opened the door and started to leave. Alexi

nearly tripped over the kittens to reach him, bracing herself against it as she called him back.

"Rex!"

"Yeah?" Shading his eyes from the sun, he turned back to her.

"Thank you. For the kittens, for the house…thank you very much."

"How much?"

She merely smiled at the innuendo. "Dinner? I really can cook."

"I believe you. But not tonight. Let's go out."

"Tonight?"

"Tonight." His expression turned strangely serious. "I want to ask you a few questions."

"About what?"

"We'll eat at about eight; I'll come by here by six-thirty."

"Why so early?"

"I have all your clothing, remember?"

"Oh!"

He was right; her suitcase was now at his house, and she was here.

"See you then." He turned and walked away then. Samson barked, as if saying goodbye, too.

Alexi didn't leave the doorway. She watched them walk away, the man and his massive dog. She looked at Rex's broad, bronzed shoulders and at the ripple of muscle as he moved, and she shivered. He was right; she was very afraid of herself.

At precisely six-thirty, Alexi heard him knocking at the door. She answered it in one of Gene's scruffy old velvet smoking jackets, but apart from that she was ready. She had showered for nearly an hour, washed and blow-dried her hair and carefully applied her Helen of Troy makeup. She was smiling and radiant—and the warm caress of his gaze as it swept over her was a charming appreciation of her labors. He also issued a tremendous wolf whistle.

Alexi tried to whistle in return—she wasn't very good, but he did look wonderful all dressed up. His suit was a conventional pinstripe, his shirt was tailored, his tie was a charcoal gray. Color meant nothing—it was the fit upon him that was so alluring. That and the crisp scents of his clothing and after-shave.

"You're gorgeous," she said.

"So are you."

"Thanks—but I really do have to change. Where are we going?" He had a bouquet of flowers for her in one hand and her suitcase in another. She smiled and thanked him, and he followed her into the kitchen so that she could put them in water.

"Can I help?" he offered.

"I've got a vase—"

"I meant with the changing."

"You would," Alexi retorted, but she was still smiling. It seemed fun. She felt curiously secure with him, even though she didn't doubt his intent for a moment.

And somehow it was tremendously exciting. He definitely let her know he wanted her; he also let her know that it would be at her time, when she was ready.

And that she wouldn't have to be frightened.

"You seem happy," he said.

Alexi poured water into the vase. "I am. I've been studying the original blueprints all day. I talked to

Gene, and I checked on some contractors. I thought you might know something about them."

"I know a few."

"How about a glass of wine? I found a super-looking Riesling down in the cellar."

His brows flew up. "You ventured into the cellar?"

She chuckled softly. "I took the kittens with me. Your bug man did a good job—there's nothing crawling down there."

He smiled and said lightly, "A Riesling sounds great."

Alexi set the flowers in the water and made a little face at him. "Good. You open and pour. I'll run up and get dressed."

He nodded, reaching into the right drawer for the corkscrew. "Call me if you need any help," he told her.

"I'll do that," she promised sweetly.

He'd left her suitcase in the hall. Alexi grabbed it and raced up the stairs. She set it on the bed in the room she had chosen and quickly opened it. She wished she had followed him back earlier, for then her things wouldn't be so crushed.

She dumped everything, trying to decide what to wear. She settled on a cream knit dress, since it wouldn't need to be ironed, and then brushed aside other things to find stockings to go with it. Slipping into her underwear, she wondered if it was Rex who had repacked for her; then she knew that it must have been, because Emily had left to run errands right after breakfast this morning. She colored slightly, wondering what he must have thought. Her slips, chemises, panties and bras were all very feminine and exotic— her agent's sister owned a lingerie shop, and for every occasion, from her birthday to Valentine's Day, Alexi received some frothy bit of underwear. She smiled, glad that her things were respectable.

She hadn't realized that she was trembling with excitement until she tried to put her stockings on. She paused, inhaling a long breath. She was frightened. Rex was new to her, completely new. He was overwhelmingly male, yet there was that wonderful streak of honesty to him. She was excited, maybe dangerously so. But it was nice, too. The feeling was as wonderful as a fresh sea breeze, and it touched all of her. It was wonderful, and she felt that if it was dangerous, too, she really had no choice. She couldn't resist. He was as compelling as the relentless pull of the tide.

Alexi slipped into a pair of high heels, dumped her things from her large purse into a smaller, beaded evening bag and hurried downstairs, afraid to sit and ponder her feelings too long. She glanced at her watch; it was barely seven. She was pleased that she had gotten ready so quickly.

Rex was in the kitchen, leaning against the counter, sipping his wine and watching the kittens as they tumbled over each other. He smiled when Alexi walked in, and his eyes fell over her with the same provocative warmth once again. He lifted his wineglass to her. "Stunning."

"Thank you."

He picked up a second glass of wine and handed it to her. She murmured a thank-you, then sipped at it far too quickly. Rex watched her, amused.

"Did you name them?"

She picked up one of the little silver bundles. "I went with Silver and Blacky—so far." She gazed at Rex and admitted. "I, uh, wasn't sure about their sexes, so I wanted to be careful."

Rex chuckled. "You've got one of each. Silver here is a—" he paused, picking up the kitten "—a girl. Blacky must be the male."

Alexi nodded, set her wineglass down and retrieved both kittens. She went to the back door with them and set them both outside. They tried to come in; she wouldn't let them.

"Cruel!" Rex said.

"Hmph!" Alexi retorted. "You didn't get me a litter box for them," she reminded him.

"How could I have been so remiss! We can stop by the store on our way to the restaurant."

Alexi picked up her wine again, swirling the pale liquid as she said, "I thought you hid out a lot, Mr. Fame and Fortune."

He winced. "That sounded like a low blow. I probably should be hiding out with *you*. But we're going to an Asian restaurant just north of Jacksonville where every table is secluded."

"You didn't recognize me when you first saw me," Alexi reminded him. "And people just point at me, anyway. They don't want my autograph."

"People don't usually recognize me, either. And not everyone is a mystery fan. The only reason I 'hide out' here is that there are a few nuts out there."

"Excuse me," Alexi teased. She bit her lip then, wishing that she hadn't spoken. She remembered him telling her that someone had actually shot his horse. No wonder he liked solitude.

But he didn't seem bothered by her words. He came closer to her and touched his glass to hers. "This time you're excused," he promised solemnly. He didn't move away from her. His eyes were on hers, dark and deep. Again she was aware of the delicious scent of him. For the longest time, she thought he was going to kiss her, and she didn't think she would protest. She wouldn't have the mind left to do so.

But he didn't. He turned around suddenly, going to the door. He started to call the kittens, but they were right there, tumbling over each other to get back into the house.

"They have to be locked in the cellar," Alexi said. She wrinkled her nose. "I don't want to have to search the whole house for what they might have needed to do."

"Sorry, guys," Rex told the playful pair. "You're being jailed for the evening."

"Well, where's Samson?" Alexi challenged.

"Probably lolled out on the leather sofa," Rex admitted. "I forgot to tell him when he was a puppy that he was a dog." With that, he led her out.

His car was a sporty little Maserati. He asked Alexi if she minded the top down, and she assured him that she loved the air. They didn't speak much on the thirty-minute drive to the restaurant; the wind did feel good, and Alexi found herself content to lean her head back on the fine leather upholstery and close her eyes. He had a good sound system, and the music and air seemed to blanket her in a shroud of comfort and lethargy.

"We're here—if you're awake," Rex told her when he parked.

"I'm awake—just a mess," she replied, fumbling in her bag for her comb. Rex came around to open the passenger door; when she stepped out, he took her hand, then smoothed back all the straying gold strands. Alexi didn't move; she just let him do that, wondering how such a simple service could feel so intimate and sensual.

"Ready?" he asked huskily.

She was ready...for almost anything.

The restaurant was beautiful. The lobby was dusky and intimate with ornately carved and very heavy chairs. A hostess in black silk trousers greeted Rex like an old friend, and Alexi experienced a moment's jealousy, wondering how often he came here—and with whom.

They were led down a little hallway. It was very intimate; silk screens and paneling divided each little room. The music was soft. When they reached their room, Alexi saw that the tables were low; she was to remove her shoes, and she and Rex would sit on cushions on the floor. The table was round, and they were seated very close to each other. Rex asked her if he could order the wine, and she said sweetly that since he knew the place so well, he should certainly do so.

Their hostess left them. Rex reached for her fingers and played with them idly in the small space between them.

"Jealous?" he asked.

"Why should I be?"

"I see...just naturally catty."

Alexi pulled her fingers back. "You forget, Mr. Morrow, I was in the most uncomfortable position of getting to hear all about your sex life."

"You didn't hear all about it. But if you want the finer details, I can always give them to you."

Their hostess bringing in the wine saved Alexi from having to reply. Once she had left again, Alexi turned her attention to the menu. Rex suggested the house specialty, which included samplings of their honey-garlic chicken and beef, and another platter with their mu-shu pork Cantonese and their spicy grilled fish.

Alexi closed the menu. "You know the place, Mr. Morrow."

He lifted her wineglass and handed it to her. "I wonder if you'll mellow out with age."

The way he said it, she had to laugh. She sipped the wine and found it delicious. And suddenly the whole evening seemed wonderful. The muted light, the soft music, the plush cushion beneath her...the man beside her. She felt as if one sip of the wine had given her senses greater power; she could hear more keenly, see more clearly and inhale and feel his scent sweep into her. She could have swirled around very easily, laid her head in his lap, closed her eyes—and luxuriated in the feel of it all.

"Who knows you're in Gene's house?" he asked.

"What?" Alexi shook her head to clear it. Rex was serious and intent; his eyes were brooding.

"Who knows you're here?"

She shrugged. "Gene. My agent. My family."

"Anyone else?"

"No—no, I don't think so. I wanted—I wanted to be alone for a while." Alexi hesitated, wondering. "Why?"

He shrugged. "Oh, I don't know. I was just curious, I suppose."

Alexi studied him. "You're lying to me. Why?"

He shrugged again, looking toward the doorway. Alexi followed his gaze and saw that their pretty hostess was returning again with another woman and half a dozen small chafing dishes.

The woman opened the dishes to describe the food, then closed them again to maintain the heat. Rex thanked them both, but when they had gone, he still seemed to hesitate.

"Rex!"

"What?"

"Why? Why did you ask me that?"

He didn't answer her. Alexi saw that he was still frowning as he stared at the thin screen that separated their little room from the hallway.

"Rex...?"

He didn't look at her, but he pressed his finger to her lips and indicated the screen. He silently began to rise.

Alexi thought he had lost his mind. But then she saw it; the shadow of a figure standing in the hallway. There was something secretive about the shadow—someone had been listening to them.

Alexi didn't know that she was gasping until Rex swore softly at her, then bounded over the table like a talented linebacker and raced toward the door.

But the shadow, too, had obviously heard her gasp.

It straightened and disappeared just seconds before Rex went racing out after it.

Chapter 7

Rex didn't return. Confused, Alexi waited for several moments, then rose and hurried out to the hall. There was no sign of any shadow man, nor of Rex. As Alexi stood in the hallway, a group of slightly inebriated businessmen made an appearance from a room farther down the corridor. It was a narrow hallway, and Alexi stepped inside again to allow them to pass.

A short, stout man named Harold was telling a tall, lean, bald man he called Bert that now was the time to dump his electrical stock. And while he was at it, Bert should dump his wife, too.

They passed Alexi, and Harold caught sight of her.

"Oh, I am in heaven!" Harold slurred out. He had small eyes, which lit up to look like pennies. "Are you th' dessert, darlin'?" He braced himself in the slender doorway, leering in at her.

"No, I'm not the dessert," Alexi told him. He reminded her of her uncle Bob. Mild mannered by day—a lecher after one beer too many.

"You sure look like dessert."

"Go home," Alexi said. She couldn't help adding, "And, Bert—I wouldn't dump your wife if I were you."

"You know Gertrude, huh?" Harold swung on into the room, staring at her incredulously. "Honey, you are cute. Come to think of it, I'm sure I know you. Don't we know her, Harry? Hey—aren't you from that massage parlor downtown?"

"No! I'm not from any massage parlor! Bert, go home and sleep it off."

"I'm in heaven!" Bert claimed. He winked. "We did, honey. We met before." He turned around to nudge one of the other men in the ribs. "She remembers me! She gave me the best little, er, massage I ever did have. You here with a loser, honey? You come on now, and Harry and Bert will make it worth your while."

He clamped sweaty, sausagelike little fingers around her wrist. Alexi sighed. So much for her Helen of Troy fame. He thought that she was a, er, massage artist.

"Bert, I'm not—"

She broke off. A pair of heavy hands had taken hold of Bert. He was lifted off his feet and set down in the hallway. Rex was there, rigid and scowling angrily.

"Hey, bud, I was just—"

Harold broke in nervously. "Bert, let's get home, huh?"

Rex crossed his arms over his chest. "Bert, I do highly suggest you leave—now."

Bert wasn't about to be put off. He straightened

his coat and looked around the wall of Rex's chest. "Honey, you wanna stay here with this animal?"

"Now!" The command sounded like a bark; Rex took a lethally charged step toward Bert.

"Rex!" Alexi protested.

"Gentlemen, gentlemen! Have we a problem? How may I help you?" The pretty hostess, anxious and distressed, came running down the hallway, speaking softly.

"Rex!" one of the other men said. "Hey, you're Rex Morrow, aren't you? I've seen your picture on the book covers! Hey, I hate to bother you, but could I have an autograph? My wife would be so thrilled. She buys all your books. In hardcover. And we both read them, every word."

Bert stepped back as if he had been slapped. "You're him?" He gaped. Alexi thought that at any second he would stutter and say "Gaw-ly," just like Gomer Pyle.

"Gentlemen?" the hostess asked anxiously. She glanced at Rex pleadingly.

Alexi saw him relax, and then he laughed. "I'm sorry. I haven't paper or a pen—"

They were quickly supplied. Rex scrawled out his name several times. When he had finished and the men started walking away, Bert paused long enough to look at Alexi longingly.

"So you're with him tonight, huh?" He gazed back at Rex. "She's expensive, but she's worth every penny."

"What?" Rex murmured.

"Good night, Bert," Alexi said sweetly.

Bert followed the others. Alexi turned on Rex. "That wasn't necessary."

"They asked me—"

"Manhandling that poor drunken sot wasn't necessary."

He was silent for a long moment, walking around to sink back into his seat at the table. Once there, he crossed his arms over his chest to stare at her. "So you enjoyed teasing that drunken sot, huh?"

"No—but I can take care of myself."

"Great. Next time four men are descending upon you, remind me that you can take care of yourself."

"You would've gotten into a fight if your ego wasn't so colossal that you were more determined to sign your name."

He stared at her a moment longer and then reached for one of the chafing dishes. Alexi didn't sit again, and he didn't pay her any attention. He dished out fried rice and then crisp, succulent little pieces of honey-garlic beef. The smell reminded Alexi that she was starving, and she wasn't sure whether she was still angry or embarrassed—or even a bit awed, since she had been taken for a prostitute and the whole explosive moment had been defused by his lousy signature.

At last his gaze fell on her again, and as it flickered over her length, the corners of his lips twitched with amusement. "So you're expensive, huh?"

"Maybe I should have gotten the old dear to take me home," Alexi said, sitting at last.

"Dear child, he was after one thing."

"Mmm. And what are you after?"

He grinned. "Several things." Then he sobered again, mechanically moving chafing dishes around to fill Alexi's plate. "I couldn't find him."

"Him who?"

"Him who was spying on us."

"Oh." Alexi shrugged. She was beginning to think that either Rex or she was crazy—or perhaps they were both imagining things. He was a mystery writer. Maybe—after a certain amount of time—that type of work played havoc with the brain. So there had been someone in the hallway. So what? Probably a hundred people walked down the hallway during the day.

"Rex—" She paused as she discovered that the honey-garlic beef was really delicious. "This is wonderful."

"Thank you."

"Rex, I don't think it's anything to worry about. Maybe it was another fan—"

"Yeah. And that was a fan running downstairs at Gene's the minute the lights went," he said.

Alexi set her fork down. Rex was eating with the chopsticks; she had decided not to make a fool out of herself with the effort. And now, on top of everything else, she was trembling.

"I thought you didn't believe me," she murmured.

"I never said that."

"You implied—"

"I implied nothing. You might have been reading me wrong."

She shook her head. "No. You didn't believe me. But I think you do now. Why? What changed your mind?"

"Nothing. Really. All right—I am worried about you. Nothing has happened out on the peninsula in all the time that I've been there, and you show up and it's a three-ring circus. Footsteps on the road, footsteps in the house, snakes, etcetera. And it's not as if the girl next door or Mary Poppins moved in. You're Alexi Jordan."

"Not Mary Poppins," Alexi agreed sardonically.

"I didn't say you were Jezebel—just not Mary Poppins. Alexi, do you have any enemies?"

She lowered her head over her chicken and shook her head. Did she? No, not real enemies. She had never stepped over anyone to get anywhere. The only enemy she could possibly have was—

"Alexi, what about your ex? Was he mad enough at you to come here and try to scare you? Make you a little crazy?"

John? She shook her head again. She trembled. John could be violent—but she couldn't see him being stealthy. When he had decided to accost her, he hadn't played any games. He had come straight to the apartment—and straight to the point.

"I—I don't think so."

Rex sighed softly. "Well, maybe we are imagining things, huh?"

She nodded woodenly.

"You're not eating."

"Oh. It's wonderful. It really is, Rex. I'm sorry."

Alexi was startled when he touched her very gently. With his knuckle he raised her chin. For the longest time his dark eyes gazed into hers; for the longest time he seemed to question what he saw there and to muse tenderly upon her.

Then he moved, lowering his face toward hers. His lips touched hers. She knew her mouth was sweet with the taste of plum wine and honey. His lips hovered just above hers, tasting them.

She felt his hand caressing her cheek. Then she felt

the movement of his tongue within her mouth, hot and supple and sensual. She trembled, neither protesting the movement nor joining it, but feeling the rise of excitement inside of her, a longing, a sexual tension that knotted in the pit of her belly and seemed to flare throughout her.

His hand still at her nape, he moved back. His dark eyes surveyed hers again. She didn't know what he sought or what he saw.

Or what he felt. Perhaps he was thinking that it was all a loss. That she didn't even know how to return a kiss decently.

Her mouth went dry. She drew her eyes from his to look down at her hands. A tiny glass of plum wine sat before her; aware that he was watching her, she drank it quickly, not sure of what to say or do.

"Maybe you should leave the peninsula," he said.

She shook her head.

"Footsteps in the dark. Maybe something frightening is happening."

"I—I don't want to leave."

"Mmm. But you won't protest if I sleep on your sofa again, huh?"

Alexi stiffened. "You're being obnoxious again. I won't ever let you sleep on my sofa again. I promise."

"Damned right. If I sleep there again, Alexi, it won't be on the sofa."

She raised her head, staring at him, a brow arched challengingly. She was still trembling, but she hoped that he didn't know it. Why not? She was certainly of legal age, and she wanted him. She ached for him. His lightest touch had been magic.

Why not? Because she trembled too easily, because

she was very afraid that she couldn't go through with it, that she would make an absolute fool of herself. She hadn't even been able to return his kiss.

She smiled, sweetly, seductively. Fever was alive in her veins, racing rampantly through her blood. "You're right, Mr. Morrow. If you ever sleep in my house again, it will be in my bed."

Startled, he drew back, a slow, entirely wicked smile curling the corner of his mouth.

"Do you mean that, Ms. Jordan?"

"I do."

"Then let's go."

He was up abruptly, a strong, bronzed hand reaching out to help her rise. Panic surged inside her; she stared at his hand for several seconds, completely at a loss.

Then she placed her own hand within it. His fingers curled around hers and she was standing beside him. For the longest time they looked at each other, standing together in that rice paper-screened section of the restaurant. She could hear his heart, and she could see his eyes, and she could see the hunger there, and the longing.

He wanted her. Badly.

And she wanted him.

He didn't say anything else. He turned, his fingers still wound around hers, leading her toward the hall. At the entryway he offered the hostess his credit card. Alexi escaped him to study a display of swords encased in a glass cabinet. She pressed her palm against her breast and felt her own heart surging. She must have been mad. He had teased her, but he'd never pressed her. And she had just all but whistled out an invitation to make love....

He caught her hand again. He smiled when she darted a quick, scared look his way. He wound his fingers around hers again as he led her out into the parking lot and to his car.

It was a beautiful night. Stars abounded in the heavens. Alexi sat stiffly in the Maserati, staring straight ahead. Rex talked casually as he gunned the motor. He pointed out a few of the constellations in the heavens. "Not a bit of fog tonight," he murmured.

"Not a trace of it," Alexi agreed.

Oh, he was so casual! So comfortable. But then, he was good at this, Alexi reminded herself, while she was only playing at it. She didn't really know the first thing about having a casual affair. She was deathly afraid that when he touched her she was going to scream.

No. She would not. It was all in her mind. She liked him so much, and she ached for him, feeling that sense of sexual arousal when he merely whispered her name. Like a coil inside of her, winding, sweet and heightened, yearning, when he was near. If she could not lie down beside him, she would never know what it was to make love again.

"Where?"

"Pardon?" She had to glance his way. And with a whole new sense of panic she realized that they were just about on the road leading out to the peninsula.

"Your place or mine?"

"Er...er..."

"Mine," he decided softly.

"Fine. Except—"

"Except what?"

"Isn't Emily there?"

Against the shadow and glow of the lights, she saw him shake his head ruefully. "Emily has gone home. She usually only works for me two days a week. She stayed longer this week because of you, but now she's gone home. The whole place is ours."

"Oh."

They were on the road out to their houses. Alexi closed her eyes and wondered what it had been like more than a century before. When Pierre had taken his Eugenia here, a bride, alone. Surely it had been completely barren then. It must have seemed as if the world were theirs, as if they owned paradise. The pines would have been the same, and the palms. The moon, rising clear and beautiful against the sky, must have been the same, too. And the stars… diamonds glittering against a panoply of black velvet.

The Maserati stopped. They were in front of the Brandywine house. Rex was smiling at her gently and was twisted slightly toward her. His fingers played idly in her hair.

"I'll walk you to your door."

"What?" She swallowed.

"You're all talk and no action, kid. You didn't mean it. Come on, I'll walk you to your door."

Startled, Alexi crossed her arms over her chest and sat grimly. Rex opened his door and came around for her. He opened her door. Alexi didn't move; she stared straight ahead.

He had just offered her an out. She couldn't take it. It was her chance to run, offered in tenderness.

"You're the one who is all talk, Mr. Morrow," Alexi murmured.

She heard him inhale sharply. "Last chance, Ms. Jordan. I'm a pretty nice guy, nine times out of ten. But if you don't get out of this car right now, I won't answer for the consequences."

Alexi didn't move. "Promises, promises, Morrow."

Her door slammed sharply. A second later, his did the same after he sank back into the bucket seat beside her. She felt his eyes on her, but she couldn't turn.

"Well, you know you're committed now, huh, Alexi?" She felt the anger that edged his words. "Is that what you want? Or is that what you need? 'Push the guy so far that there is no backing down'? Make sure it's what you want, Alexi. I'll be damned if I understand you. Make sure."

"Drive, would you, Rex?"

He shook his head. She felt herself pulled into his arms, pulled hard. His mouth came down hard on hers. Her lips parted; she felt the demand of his, forceful, hungry and entirely persuasive.

And it was good. Deliciously, wonderfully good. He tasted of the honeyed chicken and the plum wine and, beyond that, completely, tantalizingly male. This time she could respond. She trembled when his tongue thrust into the crevices of her mouth, filling her, arousing her. She grew bold and she herself explored, running the tip of her tongue along his lower lip and then his upper lip, against his teeth, against his tongue, in a sleek, sensual persuasion of her own. It was really wonderful. The scent of him filled her, as male as the taste of him, unique. Her fingertips played against the hair at his nape, over the strong structure of his cheek, to the fascinating breadth of his shoulders. And all the while she felt his kiss. Against her lip, against her throat, against the beat of her pulse there. She felt his fingers, feather-light, against her flesh; his knuckles, stroking her shoulder, drawing a line lightly over her collarbone. She nearly cried, the kiss alone was so very good....

She had never known this type of arousal. Aching in all parts of her, longing to touch and be touched... everywhere. He had her in his arms, on his lap. She was barely aware of moving, of being moved. The sense of being drugged with the pleasure of it was an encompassing one, overpowering all else, giving her the wonderful feel of perfect fantasy. This was it, the way of dreams. The need and the desire, the feeling that she would simply die if she could not have him. All of him.

It remained with her, all the magic, while he held her. While his lips touched hers again and again. Even when his eyes met hers, as dark and mysterious as the night, as probing, as curious, and still as seductive. She felt the palm of his hand flat against her breast; she felt his fingers curl around its weight, and his thumb as he sought her nipple through the knit of her dress and the lace of her bra. She buried her face against his neck, warmed by the intimacy, unable to meet his eyes yet instinctively grazing her teeth against his throat in response. It was a dream; it was magic. She was alive and explosive and soaring with desire and relief.

But then she felt his hand again. Against her stocking. A touch that made her shiver, a touch that wound the core of her tightly, tightly. She wanted him. She wanted his touch, an intimate touch, so badly. But even as his fingers roamed along her nyloned thigh, she felt the overwhelming panic begin to seize her.

She couldn't move at first.

She just felt his hand...his fingers. Higher, higher along her thigh. Fingers rimming the elastic of her panties. Light against her flesh again—bare flesh—as he slowly, seductively drew the nylons from her. She couldn't move. She could only feel the panic welling, growing, sweeping through her....

For God's sake, they were still in the car, she registered dimly. They were still merely playing.

Playing very, very intimately. The darkness seemed to surround her.

She stiffened and drew away from him abruptly.

"Alexi!"

He caught her hands. She stared into his eyes. At that very moment, she wanted the earth to open up and swallow her. She groaned.

"Alexi, shh—"

She couldn't understand that he meant to soothe her; she knew only that she had led him where he had gone and that she had then pulled away from him.

She tore at the door handle and wrenched it open. She was so awkward, caught upon his lap in the small bucket seat.

"Alexi!"

Sobbing, she stumbled over him. Her shoes were lost; her nylons were a tangle. She yanked them off and set out upon the sand, running. The night was dark, with only the moon and the stars to guide her, but it didn't matter; she didn't know where she was running to, only that she had to escape.

Pine and sand were beneath her feet. Bare feet.

The beach was out there, through a trail of pines that both sheltered and mysteriously darkened. Ahead, she could hear the waves, so soft and gentle here. Waves of the mighty Atlantic.

She reached the beach, the sand soft and cool now beneath her feet. She looked up and saw the stars and the crescent of the moon, and she inhaled raggedly, desperately.

She gasped, startled, as arms swept around her. Rex's arms.

"Oh, don't!" she pleaded. She couldn't look at him. He turned her around anyway, pulling her to his chest, running his fingers down the length of her hair.

"Please, don't. I'm so sorry. I—" she said brokenly.

"Alexi, stop. Listen to me. Stop."

She tried; she couldn't. She felt as if she sobbed raggedly for the longest time, yet she couldn't pull away from him; he held her firm. Then she tried again to tell him how embarrassed she was and how sorry, and he comforted her again. At last she inhaled a long, ragged breath and exhaled it and stood still.

Rex pulled off his shoes and socks and took her elbow. "Let's sit in the surf. And you can tell me about it."

"No!"

"Yes. I deserve that much."

"No, no, just forget about me, please. Believe that I didn't mean to do what I did—"

"Come on, Alexi."

She had little choice. Before she knew it she was sitting in the surf beside him and the waves were rippling over their feet and he was as unconcerned about his dress trousers as she was about the hem of her knit.

He didn't make her talk at first; he just held her against him, her head against his chest, his arms around her waist, his chin resting upon the top of her hair.

"John Vinto?" he asked.

She shuddered.

"What in God's name did he do to you?" Rex exploded.

She didn't want to start crying again—and she knew he wasn't going to let her go. When she started to talk, she discovered that she could do it almost impersonally, as if it had happened to someone else, as if it were history, long gone.

"I, uh, I knew a lot of what he was doing. Granted, it took me a while. The spouse is always the last to know it all. And I was so desperate to make my marriage work, you know. I had more or less run away from a great home to make it on my own. My parents hadn't wanted me to marry John. Gene didn't even approve of him. It was simply so hard to admit I'd made a mistake...."

Her voice trailed away for a moment, and then she shrugged. "I became ill during a makeup session one day and came home. John was in bed with another of his models. I think it was then that I realized he probably fell a little bit in love with every woman he photographed. It hurt, though. A lot. I didn't make any threats or accusations or anything. I just turned away. I tried to call for a cab. By then the girl was running out of the house only half-dressed, and John was slamming down the receiver. He said that we had to talk. I said there was nothing to talk about; nothing would change my mind. I wanted a divorce. He became irate. He kept telling me that I didn't want a divorce. I tried to call a cab again, and he told me that I couldn't live without him, I couldn't survive without him, that I wanted him—and that he'd prove it to me." She stopped speaking, staring out at the ocean, wincing. It seemed so horrible even to say aloud. So humiliating. So degrading.

Rex didn't say anything. He tightened his arms around her. She wasn't even aware that she was speaking again.

"It was an awful fight. I realized what he meant, and I threw the phone at him and ran. He caught me and dragged me through half the house. He kept telling me that I was still his wife." She lowered her head. "And, of course, I was his wife, and just the night before, I'd loved him. I just can't describe the terror of being powerless. Of having no control over being forced…"

"My God," Rex whispered. Like quicksilver, he moved his fingers gently over her cheek. "To think that I accosted you like that on your first night at the house. Alexi, I'm so sorry. So, so sorry." He was silent for a moment. She felt his kiss, tender and light, over her brow. She felt his arms around her, and she wasn't afraid; she felt secure.

"You kept working with him!" Rex said incredulously. "You should have taken the bastard to court."

She shook her head. "Do you know how hard it is to prove spousal assault? I would probably have lost—and the publicity would have marked me for the rest of my life." She sighed softly. "John didn't want the divorce. I did threaten to take him to court. That was the only reason he agreed to the divorce—no-fault and quick. I agreed to finish out the Helen of Troy campaign as long as he swore never to touch me or come near me again."

"Alexi, Alexi…"

She felt the soft brush of his kiss again; she felt the strength of his arms. The night was cool with the breeze, but the water was warm as it washed over her feet.

"I'll kill him!" Rex swore suddenly, savagely. He was tense, as taut as piano wire. "I swear, I'll damned well kill him!"

Alexi twisted, startled by the vehemence, by the passion, by the caring in his tone. He was her willing champion, a fury in the night. Touched, she stroked his cheek, somewhat amazed that he could show such fierce concern.

He caught her fingers and kissed them, and she met the dark fires of his eyes. She inhaled sharply, feeling everything within her quicken. She wanted him so badly! So very badly. And she was so frightened that she would pull away again. He wouldn't want her. He was fierce against brutality and injustice, but he could not want her again. A neurotic who teased.

But he was smiling, and smiling so gently, while the starfire blazed in the depths of his night-dark eyes. He kissed her fingers again, reverently, then dropped them, and to her amazement he was up beside her, struggling out of his jacket and vest and then his shirt as she stared up at him, incredulous of his strange, abrupt behavior.

"Ever been skinny-dipping?" he demanded.

She flushed, staring at the ocean while he stripped. "Rex, you saw what just happened!"

His trousers landed in her lap, then his briefs. In

the darkness she saw the bright flash of his muscled buttocks as he raced past her, splashing seawater all over her knit.

In seconds he had swum out into the surf. "Come on!"

"Didn't you ever watch *Jaws*?" she retorted.

"I promise you—no great white is in water this hot!"

"How about a small shark?"

"Minutely possible, but highly implausible. Come on! I dare you. I double-dare you."

"Rex…"

"Alexi! Come on! The least you owe me is a bit of good ogling."

She bit her lower lip, then recklessly stood. What else could happen? He knew the truth now. Her worst nightmare had already happened. Rex knew that she was basically asexual. And that she couldn't really help it—and why.

He'd sworn he'd kill John. She trembled suddenly, remembering his vehemence. It had just been a turn of phrase, she told herself. Rex didn't even know John.

"Come on!" Rex called to her.

She hesitated only a second longer. She pulled her knit over her shoulders, then hastened out of her lacy undergarments. Even in the darkness, she could see the rich grin that slashed across Rex's features where his head bobbed along with the waves.

This was crazy. It was so dark. But she plunged into the water anyway. It was cool with her whole body immersed. Alexi had never been skinny-dipping. It felt divine. She dived and swam, shivering as she broke the surface again.

She looked around. She couldn't see Rex anymore. His head wasn't above the water.

Then she felt him. Below her. Far below her. He tugged on her foot, and she gasped, laughing as her face almost slipped beneath the waves. But he didn't pull her down.

He explored her.

She felt his hands all along her legs. Felt his touch as he cradled her buttocks, felt his mouth grazing her belly, felt his kiss against her thighs....

She gasped, alive, electric, kinetic against the warmth of the Atlantic and the sheen of the moon. He had to breathe; surely the man had to breathe. He couldn't stay down forever....

But he could stay down a long time. A long, long time. Long enough to part her legs. Long enough to dive between them. To touch, to stroke, to glide...

He broke the surface, pulling her against him. She could barely stand against the sand and the water, the coil of sweetness was so tight within her.

"I'm going to drown," she warned him.

"No," he told her.

She barely knew the feel of his chest; she discovered it then: thick, dark hair a rich wet mat upon it. He let her touch him, then he swept his arms around her, and his kiss on her lips was demanding and thirsting and merciless, sweeping her away. She couldn't breathe; she couldn't protest. He broke from her, lifting her, and his mouth encircled her breast, drawing it in. She arched back, gasping, moaning.

"Rex..." she pleaded. "You know... I can't."

He slid her wet, sleek length against his own so that their bodies rubbed together provocatively. He waited until their eyes met, and he smiled triumphantly. "Oh, but you can."

He lifted her again, carrying her against the waves until they had just reached the shore. He laid her there and quickly stretched atop her, burrowing his weight between her thighs, kissing her hastily again, stealing breath and strength and protest from her. Kissing her so quickly, again and again. Her lips, her throat, her breast, her belly, her thighs, the very core of her, deeply, so deeply...

"Alexi."

He was above her, his eyes on her.

"Watch," he whispered. "You can. We can."

He touched her so erotically. And she watched. And she gasped again, crying out with the sheer pleasure of it, and he slowly, completely, insolently, possessively... electrically sank his body deep within hers.

Chapter 8

"Me and thee and a jug of wine."

There was the most wonderful, laconic smile on his face. He was still stark naked and not a bit bothered by it. Flat on his back, Rex lifted his hands to the heavens and sighed with contentment.

Alexi had no choice but to smile, too, curling on her side to watch him. The moon was high overhead and the stars were shimmering over the sand and the water, and she had never imagined that night could be so beautiful. She leaned on an elbow and drew a tender line down the length of Rex's cheek.

"We haven't any wine," she reminded him.

"Ah, true. Me and thee, then. In Eden. This is heaven." He drew her on top of him, lulled and sated to an exquisite point where he could pause now and savor and appreciate each little nuance of her, of the

things that passed between them. He could feel the
sand, gritty against his back, cool, fascinating. He
could feel the sand she brought with her, those tiny
pebbles against the endless silken smoothness of her
flesh. She leaned against his chest, slightly flushed.
Her eyes were as brilliant as gems, more wondrous
than all the stars in the heavens; her beautiful lips
were curled into the most awkward little smile. Her
hair was still soaked, a tangled mane swept clean from
her flesh now, yet it showed off the elegant lines of her
delicate, exquisite features. He leaned on his elbows,
laughing as she went off balance and then pouncing
on her as she lay on her back in the sand, touching
her cheek because he had to and studying the length
of her in the moonlight because he had to do that, too.

"Helen of Troy," he murmured softly, "the face that
beyond a doubt launched a thousand ships. Face and
form…" Softly, tenderly, with an awed fascination,
Rex explored her length with his fingertips as well as
with his eyes. Breasts this lovely had never graced the
pages of a fold-out magazine, he thought, then corrected himself. Well, all right, maybe they had once
in a long while, but not often. Long, lean torso, slim
waist, the most feminine flare of hips and buttocks…

Even her kneecaps were glorious.

"Sweetheart." He grinned at her. And then he
groaned softly in mock agony. "Had they seen her
body, too, they could have launched a million ships."

"Rex, stop!" Alexi protested, but he had her laughing and she couldn't help it. She laughed until his head
dipped over her and his face brushed her nipple. Then
he took it into his mouth, sliding his teeth, and then
his tongue, gently around it. She felt a sharp sizzle of

desire strike her anew just from that action, and her breath caught as she threaded her fingers through the deadly-dark wings of his hair, trying to draw him to her.

His eyes, darker than the sea at night, far darker than the midnight sky above them, met hers.

"I'm not, you know," she murmured. "I'm not anything like a real Helen of Troy at all. I'm..."

Quite ordinary. Those were the words she was looking for. She never had a chance to find them.

"No, you're not Helen of Troy. And you're not fantasy."

Rex smiled as he leisurely stroked his fingertip over her lower lip. She was really so beautiful that night. And maybe it was part fantasy. They were on the beach, and there was nothing on the horizon, nothing at all. They might have been the last man and woman on earth, or the very first. The breeze was gentle and balmy and the water was warm and the earth seemed to cradle them and blanket them in some welcoming, tender embrace. And she really didn't look like the Helen of Troy image at all; she was all natural. All...divinely natural, from wet hair and face to her gloriously naked body. Her eyes, her expression, the beauty in her features...were all innocence. The curve of her body was wanton and lush. The combination was nothing less than magical.

Rex dipped his head to kiss her mouth. He raised himself just a breath away from her.

"No, you're not Helen. You're Alexi Jordan, and I—"

He broke off abruptly.

And I love you very much.

Those had been the words he had been about to
say, he realized. They stunned him; they shocked him.
He'd known he'd wanted her. Any male over the age
of twelve who lived and breathed would have wanted
her. He'd known that he could enjoy her company, that
she could be fun and feisty and proud and temperamental, and even soft at times.

He just hadn't known that he was falling in love
with her. Nor was it a particularly bright thing to have
done. She was Helen of Troy, right? A woman who
would be returning to a certain world. A woman who
probably needed that world, had to have a certain
amount of adoration in her life. She'd stay awhile,
and then she'd go, and then he'd...

He'd spend the rest of his life missing her.

"Rex?"

Something in her tone was very soft and vulnerable. He'd forgotten. She'd come to him after a bad
finale to a bad marriage, and she was as delicate as
the fine marble she so resembled. He had to fall out
of love with her. But not now. Not tonight.

"Alexi Jordan," he whispered, "is far more beautiful than Helen of Troy could have ever been."

"Flatterer," she said accusingly.

"Mmm-hmm," he agreed. His one leg lay cast over
her. The prickly hairs of his chest tickled the soft flesh
of her breasts mercilessly. He casually cupped her
cheek and murmured huskily, "Think you want to
go again?"

His were bedroom eyes if she'd ever seen them,
and this dusky velvet patch of earth and water was
the most erotic bedroom she had ever known. She
smiled, wondering at the infinite tenderness in the

man. He'd known exactly what to say, and when. And he'd known exactly what to do, and when. She'd never known a man more the epitome of the male, and she'd never begun to imagine that such a man could show so much sensitivity.

"Think you can?" he asked.

She gazed into his eyes and stroked her fingers over his cheek, savoring the shaven flesh. "Piece of cake," she told him, and she set both palms against his face, bringing him down to her. She reached for his mouth first with the tip of her tongue, rimming his lips with that delicate touch before she molded her mouth to his. She felt the great rush of his breath and the fascinating hardening of his body, muscles tensing and stretching and tautening with his growing sexual excitement.

Earth, wind...and fire. It was Eden.

She felt his touch against her, her breasts, her hips, the curve of her buttocks, the soft flesh of her inner thigh. His kiss seared her, and when his lips left her flesh, the breeze came to kiss it afresh. He whispered words that meant nothing and everything, and she knew that she whispered in return, like a breath of the sea, like the cry of the waves. Each cry, each whisper, was fuel to the fire, and each fire was a lapping flame creating sensation anew, a heightened tension. She dared anything. She touched him intimately; she exulted in the swell and pulse of him. She soared to the heat and thunder of his rhythm, and she felt the tiny little piece of death that blacked out the world with the wondrous force of the climax that he brought to her upon the beach just as the very first touch of dawn burst upon it to bathe their Eden in beauteous magenta.

Floating as if she were indeed adrift upon the

waves, Alexi returned slowly to the earth beneath her, feeling again the fine grit of the sand and the coolness of the ocean at her feet. His arms went around her, and she rested on them. Only then did she shiver, watching the sky as the first tiny arc of the sun peeked out over the horizon like a shy young maiden.

"It's morning," Rex murmured.

"It certainly is," Alexi agreed. She shifted up onto her elbows. Rex stood and walked into the water, hunching down to splash water against his face, then standing again to stare out at the rising sun.

Alexi smiled, biting her lower lip. The sun was beautiful—but not nearly so magnificent as the man who stood before it, a tall, strong silhouette against that golden arc. She liked the whole of him very much, she decided, from the breadth of his shoulders to the muscles of his buttocks and thighs. She wondered if there was any more wonderful way to meet a lover than to come to him in this Eden, as he termed it.

He turned back to her. At her expression, he arched a brow.

"I'm deciding," she told him.

"Oh?"

"Mmm." She hesitated just a moment longer. "Can't decide. I like the frontside as much as the backside," she told him at last.

His dark brow arched higher. "Saucy wench, aren't you?"

"I tell it like it is."

He laughed and reached a hand down to her. She took it and stood and slid her arms around his neck and enjoyed kissing him in the light bath of sunlight. She loved feeling their naked, sandy flesh brush together.

He loved the feel of her breasts and hips against him, the feel of his sex against hers....

No, no, no, no, no, he thought. He could fairly well guarantee the privacy of his Eden by night, but not by daylight. God alone knew when the meter reader might decide to show up.

He broke away from her, found her dress and slipped it quickly over her head, then hurriedly searched for his trousers.

"All that talk and time to get my clothes off!" Alexi complained. "Now you're shoving me back into them!"

"I'm the jealous type," he told her, stumbling into his briefs. Alexi, still searching for her panties but comfortably clad in her dress, had to laugh as she watched him. He cast her an indignant glare that offered a definite threat once he was capable of standing straight.

Alexi held out a hand in a defensive gesture but kept laughing. "Don't be offended. I was watching you before, and you were just wonderful. Primal man—Atlas in the flesh. You really were just beautiful against the rising sun."

"Thanks," Rex muttered. He glanced up at her as he zippered his fly; then he started to laugh.

"What?" Alexi demanded.

"Green hair."

"What?"

"You have a lump of seaweed there. Left side—ah, you've got it."

She stared at him reproachfully, then started to smile. He stretched out his hand again and said, "I could stay here forever. But I'm afraid we might have some company."

Alexi nodded happily, curling her fingers around his. "Breakfast, Mr. Morrow? My place?"

"Sounds good. Let's pick up Samson first, though, huh? Emily went home yesterday, so he's been locked up all night."

Alexi nodded, lacing her fingers through his. She smiled as they started walking barefoot over the carpet of pine that led to the beach. "My purse and shoes are in the car. It's morning and you can't hear a thing but the breeze and the seabirds. I really do love it here."

Rex shot her a quick glance. Alexi, staring at the sky, didn't notice the penetrating quality of his gaze.

"Do you?" he said.

"Hmm?"

"No city lights."

"Well, everyone likes the city now and then. But, Rex—" She paused, looking at him with a very slight but honest, open smile. "This is like Eden. Don't you imagine that Pierre Brandywine must have thought the very thing when he first built the house for Eugenia?"

"You're a romantic," he told her.

"So are you," she said challengingly.

Was he? he wondered. Surely not.

They had reached his house. Samson came bounding out when Rex whistled. Rex asked her to hang on a minute while he got some clothes. "I'm really into sand when we're playing in it," he told her with a grimace, "and salt and all the rest. But I think I need a shower now, huh?"

"And where are you taking that shower?"

"With you."

"Presumptuous," she said with a sigh. But when they started out again, she had to stop. It was broad daylight now, with the bright, bright morning sun climbing higher in the sky. She stood in front of him, and she only hesitated for the fraction of a second. "Thank you, Rex. Thank you so very much. I—"

She hesitated again. Only the fraction of a second again, but the wheels of her heart and mind spun.

I love you.

The words almost spilled from her. Were they such easy words, then? she taunted herself. No, a heartbeat told her that they were not. She did love him. His smile, his dark eyes, the way he had looked, primitive and exciting and male, in the broad arc of the brimming sun. But that wasn't it. She loved him because he had been there. Hostile at first. Audacious at best. But he had been there for her in every sense of the words, sensitive, caring. Gentle and tender.

But he was good at that, she reminded herself. He was an accomplished lover. A good man, a practiced lover. Be his friend! she warned herself. Don't expect much; it will hurt too much if you let your feelings get out of hand.

Too late; her feelings were out of hand. She just had to take care not to let it show.

"You're very special," she finished quickly, feeling the probing of his ebony eyes. She smiled and stood on her toes to kiss him quickly. "Very special."

"Hey, I'm an obliging fellow," he said lightly. "Come on—the kittens must need an outing as badly as Samson."

"And the cellar will need a cleaning," Alexi moaned.

Rex didn't argue the point. When they reached the Brandywine house, Alexi retrieved her things from the car while Rex opened the house. By the time she reached the door, she practically tripped over the kittens to enter. Rex had let them up first thing, it seemed. Alexi quickly scooped the pair of them into her arms.

"Hi, sweeties. Did you think that you had been deserted? I'm sorry!"

Samson came running out of the kitchen and slid down the hallway, barking enthusiastically. The kittens squirmed in Alexi's arms, and she set them down to bat away at Samson. Samson tried to make a hasty retreat, but it was too late. The kittens tumbled after him.

"You asked for it this time, Samson!" Alexi laughed.

She started off for the kitchen herself, smiling as she inhaled the aroma of the coffee. Rex had gotten it going quickly.

She liked the way he looked in the kitchen, too. She paused in the doorway, watching as he moved from the cupboards to the refrigerator, barefoot and bare chested—and wearing his dress trousers.

Alexi went swiftly to the refrigerator herself and took out a carton of eggs and some cheese and bacon. Rex let her start the bacon and eggs, and he poured them each a mug of coffee.

"I'm probably the better cook," he warned her.

"Good. You can prove it tomorrow," she told him. Then she quickly lowered her head, letting her drying hair hide her features. What was she doing? She'd just come to the mature acceptance that he was a free agent, and here she was, assuming they'd be together for breakfast tomorrow.

"I will," he promised her smugly.

She breathed a little more easily and asked him to hand her the grater for the cheese. He did, then told her that she was only cooking so that he would have to go down to the cellar to see what kind of mess the kittens had made.

She watched him when he started down the stairs. She thought about the burnt brown hue of his shoulders and the weathered tan of his features and knew the color had come from endless hours in the sun he loved so much. Then she realized that she was daydreaming and about to burn something, so she turned her attention back to the stove. But as she did so she frowned, noting that the tea and sugar canisters were out of place, and she could have sworn that she had left the kitchen spotless the night before.

Alexi grated cheese over the eggs, then shook her head. Something about the kitchen didn't feel right. She couldn't explain it—after all, Rex had entered the kitchen before she had; maybe he had moved things.

She scooped the eggs off the frying pan and onto plates and quickly turned several pieces of bacon that were starting to burn. She should have started the bacon first, she told herself reproachfully. Rex probably was the better cook.

She heard a slight noise behind her and turned around. Rex had come up the stairway from the cellar and was watching her; on his lips was a curiously tender smile that brought a tug to her heart. He swung away from the doorframe, sauntered over to her, took her into his arms and met her eyes with his smile intact.

"Your hair looks like hell."

"I'm ever so sorry. I've just come from the most incredible night of my life."

"Thank you, ma'am."

She laughed and grew breathless and he started to kiss her, but they both smelled the bacon starting to burn. Alexi quickly retrieved it and popped bread into the toaster while Rex poured juice and more coffee.

While they ate, Alexi told him some of the things she wanted to do with the place. Rex listened and asked questions, and she grew more and more excited, trying to describe what she envisioned in the end. "I love this house. I always have. There's something about knowing that it belonged to my great-great-great-grandparents that just fascinates me."

"It is nice," Rex agreed. He caught her fingers across the table. "Were you going to start today, though?"

"I was."

"Is that negotiable?"

"Very."

They'd eaten every scrap of food. Alexi decided that being in love created enormous appetites. They'd barely picked up the dishes before they were both calmly and breathlessly discussing the need for a shower, and then they were in the shower—together, of course. Rex couldn't begin to make up his mind whether he preferred making love to her on the beach or against the steamy spray of the shower or in the bed she had chosen for her own with the fresh-smelling sheets and the sweet scent of shampoo and cologne dusting her flesh.

It didn't matter, he was certain. They were both drugged with it, and in the end it was about noon when they fell asleep, exhausted and content, and nearly dark again when he awoke.

Alexi was still sleeping. Her hair, dry and fragrant now, lay in tousled waves upon his shoulders and hers. He brought a lock of it to his lips, then silently held his breath while he admired the way it fell over her breasts as she slept.

He crawled from the bed, stared out at the dusk, then pulled on his clean pair of jeans and started down the stairs. He rummaged in the refrigerator and found some frozen steaks. He set them on the counter, shoved a few potatoes in the oven and made a fresh pot of coffee. That completed, he decided to grab some paper and make a family chart so that he could determine just which one of his characters was actually the murderer of all the others.

Alexi awoke first with the most marvelous sense of peace and warmth and contentment and security. Naturally, she reached out to touch him. Then her eyes flew open and she was not quite so warm and content, for she realized that he was gone.

She bolted out of bed and rushed to the window and saw that it was already dark, and ruefully admitted that maybe she hadn't slept all that much after all, since she had been up all night and all morning. Her heart began to beat, a little painfully, as she hoped that Rex had not left her. She wasn't afraid tonight; she just wanted to be with him.

She slipped quickly into a terry robe, ran her brush through her hair with a lick and a promise and started for the stairway. At the top landing she paused, gripping the banister and breathing with a sigh of relief and pleasure. He was still there. She could hear him. He was talking to someone, but who—?

She frowned, instinctively clutching her robe to her throat and silently coming down the stairs. She could hear him clearly. But who on earth was he talking to? His voice was rising and falling, rising and falling.

He was in the parlor. Alexi crossed the downstairs hallway quickly to go there, and then she paused, amused but determined not to laugh until he saw her.

Rex, scratching his head, paper and pencil in hand, was pacing from one side of the room to the other.

"No, no, no, no, no. That leaves just the butler. And the butler can't do it. I mean, the damn butler just can't do it!"

"Oooh, but he can! He can! Give the poor man a break!" Alexi cried.

Startled, Rex swung around to her. First he wore a very severe expression; then he swore softly at her—and then he laughed. "Caught in the act, huh?"

"Do you always talk to yourself?"

"You talk to paintings."

"Okay, okay—we're even," she promised. She stepped into the room and curled up on the steam-cleaned sofa in perfect comfort. She hugged her knees and asked him wistfully, "Tell me about it. Why can't the butler do it? Maybe I can help."

Rex looked at her doubtfully for a moment, then shrugged, smiled and joined her. He explained that having the butler do it would really be a cliché—unless it could be entirely justified. Of course, he might *want* it to be a cliché, if the book was to be a spoof. This wasn't going to be a spoof, though, so he had to be very careful that people didn't laugh at what was not intended to be funny.

Alexi listened while he went through his plot. To her amazement, his people quickly became as real to her as they were to him, and she could tell him why a certain character would or wouldn't behave in a certain way. She was excited to see that Rex was listening to her, and she was really pleased when he snapped his fingers, kissed her, picked up his paper and pencil and started back to work.

"You've got something?" she asked.

"I've got something." He paused, looking up at her. "The potatoes are already baking. The steaks are on the counter. Put them in and toss up a salad, and I promise I'll be ready to come and eat when you're ready."

Alexi smiled and nodded. She gave him a kiss on the top of the head, but she wasn't sure that he noticed. She asked if he didn't need to get the information down on his computer, but he absently assured her he was just writing notes and would transfer his work in the morning. Still smiling, Alexi went out to heat up the broiler for the steaks.

Samson and the kittens were in the kitchen. The big shepherd was stretched out on the floor; the little puffballs were audaciously curled right beneath his powerful jaws. Alexi shook her head and started to work again.

She put together a salad, then paused, perplexed, as she went through the cabinets again. She'd left them so organized. She'd spent yesterday really knowing what she had done with everything. It just didn't seem right that so many things had been moved.

When she went down to the cellar to find another bottle of wine, she had the same feeling. She didn't know what exactly was out of place, only that it was. The kittens had been down there, she reminded herself. And Rex had been down there, too—to let the kittens out, then to clean up after them. But she couldn't imagine the strange little chills running down her spine being caused by Rex's having been there. It was stupid—or perhaps it was instinct or a sixth sense. She was certain that someone else had been there.

She had just slipped the steaks into the oven when a pair of strong brown arms encircled her waist.

"What's the matter?" he asked her.

"Rex! Did you finish with your notes already?"

"I did...thanks to that wonderfully conniving little mind of yours. What an asset—beyond the obvious, of course."

"Do I know you, sir?" Alexi retorted.

"If you don't now, honey, you're going to," he replied in a wonderful imitation of Cary Grant, swinging her around in his arms. But his smile faded to a frown as he met her eyes.

"What's wrong?" he asked.

"Nothing! Really."

"No. Something is wrong."

"You can read me that well, huh?" Alexi murmured, a little uneasily, her lashes sweeping over her eyes. She smiled at him, telling him he'd better get out of the way so she could turn the steaks. He obliged, but when she brought the broiling pan out and put the meat on the plates, he pressed the point.

Alexi picked up the platter with the two potatoes and the salad bowl and set them at the table. She handed Rex the bottle of wine to open and a pair of chilled glasses, then sat down.

Rex arched a brow in silence, opened the wine and poured it, then sat across from her. "Well?"

"Well, you'll never believe me," she murmured.

His mouth tightened. "I have never not believed you, Alexi. But what are you talking about now?"

She sighed and sprinkled too much salt on her steak. "I don't know. This time it really does sound silly. Rex, don't you dare laugh at me. I have a feeling that someone else has been in the house."

He chewed a piece of meat, his eyes on her. "Why?"

"Things have—moved."

"Like what?"

"The sugar and tea canisters."

He glanced across the kitchen. "Maybe I moved them when I was fixing the coffee."

She nodded. "Maybe." She shrugged. "I know, I know—I'm being ridiculous."

"Maybe not." His fingers curled around hers on the table. Her heart seemed to stop when she gazed into his eyes. He wasn't laughing at her—he wasn't even smiling. In fact, the glitter of suspicion in his eyes was far more frightening than amusing.

"Alexi, you're forgetting that I was with you in the restaurant. Someone was very definitely spying on us."

She swallowed and nodded.

He looked around the kitchen. "It's just that…why would anyone want to come in here and move things around?"

"An antique buff?"

"Was anything taken?"

"No… I don't think so."

Rex was silent for a minute. She felt his fingers moving lightly, pensively over hers.

"Alexi—would your ex-husband be jealous or spiteful enough to want to follow you?"

She inhaled sharply and stared down at her plate. She remembered holding her breath on her first day in Fernandina Beach, thinking that she had seen his handsome blond head in a crowd.

Cruel? Yes—that could be said of John. Opportunistic, callous, ruthless—determined. But this…this stealth? This senselessness?

She shook her head. "I don't think so, Rex. I really don't."

His voice seemed tight and very low. "After what you've told me about the man, Alexi…"

"I know, Rex, I know," she murmured uneasily. She met his eyes at last. She'd never felt so vulnerable, and she knew his temper, too, but she was entirely unprepared for the heat of the emotion that burned so deeply into her.

"Rex… I… John was certainly no gentleman, but the only time he really hurt me, he'd been drinking and he was in a fit. A lot of it was ego; I rejected him. It never occurred to John that his behavior was unacceptable. He wanted to hurt me for the fact that I could walk away."

"He did hurt you. Badly."

"But not like—this." Her steak was cold. She'd lost her appetite anyway. In fact, a tremendous pall seemed to be falling upon a day that had been the most magical in her life. She smiled, trying not to shiver. "I probably am imagining things."

"Well," he murmured, sitting back, and his obsidian lashes hid his immediate thoughts. When he looked at her again he, too, was smiling. His fingers covered hers once again. "No one can be around now, huh? Samson would sound an alarm as loud as a siren."

Of course. She had forgotten Samson. No one could be anywhere near them. It was a nice thought. Very relieving.

"You haven't eaten a thing," Rex reminded her. He poured more wine into her glass.

Alexi sipped it and grimaced. "I'm really not very hungry." She stood and smiled again, determined to recapture the laughter that they had shared. "I know exactly what to do with it!"

"Oh?"

"Samson? Come here, you great dog, you!"

Barking excitedly and wagging his tail a mile a minute, Samson came bounding toward her, the kittens not far behind. Alexi gave the kittens tiny pieces of the meat and the rest to Samson.

"You have a friend for life," Rex assured her.

She laughed and picked up the rest of the dishes. She and Rex decided to take a short walk, but when they had gone only a few steps, Alexi gave him a playful pinch, commenting on the fit of his jeans. He laughed and cast her over his shoulder, commenting on the lack of fit of her attire and on everything that was beneath.

They laughed all the way into the house, up the stairs and into the bedroom, and there the laughter faded to urgent whispers of passion and need.

And Alexi did forget about being nervous. This night, like the one before it, was magic.

Chapter 9

One week later, the carpenters were just finishing
up with Alexi's first project, the window seat in the
kitchen.

Alexi, in a blue flowered sundress, stood by the
butcher-block table, admiring the work and her own
design. Her hair was drawn back in a ponytail, and
she was wearing very little makeup. Joe's boy had
brought out several pizzas, and Alexi had passed out
wine coolers. Rex, coming in from the parlor, surveyed the little area of the house and admitted she
had quite a talent for design. The window seat was
perfect for the house; the upholstery and drapes were
in a colonial pattern, and the seat added something to
the entire atmosphere and warmth of the kitchen. It
hadn't been there in the past, of course, but it looked
like something that could have been.

Enthused, Alexi swung around to demand, "Well?"

"It is wonderful and perfect," he told her, slipping an arm around her. With a satisfied sigh, she leaned against him. Skip Henderson, the elder of the two Henderson carpenters, chewed a piece of onion-and-pepperoni pizza, swallowed and told Alexi, "It's a wonderful design. It's great. I might try something like it in my own place."

"Yeah?" Alexi asked him.

He was a nice-looking man with muscled shoulders—like Rex's, bare in the heat—and a toothsome grin. He offered Alexi a grave nod then, though, but grinned again when he looked over the top of her head to Rex to say, "Smart, too, huh?"

"As a whip," Rex agreed pleasantly.

Alexi kicked him.

"Hey! What was that for?"

"I'd kick Skip, too, except that I don't know him that well," Alexi retorted. "There was that nice assumption that blondes only come in 'dumb'!"

Rex wrapped his arms around her and drew her tightly against him, laughing. "I've never dared make any assumptions about you, Alexi."

"You'd be welcome to kick me if you wanted to get to know me a little better, too," offered Terry, Skip's partner and younger brother.

"No deal," Rex warned him with a mock growl. Alexi flushed slightly. She liked the note of jealousy in his voice as much as she liked the ease of the teasing repartee. Were she and Rex really becoming a couple? The thought was so pleasant that it was frightening. They'd been a couple, of course. Very much a couple. They'd barely been apart since the night on the beach.

She couldn't count the times that they had made love, and that part of it was very thrilling and exciting…but there seemed to be so much more. She liked times like these almost as much. She loved the way that she could set about a project and, if she wanted his opinion, ask for it. He would take the time to answer her—unless he was behind a closed door, and then she knew that he needed his concentration. But they'd been together—living together—all these days, and they didn't seem to encroach upon each other's space. Sometimes she was so afraid that she held her breath a bit. Then she was wondering when he would decide that Eden had been fun for a spell but a woman as more than a lover was like a brick around his neck. He wasn't a cruel or cold man—he was the opposite in every way. But Alexi knew how the scars of the past could eat into a soul. The longer she and Rex stayed together, the more domestic she came to feel.

Would he run from domesticity if it became too confining?

"Finish your pizza," Skip told his brother. "I think we're overstaying our welcome here."

Alexi laughed. "Don't be silly. You're welcome as long as you want to stay. I'm going to run down to the cellar, though, and feed the creatures. I'll be right back. You all sit and enjoy yourselves."

She spun out of Rex's arms, thinking that it was nice, too, that their neighbors—Rex's friends and acquaintances from the mainland—all appeared to think it natural and romantic that the two of them were together.

Only Emily disapproved. Well, she didn't disapprove, but she seemed unhappy. Rex had told Alexi

once that Emily didn't dislike her—Emily thought
that she was simply too nice a girl for him. Alexi was
amused—and touched. Few people would assume that
she was too nice for anyone. She had made the front
pages of too many gossip magazines.

The phone started to ring as soon as she reached
the bottom step. She could hear Rex, Skip and Terry
discussing the chances of the Tampa Bay Buccaneers
in the coming season.

"Rex! Get that, will you?" She needed an answering machine for the house, she decided. Rex seldom
thought to answer a phone just because it was ringing.

"Rex!"

The phone kept ringing. Alexi dropped the fifty-
pound bag of Samson's dog food with an oath. Samson barked at her; his tail thumped the floor, and he
stared at her with huge, reproachful eyes.

She patted him on the head. "I'll be right back, big
guy. I promise."

She almost stepped on a kitten as she started up.
"I'll be back—I promise," she said again.

Skip and Terry were at the table. Skip pointed toward the hallway. Alexi nodded her thanks and hurried toward the parlor.

Rex was saying something. He looked up and noticed that Alexi had come into the room. "Hold on,
will you? She's right here." He covered the mouthpiece
and handed the phone to Alexi. "Your agent."

"Oh."

Alexi took the phone and greeted George Beattie
with affection. George was great; five-three, stout, a
very proper British chap with a heart of gold. Alexi

didn't think that she'd have made it through the past year without him.

Rex knew he probably should have left the room, but he didn't. Alexi didn't really say much of anything; she listened mainly. She glanced at him, a little apologetically, and asked for a piece of paper and a pencil. She thanked him with a glance when he supplied them.

"September first... I don't know, George. I still don't know." She paused to listen. "I'll let you know by next week. Is that enough time?"

Rex knew he must have agreed. Alexi thanked him, asked after his wife and kids, told him to take care and hung up. She fingered the paper, then noted him standing there, watching her, his arms crossed over his chest.

"They want you back?" he asked.

There was no emotion in his tone. Alexi shrugged. "Oh, it was an offer from one of the clothing manufacturers. A new campaign."

Rex took the paper from her and looked at the dates—and the sums. "That's the money involved?"

She nodded.

"Who is the photographer on the shoot? Not Vinto."

"No, no. Once the Helen of Troy finished, George knew to make sure that such a thing couldn't happen again."

"Well," he breathed softly. "You'd be a fool not to take it, wouldn't you?"

He handed the paper back, smiled stiffly and walked back to the kitchen. Alexi watched the set of his shoulders and felt as if her heart sank a little.

He didn't care. She was falling into domestic bliss,

and he was definitely finding it all to be a brief affair—cut short conveniently by her work schedule.

She'd known; she had only herself to blame. He'd never made any promises, and she wasn't really entitled to any complaints. No man could have given her more.

She stood there, watching his broad back as he disappeared through the door to the kitchen. What was the matter with her? They were hardly strangers. All she had to do was waltz right after him and demand to know what he had meant by that. She could be frank. She could take her chances. Gene had always said that you were a loser from the beginning if you didn't even try.

She trembled suddenly, thinking how much it meant to her. This little bit of time here—these hours they had shared in his "Eden"—they meant so much to her. They were everything she had always wanted, everything she had always searched for. She'd had to defy her family at first—she'd been young. But she'd always been looking for this...this very special relationship. This quiet, far from the crowds. This life... with Rex.

She couldn't go in and accost him emotionally. Not when he and Skip and Terry were discussing football. They would all stare at her as if she had lost her senses.

Alexi exhaled a little sigh and sank back onto the sofa. She remembered that she hadn't finished feeding the animals, but decided that she didn't really have the energy to do so. Maybe if she stayed away from the kitchen for a minute, Skip and Terry would go home.

As she sat there, her chin in her hands, the phone

started to ring again. Alexi idly reached over to answer it. "Hello?"

She waited, not alarmed at first.

"Hello?" she said more impatiently.

She could hear breathing in the background. Harsh and heavy.

"Hello, dammit! Say something."

She was just about to hang up when a voice said something at last.

"Hello, Alexi."

She was startled by the power that voice still held over her. She had seen him almost daily for almost a year after it had all happened, and she had dragged up a facade of cool and cordial indifference—and she'd even managed to believe it herself. But now time had passed, and she was hearing his voice. It touched her spine and raked along it—and she was afraid.

"Alexi?"

She almost hung up. But it seemed smarter to talk, to find out what he wanted.

"John. What do you want? How did you find me?"

"Oh, you were easy to find, sweets. And I just want to talk to you."

"Why?"

"Don't sound so hostile, babe."

"I am hostile."

"Alexi, come on! Think of the good times."

"I'm sorry. I can't remember any."

"I've got to see you."

"I don't ever want to see you again."

"Alexi—"

"Where are you, John?"

"Close, babe, real close."

How close? she wondered. She felt the tremors rake along her spine again. Her tongue and throat felt dry; her palms were damp.

"Well, John, forget it. I—"

She was startled when the receiver was wrenched from her hand. She gasped slightly and looked up to see that Rex was back. She hadn't heard him come into the room. Nor had he ever looked at her quite like that. His eyes were burning coals. His features were taut and strained, and he seemed a very hard man at that moment, striking, but cold as ice.

"What do you want, Vinto?"

"Who the hell are you?"

Even Alexi heard John's reply. She bit her lip, listening to the harsh tone of Rex's answer. He told John exactly who he was and exactly where he could be found. And then he told John to leave Alexi alone— or else.

Then he slammed down the receiver.

Alexi sat motionless for several long moments. She felt drained, and found that curious, for Rex seemed to be a mass of tension and knots, fists clenching and unclenching at his sides as he watched her.

"I didn't tread on any toes, did I?" he said.

"What?" She looked up at him at last.

"Did you want to see him?"

"No! Of course not. You know that! I—I'd like to feel that I could have handled it myself, but—"

"Sorry."

He turned around again and was gone. Miserable, Alexi continued to sit there. She got up at last and followed Rex across the hall.

Skip and Terry had gone. Rex was sitting there by

himself at the butcher-block table, staring at the window seat that had so recently given them both such pleasure.

Alexi came and sat down next to him. He glanced her way. A brief smile touched his lips and then was gone. He squeezed her fingers and rose. "I'm going out for a few hours." He started for the kitchen door.

Alexi rose, too. "Rex?"

"It's all right," he assured her. "I'm just going out for a few hours."

The kitchen door swung. She heard Rex's footsteps on the stairway, going up. Then, seconds later, she heard them coming down again. He hesitated, as if he was going to walk straight to the front door but then decided not to.

He came back into the kitchen. He'd donned a striped tailored shirt and moccasins and was busy tucking the shirt into his jeans. He came around behind Alexi. With his fingers he lightly stroked her upper arms.

"I'll be back," he promised her.

There was so much she wanted to say. She didn't seem able to say any of it. She nodded, and he kissed the top of her head.

"Alexi, I..."

"What?"

"I, uh, I'll try not to be gone too long."

She looked up at him curiously. He smiled and kissed her distractedly on the forehead again. A moment later, the kitchen door was swinging in his wake, but then he caught it again to say, "Come on out and lock the door."

Samson started barking. He raced up from the cellar stairs and brushed past Alexi and jumped on Rex.

"Get down, you monster."

"He doesn't want to be left behind," Alexi murmured.

"All right, all right, you can come for a ride," Rex told the dog impatiently. "Alexi, make sure you lock the door."

"I will, dammit, Rex. I know how to do it now."

He didn't answer her. Alexi heard him yell at Samson to get into the car; then she heard the Maserati rev. She locked the door and leaned against it and felt like crying.

She muttered fervently to herself about the absurdity of such a thing and went back into the kitchen. She threw away the pizza boxes and the empty beer bottles and swore softly as she washed down the table and the counters. She curled up on her new window seat, but she couldn't seem to take any pleasure in it. Then she heard a mewling and remembered that she still hadn't fed any of the animals—his or hers.

"Okay, my loves. I'm coming." Alexi uncurled herself and started down the cellar stairs. The kittens played around her feet. "Samson went out without any dinner. Serves him right, don't you think? Men. They're all alike, and they deserve what they get, huh?"

Alexi glanced through the shelves of food. "Chicken, tuna or liver, guys?"

She shrugged and decided on cans of chicken. She picked up the bowls to wash them in the big, ancient sink and bit her lip against the temptation to cry again.

Rex had been in such a hurry to get out, to get

away from her. He'd been counting the damn days, she thought spitefully. He wanted her to go back to work.

And then he'd grabbed the phone away from her. He hadn't thought her capable of dealing with John. But then, really, just what did he think of her, and what could she really expect? They'd met because she'd broken in—because she hadn't been able to get that stupid old key to work. Then she'd heard the footsteps of someone chasing her in the sand. And she'd been convinced that someone was in the house that night the lights had gone out. And then again, when they'd come back after their night out on the beach, she'd been so sure...

He thought she was neurotic, surely. He'd run out tonight because he just had to have a break from a neurotic woman who was perhaps becoming just a little bit too much like a clinging vine.

Alexi ruefully turned the water off, thinking that the kittens would surely have the cleanest bowls in the state. Then she paused, startled, her heart soaring with hope as she thought she heard the door open and close.

She dropped the bowls into the sink and hurried back to the bottom of the stairs. "Rex?"

She didn't hear anything, but she could have sworn that the front door had opened. Alexi started up the stairs and entered the kitchen. There was no one there. She hurried out into the hallway and saw that it was growing dark. The stairs to the second floor and the landing above them loomed before her like a giant, empty cavern, waiting to swallow her whole.

"You are neurotic!" she charged herself aloud. In a businesslike manner she turned on the hallway light, and she felt better. She moved on into the parlor and turned on the globe lamp behind the Victorian sofa.

"A little light shed on the matter," she murmured. Then she paused uneasily again, shivering. It felt as if someone was near. She couldn't really describe why— it just felt that way.

John.

Ice seemed to course through her veins. He had said that he was near, hadn't he? Had he been here all along, stalking her? Running after her on the sand the second night she was there, somehow slipping into the house once she had run into Rex, escaping when she had screamed...

No. It just couldn't be John. What could he want with her?

He said that he wanted to talk to her....

The shadow in the Asian restaurant, watching them through the screen...could that have been John?

Who else? She gave herself a shake, then stood very still. She hadn't heard a thing. She was just nervous because Rex was gone and she was so accustomed to being with him now.

Alexi cut across the hall. She meant to go into the kitchen, but paused and walked into the ballroom instead. She turned on the lights and walked down to stand beneath the portraits of Pierre and Eugenia.

"You were really so beautiful!" she told them both softly. And she smiled, wondering if they had ever loved each other on the beach, watching as the sun came up in an arc of beauty. Had they laughed in the waves, played in the surf?

They had been great lovers, she knew, according to family legend and some documented fact. Eugenia's father had been a rich Baltimore merchant, but she had defied him to marry Pierre Brandywine, a Southern sea captain. They had eloped and run away to Jamaica to honeymoon, even as the conflicts between the states had simmered and exploded. In 1859, Pierre had brought Eugenia to the Brandywine house on the peninsula and carried her over the threshold of his creation.

Alexi studied her great-great-great-grandfather's handsome features and deep blue eyes. He seemed to be looking at her with grave concentration. Alexi smiled. "I don't believe you haunt this place, Pierre. And truly, if you did, you would surely never hurt me! Flesh and blood and all that, Pierre!"

She looked over at the picture of Eugenia. She loved that picture. She must have been such a sweet and gentle woman, so lovely, so fragile—and so very strong. She had been here alone with one maid and an infant through much of the war.

"I suppose I can deal with a night's solitude," Alexi told the portraits dryly. She turned around, squaring her shoulders, and left the ballroom. The poor kittens. She really had to forget her problems and her fears and feed the little things.

To her annoyance, she paused in the kitchen again. Now she could have sworn that she had heard a board creak on the staircase in the hallway. She hesitated a long moment, swearing silently that she was a fool; then she rushed back out to the hallway again. There was no one there.

She went into the kitchen and didn't hesitate for a second. She went straight to the cellar doorway, threw it open and started down the stairs.

She was about five steps from the cellar floor when the room was suddenly pitched into total darkness.

And even as she stood there, fear rushing upon her as cold and icy as a winter's storm, she heard a sound on the steps behind her. A definite sound. She wasn't imagining things, nor was it a ghostly tread.

Someone was in the room with her.

She turned, a scream upon her lips, determined to defend herself. But she never had a chance. Something crashed against her nape, hard and sure. Stars appeared before her momentarily in the darkness; then she pitched forward, falling the last few steps to land upon the cold stone floor below.

Rex kept the gas pedal close to the floor. He was going way too fast in the Maserati, he knew, but tonight it felt good. He'd felt so hot in the house, so hot and tense, and had been winding tighter and tighter, until he felt he might explode.

What the hell was the matter with him? He'd known she didn't really belong on the peninsula. He'd known she'd come to the place looking for a safe harbor, a place to lick her wounds, a place to stand up on her own two feet. He'd helped her to do that. Yeah. He'd helped her. And it was nothing to feel bitter about; he was glad.

He had to be. He loved her.

He just hadn't realized, not really, that she would be leaving. That she came from another world. A busy world of schedules, of ten-hour days. Hell, she had the face that could launch a thousand ships, right? She enjoyed her work, all right—she'd run from John

Vinto, not the work. She was beautiful; the world had a right to her.

"Wrong, Samson, wrong," Rex sighed.

Samson, his nose out the window, barked.

He didn't want to share her. Ever again. Maybe that was selfish. He wanted her forever and forever. On the peninsula with him. With her hair down and barefoot and no makeup and—hell, yes!—barefoot and pregnant and together with him in their little Eden. He hadn't thought that he'd ever want to marry again. To take that chance, make that commitment. But nothing from the past mattered. It was all unimportant. Because he loved Alexi.

She didn't intend to stay. He'd known that. He'd known it, but it was a painful blow....

And that was nowhere near the worst of it, Rex reminded himself. He glanced at the road sign and saw that he was south of Jacksonville; and he'd been gone about thirty minutes. He was making good time.

John Vinto.

He scowled thinking of the name. His fingers tightened fiercely around the steering wheel, and the world was covered in a sudden shade of red. He'd like to take his hands and wind them around the guy's neck and squeeze and squeeze....

"You won't touch her again, Vinto—I swear it!" he muttered aloud. Samson turned around, panting and whining, trying to get his big haunches into the little bucket seat. He licked Rex's hand.

"I sound like a lunatic, huh?" Rex asked the dog. He inhaled and exhaled slowly, reminded himself that he'd never met the guy; he'd never even seen him, except on the covers of the gossip rags. Still, the guy had problems. Anyone who behaved the way he had with Alexi had problems. Were those problems severe enough for him to be playing a game of nerves with her now?

He glanced at the sign he was passing. St. Augustine was just ahead. Rex drove on by the main road, heading south. At last he came to the turnoff he wanted and slowed considerably, watching for the small lettering that would warn him he was coming closer and closer to the Pines.

He pulled beneath an arcade. A handsomely uniformed young man came to take the car, greeting Rex by name. Rex returned the salute, asking how Mr. Brandywine had been doing.

"Spry as an old fox, if you ask me!" the valet told Rex. "You just watch, Mr. Morrow—he'll outlive the lot of us!"

Rex laughed and asked the valet if he'd mind giving Samson a run, then entered the elegant lobby of the Pines home. It didn't appear in the least like a nursing home—more like a very elegant hotel. Rex went to the front desk and asked for Gene, and the pretty young receptionist called his room. A moment later she told him that Mr. Brandywine was delighted to hear that he was there. "Go on up, Mr. Morrow. You know the way."

Gene's place was on the eighteenth floor. He had one of the most glorious views of the beaches and the Atlantic that Rex had ever seen. The balcony was a site of contemporary beauty, with a built-in wet bar and steel mesh chairs. Rex found Gene there.

"Rex! Glad to see you, boy. Didn't know you were coming!"

Rex embraced Gene Brandywine. He was a head taller and pounds heavier than the slim, elderly man, but Gene would have expected no less. With real pleasure he patted Rex on the back, then stood away, looking him over.

"I've missed you, Rex." He winked, taking a seat after he'd made them both a Scotch and water. "But I've been hoping that you've still been keeping an eye on that ornery great-granddaughter of mine."

Rex lowered his head, sipping quietly at his drink. "Uh…yeah, I've been keeping an eye on her."

"A good eye, I take it?"

Something about his tone of voice caused Rex to raise his head. Gene hadn't lost a hair on his old head, Rex thought affectionately. It was whiter than snow, but it was all there. And his face was crinkled like used tissue at Christmas, but he was still one hell of a good-looking old man, with his sharp, bright, all-seeing, all-knowing blue eyes.

"Why, you old coot!" Rex charged him. "Seems to me you planned it that way, didn't you?"

Gene waved a hand in the air. "Planned? Now, how can any man do that, boy? You tell me. I kind of hoped that the two of you might hit it off. You didn't know what a good woman was anymore, Morrow. And she needed real bad to know that there was still some strength and character…and tenderness…in the world. You're going to marry her, I take it?"

Rex choked on his Scotch, coughing to clear his throat as Gene patted him on the back.

"Gene…we've only known each other a few weeks."

"Don't take much, boy. Why, I knew my Molly just a day before I knew she was the one and only woman in the world for me. We Brandywines are like that. We know real quick where the heart lies."

Rex straightened, twirling his glass idly in his hands. "Gene, I'm out here because I'm kind of worried about her. A couple of strange things have happened."

"Strange?"

"Nothing serious. Alexi has thought that she's heard footsteps now and then. And we were watched one night at a restaurant. Then tonight…"

"Tonight what? Don't do this to me, Rex. Spit it all out, boy!"

"John Vinto called her. He said he wanted to see her."

"And?"

"And I snatched the phone out of her hand. I talked to him myself. I said that he should leave her alone, and that if he didn't he'd have to deal with me."

Gene didn't say anything for a long time. He studied the ice floating in his glass. "Good!" he said at last.

Rex watched him, perplexed. "Gene?"

"Yeah?"

"Do you think that this guy could be really dangerous?"

Gene inhaled and exhaled slowly. "I don't know. I wanted her down here badly when this stuff first hit. I don't know exactly what happened—" He paused, giving Rex a shrewd assessment. "Her mother didn't even know, but I'm willing to bet you're in on more than we were. Still, I know Alexi pretty good. She's always been kind of my favorite—an old man's prerogative. I know he hurt her. I know he scared her, and I was glad in a way that she stood up to him to finish off that campaign. But I never did like Vinto. Smart, handsome, slick—and cruel. There's not a hell of a lot that I would put past the man."

Rex looked down at his hands. His knuckles were taut and white. He forced himself to loosen his grip on the glass. He stood and set it down on an elegant little coffee table. "I'm going to get back to her, Gene."

"You do that, Rex. I think you should."

"When are you coming out for a visit?"

"Soon. Real soon. I was trying to give Alexi a chance to finish something she wanted to get done."

"The window seat in the kitchen," Rex said. "The carpenters were there today. It's all finished up."

"Then I'll be by soon," Gene promised. He shook Rex's hand. "Thanks for coming out. And thanks for being there. I love that girl. I'd be the cavalier for her myself, but I'm just a bit old for the job." He shook his head. "Strange things, huh? You make sure that you stay right with her."

Rex nodded. He hesitated at the doorway. "Gene, you don't think there's any other reason that strange things could be happening out there, do you?"

"What do you mean by that?"

Rex considered, then shrugged. "I don't know. I've been there years myself—and I've never had anything happen before."

"Pierre isn't haunting the place, if that's what you mean," Gene assured him. Rex thought his eyes looked a little rheumy as he reminisced. "Eugenia always said he was the most gallant gentleman she ever did know. She outlived him for more than sixty years, and never did look at another man. No, Pierre Brandywine just isn't the type to be haunting his own great-great-great-granddaughter."

Rex smiled. "I didn't really think that Pierre could be haunting the house. I was just wondering…"

"There's nothing strange about that house. I lived there for years and years!" Gene insisted.

"I was thinking about Pierre's 'treasure.'"

"Confederate bills. Worthless."

"Yeah, I suppose you're right." Rex offered Gene his hand. They shook, old friends.

"See you soon."

"It's a promise," Gene agreed. Rex stepped out. "It's a good thing I know you're living with her!" Gene called to Rex. "This is an old heart, you know! Not real good with surprises."

Rex paused, then smiled slowly and waved.

Downstairs he picked up his car, thanked the valet, whistled for Samson—and, as he headed back northward, felt ten times lighter in spirit. So Gene had planned it all, that old fox.

Whatever "it" was. All Rex knew was that he wasn't going to give it all up quite so easily. Not only that, but she needed him, and he sure as hell intended to be there for her.

He drove even faster going back. It should have taken at least two hours, but he made it in less than an hour and a half, whistling as he drove onto the peninsula and approached the house.

His whistle faded on the breeze as he pulled in front of the Brandywine house. Samson panted and whined unhappily. Rex stared, freezing as a whisper of fear snaked its way down his spine.

The house was in total darkness.

Interlude

He wasn't even supposed to be there.

As a lieutenant general in the cavalry, Pierre served under Jeb Stuart. But, returning from his leave of absence, he'd been assigned to Longstreet's division, under Lee. They'd been heading up farther north—toward Harrisburg—but one of the bigwigs had seen in the paper that there were shoes to be had in Gettysburg, and before long the Yanks were coming in from one side and the rebs were pouring in from the other. The first day had gone okay—if one could consider thousands of bodies okay—as a stalemate. Even the second day. But here it was July 3, and the Old Man—Lee—was saying that they were desperate, and desperate times called for some bold and desperate actions.

Pierre, unmounted, was commanding a small force under a temperamental young general called Picket. A. P. Hill was complaining loudly; Longstreet—with more respect for Lee—was taking the situation quietly.

It was suicide. Pierre knew it before they ever started the charge down into the enemy lines. Pure, raw suicide.

But he was an officer and a Southern gentleman. Hell, Jeb had said time and time again that they were the last of the cavaliers.

And so, when the charge was sounded, Pierre raised his sword high. The powder was already thick and black; enemy cannon fire cut them down where they stood, where they moved, and still they pressed onward. He smelled the smoke. He smelled the charred flesh and heard the screams of his fellows, along with the deadly pulse of the drums and the sweet music of the piper.

He could no longer see where he was going. The air was black around him. It burned when he inhaled.

"Onward, boys! Onward! There's been no retreat called!" he ordered.

He led them—to their deaths. His eyes filled with tears that had nothing to do with the black powder. He knew he was going to die.

Fernandina Beach, Florida

Eugenia screamed.

Mary, startled from her task of stirring the boiling lye for soap, dropped her huge wooden spoon and streaked out to the lawn, where Eugenia had been hanging fresh-washed sheets beneath the summer sun. She was doubled over then, hands clasped to her belly, in some ungodly pain.

"Miz Eugenia!" Mary put her arms around her mistress, desperately anxious. Maybe it was the baby, coming long before its time. And here they were, so far from anywhere, when they would need help.

"Miz Eugenia, let me get you to the porch. Water, I'll fetch some water, ma'am, and be right back—"

Eugenia straightened. She stared out toward the ocean, seeing nothing. She shook her head. "I'm all right, Mary."

"The baby—"

"The baby is fine."

"Then—"

"He's dead, Mary."

"Miz Eugenia—"

Eugenia shook off Mary's touch. "He's dead, Mary, I tell you."

"Come to the porch, ma'am. That sun's gettin' to you, girl!"

Eugenia shook her head again. "Watch Gene for me, please."

"But where—?"

Eugenia did not look back. She walked to the trail of pines where she had last seen her love when he had come to her. She came to the shore of the beach he had so loved. Where he had first brought her. Where they had first made love upon the sand and he had teased her so fiercely about her Northern inhibitions. She remembered his face when he had laughed, and she remembered the sapphire-blue intensity and beauty of his eyes when he had risen above her in passion.

She sank to the sand and wept.

Grapeshot.

It caught him in the gut, and it was not clean, nor neat, nor merciful.

He opened his eyes, and he could see a Yank surgeon looking down at him, and he knew from the man's eyes and he knew because he'd been living with it night and day for years that death had come for him and there was no denying it.

"Water, General?"

Pierre nodded. It didn't seem necessary to tell the Yank that he was a Lieutenant General. Not much of anything seemed necessary now.

"I'm dying," he said flatly.

The young Yankee surgeon looked at him unhappily. He knew when you could lie to a man and when you couldn't.

"Yes, sir."

Pierre closed his eyes. They must have given him some morphine. The Yanks still had the stuff. He didn't see powder anymore, and he didn't see black. The world was in fog, but it was a beautiful fog. A swirling place of mist and splendor.

He could see Eugenia. He could see the long trail that led from the beach along the pines.

She was running to him. He could see the fine and fragile lines of her beautiful face, and he could see her lips, curled in a smile of welcome. He lifted his hand to wave, and he ran....

She was coming closer and closer to him. Soon

he would reach out and touch the silk of her skin. He would wrap his arms around her and feel her woman's warmth as she kissed him....

"General."

Eugenia vanished into the mist. Pain slashed through his consciousness.

He opened his eyes. The surgeon was gone. He had moved on to those who had a chance to live, Pierre knew. A young bugler stood before him. "Sir, is there any—?"

Pierre could barely see; blood clouded his vision. He reached out to grab the boy's hand.

"I need paper. Please."

"Sir, I don't know that I can—"

"Please. Please."

The boy brought paper and a stub of lead. Pierre nearly screamed aloud when he tried to sit. Then the pain eased. His life was ebbing away.

Eugenia, my love, my life,
I cannot be with you, but I will always be with you. Love, for the children, do not forget the gold that is buried in the house. Use it to raise them well, love. And teach them that ours was once a glorious cause of dreamers, if an ill-fated and doomed one, too. Ever yours, Eugenia, in life and in death.
Pierre

He fell back. "Take this for me, boy, will you? Please. See that it gets to Eugenia Brandywine, Brandywine House, Fernandina Beach, Florida. Will you do it for me, boy?"

"Yes, sir!" The young boy saluted promptly.

Pierre fell back and closed his eyes. He prayed for the dream to come again. For the mist to come.

And it did. He saw her. He saw her smile. He saw her on the beach, and he saw her running to him. Running, running, running...

Three days later, an officer was sent out from Jacksonville to tell Eugenia Brandywine of her husband's death on the field of valor. The words meant nothing to her. Her expression was blank as she listened; her tears were gone. She had already cried until her heart was dry. She had already buried her love tenderly beneath the sands of time. When his body reached her, weeks later, it was nothing more than a formality to inter him in the cemetery on the mainland.

Pierre's second child, a girl, was born in October. By then the South was already strangling, dying a death as slow and painful and merciless as Pierre's. Eugenia's father sent for her, and with two small mouths to feed and little spirit for life, she decided to return home. Her mother would love her children and care for them when she had so little heart left for life.

One more time she went to the beach. One more time she allowed herself to smile wistfully and lose herself in memory and in dreams. She would always remember him as he had been that day. Her dashing, handsome, beautiful cavalier. Her ever-gallant lover.

She would never come back. She knew it. But she would tell the children about their inheritance. And they would come here. And then their children's children could come. And they could savor the sea breeze and the warmth of the water by night and the crystal beauty of the stars. In a better time, a better world.

Eugenia left in January of 1863. By the time the war ended and the young bugler—a certain Robert W. Matheson—reached Fernandina Beach in November of 1865, there was no one there except a testy maid who assured him that the lady of the house—Mrs. P. T. Brandywine—had gone north long ago and would never return.

"Well, can you see that she gets this, then? It's very important. It's from her husband. He entrusted it to me when he died."

"Yes, young man. Yes. Now, go along with you."

Sergeant Matheson, his quest complete, went on. The maid—hired by Eugenia's father and very aware that he didn't want his daughter reminded of the death—tossed the note into the cupboard, where it lay unopened for decade upon decade upon decade.

Chapter 10

Rex ran up to the house, Samson barking at his heels. "Alexi!" he called, but all that greeted him was silence. In rising panic he shouted her name again, trying the door only to discover that it was locked. He dug for his own key, carefully twisted it in the lock and shoved the door open. Samson kept barking excitedly. His tail thumped the floor in such a way that Rex knew damn well there were no strangers around now. Rex was certain that if there had been a stranger about the place, Samson would be tearing after him—or her.

"Alexi!" He switched on the hall light. There was no sign of anything being wrong. Nothing seemed to be out of place. "Alexi!" He pushed open the door to the parlor and switched on the light. She wasn't there. He hurried on to the library, the ballroom, the powder room, and then up the stairs. "Alexi!" She wasn't in any of the bedrooms, he discovered as he swept through the place, turning on every light he passed.

He should never have left her. Something was wrong; he could feel it.

Maybe nothing was wrong. Nothing at all. Maybe she had just decided that it was time to call it quits with the small-town stuff, with the spooky old creepy house and the eccentric horror writer who seemed to come with it. Maybe she felt that Vinto was a threat and that she needed far more protection than she could ever find here.

Maybe, maybe—damn!

She hadn't gone anywhere. Not on purpose. She would have left him a note…something. She wouldn't have left him to run through the house like a madman, tearing out his hair.

He stormed down the stairs and burst into the kitchen. She wasn't there. Rex pulled out a chair and sank into it, debating his next movement. The police. He had to call the police. He never should have left her. Never. Or—oh, God, he groaned inwardly. At the very least, he should have left Samson with her. He'd blown the whole thing, all the way around. He'd gone out and gotten her a pair of kittens—kittens!—when he should have come back around with a Doberman. Or a pit bull. Yeah…with Vinto, it would have to be a pit bull.

"Where the hell is she?" he whispered aloud, desperately.

Samson, at his feet, thumped his tail against the floor and whined. Rex gazed absently at his dog and patted him on the head. Samson barked again loudly.

Rex jumped up.

"Where is she, boy? Where's Alexi?"

Samson started barking wildly again. Rex decided he was an idiot to be talking to the dog that way. Samson was a good old dog—but he wasn't exactly Lassie.

But then Samson barked again and ran over to the cellar door, whining. He came back and jumped on Rex, practically knocking him over. Then he ran back to the cellar door.

"And I said that you weren't Lassie!" Rex muttered. The cellar. Of course.

But he felt as if his heart were in his throat. He hadn't believed her. Not when she had told him that someone had chased her from the car. Not when she had been convinced that someone had been in the house. He had barely given her the benefit of the doubt when she had been certain that the snakes had been brought in.

And it was highly likely that John Vinto knew that she was terrified of snakes.

He had left her tonight.

And now he knew that she was in the cellar. But the cellar was pitch-dark, and he was in mortal terror of how he would find her.

"Alexi!" he screamed, and ripped open the door and nearly tumbled down the steps. Samson went racing down as Rex fumbled for the light switch.

The room was flooded with bright illumination.

And Rex found Alexi at last.

She was at the foot of the stairs, on her back, her elbow cast over her eyes, almost as if she were sleeping, one of her knees slightly bent over the other. The kittens, like little sentinels, sat on either side of her, meowing away now that he was there.

"Alexi!" This time, he whispered in fear. Then he found motion and ran down the steps to drop by her side. She was so white. Pasty white. How long had she been lying there? Swallowing frantically, he reached for her wrist, forcing himself to be calm. She had a pulse. A strong pulse.

"Oh, God," he breathed. "Oh, God. Thank you."

What had happened? He glanced quickly up the stairs, wondering if she had tripped and fallen. That didn't seem right. Why would she turn off every light in the house to come down to the cellar?

"Alexi...?" He touched her carefully, trying to ascertain whether she had broken any bones. She moaned softly, and he paused, inhaling sharply. She blinked and stared up at him in a daze, groaning as the light hit her eyes.

"Rex?"

"Alexi...stay still. I think I should call for an ambulance—"

"No! No!" Alexi sat up a little shakily, gripping her head between her hands and groaning again.

"Alexi!"

"I'm all right, really I am. I think." She stretched out her arms and legs and tried to smile at him, proving that nothing was broken. But he didn't like her color, and he was worried about a head injury that had left her unconscious.

She gasped suddenly, her eyes going very wide as she stared at him. "Did you see him, Rex?"

"Who?"

"Someone was here. Really, Rex, I swear it."

"Alexi, maybe you just fell—"

"I didn't! I heard someone in the house after you

left. I kept trying to assume that I was imagining things, too. But there was someone here, Rex. Behind me on the stairs. I came down to feed the kittens, and when I tried to turn... I was struck on the head."

"You're...sure?"

"Damn you, Rex!" She tried to stand, to swear down at him. But the effort was too dizzying, and before she could get any further, she felt herself falling.

She didn't fall. He caught her and lifted her into his arms.

"I'm...all right," she tried to tell him.

"No, you're not," he told her bluntly, starting up the stairs. She laced her fingers around his neck as he carried her and studied his face as he emitted a soft oath at Samson to get out of his way so that he wouldn't trip.

"There's no one here now?" she asked.

"There's definitely no one here now. But I am going to call the police."

A silence fell for a moment as he reached the top of the stairs and closed the cellar door behind him. Alexi, cradled in his arms, kept staring at the contours of his face. She reached up to brush his cheek lightly with her knuckles.

"Were you angry, Rex? Or did you just need to escape?"

"I was angry," he told her. He carried her on through the kitchen and out to the parlor, laying her down carefully on the sofa. He told her to hold still, and ran his fingers over her skull, wincing when he found the lump at her nape.

"Police first, then the hospital."

"Rex—"

He ignored her and picked up the phone. Alexi closed her eyes for a moment. Maybe he was right. She still felt the most awful pain throbbing in her head.

But, curiously, she felt like smiling. He had come back—all somber and gruff and very worried—but back nonetheless. And he hadn't been running away from her—he had left because he had been angry, and for him, walking away had probably been the best way to deal with it.

He set the phone down and came back to her.

"With me?" she asked him.

"What?"

"Were you angry with me?"

He frowned, as if he wasn't at all sure what she was talking about. "I'm going to get a cold cloth for your temple. That might make you feel a little better." He started out of the room.

"Rex!"

"What!"

"Where did you go?"

He held in the doorway and arched a dark brow, smiling slowly as he looked at her. "I beg your pardon?"

She flushed and repeated herself softly.

He hesitated, still smiling. "Inquisitive, aren't you?"

"Not usually."

"Well, that rather remains to be seen, doesn't it?" he asked her huskily. Then he said, "I went out to see Gene."

"Gene?" She sat up abruptly, then moaned and slid down again. "Gene? He's my great-grandparent."

"Yeah, but he's my very good friend. I saw him

every day, you know. I lived here. You were off in New York."

There was a strange sound to his voice as he said that; Alexi didn't have time to ponder it, because he went on to say, "I'm sorry. Maybe I had no right. I went out to ask him if he thought John Vinto could be behind all these strange occurrences."

Alexi watched him, then offered up a soft smile that Rex knew was not for him.

"How is he?" she asked.

"Gene?"

"Of course Gene."

"He's fine. He'll be out soon. He wanted to give you time to surprise him."

She was still smiling when he left the room. By the time he came back with a cloth for her head, they could hear the sound of a siren as the sheriff's car headed for the house. Alexi closed her eyes as Rex placed the cold cloth on her head.

"Mark's here," he told her, listening as the sound came closer and closer.

"Mark?"

"Mark Eliot. A friend of mine."

He saw the deep smile that touched her lips. "You have a lot of friends around here, Mr. Morrow—an awful lot of friends for a recluse."

"It's a friendly place," he said lightly. He squeezed her hand and went on to answer the door.

Mark Eliot was a tall man with sandy-blond hair and a drooping mustache. Rex shook hands with him at the door and was glad to see that Mark seemed to be taking it all very seriously—not with the humor he had shown when Rex had suggested that the snakes might have been set loose in the house purposely.

"Was anything taken?" Mark asked as they came into the parlor.

"Not that we know of," Rex said. He frowned as they came in, noting that Alexi had chosen to sit up. She still seemed very pale.

"Alexi, Mark Eliot, with the sheriff's office. Mark, Alexi—"

"Alexi Jordan." Mark took her hand. He didn't let it go. "Anything, ma'am. Anything at all that we can do for you, you just let us know."

"Mark—we're trying to report a break and enter and assault."

"Oh, yeah. Yeah."

He sat down beside Alexi. Rex crossed his arms over his chest and leaned back against the wall and watched and waited. Mark did manage to get through the proper routine of questions. He even scribbled notes on a piece of paper, and when he was done, Rex had to admit that even tripping over his own tongue, Mark was all right at his job.

"There is no sign of forced entry. Nothing was taken. Rex, when you came back, the house was still locked tight as a drum. Miss Jordan..." He hesitated.

"I didn't imagine a knock to my own head," Alexi said indignantly.

"Well, no..." Mark murmured. He looked to Rex for assistance. Rex didn't intend to give him any.

"You did fall down the stairs," Mark said.

"After I was struck," Alexi insisted quietly.

"Well, then..." He stood up, smiling down at her. "I can call out the print boys. May I use the phone?"

"Of course. Please."

Mark Eliot called his office. Rex offered to make coffee. In very little time, the fingerprint experts were out and the house was dusted. Alexi insisted on coming into the kitchen with the men. While the house was dusted, Mark excitedly told Rex about the book he was working on, and Rex gave him a few suggestions. Alexi put in a few, too, and was somewhat surprised when they both paid attention to her.

It was late when the men from the sheriff's department left. Alexi started picking up the coffee cups that littered the kitchen. Rex caught her hand.

"Come on."

"Where?"

"Hospital."

"Rex, I'm fine—" she protested.

"You're not."

"I don't—"

"You will."

She set her jaw stubbornly. "Rex, dammit—"

"Alexi, dammit."

"I'm not going anywhere. It's been hours now, and I feel just fine."

Rex leaned back and thought about it for a minute. Independent. She was accustomed to being independent. She really didn't like to be told what to do. If he forced her hand, it could stand against him.

But she really needed to go to a hospital. Just as a precautionary measure. She'd be mad at him, but...

"Rex...?"

Alexi didn't like the way he was looking at her as he came toward her. "Rex!" She screamed out her protest when he scooped her up into his arms. "Rex, damn you, I said—"

"Yeah, yeah, yeah. I heard you."

"You can't do this!"

"Apparently I can."

He stopped by the kitchen table to slip his pinky around the strap of her purse. He hurried through the house, yelling at Samson to get back when the shepherd tried to follow him. Alexi struggled against him, but he didn't give her much leverage. A moment later he deposited her in the car and locked the door. He slid into the driver's seat and revved the car into motion before she could think about hopping out.

She didn't say anything to him. She stared straight ahead, rubbing her wrist where he had gripped it.

Rex put the car into gear and glanced her way. "Alexi, your face is pale gray!"

She didn't say anything. She just kept staring ahead, watching as they left the peninsula behind and sped on to the highway.

"Gray, mind you—ashen."

She cast him a rebellious stare, her blue eyes sizzling.

"Sickly, ash gray."

She sighed and sank into the seat. "You could have at least let me get my toothbrush!"

Rex laughed and turned his attention back to the road. She would, he felt sure, forgive him for this one.

"Maybe they'll say that you're fine and that you can go right home."

She smiled at that. But when they reached the hospital, the doctor determined that she did have a minor concussion and that she should stay at least overnight

for observation. Alexi cast Rex a definitely malignant
stare, but he ignored her—and promised to run down
to the gift shop and buy her a toothbrush.

He had no intention of leaving her. From the coffee shop, Rex called Gene and very carefully chose
the words to tell him what had happened. Gene was
in good health, but Rex was wary, never forgetting
that the man was in his nineties and didn't need any
shocks in his life.

Rex told Gene that he was wondering if there wasn't
a way to get her out of the house. Gene shrewdly
warned him that if the danger was directed at Alexi,
it wouldn't help to get her out of the house.

Rex asked him harshly, "Then you think that it is
John Vinto?"

"I didn't say that," Gene protested. He paused a
moment. "I don't know what to think."

"Just for the weekend, then," Rex murmured.

"What? What, boy? Speak up there. I can't hear
you!"

"Oh. I said just for the weekend. I've got the sloop
in berth in town. Maybe we'll take her out for a sail.
Just to have a few days without anything else happening. I'll leave Samson at the house to guard it, and
Emily can come over to feed him and the kittens."

Gene was very silent. Rex barely noticed, he was so
busy taking flight with his plans in his imagination.

"I'll be there to see you off," Gene said. "We'll
have lunch."

"I haven't even mentioned it to Alexi yet," Rex
cautioned Gene.

"You'll figure something out," Gene said. "I'm a man of boundless faith."

Rex stayed at Alexi's side, watching her as she slept, and as the night passed he felt as if more and more of her stole into his soul. It seemed to him that she remained too pale, and yet there was an ethereal quality about her that was beautiful. He was afraid to touch; she was so very fine. Small and fine boned and delicate to look at—golden, like exquisite porcelain or china. But she wasn't really so delicate, he knew. Despite the battles she had waged and lost in life, she was still fighting, a golden girl, a glittering, shimmering beauty.

He was in love, he realized as he watched the swell of her chest while she breathed. He folded his hands prayer-fashion and tapped his fingers against his chin and wondered how it had happened. He could remember loving Shelley. Vaguely. It had been a different feeling. They had been growing apart, and he hadn't even known it. She'd whispered at night that she had loved him, too.

And then she had been gone.

Alexi was different. Very different. She didn't bother with the lies. She'd never whispered that she loved him, and he'd been careful to guard his own heart. All good things came to an end. He was a fool if he thought that she would stay. Hers was perhaps the face of the century. He couldn't make her stay. He couldn't make her love him.

But, he decided grimly, he could make her get on his boat for a few days. A little time for dreams and the imagination, time enough to savor all the could-have-beens.

When dawn came he stroked a length of her hair and smoothed the golden tendril over her shoulder. A smile curved her lips. He leaned over to kiss her lightly, then stood and tiptoed out of the room, telling the nurse he'd be back soon.

He drove quickly back to the Brandywine house. Samson nearly attacked him. Rex patted the dog absently and hurried upstairs to the bedroom. He found his duffel bag in the closet and hastily chose a few things for himself, then paused, wondering what Alexi would want for a few days on a boat.

Underwear, of course. He looked through her drawers, then paused again, fascinated by the beautiful collection of slips and panties and bras. Then he smiled—and chose his favorites.

Another few minutes and he had found a few short sets, a bathing suit, sneakers, shirts and jeans. Samson barked when he tried to leave the house. Rex paused, knowing that he was seeing Samson's hungry look.

"Okay, boy. Come on. I'll feed you."

He had just finished feeding Samson and the kittens when he heard the phone ringing. He reached the parlor to answer it—only to hear a breath, then have it go dead.

He swore at the empty line. When it began to ring again, Rex almost chose not to answer it. But when he picked it up that time, Emily's concerned voice came over the phone.

"Oh, Rex! I've been calling and calling. I tried all night. Is everything all right?"

"Emily! Good, good." He'd needed to talk to her to see that the animals were fed, he remembered. He told her quickly what had happened—and he admitted that he suspected Alexi's ex-husband. Emily was very upset but thought that Rex was right—getting away for a few days might be best for the both of them.

"Samson will be in the house, Emily. I don't think anyone would dare try anything with him around. Think you'd mind coming by to feed him and the kittens? If you're in the least nervous, I'm sure that Mark Eliot will come out with you."

Emily told him that she wasn't nervous at all when Samson was around and promised to come and feed the dog and the kittens and let them out for exercise and their daily "constitutionals." Rex thanked her, then hurried on out, anxious to return before Alexi could awaken. Alexi wasn't at all fond of the idea. "Leave? Rex, I don't think that's a good idea at all." A frown puckered her brow. "It's like giving up."

"It's not giving up. It's taking a breather."

"Or," Alexi murmured skeptically, "it's like a rest home for a neurotic."

Rex swore impatiently and walked over to the window, shoving his hands in his pockets. He spun around to her. "Alexi, I believe you—I believe you a thousand times over. I don't think you're a neurotic—I think you were married to a very dangerous man. I need the break if you don't."

"A break from what? We live in Eden, remember."

Rex decided to change his tactics. "I'm asking you to do it, Alexi. Just for me."

"What?"

"You're going back soon, right? Summer ends. Beach bunnies go back to their Northern retreats. Helen has to go launch a few more ships. Let's do it for us."

Alexi looked down quickly, allowing a fall of her hair to shield her face. She braced herself, then looked up again.

"Sure. Why not? A last fling, more or less."

They stood there staring at each other for a long moment. Rex wondered how they could be planning any kind of a "fling" when hostility seemed to be raking the air about them with bolts of electric tension.

A crisp-coated doctor stuck his head in to smile and tell Alexi that her release papers were all ready. She was chagrined to be forced to leave in a wheelchair, and Rex tightened his lips with a certain grim satisfaction—someone else had told her what to do that time.

Rex drove his Maserati up to the door to collect her downstairs. She exhaled with a great deal of pleasure when she was out of the wheelchair. Rex turned the car out of the drive, noting that it was going to be a beautiful—but deadly hot—day. There wasn't a sign of a cloud.

"Where are we going now?"

"To the club at the dock."

"What if I were to tell you that I get seasick?"

"I wouldn't believe you."

She hesitated, looking down at her hands. "I really don't think that this is such a good idea, Rex. I mean, I was even thinking that I should go home...and that you should go to your own house."

He had never known that words could cut so deeply. The wheel jerked in his hands, and it took everything within him to straighten out the car and keep his eyes on the road ahead.

"I kind of thought you liked me around," he said.

She remained silent.

"I can't leave you alone right now, Alexi. You could be dead next time."

"I can't keep sleeping with you because I'm afraid to be alone in my own house, either."

This time he did drive the car off the road. The gearshift made a horrible grinding sound as the engine died, and Rex wound his fingers around the steering wheel like steel.

"What?" he demanded in a breath of fury unlike anything she had ever heard.

"I—I—"

She didn't mean it. Not that way, of course. But the words were out and she didn't really know how to undo them. She was, at that moment, more afraid of Rex than of any mysterious entity in her house. His temper was afire, while the way he stared at her was ice; he looked as if he hated her.

"For one thing, Ms. Jordan, you haven't the God-given sense to be afraid!"

"You know I didn't mean it that way!" Alexi cried desperately.

He didn't look at her again. He shoved the car back in gear in such a manner that she wondered about the Maserati's life span, and then her own. He took to the road in a flash. She sat back, biting her lower lip so that she wouldn't cry out. She wanted it—she wanted a "last fling." But something bitter inside her—maybe common sense—warned her that she was becoming too involved—falling too deeply in love. She was spending too much time fantasizing about a forever-and-ever kind of love. It would be a good idea to end it all now, and maybe that was just what she was going to get. Rex wasn't mad—he was lethally furious. When she glanced his way, his face might have been carved in stone: eyes black as pitch; mouth grim.

Alexi gripped the leather seat, wondering if he wouldn't just head back for the peninsula. She shivered, remembering the feeling of being stalked yesterday. Yes! Yes, she did have the sense to be afraid. But she couldn't keep running away. She had come here to get away from New York and John and all her fears there. She couldn't run from here, too.

But she wasn't suicidal, either. She had to be intelligent about it all. A good security system could be installed. And she could get a wonderful big shepherd like Samson to go along with the kittens. But no other shepherd would be Samson....

Just as no other man would be his master.

But Rex Morrow didn't want to be tied down. He'd been burned once, and he was determined not to trust again. She should understand. She'd been hurt.

But he'd taught her that the world could be beautiful, too. He'd taught her to love and to laugh....

Couldn't she teach him the same things?

The car jerked violently. She didn't even know where they were. Her heart beat violently. Did he still intend for them to go away? She cleared her throat.

"Er, where are we?"

"The marina," he said curtly. "If you would deign to come into the dining room, someone wants to meet you."

He got out of the car, slamming the door. Ignoring her, he started toward a building with a painted sign that boasted of the yacht club's famous Florida lobster thermidor.

Alexi followed him slowly. She felt so numb. What

had she done? The best thing in her life, and she was letting it all slip through her fingers. Losing it all, because she didn't know how to hang on.

She got out of the car and followed Rex. He had waited for her at the restaurant door and was holding it open for her.

Curious, she stepped inside. The place was bright, pretty and air-conditioned but open to the sun, with wall-length plate-glass windows on all sides. The tables were made out of varnished woods and heavy ropes, and the scent of fine seafood was unmistakable. A hostess in navy shorts and a red-white-and-blue sailor top was just coming toward them when Rex waved toward the back of the restaurant.

Alexi followed his gaze, then gave a glad little cry as she saw Gene standing there, waiting for them to join him.

She hugged him fiercely, receiving his tight hug in return. He talked in fragments, and she did, too. Then she smiled brilliantly, kissed his cheek and told him she was very glad to see him.

Rex came to the table, and they were all seated. Alexi realized after a moment that Gene was studying her as surreptitiously as she was studying him. He lifted her chin with his thumb and forefinger, openly looking her over with a thorough scrutiny.

"Still pale," he commented.

"I'm fine! The doctor let me go."

"Hmmf. Well, it's good you're going out to sea for a few days. Sea air has always been the best thing in the world."

Alexi stared at him blankly, wondering just what Rex had told him. It wasn't that she wasn't old enough to indulge in an affair; it was just that it seemed very strange to be quite so open with him.

The waitress came. Alexi quickly ordered some wine and the lobster thermidor. She sipped her wine after it was poured, not daring to look at Rex at all and nervously aware that Gene was still watching her, a good deal of humor in his deep and wonderful blue eyes now.

After a few moments, Alexi realized that Gene and Rex were going on almost as if she wasn't there. They were discussing different security systems for the place, the possibility of a big dog—all the things she had been thinking about herself.

"Hey, I'm here, you know," she reminded them. They both stared at her. She wished for a moment that she could tell Rex to go jump in a lake, that she could take care of herself. But she couldn't really do that—not then. Although Gene had turned the Brandywine place over to her to reconstruct and refurbish as she saw fit, the property belonged to him, not her.

She sipped more wine, then smiled, a little spitefully, and sat back. "Well, I am here, but please, don't let me bother you. You two just go right ahead without me."

They glanced at her again, arched their brows at each other, then thanked the waitress as she delivered their lunches. Then Rex went on to tell Gene that he thought maybe Alexi needed to have some sort of peace warrant sworn out against John Vinto.

Alexi decided to ignore them then. Her lobster was delicious, and the wine was dry and good.

Toward the end of the meal, Rex excused himself to get the check. Alexi looked down at her plate, unable to think of a thing to say to Gene. She felt a blush rising to her cheeks; she knew he was watching her.

"You're not surprised that we're together," she said.

"I'm overjoyed."

"Oh?" Alexi stared straight at him, but she quickly lowered her lashes again. Gene, it seemed, had amassed all the wisdom of the ages. She had always felt that he was incredibly wise. That his gnarled and leathered face and fantastic eyes held all the wisdom of the ages. He could read her mind—and he could read her heart.

"Let me just say this. I like you both very much."

"But, Gene!" Alexi protested softly, loving him. "Liking us both doesn't make us right for each other!"

"Haven't you been?"

She didn't answer him, and he went on. "I've lived a long time, Alexi. A long, long time. And I've known thousands of people. Thousands. And out of that, only a handful could I really call friends, could I really admire. I learned to know people from the soul, Alexi. Appearances mean little; even words can mean little. What's in a man's heart and what's in his soul, those are the important things. Rex—he just doesn't like crowds. But then, well, I'm not so fond of fuss and confusion myself."

"He has an awful temper," Alexi supplied. "And he has a way of being horrendously overbearing."

"Does he now?"

"Yes."

"Well, you have a way with you yourself, Alexi. You can't listen to good sense if you've got your mind set. Oh, here comes Rex now."

Alexi glanced up. Rex, so dark and arresting that even in his jeans and polo shirt he was drawing fascinated glances, was coming back toward them, a thoughtful expression knit into his features. He scowled, though, as he saw Alexi's eyes on him. She felt a little chill run down her spine. He was still ready to kill. She might have added to Gene that he didn't seem to be a bit forgiving. But then, of course, maybe she deserved his anger for what she had said. Even for a male ego that wasn't particularly fragile, that might have been a low blow.

I just want you to love me! she thought, watching him. Love me forever, believe in me, trust in me...

A pretty brunette in very short captain's shorts suddenly jumped up from a table, barring Rex's way. She had one of his books in her hands—a hardcover text. Rex paused, gave her a devastating smile and signed the book.

Alexi looked down at her plate again. She wasn't the jealous type. Things like that would never bother her—normally. But she couldn't help wondering what Rex was thinking as he looked at the young woman. Was she someone that he would want to call once Alexi had returned to New York?

"Before I forget," Gene was saying, "I thought you might enjoy this."

"Pardon? I'm sorry."

Alexi returned her attention to Gene. He was handing her a small, very old and fragile-looking book that had been carefully and tenderly wrapped in a plastic sheath.

"What is it?"

"Eugenia Brandywine's diary. She left it to me—I was always such a pesky kid. Interested in war and life. I thought you might enjoy it. She made entries after the war, but an awful lot is about Pierre, meeting him, running away with him. Very…romantic."

"Oh, Gene!"

Alexi stared down at the little book. She would enjoy it; she would treasure it, just as she treasured the old house and the very special history Gene had always given her. She looked up at him again. "I can't take this. It's a family treasure—"

"Alexi, you are my family." He patted her hand. "Eugenia's family. Keep the book. Take good care of it."

"I will!" Alexi promised. She leaned over to kiss his cheek. "Thank you so much."

He smiled at her, covering the softness of her hand again with the weathered calluses of his own. "No, Alexi, thank *you*." He stood then, abruptly, an amazingly handsome man of immense dignity. "I've got to go."

"Go?" Alexi echoed hollowly.

"Good heavens, yes. I have a chess match with Charles Holloway in less than half an hour, and I'll be damned if I'll let that youngster catch me napping."

"Youngster?"

"A mere eighty-eight," Gene told her. "Kiss me again, Alexi. It's an old man's last great pleasure."

She kissed his cheek. By then, Rex had finished with his fan and reached the table. He shook hands with Gene.

"Have a good sail, now," Gene said.

A streak of stubbornness flashed through Alexi. If Rex had been over at the other table, planning his future dates, then he should already be asking one of them out on the boat.

"I don't think I'm going, Gene." They both stared at her. She certainly had their attention. She smiled serenely. "Maybe I'll scout some nearby kennels for a good German shepherd."

"Alexi, you know that you are making me insane," Rex said softly.

"Really? Then I'm quite sorry."

"Alexi, you're going on the boat."

"Rex, I am not."

He looked as if he wanted to explode. At the moment, it was nice. He couldn't possibly make a move against her. They were in a public restaurant, and Gene was standing right beside him.

Rex looked at Gene. "What the hell am I supposed to do?"

Gene shook his head. "Women. They're very independent these days."

"Yes, but is a man supposed to let one get herself killed?"

"That's up to the man, I suppose," Gene mused.

Alexi, who had been watching the interplay between them, suddenly gasped. Rex caught her arm and dragged her out of the chair and threw her over his shoulder.

"You can't do this!" Alexi wailed. "We're in a public restaurant! Gene...?"

The world was tilting on her. Rex was walking quickly past tables and waitresses and startled customers.

"Have a good time, Alexi!" Gene called.

"Rex, damn you, you can't—"

"Alexi, most obviously," he promised her, "I can."

And, most obviously, he could. They were already

out in the bright sunlight again, and Rex was hurrying down the dock toward a beautiful red-white-and-black sloop with the name *Tatiana* scripted in bold black letters across her bow.

Chapter 11

Alexi was dizzy. He was walking so quickly that her chin banged against his back and the ground waved beneath her feet. She spat out his name, then swore soundly. But he didn't seem to hear a thing—he didn't even seem to notice that she was ineffectually struggling to rise against his sure motion. "Rex—"

He swung sharply—and made a little leap that seemed to Alexi like a split-second death plunge on a roller coaster.

"Rex!"

They were on the boat. He still didn't stop. Alexi had a blurred vision of a chart desk and a radio and a neat little galley with pine cabinets. They quickly passed a dining booth and a plaid-covered bunk and a little door marked Head. Then Rex barged through a slatted door and dumped her down on something soft.

For such a tiny cabin, it was a big bed, built right into the shape of the boat and full of little brown throw pillows to go with the very masculine brown-and-beige quilt that covered the bed.

"This is absurd," she told him, curling her feet beneath her and trying to rise to a dignified position. She got high enough to crack her head on the storage shelves that stretched over the bed.

"Small space," he warned her. "And you're absurd. Yes, no, yes, no—dammit, use some common sense and don't act like a school kid."

"Me?"

"You!"

"You have the nerve to say something like that to me when you're acting like a Neanderthal?"

"It's better than behaving like a jealous child."

"What?"

"This one all started because I gave out a lousy autograph."

"Oh, you know, Morrow, you really do overestimate your charms. I just don't want to be here."

He touched her face with his palm. "Don't worry, sweetie. There's nothing to be afraid of out here. You won't need to sleep with me. You can have the cabin all to yourself."

"I—"

Her rejoinder froze on her lips because—despite his bitter denunciation—he was slipping his shirt over his head. Still staring at her in a cold fury, he kicked off his shoes, then started to slide out of his jeans.

"What—what are you doing?" Alexi gasped out, pained.

"Oh, don't get excited," he tossed back irritably. Naked except for his briefs, he turned from her, bronzed and supple and so pleasantly muscled. He opened a drawer, pulled out a pair of worn denim cutoffs and climbed into them, smiling at her sudden speechlessness. "Eat your heart out, Ms. Jordan," he told her. And then he was gone, slamming the slatted door in his wake.

Alexi, numb, stared after him for several seconds. A moment later, she heard the rev of a motor and felt movement.

The cabin was lined with little windows. Alexi bolted to the left to look out and saw that the dock was fast slipping away from them.

"Why, that… SOB!" she muttered. They were passing the channel markers to the right and left and heading for the open sea. She was off with him for the duration—with or without her agreement.

She threw a pillow across the room in a sudden spate of raw fury. He couldn't do this. He really couldn't—she had said no. But he was doing it anyway. He deserved to be boiled in oil. Someone needed to tell him quickly that this was the modern world. That he couldn't do things like this.

It wouldn't matter, she decided grudgingly. Rex would do what he wanted to do anyway.

After a moment, Alexi realized that the hum of the motor had stopped. She could hear footsteps above her.

And she could hear Rex swearing.

She smiled after a moment, realizing that he had turned off the motor to catch the wind with the sails. And he was having a few problems. She kicked off her shoes and lay back on the bunk, smiling. He'd planned on her giving him a hand with the sails, she realized. And now, of course, he was presuming that she wouldn't move a muscle on his behalf.

"Right on, Mr. Morrow," she murmured.

But then her smile faded, because she was remembering how cute he had looked, stripping out of his jeans to don his cutoffs—then indignantly denying her suppositions about him. Maybe "cute" wasn't the right word. Not for Rex. He was too deadly dark, too striking, too mature, too dynamic.

No…at that moment, "cute" had been exactly the right word.

Maybe she *had* been acting like a schoolgirl, and, at the end, maybe she had balked and refused the trip because of pure and simple jealousy. No—there was definitely nothing pure and simple about it. Painful and complex. She didn't know where she stood with him. And she was afraid to make any attempt to find out.

Something dropped with a bang. She could clearly hear Rex muttering out a few choice swear words.

Alexi sat up and smiled slowly and wistfully. They were far from shore; they were together, and alone with the elements. Maybe she wouldn't exactly offer a white flag, but…

Alexi hopped off the bed and hurried through the door. The boat pitched to the right, and she had to grab the wall to keep from falling. "I hope I don't get seasick," she muttered to herself. She steadied herself and hurried down the hallway, past the head, past the neat-as-a-pin little dining room and living room and on through the galley to the short flight of ladder steps that led to the topside deck.

"Watch it!" Rex snapped, annoyed, as her head appeared.

Standing on the top step of the little ladder, she ducked as the boom of the mainsail went sweeping past her. "Grab the damn thing. Help out here!" Rex called to her.

He was at the tiller, leaning left, trying to control the wayward sail at the same time.

"What do you want me to do?"

"Trim the sail."

"What?"

"The sail!"

"I don't know what you're talking about."

He paused. The wind ripped around them, pulling his hair from his forehead, then casting it back down again. "Come on, Alexi—"

"I don't know what you're talking about. I've never been out on a sailboat in my life."

"You were born a rich kid!"

"And I play tennis and golf, and I've even been on a polo field or two, but I've never been on a sailboat!"

Rex stared at her for a long moment. "Damn!" he murmured. Then he ordered curtly, "Come over here."

She shook her head. "I don't know how to steer, either."

"Just keep both your hands on her and don't move!" he bellowed. "Alexi—"

There was something so dangerous about the way he growled her name that she decided to comply. She slid next to him on the hollowed-out seat and set her hands on the long tiller. "Don't move it!" he warned her.

He jumped up, leaving her to watch as he nimbly maneuvered around the boat. Barefoot, in cutoffs, he seemed every inch the bronzed seaman. He quickly brought the sail under control. Red-white-and-black canvas filled with wind. Alexi had to admit that it was beautiful. She lifted a hand to shield her eyes from the sun and stared out at the horizon. It seemed endless. If she looked to her right, though, she could see the coast, not so very far away.

Rex jumped down beside her. He slipped his brown hands over hers. "Thank you," he said curtly.

"Aye, aye, sir!" she said mockingly. She stood, glad she'd left her sandals below so that she could present a facsimile of coordination when she climbed forward, holding on to the mainmast, to look out at the day. With her fingers tightly clenched around the mast, she closed her eyes and inhaled and decided that the air was wonderful. The wind, alive and brisk, felt so good against her face. If only she weren't at such odds with the captain at the moment.

She decided that for the time being, no action was her best action. She went back below, and for almost an hour she immersed herself in Eugenia's diary. She was amazed to discover that Eugenia's plight could actually make her forget her own.

But she hadn't really forgotten. She set the book down pensively. She would finish it later, maybe that night. Rex hadn't tried to talk to her. Alexi realized ruefully that she was more concerned with her own life than Eugenia's.

Alexi went back topside. She pretended to ignore Rex and sat on the fiberglass decking and leaned her head against the mast. The sun beat down upon her while the breeze, salty and fresh, swept around her. Talk to me, Rex, she thought. She closed her eyes and enjoyed the warmth.

She must have dozed there, for when she opened her eyes again, the sails were down and the boat was still except for a slight rocking motion. Twisting around, she could see that the anchor had been thrown and that they were just about twenty or thirty feet off a little tree-shrouded island.

Rex was sitting at the bow, a can of beer in his hand, wearing mirrored sunglasses, his skin and hair wet from an apparent dive into the sea.

Alexi stood and stretched and hopped down to the scooped-out tiller area and then down to the ladder. She was sure he heard her, but he didn't turn. She went on into the galley and opened the pint-sized refrigerator to find a can of beer. She smiled, popped the top and crawled up the ladder again.

Perching just a few feet behind Rex, she watched his back. He turned around, arching a brow to her, but she couldn't begin to read his thoughts in the reflections of herself mirrored in his sunglasses.

She smiled sweetly and raised her beer can to him. "Cheers."

"Cheers." Solemnly he lifted his own.

He looked out to sea again, then stood and took a long swallow of the beer. Alexi set her can down and rose, too, slowly coming up behind him. She pressed her lips against the flesh at his nape, then followed along his spine…slowly. She slipped her arms around his waist and grazed her teeth against his shoulders. He tasted of salt and sun and everything wonderfully male.

"I thought you were angry," he said gruffly.

"I am. Furious." She got up on tiptoe to catch his earlobe between her teeth.

"Alexi—"

"You had no right to drag me out here. None at all."

"I had every right! You don't use your common sense. You're a little fool. You need protection now, and I'm it."

"I am not a fool!" She nipped his shoulder lightly, then laved the spot with her tongue.

"Alexi—"

"Will you please shut up?"

"Alexi—" He tried to turn and take her into his arms. Alexi pushed away from him, smiling.

She reached for the hem of her shirt and pulled it over her head, then neatly shimmied out of her shorts. "Want to go skinny-dipping?" she asked him, casually slipping from her bra and panties. She offered him one sweet smile, then posed for a fraction of a second and dived into the sea.

She swam with long, clean strokes toward the island, then paused, panting slightly and treading water as she looked back toward the *Tatiana*. Rex was nowhere in sight.

She gasped, nearly slipping beneath the surface, when she felt a tug upon her foot. Then he was with her, sliding up from beneath the surface, his body—all of it—rubbing against hers. Next to the chill of the sea, he was vibrant warmth, his arms coming around her, his legs twining with hers, his desire hot and potent and arousingly full against her thighs. She saw his eyes then for a moment, dark and glittering with the reflections of the sun. Then she saw them no more. His mouth came to hers, sealing them together in a deep, erotic kiss that sent them sinking far below, into the depths. So wonderfully hot...his tongue raked her mouth with that fire while his fingers moved over her in the exotic world of the sea. She would die...in seconds she would smother. But his touch in the watery world was already a taste of heaven.

Rex gave a powerful kick, sending them both shooting back toward the surface, still entwined. As they broke the surface, Alexi cast her head back, gasping for breath and laughing. She had barely inhaled when his lips were there again, against hers. He alternately rimmed her lips with his tongue, then whispered things to her. She and Rex did not sink, for he held her tight against him, treading water. She swallowed, weak and dizzied, as he moved his hands in concord with the warning of his whispers, teasing her breasts, working along her lower abdomen, stroking her thighs, taunting her implicitly.

"Oh..." she whispered.

"Alexi."

She leaned her head against him, closing her eyes, unable to reason against the sensations. She would sink again. Sink forever in the swirling realm of bliss where she floundered now.

"We've got to get back to the boat."

"Yes."

"Alexi."

"Yes."

"*Now*," he laughed, "or I won't have the strength left to do us justice."

"Oh!" Lost in the sensations of his loving, she realized that he had been doing all this while keeping them both afloat. "Oh!" she repeated, slightly embarrassed. She kicked away from him, hard, and began to swim. He caught her at the rope ladder by the motor at the back of the *Tatiana*. He raised her to the deck, then curled his leg around the ladder himself for balance. Alexi tried to rise. He stopped her, caught her foot and stroked the arch while he kissed her ankle.

"Rex!"

"What?" Tenderly he moved his mouth up along her calf.

"The sun is out and shining. We're in broad daylight. There's nothing to shield us—"

"And there isn't another boat around for miles," he assured her. Her kneecap received his ministrations next.

She thought that she had died. Where he did not touch her, the breeze moved erotically over her wet body. And there, in pagan splendor beneath the captivating rays of the sun, he made very thorough love to her. He treated the length of each leg with the same exotic care as he did the juncture between them, with incredible, exotic savoir faire—so sweetly that she was nearly numbed, consumed again by tiny explosions of delight. She could scarcely move...but then agility came to her and she reached for him, eager— desperate—to love him as he had loved her.

He came up beside her; they stood, damp and sleek, their fingers entwined. And she pulled him close to her and kissed him, consuming his lips again and again, savoring just that touch to the fullest, like a fine delicacy. She brushed her breasts against his chest as she tiptoed up to him, then slid against him, tasting the salt on his shoulder, all that lingered on his chest, falling to her knees and returning each subtle nuance. She moved on to his feet, his ankles...then up the length of his legs to the pulse of him. He whispered frantically—

urges, cries. She obeyed them all and gloried sweetly in her power, in the absolute intimacy. She had never loved like this; she knew that she never would again.

They sank together upon the deck at last in an inferno of mutual desires and hungers, with a need deeper than any words they could ever whisper. To Alexi the earth seemed to tremble, to shake, to explode in a blinding brilliance. The sun was the brilliance, she knew, riding high above her, very real in the sky. But it seemed to live inside her, too, a life-giving warmth, given to her...by him.

Rex turned to her at last, stroking her breast, then her cheek, a curious twist to his lips.

"Am I supposed to apologize now for dragging you out here against your will?"

"An apology would be nice."

"All right!" he said, pressing her down on the deck. "I'm sorry I dragged you. Now you can apologize."

"I beg your pardon? *I* was the abused party. But not only did I take incarceration in stride, I went way beyond the call of duty."

"That you did," Rex admitted with a broad smile. Then his smile faded and he sat up, wrapping his arms around his legs.

"Rex—"

"Why did you say that to me, Alexi!"

"What?" she asked, at a loss.

"That bit about sleeping with me because you were afraid." He twisted around to stare at her, harsh and accusing.

"You knew it wasn't true!" she cried. Please, please, she thought. Don't ruin this. This is ideal. This is the type of day that one remembers for a lifetime.

He shook his head. "No, I didn't," he said lightly. "Tell me what is and isn't true, Alexi."

"I don't know what you're talking about."

He touched her lower lip with the tip of his thumb, studying her face. "Tell me what you've felt—what you've wanted."

"I have told you," she gasped out, herself turning. She didn't want him to see her eyes. To read any of the secrets within them. Love made one so vulnerable. She wished she were dressed.

She shivered. "Rex, do you have robes aboard this boat? It's getting so chilly—"

He pulled her into the curve of his arm. "I'll keep you warm," he promised her.

"I told you," she murmured, her eyes downcast, "that you were very special."

"The Easter Bunny is special," he told her.

"I have been with you every time because I wanted desperately to be with you. Is that what you want?"

"No." He lifted her chin to force her eyes to his, holding her close against his chest. "I want more, Alexi."

Her heart seemed to thunder and stop, then race again and soar. Her lips were dry, and she moistened them with her tongue. "I hear that you're the one with a girl in every port."

"A gross exaggeration. And reasonable." He smiled ruefully. Smiled at her, deep into her soul, and she instinctively stroked his face, musing again about how she loved it. Dark and macabre... To think that she had once thought he must be that way, when he smiled at her now so openly, so ruefully, so tenderly.

"I've been scared. I've been running. And I'm still very, very scared."

"Of me?" she whispered.

He nodded. "Alexi?"

"Yes?"

"Do you have to go back? Do you have to do that commercial or whatever it is?"

"Er, no."

He hesitated. He gave her a crooked smile, dark lashes covering his eyes. He released her and stood, hands on hips, beautifully naked, staring out to the sea.

"That wasn't the right question," he said at last. "Do you want to go back?"

She had thought that she was safe; his back was to her. But he spun around swiftly, and she felt that she was seared through by the probing intensity of his eyes, by the demand within them. She felt herself blush—all of her, from head to toe—and she felt painfully, terrifyingly bare and vulnerable.

"I don't know."

It wasn't the right answer, she knew. Or she had hesitated too long. She saw the disappointment that darkened his eyes before he turned away. "Of course you want to go back," he muttered.

"Rex!" She jumped to her feet, coming to his back as she had earlier, pressing against him and groaning softly. "Rex! I'm frightened, too."

He remained tense. "You should be frightened. I keep telling you that."

She shook her head vehemently. "I don't mean that. I'm not talking about whatever is going on at the house."

"Then exactly what are you talking about?"

"You. Me." Alexi groped for an answer. "Rex, I'm afraid of you."

"Afraid of me!" The narrowing of his eyes, the glint within him, warned her that he had misunderstood.

"No, no—not that you would ever hurt me. Not that way. Let's face it. We've both been burned. In different ways, perhaps. I ran; you put up high walls around you and learned to play rough."

"I don't know—"

"Yes, you do," Alexi said softly, lowering her eyes. "I overheard you talking to Emily that morning, remember? You like the chase, Rex."

He made an impatient sound. "Alexi, dammit. So this whole thing *was* over the girl back in the restaurant—"

She shook her head furiously. "No! All right, I did feel a twinge of jealousy—"

"That was childish! I had to watch the pizza delivery boy practically trip over his tongue when he was near you!"

The way he said it, she had to laugh, her eyes meeting his. But then her laughter faded, as did the wry smile that had touched his lips. "Rex! Don't you see? It isn't like me to be like that. I enjoy you, I enjoy your success. I just…" Her voice trailed off.

He came closer and lifted her chin. "You just what?" His eyes probed hers deeply, searching. He was so close again. She wanted to lay her head against his chest and forget everything. He didn't intend to let her. "Alexi…?"

She shook her head. "I don't know. Maybe I want

to believe in magic and forever and I'm just a little too world-weary to really take the chance."

His touch, his voice, grew tense. "You just said that you knew I would never hurt you."

"But you don't trust *me*, either!"

He released her, his eyes narrowing. "What are you talking about?"

"You're not honest with me. At least, if—if you care you're not."

"Meaning?"

"You said that I should go. That I should go back to New York. You made me feel as if what we had was nothing more than a brief affair between consenting adults. Either you want me to go—or you don't want me to go."

Rex laced his fingers around his knees and stared out at the water. Then he swung around to her, heatedly intense again. "All right. I don't want you to go. Is that going to change anything? I can't really do that, Alexi. If I ask you not to go—and you don't do it because of me—you'll resent me for it in the long run."

"But I don't know if I even want to go back!"

Rex inhaled and exhaled slowly. He touched her cheek softly. "You just said it, Alexi. You don't know. I can't hold you back—"

"You could come with me."

"If something can't be solved about all these things that keep happening," Rex said harshly, "you can bet I'll come along."

"What?"

"I said—"

Alexi didn't let him finish. She laughed and caught his cheeks between her hands and kissed him. "You'd do it? You'd really do it? You'd leave all your privacy behind and come with me?"

He caught her hands and held them tight between his. "I'd do it because I'm afraid for you," he told her sternly. "I haven't changed my mind. I like the peninsula. I like the peace, and I like the privacy."

She still smiled. "But you'd leave it for a while."

"Alexi—"

"You started this! You gave out the ultimatums."

He watched her, then slowly shook his head, drawing her to him, ruffling her hair, speaking very softly. "Ultimatums don't work, Alexi. That's what I'm saying. I can't force you to live my way; I couldn't promise to stay in New York. We're on dangerous ground, you know."

Alexi felt his fingers against her hair. She closed her eyes and inhaled the scent of him and felt the warmth of his body next to hers. "I thought you wanted me to leave. You'd have your whole peninsula back."

His arms tightened around her. "I've decided that I like you there."

"Sometimes I think you've decided that I'm insane."

"Why do you say that?"

"I know you think I imagined footsteps the night I ran into you on the sand, and I know you think I imagined noises in the house when we came in from the beach. I wonder if you even believe I was hit on the head yesterday—the police, I know, think I fell down the stairs and invented the intruder."

"You're wrong. I might have doubted you once, but I believe you now."

"Because you think that John is out to—to do something."

"Yes."

"I might not be a very good deal, you know," Alexi warned him. "I could very well be neurotic myself, and I seem to come with a half-crazy ex-husband."

"I'm not worried."

"Oh?"

"No. I'm a big boy. I can handle it."

"But do you *want* to handle it?"

"Yes."

"Rex?"

"Alexi?"

"I *think* I'm falling in love with you."

His arms tightened around her so much that for a moment she couldn't breathe. Then she discovered that she was falling in his arms to lie against the deck and he was over her, his eyes afire, a smile on his lips.

"Let's hear that again." His hold was fierce; his words were full of a harsh command. She twisted against the force of his arms.

"Rex, damn you—"

"Alexi, please!"

"I said…" She paused, watching the blaze in his eyes, watching that small smile that curved his lips. "You're just terrible!" she said accusingly. "Every time you want something, you just decide that if you sit on me—"

"Not every time," he protested. But he was straddled over her and she inhaled sharply, feeling all her senses begin to swim again beneath the dazzling command of his eyes and the easy feeling of him against her—his hands upon her, his chest, muscles rippling in the golden heat of the sun, his thighs tight around her own. "Alexi!" He lowered himself against her until his lips hovered just above hers.

"I'm falling in love with you, too, you know. And you're right. It's very, very frightening," he said.

"We're both afraid of the future," she whispered in return.

"Yes," he told her, kissing her lips.

"What do we do about it?" She opened her eyes to him, very wide, very blue, trusting and innocent. She curled her arms around his neck and pressed her body against his.

"Maybe we could take a chance," he murmured, moving slightly to the side to stroke the length of her. The sun was gloriously hot upon their bodies.

"Maybe," she murmured.

"Let the feelings grow."

"For now, at least."

He tensed, staring down at her. "Sure. For now," he murmured bitterly. He rose over her again, lifting his arms to the sky. "For now. We've got the sun and the sea and a warm Atlantic breeze. What else could we possibly want?"

"We could pretend," Alexi told him. She placed her fingers on his shoulders, then let them run over the rippling muscles of his chest. She drew them lower, so that he sucked in his breath as he watched their progress. "We could pretend that this is never going to end. That there is no future, no worry over it. We could spend these few days forgetting to argue or wonder what can and can't be. We could just talk about the water and the day and the night and the sun and the moon. And laugh and relax and—"

He caught her cheeks between his palms and tenderly massaged them with the callused tips of his thumbs. He cut off her speech with a slow, deep kiss, cradling her breasts, stroking the nipples to high peaks with his fingertips.

"Make love?" he suggested.

"It's a wonderful way to explore one's feelings," she offered solemnly.

He stretched out carefully atop her, distributing his weight along her legs, moving against her hard and erotically.

"A wonderful way to explore," he repeated. He caught her lower lip between his teeth, then kissed her deeply, exploring her mouth with a sweep of his tongue and the intimate recesses of her body with his fingers.

She gasped his name, amazed at the molten fire spreading throughout her, tantalized...

"Sweetheart," he murmured, staring into her eyes, "I do *think* that I love you." He thrust himself deep inside her, shuddering at the feeling of the velvet encasement of her love. She wrapped her limbs around him, and he whispered all the things about her that he loved.

The sun started to fall, but neither of them felt the chill as the warmth left the sky. Beautiful pinks and mauves stretched out over the horizon as twilight made a gentle descent.

Alexi saw stars streaking the heavens in a splendid outburst. She whispered to Rex that she had seen them bursting out all around her.

He laughed and told her that it was night. They rose lazily at last and made spaghetti and salad for dinner in the galley, then sat out beneath the stars.

They talked about the sky and the sea, and he tried
to tell her exactly where they were, pointing out the
islands and the coast, which were alive at night with
a glow of light.

They didn't challenge each other anymore. They
had made an agreement. They were going to take a
chance.

But Rex couldn't stop worrying. Eventually, they
were going to have to go back. And nothing could ever
be right between them—

Until he found out what was really going on at the
Brandywine house.

Chapter 12

By the time they came back in, three days later, Alexi had grown fairly adept with the *Tatiana*. The sails were furled when they approached the dock, though; the motor was softly humming to bring them in at a slow, safe speed.

Alexi—ready to jump onto the dock and tie the *Tatiana* up in its berth—started, openmouthed, when she saw that Gene was waiting for them farther down the dock.

"Alexi!" Rex yelled.

"What?"

"Now! Hop off and secure her."

She obeyed him mechanically. She slipped the little nooses over the brackets just as he had shown her. When he leaped off himself to check her work and tighten the ropes, Alexi pointed down the dock. "Gene's here. Did you plan this?"

His quick look assured her that he had not. "Run and see if there's a problem while I rinse her down," Rex said. Then he abruptly changed his mind. "No. Wait. Start making sure that the boat's all in order, and I'll go tell Gene we'll be with him as soon as we rinse her off."

Hurrying off, he didn't give Alexi much of a chance to protest. She muttered something under her breath, then paused, smiling. He was darker than ever now. Striding down the dock, barefoot and in cutoffs, he was agile and smooth and dark and sleek and muscled, and, being in love with him, Alexi had to take a moment to admire him and determine that he was a perfectly beautiful male. Then she muttered beneath her breath again and hopped back onto the *Tatiana* to crawl below. She thought she'd start in the galley, making sure that the pots and pans and dishes were secured.

Approaching Gene, Rex looked back to assure himself that Alexi wasn't trailing right behind him. She was gone from the deck; below, he hoped.

"Gene!" Rex caught the old man's hand, instantly worried about the way he was standing there in the heat. "How long have you been out here? What's wrong?"

"Not that long out here in the heat," Gene said. "I've been here all morning, though. Long enough for breakfast, Bloody Marys and lunch. I knew you planned on coming back in today, and I didn't want to miss you."

"What's up?"

"John Vinto is what," Gene said worriedly. He gazed at Rex keenly. "I'm glad you came up to me alone, Rex. Vinto has called her mother, her cousin, and me—three times. He insists he has to see Alexi. He's determined to make an appointment to talk to her." He looked down the dock and lowered his voice, even though Alexi was still nowhere in sight. "I think he's going to show up at the Brandywine house. He knows she's there."

"I think he's already shown up at the Brandywine house a few times," Rex muttered.

"Maybe. Maybe not. Amy—that's Alexi's mother—is certain she saw him nosing around Alexi's apartment in New York just last week."

"One can come and go easily these days," Rex insisted. "Jet transportation. And between here and New York there are flights just about every hour."

"I don't know," Gene said. "I just don't know. And since I don't know quite what happened between them, I didn't know how worried I should be."

"I'll be there with her," Rex said grimly. "And Samson will be there, too." He didn't want to say any more to Gene. He wasn't sure whether John Vinto was a dangerous man or had just been dangerous to Alexi because she hadn't been as physically strong as he.

He thought of how she had screamed that night in the car in front of the house and what a trauma it had been for her to tell him what had happened. John Vinto had hurt her in many ways. She had stood up to him after that—but then she had run away. Rex wasn't sure Alexi should see him again.

"I'm going to take her to my house," Rex said. "I'll leave her there with Samson, and I'll meet John Vinto, see just what it is he wants from her."

"Good," Gene said, indicating with a nod something slightly past Rex's shoulder. "She's on her way over to us."

"Alexi!" Gene stepped past Rex and threw his arms out for a big hug. Alexi returned the hug and kissed his cheek. She was in white shorts and a red-white-and-blue halter top, with her hair pulled up into a high ponytail. She had on very little makeup, and her cheeks were tinged from the sun. Rex thought that she seemed exceptionally appealing, fresh and young and innocent and stunning all at once.

And delicate, slim—and vulnerable.

He tensed, thinking again that he did love her, thinking of the things he'd said to her and the things that she'd whispered to him. He was falling in love—hard. Like a rock. And he could even begin to believe in a future for them.

He couldn't let her face Vinto again. Not without him there. Because if Vinto so much as touched her…

"Gene, what are you doing here?" Alexi asked him, smiling, and quickly added, "Not that I'm not glad to see you, but it's so awfully hot out here!"

"I, uh—lunch! I knew you were coming in, and I thought I'd meet the two of you for lunch again."

Alexi cocked her head, watching him suspiciously. "What's up?"

"Nothing." Rex, safe behind Alexi's back, arched a brow as Gene flatly lied to her. "Well," Gene hedged, "I was just hoping that you weren't mad at me, after the way you left and all. I mean, Rex there was acting just like a caveman and I didn't do anything to help you."

"You both have atrocious manners, and neither of you seems to be aware that women did earn the vote,"

Alexi told him sternly. She was smiling, though, and Rex breathed a little sigh of relief. She had fallen for it. Rex knew Gene. He wasn't a bit sorry for letting Rex stride out with her over his shoulder. Gene had decided that the two of them were good for each other. When he made a decision, that was it. Good or bad, he never regretted it. "Can't go back," he always told Rex. "That leaves you with forward, boy. No other way to go."

"Why don't you two go ahead and have lunch?" Rex suggested. Alexi swung around, ready to insist that they all have lunch together. Rex caught her shoulders, dazzled by her smile, and shook his head regretfully. "Seriously. You're both dressed, and I'm a mess and I want to hose down the *Tatiana*."

"But, Rex—"

"Please, Alexi." He lowered his lips to whisper in her ear. "It's too hot for Gene to stand around out here. Go on in with him! I'll join you a little later."

"Oh!" she murmured quickly. She turned around and slipped her arm through Gene's. "Let's have lunch, then. How are their Bloody Marys?"

"Wonderful. Tall and cool and wonderful."

"Oh, Gene!" Alexi told him, full of bright-eyed enthusiasm. "I've been reading Eugenia's diary. Oh, it's so sad, the way she would wait for Pierre, wait and wait and watch the beach! It's been wonderful, Gene. I feel like I know her—and Pierre through her. She loved him so much!"

Rex waited until they had disappeared into the yacht club restaurant; then he hurried back down to the boat and put a quick call through to Mark Eliot. Mark came on the line and started a long dissertation about the latest mystery he had read. Rex tried to listen politely, but he had to cut Mark off.

"Mark, great, we'll get together soon and talk. Right now I need some help."

Mark told him he'd be happy to do anything he could. Rex explained that he wanted to know anything that Mark could find out about John Vinto. Was he in town? Had he been in town? Anything Mark could get.

Mark whistled. "That's a tall order, but I'll see what I can do. Where are you now?"

Mark told him he was at the docks and that he'd be around there for at least a half an hour. "Then I'll be in the club, then back out at my house." Rex thought grimly that it made good sense to keep Alexi away from the Brandywine house until he'd had a chance to see Vinto. He thanked Mark for his help then and hung up.

He hurried for the hose to start rinsing down the *Tatiana*. He'd barely started, though, when he heard the phone ringing. He dropped the hose, ran toward it and answered it.

"Rex?" Mark said.

"That was quick."

"I didn't have to go that far. I checked the airlines. Your friend Vinto is around here somewhere. He flew into Jacksonville yesterday morning."

"I see," Rex murmured. "Thanks, Mark."

"I'm still checking on the rest of his activities."

"Thanks. I really appreciate it."

"I'll call you tonight, at your house."

"Great."

Rex hung up. Vinto was very near—he could feel it. And he didn't want the guy anywhere near Alexi.

He was growing more certain that Vinto had been in the Brandywine house. Rex didn't know what the man's motives were, but he was sure Vinto had stalked her—had even struck her down.

And none of it was going to happen again.

He hastily finished rinsing down the boat. Then he went down into the cabin, changed into street clothes and joined Gene and Alexi in the restaurant.

He gave Alexi a kiss on the cheek and slid into the chair beside her, smiled broadly and asked them what they'd eaten.

Rex studied the menu quickly, noting that Alexi was watching him, then smiled at her and ordered.

He was acting very strange even for Rex, Alexi decided, and she couldn't quite put her finger on the problem. He was being very sweet and charming—he just seemed tense.

"So," Gene said to her, "it's all starting to look really good, huh, young lady?"

Alexi nodded eagerly. "I do love that house, Gene. And the window seat came out perfectly. Why don't you come out with us now and see it?" Alexi suggested.

"What?" Gene murmured uneasily.

"He can't!" Rex told Alexi quickly.

"Oh?" Alexi leaned back in her chair, crossing her arms over her chest. "Why can't he?"

"Chess championships," Rex supplied. Alexi gazed at him skeptically. He'd already drunk half of his Bloody Mary, and he was merely picking at his food. She looked over at Gene. "Do you really have chess championships today?"

"Oh, yes, yes."

"You're a liar. You're lying because Rex wants you to lie. What I want to know is why."

Rex made a sound of impatience. "He doesn't want to come out now, Alexi, all right?"

"No, it isn't all right—"

"Dammit!" He threw his napkin down on the table. "Do we have to make a major production out of everything?"

Alexi went dead still, staring at him in sudden fury. Gene cleared his throat, then looked at his watch. "Wow. I'm going to miss those chess championships if I don't go back. Now."

Alexi stood up. "We'll drive you—"

"No, no. I have a driver waiting," Gene assured her. He kissed her cheek, waved to them both and left. Alexi stared at Rex. He wasn't looking at her; he was glaring down at his plate. Ignoring her, he raised his hand to ask for the bill. They maintained a tense silence while he signed it. Walking out of the restaurant, Alexi jumped when he slipped a hand around her waist. She drew back from his touch and hurried ahead.

In the car, he bounced angrily into the seat beside her. As they drove along, neither of them spoke for at least ten minutes. Then Alexi burst out with a demand to know what was wrong with him.

"Nothing," he insisted, but he didn't look her way, and he didn't have another thing to say as they headed along the peninsula. She didn't know what to think or what to feel; she was simply baffled and hurt. Hadn't he said that he was falling in love, too? Hadn't they admitted the same fears and then agreed to let things blossom and grow as they naturally would?

Maybe she had closed the doors against him; maybe he had never really opened them as far as she had thought. For all that the days had been between them, they were as distant now as the sun and moon, and she couldn't begin to understand what had caused his fit of temper.

"Drop me at my house," she told him, and added softly, "then go home yourself. I think we need some time apart."

"You must be crazy!" he thundered out to her.

"No! I'm not crazy!" she retorted after several seconds of incredulous silence. "You're yelling at me, and I don't feel like being yelled at! Let me off—and go home!"

He cast her a murderous stare. The type that reminded her that she had once thought he might have a dark and wicked soul. "You were conked on the head not too long ago—being in that house by yourself. Have you forgotten that?"

She looked down at her hands, which were folded in her lap. "I—no. And I do have the good sense to be afraid of—to be afraid. Maybe it is John—and maybe it isn't. Maybe something else is going on—"

"Like what?"

"I don't know! It doesn't matter. I'll be all right; I'm not stupid. Samson is there, and you know as well as I do that no stranger could ever get past Samson."

"You'll come home with me."

"There you go again!"

"There I go again what?"

"Cracking the whip, laying down the law, whatever! Will you please quit telling me what to do? Now,

Samson is in that house. And I appreciate that, Rex, I really do—"

"You can't borrow my dog, Alexi."

"Rex! What—"

They drove right past the Brandywine house and kept going. Alexi gritted her teeth. She really wanted to land a hard punch right to his jaw. "Rex, I swear, this time you really can't do this! I want to go to my house, and so help me, I will!"

He ignored her. The car jerked to a halt before his house. Alexi turned to her door, ready to storm out. Rex's hand fell upon her arm. She started to wrench it away from him.

"Alexi!"

He turned her to him. He caught her lips in a long, burning kiss. She tried to push away from him; she couldn't. And despite her anger, or perhaps because of her anger, the heat of him took flight and seared into her. When he drew away from her, she was breathless. Furious, but breathless…

"Marry me," he said.

"What?"

Rex wasn't at all sure what had made him say that. He wanted her; he wanted her forever. And he wanted to keep her here, far from the Brandywine house. But marriage…

He really didn't know where the words had come from, but once they were out, he knew it was what he wanted. It was exactly what he wanted. She was beautiful, she was sweet, she was fire, she was a tranquil pool where he found peace.

"Marry me."

"Rex—you're crazy."

He stepped from the car and came around to her side, jerking the door open. None too gently, he caught her hands and pulled her up and into his arms and kissed her slowly and heatedly, holding her tightly to him. He lifted his lips a bare half inch from hers.

"Marry me."

"You're a temperamental bastard," she whispered in return. "You think you're some he-man. You think you can tell me what to do all of the time. I still don't believe you trust me—"

"I want your property," he told her, smiling.

"I don't even own it."

"Close enough."

He picked her up and smiled at her as he started for the house. She curled her arms around his neck, but she still watched him skeptically. "Rex, I'm going home."

"Later."

"Rex—"

"Please, Alexi. Please. I want you.... I need you."

"You're hardly deprived at the moment," she murmured. "We've been off together alone—playing—for three days now."

His arms tightened around her. She felt the keen burning flames in his eyes, glitter against ebony. It was crazy; it was mad—but she felt the touch of his eyes and the heat of his arms, and it was something that came to her, that built in her, and it was as if they had been apart for days, for months, for years. She felt the rapidly spreading wings of desire take flight, deep inside her, at her very core.

As he opened the door and brought them into the house, she was caught by the flare in his eyes, and was held by it as he headed for the bedroom. The shades were drawn and it was dark and cool, and when he put her down she couldn't remember why it had been imperative that she leave; now leaving was the last thing on her mind. He set her down upon the spread, and she was still, watching in silent fascination as he quickly stripped. She shivered in a whirlwind of anticipation and sensation then as he lay down beside her and removed her clothing with the same careless, nearly desperate abandon with which he had shed his own. She melded quickly with him in that same fierce, desperate heat. The urgency remained with them....

In moments, the culmination of something so fiercely desired burst upon them, sweet and exciting and exhausting. Alexi curled up at his side.

"Marry me," he repeated softly after a moment.

Yes! she wanted to shout. But she didn't know whether or not it was right; she knew he feared the commitment, and the question had been so sudden. And she still couldn't begin to figure out what made him tick—she had no idea why he had been so angry at the restaurant or why he had been determined to keep her away from the Brandywine house.

"I do love you," she whispered.

He turned to her, fierce, protective and somehow frightening in the shadows. "I love you, Alexi." He said it slowly, as if professing the words without qualification was difficult. "I do. I love you."

He kissed her again, running his fingers sensually over her lower abdomen and curling his naked feet around hers. Instantly she felt little flaming licks of desire light along her spine. She pulled away from him and threw her legs over the side of the bed to sit up. She and Rex should rise, she thought.

Softly, throatily, he whispered her name. He rose on his knees behind her, and she felt his lips against her shoulders. He turned her in his arms...and she was lost. This time he was very, very slow, making love like an artist. They'd been so hurried before, but now he took his time. He touched her....

And touched her. Stroking the soles of her feet, finding a fascination with the curve of her hip, laving her breasts with endless kisses that each sent waves of sensation flooding through her. He said the words to her again and again.

"I love you...."

She didn't know quite what it was about those three simple words. When the climax exploded upon her that time, it was as if a nova had burst across the heavens.

Three little words—difficult for him to say, but whispered with a joyous sureness. Difficult for him to say, and so incredibly special because of that. She whispered them in return. Sweetly and slowly and savoringly, she whispered them against his flesh. Then she curled against him and slept.

Later, she vaguely heard the phone ring. She even knew, because the warmth was gone, that he had left her. But she was so very drained and tired. She just kept sleeping.

He hadn't meant to sleep. He'd planned on Alexi doing so, but he hadn't counted on winding up quite so exhausted himself. But certain things just had a way of leading to certain other things.

The phone woke him. At first he didn't even recognize the ringing sound. He swung his legs over the side of the bed and ran his fingers through his hair, dimly aware that the machine in his office would pick it up. He heard Mark Eliot's voice, though, and leaped to his feet, anxious to catch the bedroom extension before Mark could hang up.

"Mark!"

"Rex. You know the guy you're so worried about, this Vinto character?"

"Yeah, what have you got?"

"He's out there somewhere. On the peninsula. I got a make on a rental car—a blue Mazda—and Harry Reese just told me he saw a blue Mazda turn down the road for the peninsula about half an hour ago."

"I'll be damned," Rex murmured. "Mark—thanks a lot. I'm going to get over there now—before Alexi can find out anything about him being here."

"Oh," Mark said. "*Oh!* That's the John Vinto on the pictures of the magazines! The photographer. The ex-husband!"

"Yes!" Rex said. "I'm going to run, Mark. Thanks again. I'll talk to you soon."

He hung up and glanced over at Alexi. She murmured something, curling deeper into her pillow. Her hair was a spill of gold over his sheets; her form, half draped beneath covers and half bare, was both evocative and sweet. Emotions unlike anything he had ever known rose and swirled in a tumult inside him. Rex pulled the covers up around her and kissed her on the forehead.

He'd be damned if he'd let John Vinto anywhere near her again. Ever.

Rex dressed quickly in dark jeans and a pullover,

grabbed a flashlight from his drawer and glanced at Alexi one more time. She was still sleeping. He hurried out of the house. Deciding not to take the car, he began a slow jog down the path. It was windy, he noticed, and the air had grown cool. Looking up at the sky as it grew dark with the coming of night, Rex noticed black patches against the gray. There was a storm brewing. A big one. He started running faster.

The porch and hallway lights had been left on at the Brandywine house; Emily had been taking care of the animals, and it seemed reasonable that she would leave lights on. Rex thought absently that he should have called Emily to tell her that he was back.

He saw the blue Mazda, sitting right before the path to the house. Then, right behind it, he noticed Emily's little red Toyota.

His heart began to beat too quickly. Emily. What if John Vinto *was* dangerous?

"Emily!" he called and charged up the path to the house. He swore, aware that he had forgotten his key. It didn't matter; the door was open. He pushed it inward.

"Emily! Samson! Vinto!" With a sense of déjà vu, Rex tore up the stairs. There was no one in any of the bedrooms. What really worried him the most was that Samson didn't answer his calls.

He searched the downstairs, absently noticing that the wall beneath Pierre's portrait had been torn apart. Something must have started to fall, he thought, and Emily had called in help. What the hell difference did it make now? Vinto might well be a psychopath, and he was missing, along with Emily, one massive shepherd and two kittens.

Where the hell could they be?

Rex tore out of the house and raced toward the beach, trying to search through the trees. He traveled all the way through the trail of pines until the waves of the Atlantic crashed before him. He turned back. They had to be the other way.

His gaze fell on his own house. The lights were all on upstairs.

A streak of lightning suddenly lit up the sky; a crack of thunder boomed immediately after. Through the pines, Rex saw a jagged flare of fire catch, siz-zle...and fade.

And then the lights in both houses went out. "Alexi!" he screamed. The rain began to fall as he raced back toward his house. He threw open the front door. "Alexi! Alexi! Alexi!"

There was no answer but the sure and ceaseless patter of the rain. He'd known she was gone. She was somewhere within the darkened Brandywine house.

"Alexi!" He started to run.

The bed was still warm beside her when Alexi awoke. She smiled. He was up, but he had to be nearby.

It had grown dark. She reached over to switch on the bedside lamp. "Rex?"

He didn't answer her. Alexi crawled out of bed and scrambled into her clothing. "Rex!" she called, zipping up her shorts. She started down the stairs and headed for his office. He wasn't there, and some sixth sense told her that he was nowhere in the house. She noticed that his answering machine was blinking. Curious, she went over and pressed the playback button, hop-ing that a message might give her a clue to his whereabouts. Maybe Gene had called. Maybe Rex had gone to meet him at the house.

Rex seemed to have a dozen messages. She sat through six business calls, two friends saying "hi" and then a call from Mark Eliot—a call that made her start in surprise. Rex's answers had been recorded, along with Mark's information.

Listening to the exchange, Alexi felt a numbness of fear sweep over her. John was there, on the peninsula. Why? Had he been there all along, watching her, spying on her, stalking her?

She gasped aloud, suddenly more afraid of the sound of Rex's voice. *He meant to meet John.* And God only knew what he meant to do. "No, oh, no!" She hurried toward the door. She didn't know what to do; she was too frightened to really think. John was her problem, though. Rex shouldn't be dealing with him. And she was afraid to think about just how Rex might be dealing with the man.

She ran, barefoot, toward the Brandywine house. Against the darkness of night, it seemed ablaze.

She hadn't noticed the coming storm. She screamed out, startled and cringing, as a bolt of lightning lit up the sky. Thunder cracked immediately, and then she saw a flash of fire. The fire sizzled out—and the world was pitched into an ebony darkness.

Rain started to fall against the earth in great, heavy plops.

Alexi swore softly and raced on toward the house. In a flash of lightning she saw an unfamiliar blue car and Emily's red Toyota. She kept going up the path. The front door was ajar; Alexi pushed it inward.

"Rex! Emily? Samson!" She swallowed, straining to see in the darkness. "John...?"

Alexi stumbled into the kitchen. She groped around the cabinets, reaching to the top to find a candle, then swore vociferously in her efforts to find matches. At last she came across a book of them and managed to light one with her chilled, dripping fingers. She cajoled the wick into catching, then raised the candle high. The kitchen seemed eerie in the darkness.

Something drifted over her bare foot. Alexi screamed and nearly dropped the candle, and for one instant she was convinced that her ancestral home was haunted—and that a ghost had wafted over her. Then she heard a soft, plaintive mewling.

"A kitten!" she whispered, stooping to find the little pile of fluff that had rubbed against her. She picked it up and smiled at the brilliant, scared eyes that met hers. "Silver. Where's your cohort? And where in heck is Samson? Hey, you're all wet...."

Alexi frowned and raised the candle higher. She gasped then, realizing that the back door was open. She stepped toward it and the porch beyond it, her frown deepening as she noticed a large, huddled form there. Her heart quickened with fear.

"Rex?"

She kept going. She wanted to scream, and she wanted to stop—and she could not. She set the kitten down in the kitchen and stepped out onto the back porch.

The huddled form was a body. She began to shake, terrified. She had to touch it.... Someone was hurt; someone needed help.

She went down on her knees, and her eyes widened. She saw a patch of blond hair.

"John!" She gasped. She touched his shoulder nervously. "John?" She pulled her hand away and began to shake in earnest. There was blood all over her hand.

"Oh, my God!" she breathed. She heard the front door slam. Then she heard footsteps racing through the house. A scream of terror rose to her throat.

Rex. Rex had come here, and Rex had killed John. It was her fault. John was dead. She'd hated him; she'd feared him—but, oh God, she'd never expected this....

She screamed as a figure burst out upon her.

"Alexi!"

It was Rex. He raced over to her and paused, staring at her, then at the body. He dropped to his knees beside the body and pressed a finger against John's throat. He looked at Alexi again.

"This is Vinto?" His voice had a harsh, strangling sound. Alexi gazed at him blankly. He *knew* this was John. *He had done this thing to him.*

"You...you..."

"We've got to get help out here right away," he muttered.

"Oh, Rex! Oh, God!"

"Alexi, you're going to have to tell the police everything that happened between you. Everything. From before."

"What?"

"I love you, Alexi. Whatever happens, I'll be by your side."

"What?" she repeated, amazed and ready to burst into tears. She'd fallen so in love with him. She should have known it was too good to be true. This morning they'd sailed a turquoise sea under a golden sun, and now they were sitting here, drenched and ashen, staring at each other over the body of a man....

"Samson!" he said suddenly. "I hear Samson."

She looked up. He was right. The shepherd was racing toward them, skidding across the kitchen floor so fast that he nearly flew into Rex's arms once he'd left the doorframe behind. He barked excitedly, jumping over John's body to crash into Alexi. She burst into tears, hugging the shepherd. It was too much. "Alexi—" Rex began.

"There you are!"

Rex turned to the doorframe and distractedly noticed Emily standing there in her trench coat. "Emily, thank God you're all right," he said. He reached out for Alexi. She winced, jerking from his touch. "Alexi, it's going to be all right!"

"Rex!" Emily said in a strangled voice. She'd seen the body, Rex thought.

"Emily—" He began to turn.

"Oh, my God!" Alexi shrieked. "Rex—*she's* got a gun."

But somehow that fact didn't quite penetrate Rex's mind. "Emily, what in God's name are you doing?" He started to walk toward her. She raised the barrel so it was even with his chest. "Stop where you are, Rex."

He knew from her tone that she meant it. "Emily—"

"Back up, Rex—now. I mean it. I—I'm sorry. I didn't want to hurt either of you. I've got to figure this out now. You'll all have to be found together. A love triangle. I don't know. Maybe you found the two of them together, Rex. Then shot yourself."

Fingers were touching him. Reaching for his arm.

It was Alexi. Numb, Rex encircled her with an arm, drawing her tightly to him.

"Why?" Alexi whispered. Emily looked at her and spoke as if she was trying to explain things to a half-witted child.

"Why, the treasure, child, of course. I finally found it. Today."

"It's worthless, Emily!" Rex thundered. "It's worthless paper! It's not—"

"It's not paper at all, Rex Morrow!" Emily corrected him. She sniffed. "No one knew Pierre Brandywine—not even his beloved Eugenia! It was gold he left her. Gold bars! A fortune. A real treasure. And it's been in this house all these years because some foolish little maid didn't bother to forward a letter." Emily smiled. "I found it, you see. I was cleaning up in the old kitchen before Gene had them put the new stuff in. I found Pierre's letter. Telling Eugenia he left her gold. Only Eugenia knew where it was hidden. I didn't. I had to search and search."

Alexi's fingers were a vise around Rex's arm. He could feel her trembling, but she was determinedly standing there—buying time.

"You tried to scare me out, right, Emily?" she said shakily.

"I tried."

Alexi kept stalling. In the terrible dark of the night, against the endless monotony of the rain, she was desperately stalling for time.

"You had no reason to ever be afraid of Samson. Samson was your best friend. You could search and search—and he wouldn't bark."

"It was easy before you came," Emily agreed. "I

went through the house at my leisure. I looked and looked and couldn't find it, but I knew that gold was here somewhere. I followed you when you first came. You ran right into Rex. I slipped into the house. I thought you might believe in ghosts. I had to knock you out the other night. And now this man found me. I had to shoot him. It's your fault—you just wouldn't leave. And, Rex... I am so sorry. Really."

He was going to have to jump her, Rex decided. Throw himself against her to at least give Alexi a chance to run. Alexi's fingers tightened around his arm again. She was thinking the same thing!

"Oh!" Emily let out a startled little scream. The gun rose for a split second. "Oh, you damned dog!" Samson had nudged her with a cold nose. Maybe he wasn't her best friend after all.

"Get down!" Rex shouted to Alexi. She dived for the porch just as he threw himself at Emily and knocked her down, sending the gun skidding away along the old wood of the porch. Emily screamed then, striking out at Rex with her nails. "Stop!" Rex commanded her. Alexi was there then, drawing her belt from her shorts, then slipping it around Emily's wrists. Rex caught hold of it and tied it securely.

Lights suddenly appeared, blinding them at first. A car stopped; they could hear the doors slamming. "Alexi! Rex!" It was Gene.

"Rex? Miss Jordan?"

"We're here, in the back!" Rex called out. "Mark Eliot," he told Alexi. She smiled.

"If you can give that nice boy any bit of help, you do it," Alexi said.

"I will," Rex promised. He glanced over at John's body. "He might still make it."

"He's alive?" Alexi demanded.

"Just barely." He smiled at her ruefully. "I thought you had tried to kill him."

"And I thought *you* had!"

"He hurt you so badly."

"You once said that you *would* kill him," she reminded him.

Rex groaned. "Alexi! That was a term of speech!"

"Well…" she murmured.

Emily was swearing viciously, but by that time, Gene and Mark had reached the porch. They both stared at John and then at Emily. It seemed to Alexi that everyone was talking at once. Gene looked so white that she quickly put her arms around him, anxious to assure him that she was fine. Rex was trying to explain the situation to Mark Eliot. Mark took one look at John Vinto's body and hurried to the car, calling for an ambulance. Then he returned and checked the body. "There's still a pulse—just barely," he said grimly, staring at Emily.

"Come on, Mrs. Rider. Let's go to the car." Mark exchanged the belt around her wrists for handcuffs. By then they could hear the ambulance's siren. A moment later, two paramedics were carefully working on John Vinto. Alexi stared at her ex-husband's features. She was shivering, but her fear of him was completely gone. She prayed that he would live. Rex slipped his arms around her as they took John away. "I wonder what he did want," she murmured.

"I don't know," Rex said.

"Why on earth did she shoot him?" Gene murmured.

"He just happened to come upon her when she had discovered her stash of gold at last," Rex wearily told Gene.

"Gold!"

Rex smiled ruefully. "Pierre really did leave a 'treasure,' Gene. No Confederate bills. Gold. Could I have your flashlight for a minute, Mark?"

"Take this, Rex," Mark said. "I've got to take my prisoner on in. I'll need you all in the morning. Mr. Brandywine, now, you take care."

"Thank you, Mr. Eliot," Gene said. Rex and Alexi echoed his words, waving until he was gone.

Rex led the way, and they followed him to the ballroom. The bricks around the lower mantel under the portraits had been pulled out. An ancient, rusting trunk lay amid the rubble on the floor.

"It's your trunk," Rex told Gene.

Gene stepped forward, lowered himself to his knees and flipped the lid on the old trunk. Bars and bars of gold sparkled before them in the glare of the flashlight.

"I'll be darned," Gene said, flashing his head. "All these years…"

"He meant it to go to his heirs," Rex murmured. "You're his grandson, Gene."

Gene smiled at Rex a little wearily. "Poor man. He worried so much, and his wife and his children were a lot stronger than he gave them credit for." He flashed a quick smile at Alexi. "A lot stronger, girl."

Rex slipped his arms around her waist and pulled her back against him. "Very strong," he said softly. "What are you going to do with it all?" he asked Gene.

Gene scratched his head for a minute. "A museum. Yes, I think a museum. We'll put Eugenia's diary in it, and the clothes from up in the attic—Pierre's old sword and the like. He'd approve, don't you think?"

"That I do, sir. That I do," Rex agreed.

"Well, well," Gene murmured. "It's a bit too much excitement for me for one night. Pierre's treasure almost cost me something he would have prized far, far more." He touched Alexi's cheek. "I think I'll go on up to bed here. Do you mind, dear?"

"Gene! It's your house."

"Yes. But of course you'll have a chaperone now." He cleared his throat. "Rex Morrow—just what are your intentions regarding my great-granddaughter?"

Rex laughed. "The very best, sir."

"Well?"

"I intend to marry her. As soon as possible."

"He's only after your land!" Alexi warned Gene.

"Does she ever shut up?" Rex asked Gene.

Gene smiled wickedly. "Sure she does, boy. You've got the knack, I'm quite sure."

"Do I?" Rex said, smiling down at Alexi.

"Do you?" She slipped her arms around his neck, standing on tiptoe. He kissed her. He meant just to brush her lips, but there was just something about her....

The kiss went long and deep, very long and deep, until Gene cleared his throat. Rex broke from her. His eyes were glittering ebony as he challenged her, his voice gruff with tenderness. "Will you, Alexi? Will you marry me?"

She smiled. Rex knew that treasure had never lain in gold, nor in silver—nor in any other such tangible thing. Treasure was something that any man could find on earth, if he could trust in himself enough to reach for it.

"Yes, Rex. Yes!" Alexi told him.

He stared into her eyes, dazzled. "I love you, sweetheart."

"Well, then, if it's all settled, go ahead and kiss her again," Gene said. "But excuse me. I'm an old man."

"An old fox!" Rex whispered.

"I heard that!" Gene said.

Alexi and Rex laughed and waved good-night. They heard a door close above them.

"Well, my love?" Rex whispered.

"You heard him," Alexi murmured. "Go ahead. Kiss me again. Hmm… Morrow… Alexi Morrow."

"I'll come with you to New York."

"No, we'll live here."

"But you don't have to give up your career—"

"I really don't care."

"You don't have to give it up!"

"Don't tell me what to do!"

"I'm not! I'm trying—" He broke off suddenly, staring up at the picture of Pierre. He shook his head. "Maybe there is only one way to do it."

"To do what—" Alexi began.

She never finished. He had decided to kiss her again.

Epilogue

June 2, Two Years Later
Fernandina Beach, Florida

"There he is, Alexi. Down on the beach."

Alexi stared out through the long trail of pines to the beach, where Gene's call directed her. She rose, a smile curving her lips, her heart, as always, taking flight.

Rex was alighting from one of their new acquisitions, a silver raft. The waves of the beach pounded against his bare, muscled calves as he splashed through the water. From a distance, he was beautiful and perfect.

"Rex!"

Upon the porch of the old house, Alexi called his name. He couldn't hear her, of course. He was too far away. She was certain, though, that his eyes had met her own, and that the love they shared between them sang and soared likewise in his soul.

He had seen her. He waved. He started to run. To run down the sand path carpeted in pine and shadowed by those same branches. Sun and shadow, shadow and sun; she could see his face clearly no longer.

"Gene? Take the baby for a minute?"

"With the greatest pleasure."

Carefully—he was a very old man—Gene slipped his hands beneath the squirming body of his very first great-great-grandson. Alexi smiled at him briefly, then leaped down the steps, waving to Rex.

"I'll take him inside!" Gene called to Alexi. "It's getting a little bit hot out here. And don't you two worry—I can rock the boy to sleep just as well as the next person."

Alexi turned in time to give Gene an appreciative thumbs-up sign. Then she started to run, running to meet her husband, running to meet her man.

Run…run, run, run. Sunlight continued to glitter through the trees, golden as it fell upon her love. She felt the padding of her feet against the carpet of sand and pine, and the great rush of her breath. Closer. Closer. She could see the love he bore her, the need to touch.

Her breath, ragged, in and out, in and out. Down that long, long trail of sand and pine.

"Rex!"

"Alexi!"

Laughing, she flew the last few steps; those steps that brought her into his arms. He lifted her high; he swirled her beneath the sun. He stared into her eyes, his smile soft as he cherished her and the life they had created between them.

"The baby?"

"He's with Gene."

"They're okay?"

"They're perfect."

Rex smiled and laced his fingers through his wife's. They started to walk toward the beach again. At the shore, where the warm, gentle water just rushed over their bare feet, Rex slipped his arms around Alexi's waist.

Time had been good to them; life had been good to them.

For one, John Vinto had lived. Rex had been worried when Alexi had insisted on visiting him in the hospital, but in the end he had been glad. John had wanted to see her just to apologize; he had thought there might be some way to hang on to his marriage. He'd met a new girl, but somehow he'd needed Alexi's forgiveness before he could start out in a new life. Alexi had promised her forgiveness with all her heart—if he would promise to get some counseling.

It hadn't been easy for Rex, standing there. Vinto was a handsome man, beach tan and white blond, successful—and earnest. But trust had been the ingredient he needed to instill in his heart, and when he had seen Alexi's eyes fall on him again, he had known that she loved him. She didn't need to make any comparisons between men—she loved Rex, and that was that. He had sworn to himself in a silent vow that he would give her that same unqualified love all his life.

Gene had used the gold to open a small Confederate museum. It gave him a new passion in life—the hunt for artifacts. Alexi and Rex had grown fascinated with the search themselves, and the three of them frequently traveled throughout the States to various shows to see what else they could acquire.

They'd had a wonderful wedding. A big, wonderful wedding in the Brandywine house, with Alexi's folks and his folks and cousins and aunts and uncles—and Mark Eliot and the carpenters and Joe's boy and anyone else in the world they could think of to invite. Rex had insisted on Alexi tying up some loose ends with her Helen of Troy work, and then Alexi had insisted on staying home for a while. She had a new line of work in mind. That new line of work—Jarod Eugene Morrow—was just five weeks old, and the center of their existence.

"What are you thinking?" Alexi murmured to him.

He squeezed her more tightly. "That it's been so very good here. That I love you so much. That we're so very lucky. Pierre Brandywine picked a beautiful place. I wonder if he can see that—even though he lost his own life and his own dreams—his family is still here. Jarod is his great-great-great-grandson."

"Great, great, great, great—but who's counting," Alexi murmured. "I'm sure Pierre knows," she added softly.

"Yes, I like to think so."

"Yes," Alexi whispered. She smoothed her fingers gently over his hands. "It's been good."

He nuzzled his chin against her cheek. "What were you thinking?"

"Hmmmm…well, I was thinking that Gene really is so very good with the baby."

"Yes?"

"He took him inside, you know."

"Yes?"

"It's just like we're alone in our very own Eden again."

"Yes?"

She hesitated, a charming, slightly crooked smile curving into her features in such a way that he instantly felt the heat aroused tensely in his body. His pulse skipped a beat and then thundered, and he inhaled deeply. "Yes, Alexi?"

"Want to go skinny-dipping?"

"Yes!" He twisted her around and kissed her lips and smiled down into the beauty of her eyes. "I was hoping that you might ask."

Alexi laughed as he fumbled eagerly with the zipper of her halter dress. "This is skinny-dipping. We both disrobe by mutual consent."

"I'll dip you and you can dip me," Rex retorted. The dress came over her head and landed in the sand. A moment later they were both down to their birthday suits and racing out to the water.

Rex caught Alexi beneath the benign warmth of a radiant sun. Their smiles recalled the first time—and reminded them that there would always be forever.

His arms swept around her. "I love you, Alexi."

"And I love you," she returned. Heat and salt and sea and the endless breeze swirled around them as they kissed, becoming one.

The pines dipped and rustled.

Back at the house, Gene stood beneath the beautiful old paintings of his grandparents and frowned curiously.

He wasn't superstitious, and he sure as hell didn't

believe in haunted houses. He could remember Eugenia as clear as day, even though she had been dead for years and years and years.

No, he was too old for ghost stories. But holding Jarod Eugene Morrow beneath the portraits, he could have almost sworn that a little twist of a smile came to Pierre's lips.

"More than a century later, Pierre. And the boy here—he'll grow up right here, Pierre. More than we might have dreamed, huh? More than we might have dreamed."

Gene winked at the picture.

And he was almost sure that the damned thing winked back.

* * * * *

Visit the Author Profile page
at Harlequin.com for more titles.

SHELTERED IN HIS ARMS

Tara Taylor Quinn

For Jeanine Lynn Clayton (1960–2000).

My childhoood soul mate. An integral part of my life that transcends the tragedy this temporal existence handed us. Your life was and always will be a part of me. With me. Sitting on my shoulder.

Chapter 1

Her high-heeled evening sandals hadn't been made for sprinting across gravel. And the Montfords' desert landscaping was full of it. The darkness made things even worse.

But she had to get away—get out. She had to handle this news alone.

There was an old gnarled pepper tree in the corner of the yard and she hurried toward it. One branch had grown sideways, forming a natural bench with the other branches hanging down around it. Because of the balmy late-March weather they'd been enjoying in Shelter Valley, the tree was thickly covered with leaves. She could safely hide there.

For the moment. Until someone decided to turn on the outside lights.

"Ouch!" Cassie Tate's headlong rush from the house halted abruptly.

Damn!

She bent to pull a cactus needle from her shin. One
quick jerk—a sting—and it was gone. When had her
ex-in-laws gotten that cholla plant? It hadn't been there
a few months ago, when she'd been over for a Christmas drink and gift exchange with them.

Unmindful of her new silk dress, Cassie slid onto
the rough bark of the branch, its horizontal shape familiar to her. The first time Sam had ever kissed her
had been right here...

Cassie looked around, her hands poised on the
trunk as though she were ready to push off. Maybe it
had been a mistake to come out here.

But where else could she go? The backyard was
enclosed with an eight-foot-high stucco wall. She
couldn't get out front—and to her car—without walking through the house.

Breathe, she reminded herself. She filled her lungs
as much as her tight chest muscles would allow.

She had to be calm. To assimilate what she'd just
heard. And what she was going to do about it.

One thing was for certain. She *wasn't* going to cry.
She'd cried enough tears for Samuel Montford.

Glancing through the leaves surrounding her, toward the house where strains of piano music wafted
from the living room, Cassie could see the lights of
the party twinkling merrily. As though everything
was normal.

And maybe for all those people in there, things
were just fine.

Maybe all of *them* could welcome Sam home after
his ten-year desertion. Maybe they could forgive. Forget.

Maybe she could, too. If she had a million years to try.

Sitting out here, on their tree, her mind wandered back to the boy she'd known and loved with all her heart. She thought of the passionate dreams he'd poured out to her beneath these branches. He'd wanted to save the world back in those days. Get rid of poverty, pain, injustice.

He'd promised to love her forever.

"Oh, God, Sam. Why?"

Her words sounded shockingly loud in the night. Cassie took a long, shuddering breath. How many times had she asked the same question over the past ten years?

"Can't you at least just leave me in peace?" she whispered, tears pooling in her eyes.

She used to dream of great things. Of love and family and children. Of happiness and warmth. Now all she hoped for was peace. It was the only option left.

"Cassie? You out here?"

It was Zack. Her partner. Her friend. He'd know how she was feeling. Without her saying a word, he'd know.

His footsteps were getting closer. Cassie pulled herself in, hardly daring to breathe as she waited for him to pass. She couldn't face him yet. Couldn't face anyone.

Not until she was sure she wouldn't fall apart. She'd done that once, back then, suffered a debilitating breakdown, and emotional collapse.

She'd done it after Sam had left her, after her baby girl had died, after she'd been told she'd probably never be able to conceive again.

But those dark days had helped her find the strength and awareness she needed. She'd gone on to finish college, to become a nationally renowned doctor of veterinary science. She was successful. She wasn't going to fall apart again just because her adulterous ex-husband had decided to return to town.

Though she couldn't help wondering why he was coming back. The way she remembered it, he hadn't been able to leave fast enough. And he hadn't been in touch with any of them since—other than infrequent calls to his parents to let them know he was okay. And to make certain that they were.

What had he been doing all these years? And with whom?

These were questions Cassie had tried so hard never to ask.

What had the years done to him? Another question she'd shied away from. But one that was apparently to be answered soon.

Were his eyes still that deep green? Did they still have that penetrating directness? Her stomach tightened just thinking about them. About what a look from him used to do to her.

One time, she'd been looking for him in the high-school cafeteria. Her class right before lunch had gotten out late and she hadn't seen him in line. She'd gone through, anyway. Bought a salad and a soda, and was standing there with her tray, wondering what to do when she'd seen him come in through the door at the back of the room. He'd been frowning—until he saw her. And then his eyes had lighted with such familiar, knowing warmth that her belly had fluttered, her knees had fluttered—and she'd dropped her tray.

Sam had always been a looker. Was he still?

Was his dark hair still as soft as the finest silk, still as thick?

Did he have any of the wrinkles she'd been noticing around her own eyes lately? Had he gained any weight?

Sniffling, Cassie wiped the tears from her cheeks. God, she missed him.

Missed the boy she'd loved since she was twelve years old. The man she'd married—and lost—more than a decade ago.

She missed the dreams. And the dreaming.

"Damn you, Sam Montford," she whispered, sniffling again. "Damn you for what you did. And for coming back now…"

The man might return to Shelter Valley, but as far as Cassie was concerned, he'd lost the right to call this town home.

Mariah was still asleep. Sam's heart swelled with love—and worry—as he glanced over at the child on the reclining passenger seat beside him. He should have sold the truck, bought a car. Something she could get into without climbing up on hands and knees.

Something that felt more like it belonged to a family than a roaming man.

Mariah might not know it, might not believe him when he told her, but they were almost home. At last.

In all the years he'd lived in Shelter Valley, the place had never felt as much like home as it did now. This journey back was so important. So life-changing. So right.

And so damn scary.

But he was ready.

The little girl stirred, her skinny legs stiffening as she stretched. Their boniness, visible beneath her new denim shorts, scared him. She'd been wearing pants all winter, and her loss of weight hadn't been as noticeable. Or maybe he'd just been too afraid to acknowledge that she was wasting away.

He had to get her to eat more. To eat, period. He wasn't going to let her die. He wasn't going to lose her, too.

"Good afternoon, sleepyhead," Sam said cheerfully, smiling at the little girl who'd stolen his heart in the delivery room seven years before. Her parents, his closest friends in the world, had insisted he be there with them. "How's my girl?"

Mariah looked at him.

That was all. Just looked. It was all she ever did anymore.

Heart heavy, Sam continued with cheerful chatter. Keep talking to her, the doctors had told him. Surround her with love. She'll never forget the tragedy, but she can recover.

He'd been talking for six months.

And Mariah had yet to say a word.

"You just wait until you meet your new grandparents," Sam told the child. "I was an only child, too, just like you. And my mom and dad were the greatest. You'll love them, but they'll love you more. Not that you need to let that worry you. That's just the way they are."

The landscape was painfully, blissfully familiar. Yet different.

"Mom makes the best chocolate chip cookies in the world." He glanced over again and decided to feel encouraged by the fact that Mariah was still watching him. Even if that was about all she ever did.

Maybe she was listening, too.

"Sometimes, when I was a kid, I'd sneak down from my bed at night, just to have another one of those cookies. I tried really hard to be as quiet as a mouse so I wouldn't get caught," Sam said. The smile he'd plastered on his face, became real as he remembered those days. "Every time a step creaked, my stomach would jump and I'd stand still and not breathe until I was sure my mom hadn't heard me."

Mariah blinked, her sad little face turned up toward his. Shelter Valley was going to be good for her. It had to be. If the answers weren't there, if the love in Shelter Valley wasn't enough to heal her, nothing would.

"The cookie jar was this big glass thing and the lid was really heavy and I'd have to lift it really carefully..."

The approaching sign said Shelter Valley, One Mile. The sign was new.

At least, it hadn't been there ten years ago.

Sam wiped his palm along his denim shorts.

"...the hardest part, though, was putting the lid back without making a noise. Especially because by that time I was always afraid I'd get caught and have to put the cookie back."

Sam slowed, approaching the exit. Mariah's gaze never left his face. She didn't look around, didn't show any interest at all in the place that was going to be home to her. He wondered how it was possible for someone with her naturally dark complexion to look so pale.

"I'd creep slowly back up the stairs, the smell of that cookie in my hand teasing me the whole way."

There was a new gas station at the Shelter Valley

exit. And the huge old tree was still shading the east side of the road.

"It was sure a lot of work, but boy, when I finally made it back to my room and sank my teeth into that cookie, mmm." Sam grinned at Mariah. "It was worth it. Just for that one bite."

He passed the road that led out to the cactus jelly plant. The street sign still had those familiar BB gun dents put there by some guy who'd gone to high school with Sam's parents. No one had ever told Sam *which* guy, just "some guy."

A few scattered houses came into view, then disappeared as he drove past. He wondered what Mariah thought of them, as he tried to see Shelter Valley through her eyes. Through fresh eyes.

Not that she'd have any opinion of those houses. She wasn't seeing them. She was still staring at Sam.

"You want to know the funniest thing about my cookie escapades?" he asked, glancing over at her.

She blinked. A regular occurrence, but Sam chose to take this particular time as a yes.

"When I was in high school, my mom told me that she'd known all along I was stealing those cookies. She and my dad would sit in the family room and listen for me to come down the stairs…"

They'd smiled at each other, sharing their joy in their only son. She hadn't told Sam that, but he'd known. No parents had ever delighted in their child more than Sam's parents had.

Until the day he'd hurt them beyond belief.

"…all that work was for nothing." Sam finished his story as he slowed, entering the town proper.

Sunday afternoon had always been a sleepy time

in Shelter Valley. It still was. Sam was relieved. He welcomed the comfort born of knowing this place. Craved its predictability.

Yearning for a drive through these remembered streets, for reassurance as he reacquainted himself with the place he'd always called home, for even a glimpse of the woman who still held such a place in his heart, Sam turned his truck and headed up the mountain, instead.

To the home he'd grown up in. He and Mariah had been driving for three days. His little girl needed to get those legs on solid ground—and since it had been two hours since their last stop, probably needed to go to the bathroom, too.

She didn't need a trip down her father's memory lane. Her father of only a few months…

"There it is, honey," he said, his throat tight as the huge house became visible, off in the distance. "See, it's just like I told you. A big beautiful castle up on the mountain."

Montford Mansion. The place he'd loved and hated with equal fervor.

Mariah had been staring at the insignia on his glove compartment, but when Sam spoke, her eyes turned toward him again.

"Look, Mariah, the orange trees are filled with blossoms."

Damn, it felt good to be home, in spite of all the resurrected pain the old sights were bringing him. The regrets.

The knowledge that he was going to have to see his Cassie with another man, married to another man. After all this time, she would've found someone to love. Someone who wouldn't betray her faith in him, her loyalty. She'd probably have several kids by now. She'd wanted at least four.

Reaching out, he stroked a couple of fingers lightly down Mariah's cheek. "You're the princess of the castle now, remember, sweetie?" he said, trying his damndest to help his daughter feel a little magic again, to believe in the fairy tales that thrilled most seven-year-old girls. He fingered one of the waist-length black braids he'd painstakingly tied when they were back in their hotel room in Albuquerque this morning. "That's why we did the braids, remember?" he coaxed. "So you can wear your crown like a real princess."

He'd bought the crown more than a week ago, before they'd left Wilmington, Delaware. With its glittering glass jewels, it had cost him almost a hundred dollars—no plastic piece of junk for his little girl. He'd have paid ten times that amount if it would make Mariah smile again.

Slowing the truck, overwhelmed by unexpected emotion, Sam wound around the curves that would take him up the mountain to his parents' driveway. His driveway, really. He was the only living heir to Montford Mansion.

Not that any of it meant a whole lot to Sam. He was the fourth-generation descendant of Shelter Valley's founder, but his heritage had been far more of a burden to him than a blessing.

That burden wasn't going to stop him from coming home. Shelter Valley was Mariah's only hope.

And maybe Sam's, too.

The house looked exactly as he'd left it. Driving slowly, Sam approached the circular drive, heart pounding in spite of his admonitions to the contrary. This wasn't going to be easy. He knew that. He'd come fully prepared to accept the hostility that was his due. Prepared to make amends as far as was humanly possible for destroying the hopes and dreams of those who'd loved him so faithfully.

Parking in front of the house, Sam sat and stared, taking in the heavy double doors, the stucco walls, the shrubbery under the huge picture windows. As a little kid, he'd been paid a buck an hour to clean up behind the gardener who trimmed those shrubs.

A buck an hour. To a kid who was a millionaire in his own right. But what had *he* known? He'd wanted to grow up and be a gardener someday. To make some of the dingy houses in town look as beautiful as his did. Even then, working with his hands had been all Sam cared about.

Sam's finger itched now, for the drawing pencil that was never far away these days. His mind was reeling with stories for next week's strip.

Mariah's small brown hand slid across the seat and stole into Sam's. Turning, he met the frightened eyes of his little girl—and felt traces of the heartache that would never ease.

"You're going to love it here, honey. See all the pretty flowers your grandma has growing in the yard?"

Mariah continued to gaze at him, unblinking now, and suddenly Sam wasn't at all sure about what he was doing. Unbuckling Mariah's belt, he pulled her across the seat and onto his lap, cradling her protectively in his arms.

Shelter Valley was her only hope. He knew that.

The people in this town, with their huge hearts and warm smiles, would coax his little girl out of the silent world of terror into which she'd sunk. They'd teach her to smile again. To play. They'd make her laugh. Forget.

Maybe, someday, she'd even find the courage to love.

He wondered if his parents still had Muffy, the cocker spaniel he and Cassie had bought them shortly after Sam had left home to marry Cassie. The dog would be almost twelve years old.

Best not get Mariah's hopes up on that one. Or Sam's, either. He'd been very partial to that dog.

"It's going to be okay, baby, it's going to be okay."

Mariah shuddered, her little hand coming to rest in his again. Sam could only imagine the thoughts running through the child's mind—terrifying images of the tragedy that had torn her life apart.

Looking at the familiar front door of the big house that had been both prison and haven to Sam, he wondered if maybe he should go back to Phoenix, get a hotel room, tuck Mariah in for a nap and call his parents from there.

He'd sent them a brief note, almost three weeks ago, telling them he'd be arriving some time soon.

A brief note. That and a few very short phone calls were all the communication he'd had with them in the ten years since he'd left home in disgrace. They knew nothing about his life since. Nothing about Mariah.

And he knew nothing about them, other than that they were both healthy. Nothing about the state of his father's business, the small but prestigious investment firm James had founded thirty years ago. He knew nothing about Shelter Valley, except for what he'd seen on the drive in. From the moment he'd walked out of his and Cassie's house that Saturday morning, his parents had never mentioned her again. And after he'd left town two weeks later, they'd never mentioned Shelter Valley, either.

He'd never even received divorce papers, although he'd signed documents before he left town, allowing Cassie to terminate their marriage. He'd never given anyone a forwarding address.

He'd never expected to come home.

He'd purposely kept the time of his arrival vague. Hadn't wanted them to be waiting for him, or to have anyone else waiting to welcome him home. Hadn't been able to bear the thought of their *not* waiting, either, if truth be known.

But for Mariah's sake, he'd needed to arrive in town with as little fuss as possible.

Now, sitting outside his childhood home, he felt like a fool. How could he take his fragile little girl in there, with no idea of what she'd have to face. Sam was all she had left in the world. How would she react if his parents were rude to him?

Or worse, indifferent? Cold?

A chill swept through him, in spite of the child sweating against him and the Arizona sunshine beating down on his truck. He had to turn around. Go back to Phoenix. He couldn't risk creating any more anxiety or tension in Mariah's life.

His parents were going to love her. He knew that. But he also knew he had to smooth her way. Give them a chance to speak their piece against him without her witnessing it.

And maybe he needed a little more time than he'd realized, as well—

"Sam?" The voice came from far off, but Sam's heart recognized the call immediately. "Sam, is that really you, son?"

His mother came running out of the big front doors of Montford Mansion, almost tripped over her own feet as she came around to his side of the truck.

"Yeah, Mom, it's me," he said under his breath, before pulling open the door. Mariah's fingers dug into him, and she buried her face against his shoulder, just as his mother threw her arms around his neck and kissed him.

"Oh, son, let me look at you," she said, crying, smiling, trembling all at once. "I've missed you so mu—"

Her words broke off, and Sam, watching her face, knew she'd seen Mariah. Her eyes filled with wonder, with curiosity—and fresh tears—as she pulled back.

Sam grabbed hold of her hand.

Taking a deep breath, offering a short silent prayer, he ran his other hand down his daughter's coal-black hair. "This is Mariah, Mom. I adopted her three months ago. She's been waiting to meet you."

Chapter 2

"Hey! Zack and I are on our way to my folks' for a barbecue and swim. You want to come along?"

Cassie jumped, her pen slashing across the journal subscription form she'd been filling out. The voice coming from her office doorway—when she'd thought herself alone in the clinic—gave her a shock. Not her partner's voice, as she might have expected, but his wife's. Zack would have made a lot of noise as he entered, to warn her that she wasn't alone.

In case she'd been doing something private. Like crying.... Reaching for the remote just beyond her right hand, Cassie turned down the volume on the small television she'd been listening to while she worked.

"I've got reports to catch up on," she said, smiling in spite of her refusal. Zack Foster had been her sole confidante and best friend for more than nine years. They'd met after she'd left Shelter Valley to finish her education in Phoenix. Now that he'd married Randi, she had a second best friend.

A friend who was far less predictable than Zack—

Randi leaned over Cassie's desk, peering at the paperwork she'd just messed up. "Looks like important stuff to me," Randi said, raising both eyebrows.

Cassie pointed to the pile of manila folders stacked in the tray on the far corner of her desk. "Those are the reports."

"That pile doesn't look as big as Zack's."

And he has time to take the day off, Cassie finished for her.

"He writes faster than I do." She had no intention of crashing her friends' family gathering, but Cassie didn't mind continuing their banter. Even though she intended to stand by her refusal, she was actually enjoying herself. She enjoyed arguing with Randi over big issues and small ones. Randi's professional sport days might be over, but the woman was a born competitor.

"Ah," she was saying now, "but it takes Zack longer to figure out what to say."

"And I have to supply forms to fill out. My medical supply rep is coming by first thing in the morning. Your husband tends to get a little testy when he doesn't have the syringes he needs."

Randi shoved aside the folders and perched on the corner of Cassie's desk. "It's not good for you to be here alone on a Sunday afternoon."

Though Randi's concern wasn't necessary, Cassie

was warmed by it. "The last million or so haven't hurt me any."

"That's debatable."

"I'm fine, Randi, really," Cassie said, brushing a lock of red hair away from her face. She usually wore it pinned up or tied back, but since she'd been planning to spend the day alone, she hadn't bothered with her hair. Or her clothes, either. She was wearing jeans she'd owned since high school.

Randi frowned, apparently not satisfied with Cassie's assurances. But then, Randi was stubborn. It was hard for her to accept being wrong. It usually took her a couple of minutes to figure out that she was.

"How'd your meeting with Phyllis go yesterday?" Randi asked, referring to a mutual friend, psychiatrist Phyllis Langford.

"Wonderful," Cassie said. "Even better than I'd expected." Her enthusiasm for the pet therapy project she and Phyllis had discussed infused Cassie's voice. "She gave me some great insights that I'm going to incorporate into my next article. And an idea for a case I worked on back east this winter. A woman who'd lost several babies and was suffering from acute depression. Phyllis thinks a puppy might satisfy her mothering instinct to some extent, perhaps helping her accept adoption as another choice."

Randi scoffed, though Cassie knew full well that during the past months, working with Zack on his nursing-home project, Randi had been won over to the miracles that happened regularly through pet therapy. "You think a puppy who pees everywhere in the house, chews up her shoes and bites at her ankles is going to help the poor woman?"

"Brat's giving you problems, eh?" Cassie grinned. Zack had adopted the dalmatian puppy the week before, when the owner of its mother had despaired of finding the runt of the litter a home. Randi, though, had been the one to name him—Miserable Little Brat, or Brat for short.

"It's Zack's dog," Randi said, rubbing at the leather on her pristine white tennis shoe.

Cassie knew better. She'd been over at Randi and Zack's for pizza a few days earlier and had seen Montford University's seemingly tough women's athletic director cuddling that puppy.

Until Randi had noticed Zack and Cassie looking. Then she'd shooed him away, pretending to scold, while passing him a pepperoni slice under the table by way of apology.

"I don't know why he thought we needed another dog," she muttered. "As if Sammie and Bear aren't trouble enough."

Two of their trained pet therapy dogs, Sammie and Bear weren't any trouble at all. In fact, Zack had told Cassie that on a couple of occasions Randi had made excuses to take Sammie to work with her. Apparently, the dog was quickly becoming the mascot of the women's athletic department.

Cassie had Randi's number. The woman was strong when she needed to be and maintained an effective façade of toughness. But in reality, she was indeed the princess her family had always thought her. Tender, loving, frequently indulged. And kinder than anyone Cassie had ever known. With Zack's encouragement, she'd gotten over her lifelong fear of dogs, and a latent love of animals had begun to emerge.

Although she and Cassie had graduated from Shelter Valley High School the same year, had grown up together in Shelter Valley—population two thousand when the university wasn't in session—the two women had hardly known each other. Cassie had been completely besotted with her one true love, Samuel Montford the fourth, the town's esteemed future mayor and savior of the world. And Randi had been absent a lot of the time, training for her career in professional women's golf.

Neither woman's life had turned out the way she'd planned. They were both back in Shelter Valley, Cassie without Sam, and Randi with a bum rotator cuff that had ruined her swing.

"You'd better get back to your husband, or he's going to be in here looking for you," Cassie told her friend. Cassie knew her partner. Zack had all the patience in the world; he just didn't like to wait.

Randi shook her head. "No, he won't. He said you were going to be pissed if we kept hounding you, so he refused to come in. As a matter of fact, he went to get some gas and wash the Explorer."

Glancing at her watch, Cassie said, "Which means he should be pulling in right about now."

Randi didn't budge. "Other than the few times Zack and I've been able to coerce you over to our place, you've been hiding out in this clinic ever since you heard Sam was coming home," she said bluntly. "You can't keep hiding."

Retrieving another subscription form from a sample issue of the journal, Cassie started to fill it in. "I'm not hiding out. And I can do whatever I damn well please. That's the great thing about being single and living alone."

At least, she told herself that often enough. And it was true. Sort of. She *enjoyed* living alone. She had to. Or live her life without enjoyment.

"It's been three weeks," Randi said. "He's probably not coming back, after all."

"It doesn't matter to me one way or the other," Cassie lied.

"Uh-huh."

"Isn't your family going to be getting mighty hungry?" Cassie asked, still concentrating on the form in front of her.

"Dinner's not until five."

Oh. Great.

"Look," Cassie said, putting down her pen as she met her friend's gaze. "My life with Sam was a long time ago. I'm a different person now, and I'm sure he is, too."

"But that doesn't mean—"

"He killed any feelings I had for him when he went to another woman's bed," Cassie interrupted, before Randi could say anything she might have a hard time denying.

It was taking everything she had to keep her mind on the right track. And her heart from splintering into a million pieces with the force of bitterness and regret.

Randi stood up, headed for the door. "You need to learn how to lie better before you go trying it again," she said, getting the last word. "We'll bring some barbecue by your place later tonight. You'd better be there, or I'll make Zack come here and drag you out."

No question, Randi had won that round.

But Cassie would have her turn. She wasn't going to let anyone get the better of her again. Not her partner's new wife. And not the ex-husband she hadn't heard from in ten long years.

After three weeks of waiting, of constantly looking over her shoulder, of hiding out to avoid the chance of inadvertently running into Sam, Cassie's nerves were a little raw.

But maybe Randi was right. Maybe he wasn't coming, after all. His cryptic note had come three weeks ago. Surely it didn't take that long to get to Shelter Valley, no matter where he'd been.

It was time to get on with her life. She wouldn't give Sam the opportunity to rob her of it again.

Sam. Where had his letter come from, anyway? The postmark had been someplace back east. But the letter had been sitting on James Montford's desk for a day or two before his wife had happened upon it in the middle of a party—a celebration to welcome their long-lost nephew into the fold. She'd gone to the library to check on her guests' sleeping babies, had come through James's office on her way back to the party, and had been reaching for a tissue on his desk, when she'd knocked a pile of unopened mail onto the floor.

She'd recognized her son's handwriting on the envelope with no return address. After ten years, she still recognized Sam's handwriting.

Cassie knew she'd have recognized it, too.

What else about Sam would be recognizable?

No. She shook her head, pulled the stack of files toward her. She wasn't going to spend another minute of her life thinking about something that hadn't been real for a very long time.

He wasn't coming, anyway.

* * *

The clinic was new, built since he'd left town. Not too far off Main Street, it sat on a lot that had been vacant Sam's entire life. With its fresh stucco finish and smoothly paved parking lot, the clinic spoke of success.

It spoke of Cassie.

Leaving his truck parked under the shade of a tree, Sam took Mariah's hand, drawing as much comfort as he gave. Somehow, his having a child made facing Cassie more tolerable. He didn't question that Cassie would have a family; it was all she'd ever wanted. He wondered briefly about the man she must have married—someone he knew?—then dismissed the thought. It occurred to him that in some ways, Mariah's presence put him and Cassie on a more equal footing. They'd both moved on. She wouldn't be the only one who was a parent now. They were both parents... although not of each other's children. He slowly approached the door of the veterinary clinic. It was Monday morning; he wasn't ready for this. Could hardly drag the air through his lungs. But he'd become a man who faced hardships and challenges head-on, and this was one of the biggest.

There were only a couple of cars in the parking lot. He hoped one was Cassie's. And that she'd have a minute or two to spare for him. While he and his parents had spent a miraculous five hours talking the night before—about their lives and his, about Mariah—they'd never mentioned Cassie.

The unspoken message was very clear.

He'd have to clean up this mess on his own. And until he did, his parents weren't going to give him anything where Cassie was concerned. They loved her like their own daughter. Always had.

They were on her side.

Sam couldn't blame them. He'd be on her side, too, if there were any way for a man to be in two places at once.

"We're going to see an old…friend of Daddy's," he told the silent child who'd refused to leave his side in the eighteen hours they'd been in town.

His mother had been enchanted—as Sam had known she would be—with Mariah. Though the little girl was completely unresponsive, at least outwardly, Carol Montford hadn't lost any opportunity to make contact. To touch Mariah's hand. To smile at her, tend to her, stroke her hair. To get some food—any food—into the child's stomach.

His father was already wrapped around Mariah's little finger.

Mariah just didn't know it yet.

She didn't know she'd met her match in those two. They were going to love Mariah back to life. Period. Between him and his parents, she wouldn't have a chance *not* to become the vivacious, happy child she'd once been.

They walked across the parking lot. "Her name is Cassie and she's just about the prettiest woman you've ever seen," Sam said, remembering.

He had to do this, to see her first thing. It wouldn't be fair to either of them to accidentally bump into each other in town. And he hoped that seeing her at work would mean he wouldn't be face to face with her children. Or her husband. At least not yet. Unless it was in the form of a photo on her desk.

It was what he wanted for her, what he'd been imagining all these years. A husband who deserved her love, who cherished her as Sam had promised *he* would. All the children she'd dreamed of raising. It was the only way he could live with himself, believing that without him she'd managed to have everything she wanted. That she was happy.

"She used to be Daddy's best friend, a long time ago."

Mariah walked solemnly beside him, her long black hair in a high ponytail tied with a blue bow that matched the jeans overalls and pink-flowered top he'd chosen for her that morning. Before the disaster that had changed her life so completely, Mariah had insisted on choosing her own outfits every day. And on doing her own hair, as well. She'd looked a little lopsided a time or two—but Sam would trade that for the smile she'd worn any day.

She'd been so proud of herself back then. So sure that life was there just for her. Sure there wasn't anything she couldn't do, couldn't have, if she just got big enough.

She'd been sassy and confident and too smart for her own good.

And she'd chattered from the time she got up in the morning until she'd gone to bed at night, innocently sharing her every thought with anyone lucky enough to be around.

Sam had never tired of listening.

"Cassie is an animal doctor," Sam told Mariah now, as she hesitated outside the door of the clinic. "She's the one who gave Muffy to Grandma and Grandpa."

Muffy hadn't worked the magic on Mariah that

Sam had hoped. The child, having always begged for a dog, had shown no pleasure at finding herself finally living with one.

But then, Muffy was old. And fat.

Sam had been saddened to see such obvious signs of the years he'd lost.

His parents had aged, too, but they still looked great. A little grayer, perhaps, a little more lined, but robust and healthy.

Apparently they walked a couple of miles every morning. And swam every afternoon. They were hoping to take Mariah out to the heated pool in the backyard with them this afternoon.

Sam wasn't sure he could persuade the little girl to let go of his hand long enough to walk into the next room, let alone outside the house. But he was willing to try. If anyone could reach Mariah, his mother could.

"Look, honey." He gently guided Mariah's head in the direction his finger was pointing. "See the plastic fire hydrant? That's for boy doggies to go to the bathroom."

Mariah might have been facing the fake hydrant, but he could see that she was still watching him out of the corner of her eye. Sam wished he knew what kind of expression could reassure the frightened child. A big smile? A calm, neutral look? A devil-may-care grin? He had no idea.

The inside of the clinic was as pristine and plush-looking as the outside. Brightly upholstered chairs lined the walls of the waiting room. At the moment, they were all empty.

There was a fancy digital four-foot scale along one wall. Sam supposed it was for animals. He liked the decor, the bright yellows and oranges, the tile floor that would serve for easy cleanup.

With Mariah by his side, Sam walked up to the waist-high solid oak receptionist's counter.

"Is Cassie in?" he asked, as though he stopped by often. As though he wasn't asking a question he'd been yearning to ask for the past ten years.

"Dr. Tate?" the college-age girl asked. "Yes, she's in her office." She glanced down at the appointment book open in front of her. "Is she expecting you?"

"No," Sam said, glancing down at Mariah's head. "I grew up with her here in Shelter Valley. I'm an old friend, just dropping in to say hello."

"Oh!" The girl's expression changed from professionally polite to warm and friendly. "You're visiting?" she asked, rising to her feet.

Again, Sam glanced at Mariah. "Uh, no," he said. "I'm moving back to town. Just arrived yesterday afternoon."

"Welcome back, then," she said. "My name's Sheila." She grinned. "I've only been in Shelter Valley a couple of years, but I feel like it's been my town forever. I love it here."

The town had a way of doing that to people. Unless you were the "savior of the world," as Cassie had jokingly called Sam. The heir apparent, future mayor and all-around best guy for the job. The man loaded down with everyone else's expectations.

"Hi, Sheila. I'm Sam. You going to Montford?" he asked, years of Shelter Valley friendliness automatically kicking in.

The girl nodded. "I was, but I got married and just recently had a baby. Now I work here full time."

Mariah's little hand was getting sweaty inside his. Releasing it, Sam slid his arm around her shoulders, as he smiled at the receptionist. "She's in her office, you said?"

"Shall I tell her you're here?"

"No," Sam said quickly, and then added, "I'd like to surprise her, if you don't mind."

He didn't want to take the chance that Cassie would refuse to see him.

"Oh. Sure." Sheila grinned at him again. "You just go through that door, and down the hall. Her office is on the right."

"Thanks." Sam led Mariah through the open door. "Is her partner in?" he thought to ask as he passed Sheila. There had been two names on the placard out front.

"Zack?" the girl said. "Not yet. His first appointment today is at eleven."

Wondering if Zack was her husband as well as her partner, Sam braced his shoulders and strode forward. As a Peace Corps member and then a national disaster-relief volunteer, he'd spent the past ten years rescuing people from sickening, tragic situations.

He could handle a ten-minute meeting with his ex-wife.

Chapter 3

No matter how many times Cassie flipped through the pages of her calendar, there were no upcoming trips written in anywhere. She'd traveled so much over the past eighteen months, launching her nationwide pet therapy program in cities and universities across the United States, that Zack had been left to handle much of their Shelter Valley veterinary practice by himself. Her travel schedule was why she'd invited Zack, who'd been working at a practice in Phoenix, to go into partnership with her in Shelter Valley. His first marriage had just ended, and he'd been eager for a new start. And now, two years later, Cassie's wedding present to him and Randi was to stay in town a while.

But damn, a trip sure would be nice. Help her put life in perspective again.

"Hey, stranger."

Planner pages between her fingers, Cassie froze, staring at the month of May. It was coming up in a matter of weeks. She'd be—

"Cassie?"

She hadn't imagined the voice. There was only one man who said her name in just that way. With that slight emphasis on the second syllable.

Heart pounding, Cassie didn't know what to do. Sam was really back. After all this time.

She had to look up. To get through this. Making plans for May seemed so much safer.

Thank God, she was in her office. Private. No one was going to see if she messed up.

Except Sam.

He was standing in front of her desk. She could feel him there. She just couldn't bear to look at him. Couldn't be sure she wouldn't make a total idiot of herself and start to cry.

Sam hated it when she cried. Nearly as much as she did.

There was movement over there, close to Sam, but not really where he was standing. It drew Cassie's eye.

There, with her little hand clasped in a bigger one that could only belong to Cassie's ex-husband, stood a little girl. A very solemn, beautiful, dark-eyed little girl. She appeared to be part Native American.

"We—" Sam raised the child's hand "—Mariah and I just got into town last night. I couldn't be in Shelter Valley without seeing you first thing."

Oddly enough, Cassie understood that. She didn't like it, but she understood. She and Sam would never truly be strangers, or casual acquaintances who just had chance meetings on the street.

"You could have called first," she said, her eyes riveted on the child. His daughter? *His* daughter?

Pain knifed through Cassie, so sharp she couldn't breathe. When he'd left her all those years ago, he'd taken from her any hope that she might have children of her own. Taken away any hope of the family and the life she'd wanted. And now he had the nerve to waltz back into town with a child who should have been theirs.

"I was afraid you wouldn't see me," he murmured.

"You were probably right."

Was the child his? With her obvious coloring and that coal-black hair, the girl didn't look anything like him. Yet her white heritage was noticeable in those striking blue eyes.

Sam had green eyes.

"This is Mariah," Sam said, sounding less sure of himself as she continued to watch the silent little girl. "She's my daughter."

The knife sliced a second time. Lips trembling, Cassie nodded. And tried to smile at the child. After all, it wasn't Mariah's fault her father had hurt Cassie so badly.

"Hello, Mariah."

The little girl stared wordlessly at her father's waistline. Which, now that Cassie noticed it, looked as firm and solid as it always had. Clearly, Sam was still in remarkably good shape.

"You're looking great, Cass," Sam said, an old familiar warmth enlivening the words.

"Thanks." Taking a deep, shuddering breath, Cassie forced herself to look up, to meet Sam's gaze.

And then looked away again almost immediately.

His eyes were exactly the same. They met hers—and touched her all the way inside.

Without waiting for an invitation, Sam sat in one of the leather chairs facing her desk, pulling Mariah onto his lap.

"How old is she?" she asked. Morbid curiosity.

"Seven."

Cassie's daughter would have been ten this year.

"So how've you been, Cass?" Sam asked, glancing around her office at the degrees on the wall behind her, the thick texts lining her shelves. "You've accomplished a lot."

Cassie stared at the little television in the corner. Wishing she hadn't turned it off after the news ended half an hour ago. It would have given her something to focus on. Taken her thoughts off the bitter pain that had already seized her.

Off the man in front of her.

"Your parents told you about the pet therapy program, I imagine," she said. It was the sum total of her life's accomplishments. Had they told him that, as well?

If this was just a guilt-induced duty call, he could leave now. She didn't need his polite compliments. Or his pity.

The flood of anger felt good.

"They haven't mentioned you at all," he said quietly. "I don't know the first thing about a pet therapy program. I'm just impressed with this office, the clinic, your degrees."

Cassie shrugged. "I imagine you went on to greater things. You're probably a lawyer by now."

Not that she cared. She just figured he'd finished

college and pursued postgraduate work. Entered some highly regarded profession. Sam had been the more intelligent of the two of them. He hadn't particularly liked to hit the books, hadn't enjoyed learning as much as she had, but it had all come so naturally to him. Even in high school he could ace a test with a five-minute look over his notes, while Cassie would study for an entire evening to get the same grade.

"I don't even have a bachelor's degree."

Shocked, Cassie frowned at him. His hair was longer, his face lined with experiences she knew nothing about. "Why not?"

"I never went back to school after I left here." There was no apology in the words. No excuse, either.

"But you had a perfect grade point, a future..."

"...that I didn't want," Sam finished for her, his jaw firm. Then he smiled, which instantly softened his face. It was as though he'd learned to control the emotions that had once flowed so freely.

When they were young, Sam had been the most passionate man she'd known. Passionate about everything, from kissing her to saving an abandoned dog on the outskirts of town. She'd loved that about him.

"So what's this pet therapy business?" he asked. "Analyzing neurotic poodles?" He grinned in an obvious attempt to lighten the atmosphere, but his expression sobered when she didn't respond. "Seriously," he muttered. "Tell me."

Mariah's arm slid up around Sam's neck, and she laid her head against his chest.

She was too skinny. And quieter than any child Cassie had ever seen. It almost seemed as though something was wrong with her. Her stomach seized at the thought. The little girl was so beautiful.

She couldn't imagine Sam with a handicapped child. Everything had always come easy to him. Perfection had been his for the taking.

"I, uh, developed a bit of a name for myself by using animals as a way to treat mentally, and sometimes physically, ill patients," she said slowly, her attention on Sam's little girl.

There was something heart-wrenching about her. Something pathetic in seeing her tucked so securely in Sam's arms.

Sam. She couldn't believe he was here. Sitting in her office. *Damn him.*

Her life wasn't ever going to be the same again, with Sam back in town. The memories, the reminders—they'd all be right in front of her. Mocking her. He'd just shot her carefully won peace all to hell.

Sam asked a few more questions—intelligent, thoughtful questions—about pet therapy, which Cassie managed to answer. Somehow, with him sitting there, work wasn't the first thing on her mind. It was an odd sensation.

A very unwelcome one.

Sam didn't know what he'd been expecting to find that morning, but the woman sitting across from him wasn't it. Her beauty was still as potent, her figure perfect, her hair still that glorious red. But despite all the similarities, he could hardly believe how much ten years had changed her. Was it just growing up that had made her so self-composed? So unemotional?

Or was it only with him that she was this way?

The thought sickened him. Saddened him. He'd carried the image of his vivacious and tender ex-wife with him every day of the past ten years, used it as a sword to punish himself—and as a reminder of the penance he owed.

"So who'd you end up marrying?" he asked now, forcing himself to confront reality, to see the woman Cassie had become, to not linger on memories of the days when he'd known her as well as she'd known herself. "You are married, right?"

Cassie shook her head, and Sam froze.

"You aren't married?" he asked, his shock more evident than he would have liked. She *had* to be married. It was all Cassie had ever wanted. Marriage and a family.

"There are a lot of successful single women these days," she said, her tone tinged with sharpness. "I would never have been able to accomplish everything I have if I was married. I've spent the past couple of years traveling all over the country, setting up pet therapy programs in universities and in hundreds of mental-health facilities."

Sam stared at her, not understanding. "But you wanted to be a wife and mother more than anything in the world," he said.

He hadn't been wrong about that. Had he?

Cassie's gaze slid away from him, her shoulders stiffening. "People change, Sam."

Mariah's fingers dug into Sam's neck; he rubbed her back reassuringly.

"You never had children?" He just couldn't take it in. Didn't want to. Didn't want to believe he'd had anything to do with her decision. It was one of the reasons he'd left town and never come back. So that Cassie could get on with her life.

Or that was what he'd always told himself. He'd assumed, without question, that she'd meet someone, marry, have kids. He thought briefly of his syndicated comic strip—another secret. The origins of the Borough Bantam were unknown to the people of Shelter Valley and yet it was based on them. Cassie was the gazelle. And in one of last month's episodes, the gazelle had given birth to twins.

"I don't have any children," she said, then stood as though dismissing him. "I'm happy your parents finally have you back, Sam," she said, then added, "You always were the light of their life."

Another too-familiar stab of guilt hit its mark. Sam also stood, sliding Mariah down to the floor beside him. The child's eyes were pleading when he looked down at her. She was ready to go. Now.

Odd. He hadn't realized that he was learning to communicate with her, to understand her, even without words. The thought brought a strange sort of comfort.

"I guess I'll be seeing you around," he said, guiding Mariah back into the hallway. He needed to tell Cassie about Mariah. And he would, as soon as he had a chance to talk to her alone. He needed to tell her the child wasn't his. Or not biologically, in any case.

Cassie had never married. God, he felt sick. And ashamed. A bone-deep shame.

"Okay" was all she said. So why did he hear, *Not if I can help it?*

After ten years, she still hated him so much. He deserved it; he knew that. Why had he been foolish enough to hope that the years might have dulled the consequences of his sins?

Mariah walked stoically beside him down the hall, which seemed to have grown a mile longer during his stay in Cassie's office, and he realized that if he was going to get through this, he had to concentrate solely on his new daughter—her needs, not his own. Just as they reached the door that would lead them back to the waiting room, she turned, looking over her shoulder.

"Cassie's a nice lady, don't you think?" he asked gently, his heart rate speeding up.

Mariah didn't answer him, but for the first time since her parents were killed, she'd shown an interest in something. It might not be much, but it was a start.

At that moment, Sam was willing to settle for anything.

"Let's go see if Grandma has lunch ready, okay?" he asked, squeezing Mariah's hand.

He might as well have been talking to himself.

Cassie didn't see Sam again for two days. She was walking home from the clinic on Wednesday evening—since she'd left her car at home that morning—enjoying the balmy Arizona spring day, trying to work up some enthusiasm for the cabbage rolls she'd made over the weekend and was going to have for dinner.

She'd had a good day. Had helped a collie through a difficult birth, managing to save all six puppies and the mother, as well. They'd been so adorable, she hadn't been able to resist when the collie's owner had offered Cassie pick of the litter. Now that she wasn't going to be traveling so much, she'd been planning to get a dog. And she'd always loved collies.

"Can we give you a ride home?"

Still reacting to that familiar voice, even after all these years, Cassie didn't stop walking. "No, thanks," she called, barely glancing Sam's way.

He drove a white truck.

She'd have expected him to drive a Lincoln Continental, or some other expensive car. But the truck seemed to suit him. Not that she really knew anything about Sam, or what would suit him. Nor did she want to.

Back to cabbage rolls. Yes, they'd be good. She'd treat herself to two. That would leave two more meals' worth in the freezer. It was a good thing they'd only take a few minutes to microwave. She was getting hungry and—

"I have a cousin."

Sam came up behind her, on foot, Mariah's bony little legs moving quickly beside him. Glancing back, Cassie saw his truck parked at the curb.

What did he want with her, for God's sake?

"I know you do," she said aloud. She realized that the news had to be a shock. When he'd left, he was the sole Montford descendant, the family's one hope. Now he'd come home to discover that an unknown cousin had shown up.

"You've met him?"

"No."

Mariah's hair was braided today. Cassie could just picture Carol fussing over the little girl. Her ex-mother-in-law must be about the happiest woman in Shelter Valley these days.

Cassie was genuinely thrilled for Carol. She'd always loved the woman like a second mother.

Her own mother didn't even know Sam was in town. Her parents had left at the end of March for the six-month cruise around the world that they'd been saving half their lives to take. Cassie was glad they were gone. She had no idea how they'd react to Sam's reappearance. Her father, who'd had four daughters and no sons, had taken Sam's defection personally.

He'd also been the one who had to tell Cassie that her baby girl had died.

"What's he like?" Sam asked, slowing his pace now that he was even with her. Mariah walked between them, staring ahead, it seemed, at nothing. "Ben, I mean. My cousin."

Watching the child, Cassie frowned. "He's very nice," she said, wondering what was wrong with Sam's daughter. Wondering how to ask. "He came to town last fall, fell in love with his English teacher—who wasn't really a teacher at all, it turned out." She gave a quick shrug. "It's a long story. They're married now."

"Mom said he's got a daughter Mariah's age."

Cassie nodded, wishing her house wasn't still two streets away. She couldn't do this. Walk casually with Sam and the child who'd never be hers, pretending they could be friends. "She's not actually his, biologically. Did your mom tell you that?"

"Yeah." Sam nodded, his free hand in the pocket of his jean-shorts. His long legs were more muscled than she remembered. "She said he married a girl his senior year in high school who claimed he was the father of her child."

"She let him support her for almost eight years before she told him Alex belonged to her boyfriend, who was in prison."

"Mom said that Ben's being awarded full and permanent custody of her, though."

"Her real father beat—" Glancing down at the head bobbing between them, Cassie broke off. "He wasn't a very good father."

"I gather Ben is."

"Obviously you haven't met him yet," Cassie said, "or you'd *know* he was."

Sam nodded again. "You're right, I haven't met him, but Mom's pushing for a get-together."

"Ben's a great guy. Looks a bit like you." In fact he resembled Sam enough that Cassie had had a hard time liking the man when she'd first met him. But he was Zack's closest friend. Nowadays Cassie not only liked and respected him, she admired the hell out of him. Ben Sanders was a real man in the true sense of the word.

Too bad Sam didn't share those particular genes.... Cassie stopped her reaction even as it took shape. She wasn't going to do this. She wasn't going to grow old and hard with bitterness, entertaining nasty thoughts. She was okay now. Happy with her life. Surrounded by friends and family who loved her.

"Just seems odd, after a lifetime of being the only Montford heir, to find out that I'm not."

"It's not like your inheritance meant a whole lot to you the past ten years." Damn her tongue. She turned the corner, Sam and Mariah staying in step beside her.

"It doesn't mean squat to me."

He'd certainly said so with great frequency. But until he'd left, turning his back on the money, the position, the town, she'd never really thought he believed it. She'd always thought the complaints were just a habit left over from when he was a kid, railing against expectations.

Everyone did that. Complained about what their parents expected of them. It was a normal part of growing up.

"Then what's the problem with sharing it?" she asked him now, thinking how little Sam appeared to need the Montford fortune, and how much Ben and his new family did.

"He can have it all," Sam said without bitterness, as though he still meant the words completely. "It just feels odd to have been one thing your entire life, only to find that it's not what you are at all."

Cassie nodded, glancing down as Mariah's arm brushed against her leg. The child, moving silently between them, didn't seem to notice.

Relieved when they reached her block, Cassie firmly turned her thoughts once again to cabbage rolls. They'd smelled so good when they were baking on Saturday night.

"This is it," she said, stopping at the bottom of her driveway. If he expected her to ask him in, he was mistaken.

Sam hesitated, looking at the house she'd bought a few years before, in one of the more affluent neighborhoods in Shelter Valley.

"Nice place."

"I like it."

"It's big."

"Yeah." She did most of her pet therapy work from an office here at home. And used the rest of the rooms to indulge her amateur interest in interior decorating.

Cassie was beginning to think Sam's daughter

couldn't hear. The child didn't even turn toward the house they were discussing. Cassie had heard the adage about children being seen and not heard, but this was too much.

Besides, she'd never figured Sam for that kind of parent.

A familiar pain tore through her at the thought of Sam as a father. She had to stay away from this man, dammit! He could destroy every bit of her hard-won composure, and his very presence threatened the contentment she'd so carefully pieced together.

The child, however, shouldn't suffer for her father's sins. Her silence tugged at Cassie. Bending down, face level with the striking little girl, Cassie smiled. "It was nice to see you again, Mariah."

Mariah didn't respond. And Sam gave no explanation. Surely if the child was deaf, Sam would have said. And how could she ask, in case the little girl *could* hear and know they were talking about her?

"Have you had any of your grandma's cookies yet?" she tried again.

Neither a nod nor a shake of the head. Mariah's gaze seemed intent on the T-shirt tucked into Sam's shorts. Her fingers were clutching it. Hard.

Meeting Cassie's questioning gaze, Sam just shook his head.

"Well, if you haven't, you've got a treat in store," Cassie continued, simply because she didn't know what else to do. "They're the best."

"I told her."

Of course. He would have. He'd grown up with them.

They both had.

"Well, good night," Cassie said awkwardly.

"'Night."

She didn't look back as she walked to her door, let herself in and locked it behind her.

But she knew Sam stood there watching her.

Chapter 4

Mariah didn't want to go back to that house. Sam was driving up the hill, so she knew they were going back there. She didn't want to. She didn't belong there.

Sam's house was for happy kids who didn't know bad stuff. And grandmas were for happy kids, too. Mariah wasn't like that anymore. She'd cried, made too much noise when the bad men came. That was why they'd killed her mommy.

Sam's mouth was all tight, except when he seemed to remember that Mariah was looking at him. Then he smiled a good Sam smile.

She used to think Sam's smiles made her feel happy. Now she didn't care whether he smiled or not. Smiles couldn't really do anything. They couldn't stop bad stuff. They couldn't save you from the horrible men.

Sam didn't have to smile. He just had to stay breathing. Mostly that was what she watched. To make sure he was always breathing.

Mommy had been still holding Mariah's hand but she hadn't been breathing—and the men had made Mariah let go of her. That was when they said Mommy wasn't coming back. But Mommy hadn't gone anywhere, she'd been right there with Mariah the whole time—so how could she come back, anyway?

Daddy had gone away with them after they hit him so many times and made his face bleed. When Mariah cried out for him, they yelled back at her and told her to shut up. If she made a sound, they were going to hurt Mommy. They said Daddy wasn't ever coming back, either. Sam said he'd stopped breathing, too. She hadn't known that about breathing before.

Daddy was put into a hole in the ground—

"You hungry, honey?"

Sam smiled at her now. Mariah didn't get hungry anymore. She just got tired from watching Sam's breathing.

Breathing stopped, and then some men shoved you into a hole in the ground. But first, sometimes, they cut you and made you bleed so much that a Band-Aid didn't work.

They scared you and did other things Mariah couldn't think about.

So she just thought about breathing. If she stopped breathing, they'd shove her in a hole, too.

Sam's pencil slid easily around the page, making a mark here, another there, until the familiar figures began to take shape. After so many years of drawing this cartoon strip, he was seeing it differently tonight.

He was on overload with the past four days of memory and stimulation.

Borough Bantam. Sam's imaginary world was filled with non-human life, of the animal variety, mostly—each creature representative to Sam of the people he'd known all his life in Shelter Valley. There was the king—a grizzly bear—his father. His mother, the queen, a gentle brown bear. Will Parsons was a lion. His wife, Becca, Sam's readers knew as a book-reading lioness. There was Nancy Garland, a girl they'd known in high school; she was a gopher. Sam's parents had told him she was still in town, hostessing at the Valley Diner. Jim Weber, owner of Weber's Department Store, was a penguin. Hank Harmon was the big friendly skunk everyone in the Borough loved, in spite of his smell. Chuck Taylor was a leopard. And on and on...

Cassie was the gazelle. Graceful. Lovely. And unattainable.

He still hadn't found a moment away from Mariah—a chance to see Cassie alone. Although the more he thought about the whole damn mess, the more he wondered whether it would make a difference to her whether or not Mariah was his biological daughter. She was still his daughter. He had a child to raise, while Cassie did not.

And yet he couldn't understand why Cassie had made that choice—to remain unmarried and childless. Nor could he stomach the irrational fear that he was at least partially to blame.

Mariah was finally asleep; Sam had put her in the bed across from the desk at which he sat. His parents had given him a guest suite, as it had two beds and plenty of room for him and Mariah.

Sam hoped that it wouldn't be too long before Mariah hankered after the princess room down the hall. Its lacy white canopy, yellow walls, and pictures of tea parties were enough to tempt any little girl. Weren't they? As a teenager, Cassie had always loved his mother's fanciful guest room. The couple of times her family had been out of town and she'd stayed with them, she'd chosen that room. It had been updated since he left town—with new paint, different pictures, some fancy ladies' hats on a rack—but his impression was the same. He still felt like a clumsy oaf in ten-pound mountain boots whenever he walked in the door.

Characters appeared on the page in front of Sam, seemingly of their own accord. The pencil moved swiftly, filling in thought bubbles almost faster then he could think them....

The castle was in chaos. There was a stranger in their midst, a wild stallion. He claimed to know them. The king and queen had offered their usual warm-hearted welcome. Always trusting. Seeing good in the visitor although his heart might harbor unclean things.

The half-witted magistrate, so full of his own importance, didn't know that Borough Bantam had been invaded yet. Sam grinned as the rotund little worm slithered around his circle, certain that he was circling the world. That he controlled the entire globe. His bubble was easiest of all to fill. *I am. I am. I am.*

It was rumored that the newcomer—the stallion—posed a threat to the magistrate. The worm—Sam's version of Shelter Valley's mayor, Junior Smith.

Ten years older than Sam, Junior had just become mayor when Sam's father retired. That was the year before Sam left town. James Montford had suffered a bout of Crohn's Disease and needed to lower his stress level; as a result he'd stepped down from the mayoralty. That was when Sam really started to feel the pressure to run for mayor. The fact that he would win was a foregone conclusion. The office of mayor was of course an elected position, but politics in Shelter Valley had more to do with tradition than democracy. The town's mayor had almost always been a Montford—although, occasionally, a member of the less-reputable Smith branch of the family held office.

The newcomer sat off by himself, watching the confusion, detached. He couldn't care less about the worm. He was waiting. Though he didn't know for what. The plan would be made known to him in due time. He just had to be patient.

Sighing, Sam scribbled the finishing touch, the signature of Bantam's creator, *S.N.C.*, and dropped his pencil. Then he tore off the piece of drawing paper, folding it carefully and sealing it in an envelope for mailing in the morning—on time to meet his deadline. He methodically put all evidence of the work he'd been doing in the battered satchel, which he placed back on the closet shelf. Patience was the lesson of the week—for the comic strip's new character *and* for him.

Sam needed to find a truckload of it somewhere.

On Thursday night, Cassie was getting ready for bed with the eleven o'clock news playing in the background—from the console television in her bedroom, the little portable in her luxurious ensuite bathroom and the nineteen-inch set out in her kitchen—when the doorbell rang.

Assuming the caller was a patient with an emergency, she quickly spit out her toothpaste, wiped her mouth and pulled a pair of jeans on over her nightgown. Grabbing from the hamper the black, short-sleeved cotton shirt she'd worn to work that day, she drew it over her head while she made her way to the front of the house. It never occurred to her to be alarmed, to think anything dangerous might be waiting on her porch. This was Shelter Valley. A lot of people didn't even lock their doors at night.

She opened the door, and when she saw who was standing there with his hands in the pockets of his jeans, her heart started to pound so hard she actually felt sick.

"Why are you here?" she asked. It was too late to go back, to return to the lives they'd once lived. And for her and Sam, there was no going forward.

He shrugged, the dark strands of his hair almost touching the shoulders of his white shirt. His eyes glistened beneath the porch light. "I'm a little lost here, Cass," he said, giving her a glimpse of the past—a glimpse of who they used to be. Two people who told each other everything.

She couldn't do that anymore, could no longer be that person. Her hold on happiness was too fragile. Too tenuous.

"Perhaps you should go back where you came from, then," she said, trying not to cry as she rejected the intimacy he was offering.

"I belong here."

"Since when?"

He looked down at his tennis shoes and then back up at her. "Can I come in?" he asked softly.

"No!" There was nothing for them. No point. She'd built a life for herself inside this house—a house in which there was not one bit of evidence that Sam Montford had ever existed.

"Please, Cass," he said, his eyes begging her. "You know if we keep standing out here, everyone'll have us married again by morning."

"Which is why you need to leave. Now."

"I can't."

"Sure you can."

"I find myself needing a friend tonight, Cass. And you're the best friend I ever had in this town."

Why tonight in particular? Why did he need a friend now?

"Then why don't you go back where you and Mariah came from? You obviously have friends there." God, she hated what he was doing to her. How she was acting around him. But if she didn't get defensive, she'd crumble into little pieces at his feet.

She'd needed him so badly for so many years. And had broken down when she'd lost him. She'd learned that *breakdown* was not an exaggerated or metaphorical description. It was exactly what had happened. And it had taken a lot of years to rebuild herself, to repair all the damage. She just couldn't afford to allow Sam Montford to enter her life again.

"There's nobody back there. I'm all Mariah's got. Her family was killed six months ago," he said, and then rushed on as though he knew his time with her was limited. "Mariah saw the whole thing, Cassie, and I'm losing her."

Sagging against the big oak door, Cassie slowly pulled it back, gesturing Sam inside.

Not for him. Never again for him. But for that sweet child with the haunted eyes.

"Where is she now?" Cassie asked, leading Sam from the homey comfort of her living room in to the library she'd decorated with impeccable formality and never used. She took one of the leather chairs; Sam slouched down in the other.

"She's asleep," Sam said. "Thankfully, once I get her to give in and go to sleep, she usually stays that way. She used to have a lot of nightmares, but they've decreased in the past month or so. My mother's sitting with her."

Cassie sat forward, already preparing to kick him out. "Carol knows you're here?"

"No." He shook his head. "I told her I was going out for some air. She encouraged me to take an hour or two for myself." That sounded like Carol Montford. Tending to her family made her happy. And she'd had so few opportunities in the past ten years. There'd only been her husband, James, who needed little—and Cassie.

Sam grinned suddenly, shocking her with the intensity of the effect that smile had on her. "She warned me not to drink and drive."

In the grip of remembered companionship, Cassie said, "As if you ever would." Sam had always been responsible about stuff like that.

About everything.

Except fidelity.

"Is Mariah deaf?" she blurted out, nervous, needing to get him out of her house.

Eyes clouded, Sam shook his head. "No." And then, looking around, said, "You don't have a dog?"

Cassie's toes were cold. She pulled her feet up on the chair, covered them with her hands.

"I've been traveling more than I've been home during the past couple of years," she said. "It wouldn't have been fair to have a pet and then desert it so often, but I did recently acquire a collie puppy. I'm waiting for her to be weaned from her mother before I bring her home."

Why did it matter that he know this? That he not think her lacking—cold and immune to the animals she'd dedicated her life to assisting?

"I can't believe how fat Muffy is."

"You need to convince your parents to put her on a diet, Sam. She almost died a few months ago."

They shared a concerned look. Muffy was special to both of them. They'd picked her out together as a comfort to Sam's mother, who'd been so sad after Sam moved out.

"Her food was cut in half as of yesterday."

That reminded her of Sam, the old Sam. See a need, take charge, make it better.

Or at least try....

"Why doesn't Mariah speak?" she asked, focusing somewhere just to the right of his chin. There could be no more meeting of the eyes. Sam's looks touched her in ways she could no longer welcome. "Does she talk to you? Is it just strangers she's so shy with?"

Frowning, Sam lifted his hands, then let them drop back to his knees. "She hasn't said a word in six months. To me or anyone."

"You said her family died. What happened? A car

accident?" The tragedy sure explained some of the sadness she saw in Sam's eyes. The sadness reached out to her in ways she wanted to resist.

"They didn't just die—they were murdered by a band of terrorist thugs hijacking the airplane Moira and her husband, Brian, and Mariah were on." He shook his head. "They were the only family Mariah had, and my closest friends."

Cassie swallowed, her throat suddenly dry. *Mariah's mother had a husband.* "Where were they?"

"It was a small jumper plane leaving Afghanistan. The Glorys were the only Americans on board. The terrorists were part of an extremist group fighting for recognition."

Cassie remembered with horror the reports she'd seen on the news. "Out of forty people on the plane, only ten survived," she continued slowly, her heart heavy as she watched the despair on Sam's face. "Six women, three men—and an American child…" Her voice trailed off. Mariah. "At least those terrorists were caught," she said, the thought bringing little comfort.

Sam clenched his jaw, and his hands tightened into fists. "It was all over the news—another terrorist incident. Mom and Dad heard about it in Germany, but they had no idea, of course, that the tragedy had anything to do with me."

"You weren't with them?"

Sam shook his head, eyes dulled and faraway. Cassie had all but forgotten that she wasn't going to look into his face anymore.

"I was in New Jersey. I'd been there a couple of years, working with a guy who's restoring old houses. I came home from work one day to a call from an attorney in Delaware—which is where the Glorys lived when they weren't on assignment somewhere in the Third World. Their will named me Mariah's legal guardian."

"You didn't know that?" Cassie was confused. Apparently, he hadn't been able to make a go of marriage with this Moira, either. It must have complicated things when she'd married his good friend—not that Cassie wanted to hear anything about that. But wouldn't he, as Mariah's natural father, *expect* to have custody of her in the event her mother could no longer care for the child?

Sam nodded. "I knew," he said hoarsely. "I just didn't think there'd ever be a need...."

His voice broke off, and he lowered his chin as though holding back deep emotion. He'd loved the woman so much?

Another stab of pain left Cassie feeling weak and tired.

"When I got to Afghanistan to collect Mariah, she was this silent huddle with big frightened eyes." He paused. "Immediately after the funeral, I moved into the Glorys' home and began adoption proceedings. I tried to make her life as normal as possible, surrounding her with familiar things, but she hasn't responded very much. She's been in counseling since the beginning, but there's only so much medical science can do. She's suffering emotional pain, not some kind of chemical imbalance they can medicate. There is no diagnosis of a disease. There are always medications, of course, but some things you have to come out of naturally, on your own. Mariah has to *want* to return to us."

"So she hasn't spoken at all?"

"Not a word."

"Not even when she saw you?"

Sam shook his head.

"It's obvious she adores you."

"We've always been close," Sam said softly, almost apologetically, as his eyes met Cassie's. "Without you, she was my only shot at having a child in my life."

Cassie ignored the first part of that statement. "You and her mother split before she was born?"

"Her mother and I were never together," he said, his expression gentle. "At least, not in any child-making sense. Mariah's not my biological daughter, Cass."

The breath slowly left Cassie's lungs. She felt dizzy, light-headed. But not relieved. Whether or not Sam had had sex with Mariah's mother made no difference to her; he'd certainly had sex with other women.

At least one while he and Cassie were married.

Because she didn't know what else to do, Cassie sat and listened while Sam told her about his best friends, the Glorys. All three of them—Brian, who was full-blooded Chippewa, Moira, a Peace Corps brat, and Sam—had met when they'd been leaving for a two-year stint overseas as Peace Corps volunteers.

Mariah's name came from a song she'd always loved. It referred to the wind. Sam said Mariah blew into their lives unexpectedly, but that she was vital to the very air they breathed.

While Cassie had been mourning their lost child, fighting to recover her life, Sam had been overseas making friends and helping other people, instead of caring for the wife he'd promised to love, honor and cherish. He'd been taking part in raising another child.

She'd have to tell him about that someday. When she was ready. When she felt she could get through the telling without falling apart. Emily's premature birth—and subsequent death a month later—wasn't something she spoke about. Ever. Even after all this time, the wounds were too raw. And it wasn't as though she owed Sam an explanation. He'd lost all rights to Emily when he'd deserted them.

Although she knew Sam wasn't responsible for the death of their child, any more than she was, she couldn't stop believing that if only he'd been there...

Yet, no matter how frozen her heart felt at this moment, Cassie was still glad to hear that he'd been doing something worthwhile during those years. Glad to know that, while he hadn't been there for his own child, little Mariah had been able to count on him.

Cassie had always figured he'd been enjoying the beds of coeds, like the girl he'd been with the night he should have been home with Cassie. Despite everything, she felt somehow consoled that this wasn't the case.

"We were pretty much the only family any of us had," Sam said, obviously lost in time. Cassie hated the stab of jealousy she felt as she heard the affection in Sam's voice for these unknown people.

She'd never been petty. Or possessive. She sure as hell wasn't going to start now. Sam was nothing to her. Less than nothing.

He'd betrayed her trust. Nothing was going to change that. Ever.

She might someday be able to forgive him. Had been aiming toward that goal for the past several years. But even if the day came when she could be truly free of the pain he'd caused her, the trust was gone. Once trust was broken, it couldn't be restored. It simply ceased to exist. How could you believe in someone you couldn't believe?

"Moira's parents were still alive back then, though they're both gone now." He shook his head grimly. "I'm glad they weren't around to know what happened to their daughter. They died of a viral infection in Africa, within a week of each other. Even when they were alive, they were always in service somewhere obscure. She saw them once a year if she was lucky. And Brian was an orphan."

Sam didn't bother to explain about his own aloneness. Perhaps there wasn't any point.

He gave a sudden laugh, and Cassie sensed sadness there as well as mirth. "I was the one who proposed," he said.

"To Moira, you mean?" So he and Brian had both been in love with the woman?

"No." He steepled his fingers in front of his chest. "They were such blind fools. Even after they were expecting Mariah, they couldn't figure out that they were crazy about each other. I had to point out the obvious and then drag them off to Atlantic City to tie the knot before they could talk themselves out of it."

Cassie had never had a friendship that close. Not since Sam. She envied him.

She had Zack, though. And Randi now, too. Zack had pulled her through some rough times in those first days after she'd made the decision to get on with her life and reenter college. At Arizona State, not Montford University. There was no way she could have gone back to Montford.

"When Mariah was born, I had to do most of the coaching because poor Brian was so scared seeing Moira in pain, it made him sick."

Sam had witnessed a birth, had coached an-other woman through those hours of pain. Another woman... This was why she couldn't be with him, why she couldn't spend any more time with him. Ev-erything he said hurt too much.

"Tell me about Mariah," she said now, needing to get him back to the only thing that could matter.

Her life's work involved helping emotionally dev-astated people. And she hadn't been able to get that little girl out of her mind. Couldn't bear to have the child living so close, to run the risk of running into her over and over, without finding out if there was something she could do to help.

She wasn't interested for Sam's sake. Never for Sam. But because this was what Cassie did. What made her feel good about herself. What gave her a reason to get up in the morning.

Sam sat forward, his hands hanging helplessly. "Only she could tell us what's on her mind at this point. There were reports of the things that happened during the twelve hours the plane was held captive, but they varied depending on who was talking, where they were sitting. Every report was clouded by the witness's own terror. Not a lot of people noticed the mother and little girl sitting in the back of the plane—"

He paused, then continued. "Brian was beaten up pretty badly—we do know that. Used as an example, the reports said. We're guessing because he was an American. And because he tried to protect his family."

"And Mariah saw that? Saw him...hurt?"

"Who knows?" His eyes met hers, his agony evident. "I'm assuming she probably did. The plane wasn't that big."

"And Moira?"

"They slit her throat."

"Oh, God."

Feeling sick to her stomach, Cassie leaned forward, her elbows on her knees. "In front of the child?"

"We think so. Apparently, Mariah kept crying for a Band-Aid. No one else knew that Moira had been hurt at that point."

"And you said you've had Mariah in counseling."

"Of course. And we've been referred to someone in Phoenix who comes very highly recommended, but at this point, the doctors say that what she needs most is time. And to be surrounded by safety and love."

"She'll get plenty of that in Shelter Valley."

"That's why we're here."

Not for Sam, but for Mariah. He hadn't come back for his own reasons. For his parents or his town—or Cassie.

"I sure could use your help, Cass."

She'd already anticipated his request. "We'll start with Zack's dog, Sammie," she said, her mind hard at work. "But I think it'll probably be best to get her a puppy of her own, one who can be with her permanently. And I'd like to call Phyllis Langford in to help, too. She's a new psychology professor at the U. She's incredibly gifted when it comes to working with damaged emotions—"

Sam stood, grabbed Cassie's hand, pulled her up. "I meant, I could use a friend."

"No." Snatching her hand away, Cassie slipped behind the chair, her hands clutching the back of it.

"I'm not asking for anything else, Cass. Just a friend, someone to talk to."

"We are not, nor can we ever be, friends."

Nodding, Sam headed for the front door.

"Sam?"

"Yeah?" He turned, waiting.

"I'd like to try to help Mariah. Pet therapy might work."

"You don't have to do this for me. Like I said, the woman in Phoenix comes very highly recommended."

"It's not for you, Sam. It's for her." And it was. Almost completely. "We've seen some amazing results in cases like this, where people have been traumatized by other people. Rape victims. Severe spousal abuse. Instances where trust has been irrevocably broken. In such cases, counseling alone doesn't often help, since it's impossible for the patient to trust anyone, including the therapist. But we've found that sometimes these patients can trust an animal, and once trust is reborn, they slowly learn to have faith in people again, too." She paused. "Some people, anyway."

Rubbing his chin, Sam said, "I've never heard of a vet doing counseling before. I'm impressed."

"My undergraduate degree was in counseling," Cassie told him. "I'm fully certified. And I work very closely with a team of psychiatrists from around the country."

"I'm more than impressed." He was proud of her. She could see it in his eyes. Cassie looked away.

"Pet therapy might help Mariah," she said. "What could it hurt to try?"

"Nothing," he answered, his hand on the doorknob. "I'm willing to try anything if it could bring that little girl back to me."

"And back to herself," she whispered.

She saw the agony on his face, and her heart ached for him, this man who'd once been so honorable. Who was now just lonely. And alone.

"I'll talk to Zack and Phyllis, and someone will give you a call."

Sam stared at her for longer than she could handle, and when she glanced away, said, "Thanks, Cass, I owe you" very softly. And let himself out.

He was gone.

She'd survived.

Maybe.

Chapter 5

Following his patient out of the examination room, a chart in his hand, Zack Foster grinned. He'd just had the pleasure of telling Shelby's owners that their six-year-old German shepherd was going to be a mother again. They'd been trying for a couple of years.

"Just make sure she's not out in the heat too much," he reminded the man and woman who were taking turns petting Shelby and telling her she was a good dog. Zack hoped Shelby was as happy about the upcoming event as her family was.

"We will, Doctor, thanks."

In her own doggy way, Shelby looked happy. In each of her previous two litters, she'd produced seven puppies, several of them now show-ring champions. She'd mothered them possessively and tenderly.

And speaking of mothers... Zack thought of Randi

and what a great mother she'd be. They'd talked about
having a baby but hadn't decided on timing.

Zack was already in his thirties, and though he'd
been in Shelter Valley for only two years, he'd already
fallen into the town's family-oriented outlook—the
larger the better, as far as families went.

Maybe he'd bring the idea up with Randi tonight. A
romantic evening... He'd buy her a gift—a new pair
of white tennis shoes to go with the twenty other pairs
she'd lined up on her half of the closet floor. Maybe a
sweatband or two, soften her up a bit. He grinned as
he planned his seductive persuasion. Dinner in Phoenix and then—

"Zack?" Cassie called out to him from her office.
She wasn't due in until this afternoon. She was supposed to be home catching up on her sleep. Taking
care of herself.

His grin vanished. Clutching the chart with both
hands, he stopped in her doorway. "You're here ahead
of schedule, huh?"

With her crisp white blouse and navy slacks, she
was impeccably put together, as always, but she didn't
seem at all rested or relaxed. She was pale, and her
eyes were hollow and bruised-looking, as if she'd had
no sleep.

"Sam came over last night."

Zack's heart dropped. He'd never actually met Sam
Montford, but he sure hated the guy. Zack had been
the one who'd helped Cassie pick up the broken pieces
of the life Sam had left her with.

"If he's giving you a hard time..."

She held up her hand. "Not really. He just wants
to be friends."

Zack sank into a chair. "Where was he ten years ago when you needed a friend?"

"In the Peace Corps."

That surprised him. He'd expected to hear that the guy had been partying on a beach in Jamaica. "For ten years?"

Cassie shook her head, focusing on the top of her desk. "For the past couple of years he's been restoring old homes in New Jersey."

"You always said he was brilliant. Had a career in law and politics ahead of him."

"He *is* brilliant. He was attending Montford University on full academic scholarship, and he never really even tried. But apparently he'd rather waste his mind than use it."

"I'm more inclined to believe the man's an idiot," Zack said, not bothering to hide his derision. Years ago, when he and a much younger, more fragile Cassie had spent a lot of time together studying and talking, he'd experienced firsthand the damage the man had done. Montford had taken the life from a lovable, bright young woman and left her little more than an empty body. Back in those days, Zack had fantasized regularly about meeting up with Sam Montford in a dark alley someday.

He was still fantasizing about it.

Sam Montford had a lot to answer for.

Cassie had recovered very slowly, healing physically and emotionally while she found the inner strength to pursue a career. Though she'd very thoroughly and permanently closed herself off from any future romantic relationships, she'd managed to create a successful, contented, *useful* life.

Zack was not going to sit idly by and watch her lose it again.

"His little girl needs help, Zack."

Zack frowned, dropping Shelby's chart on the edge of Cassie's desk.

A couple of nights ago, Ben Sanders, Montford's cousin and Zack's good friend, had told him about Montford's adopted daughter. The details were harrowing, and Zack wasn't sure how much Cassie knew, but ever since he'd heard them, he'd been half afraid she'd want to get involved.

Ben hadn't met Sam and Mariah yet, but Carol Montford had been keeping Ben apprised of family events. Ben had an adopted daughter who was just about Mariah's age and was still recovering from the beatings inflicted by her natural father several months ago. Carol was hoping the little girls would be able to help each other heal.

"She's got a great therapist in Phoenix," Zack said now, having grilled Ben for everything his cousin knew about the situation.

Cassie leaned forward. "She's been in therapy for almost six months," she said earnestly. "And she's made virtually no progress."

Pushing back from the chair, Zack shoved his hands into the pockets of his jeans. He paced slowly in front of Cassie's crammed bookshelves. Perusing the titles. Retaining none of them.

The situation was delicate, but the answer clear.

"From what I understand, the child was severely traumatized," Zack said. "She might be beyond any sort of help until some of those memories fade."

"But we might be able to reach her." Her voice was

full of compassion. And something more. It was the "something more" that made him nervous.

He turned toward her. "You might not make any difference at all," he reminded her gently.

"As long as there's a chance that we can reach her, I have to try. And I want to use Sammie, at least to start with."

Cassie's gaze was strong, steady, unrelenting. Zack knew he'd lost before he'd even begun to fight.

"At what cost to you?" His words were softly delivered; the look he gave her was not. They'd been through too much together, too many dark days fighting demons. He couldn't just calmly let her risk her hard-won hold on happiness on such an unsubstantial possibility.

"How can I measure my own well-being against that of a child?"

Hands on her desk, Zack leaned over until his face was only inches from hers, staring her straight in the eye. "You can't save everyone in the world," he told her.

"This isn't the *world,* Zack. It's my hometown. The town that nurtured me as a child, that has loved me every day of my life. The town that helped me gain back my self-esteem when I thought I had no reason to go on."

Zack held his position. "She's not from this town."

"She's a Montford now."

"And are you sure that that isn't why you're doing this? Because she's Sam's daughter?"

Cassie shook her head. The movement conveniently broke eye contact with Zack. "I've helped people all over this country, Zack, and you know it. I certainly have to do everything I can for someone right here at home."

"For Sam…"

"For *anyone* right here at home. I'd feel the need to make this offer even if she was a total stranger. You know that."

He did. Damn it. Cassie was world-renowned for her innovative approach to emotional therapy—using animals to achieve remarkable results with emotionally traumatized people who'd lost their ability to trust.

"Maybe this one's a little too close to home."

"There's no maybe about that."

He pushed away from her desk with so much force, it moved. Why should Cassie have to risk more grief? Hadn't she already suffered enough at the hands of Sam Montford? Could she survive another assault on her emotions?

"Let me do it," he said, knowing the words were asinine even before they left his mouth. He had no training in Cassie's area of expertise. He was good at lessening the loneliness of old people, at helping a newly blind man find the courage to shower again with a dog by his side, or encouraging a quadriplegic to try to retrain his muscles. He knew next to nothing about emotional disorders.

Cassie smiled, but didn't even bother with a response. Her glorious long red hair was clipped up into some sort of twist, making her look, at that moment, like his fourth-grade teacher.

Arms folded across his chest, he stared at her. "Can you assure me that you won't get hurt?"

"Does life ever offer that assurance?"

Zack stood there for several more minutes before

settling back into the chair. "How are you going to do this, Cass?" he finally asked softly. "Seriously, how can you possibly involve yourself with Sam again? In any capacity?"

Her shrug did very little to reassure him. "I just know I have to try."

The sound of suppressed tears filled him with dread.

She was hurting already.

She'd said she was okay, but he knew better. He knew better, dammit, and there wasn't a thing he could do about it.

Except be there to hold the pieces if she fell apart.

Sam, feeling disjointed, drove his truck slowly into town. He reached for Mariah's hand, the tiny fingers lost in his big, work-roughened palm. "Are you excited to meet your new cousin, honey?" he asked, infusing his voice with a cheer he couldn't really feel. "She's seven, just like you."

Glancing sideways, he smiled at Mariah, willing her to care. If his determination could make something happen, Mariah was going to get well. Sam was sending her every bit of energy, of strength, that he possessed.

How many times in the past seven years had he been discouraged, overwhelmed with the self-hatred that was always there, and found solace in the love of this little girl? Without ever knowing, or trying, Mariah had brought a joy to his life he'd never thought he'd find again.

He'd been there for her conception—or practically, passed out in the very next room. He'd been there for her birth. For every birthday and Christmas. The first day of school. And days in between.

And how many times had he sat with her, wondering if he and Cassie would have made a child as special as Mariah?

Brian and Moira were Mariah's parents, and they'd had the privilege of listening to her childish pronouncements every day. Of being there for her first step. Of chasing her through the house in her pajamas. Of listening to her earnest prayers every night, then tucking her into bed. Drying her tears.

For him, the pleasure of Mariah's company had been, of necessity, occasional. He'd seen the Glory family as often as possible, but sometimes they were away for weeks or months at a time. Mariah always accompanied them, as Moira had accompanied her own parents on the same kinds of trips.

If he'd stayed around long enough for him and Cassie to have the family they'd always planned, he'd have known the same satisfaction as Moira and Brian. If, ten years ago, he'd known the immeasurable completeness a child brought to life, the incredible store of love and excitement, he'd never have left home.

Or would he?

Pulling onto Main Street for the first time since he'd been back, Sam wondered about that. He'd been so unsure of himself in those days, so unsure of who he was. How could he possibly have experienced—or even understood—the kind of joy Mariah now brought him?

How could he possibly have been a father, responsible for another life, when he was barely responsible for his own?

"Before we meet your new cousin and her daddy, we're going to see a statue of my great-great-grandfather," he told Mariah, slowing the truck. "Which means he's your great-great-great-grandfather." He lifted their clasped hands, tickling her neck. Though she flinched, the movement was almost imperceptible. She certainly didn't smile as he'd half hoped she might. She didn't even blink.

"I haven't seen it yet, so you and I can see it together for the very first time, okay?" he asked, squeezing her hand.

She continued to watch him.

Sam pulled into one of the angled parking slots along Main Street's curb, got out and helped Mariah climb down. They'd be meeting his cousin, Ben, and Ben's daughter Alex, in this park a few minutes from now. And though he didn't really understand why, Sam had very mixed emotions about the meeting.

Somehow Ben's existence threatened him.

The statue was easily visible from the road, but until Sam got close to it, it was just a statue that his mom and dad had told him about. Which was probably why he was so unprepared for the tremor that shot through him as he got close enough to read the inscription, to see the face.

The resemblance was immediately recognizable. And startling.

The man was a legend. Sam was not. At least, not in this town.

"Hey, Mariah, do you think he looks like me?" He lifted her up for a better view.

The child stared at him; she ignored the statue. She

had one hand around his neck, and with the other, she was clutching the collar of his shirt.

"His name is Sam Montford, too. And since your name is Montford now, he's related to you, just like he is to me," he told her, constantly trying to reinforce the fact that she wasn't alone in the world. That she had an entire family surrounding her, loving her, whether or not she let them.

"He's the man who started this whole town," he explained. Maybe a sense of history would help her. A story that was enough like one of the books Moira used to read to the child, to mean something to her now. To provide a sense of connection. "He moved out to Arizona from back East; just like you," he rattled on, repeating some of what he'd known growing up as the only Montford heir. But he'd learned much more of his ancestor's history in the five days he'd been home. The previous year, Becca Parsons, the wife of Montford University's president, had spearheaded a project to honor the original Sam Montford, which included a biography, a play and the commissioning of this sculpture. She'd apparently tried to find Sam, to bring him home for the unveiling of the statue, but Sam hadn't left a forwarding address. His phone number had been unlisted.

The only people who'd ever known where to find him were Brian, Moira and the disaster relief organization for which he'd been volunteering the past eight years.

"When your great-great-great-grandfather came out to Arizona, he lived with Indians for a while." He gave Mariah the condensed version. The first Montford had been on the run when he'd settled in Arizona. On the run from a stratified society that had killed his dark-skinned wife and biracial son in cold blood.

Mariah didn't need to know about that.

"He met a very pretty woman who was visiting the Indians with her dad, who was a missionary," he went on. "And she was your great-great-great-grandmother."

Looking at Mariah's earnest little face, Sam had no idea if he was getting through to her. Her blue eyes, once so alight with mischief and precocious pursuits, were blank.

"They had several children," Sam said, speaking his thoughts aloud. He looked back toward the likeness of his ancestor, and found himself experiencing a strange sense of pride—of belonging, almost. A *willingness* to belong.

Had that feeling always been there, waiting for him? Or had it been necessary for him to forge his own way, to witness life's extreme sorrows—in the midst of war, famine, earthquake and storm—to appreciate what he'd taken for granted all his life, growing up in Shelter Valley?

Would he ever have found the real Sam Montford if he'd stayed in this town?

"One of their children was my great-great-grandfather. And another one was your uncle Ben's great-great-grandmother."

Sam still couldn't grasp the idea that he wasn't the only Montford heir. He'd been "the only" his entire life. Carol and James's only son. Cassie's only boyfriend. Her only lover. The only Shelter Valley High graduate to score off the charts on the SAT exams. Shelter Valley's only hope for leadership...

"Let's go, hon." Putting Mariah down, he took one last glance at the statue of his namesake and headed farther into the park, holding her hand tightly. "Alex is waiting to meet you."

He spotted Ben and Alex almost instantly, across the park. It seemed fitting that they'd arrived at opposite ends.

"Your uncle Ben's little girl is adopted, too," he told her. He pondered his next remark, bit it back, then said it anyway. "She was hurt kind of bad, too," he confided, hoping that if Mariah knew she wasn't the only child to suffer, the knowledge might somehow bring her comfort. Hoping that she didn't start to think all children lived happily until the age of seven, when suddenly life turned into hell on earth and you had to wonder why you lived at all. "Alex's mom was married to Ben when Alex was born. She told Ben that he was Alex's daddy, but she wasn't always a very nice lady."

As he repeated the story his mother had related the other night, Sam felt a stirring of compassion for the man he could see across the park, throwing a Frisbee to the laughing little girl who was tripping over her feet as she tried to catch it. "But then later," he continued, walking slowly toward the pair, who hadn't seen them yet, "the man who was really Alex's dad came back from prison—he wasn't a very good person, either—and they made Ben go away and took Alex to a new place. But the new man got mad and hit Alex," he said, praying he wasn't making the biggest mistake of his life.

Sweating suddenly, he had a horrible feeling that he should have spoken to Mariah's counselor before telling her this particular truth. Yet instinct was telling him it *had* to help her to know she wasn't alone.

"Alex called Ben secretly on the phone, and he came and rescued her, and now she's his forever and ever," he said quickly, getting to the good part. "Just like you and me."

Ben abruptly stopped his game. He'd obviously noticed Sam and Mariah approaching. Holding the Frisbee in his hand, he drew Alex close to him. Sam's jaw tensed.

"Ready, honey?" he asked softly, crouching down beside his daughter.

Mariah buried her face against Sam's neck.

That Saturday morning Carol Montford paced from her living room across the foyer to the formal library on the other side and back again, peering out the huge windows in both rooms toward the curving drive beyond. Waiting.

She told herself to stop. Went out to the family room to see if her husband needed help with the crossword puzzle he was working on. He didn't. Nor did he want anything to drink—and would she *please* just relax and knit or something?

She might have tried to follow his advice. Except that she didn't knit.

And before she knew it, she'd resumed her path along the living room windows and through the library.

She so desperately wanted Sam to feel a part of things again, to know in his heart that Shelter Valley was his home. To stay.

She was afraid that Ben's being here now would just give Sam another excuse to leave.

She wanted the two boys, the cousins, to find something in each other.

"You have to trust that everything will work out for the best," James said suddenly, coming up behind her at the living-room window, his hands on her shoulders.

Carol slowly covered his hands with her own. Even after all these years, all the heartaches, she still felt a thrill at the simple touch of her husband's hand.

That was all she'd ever wanted for her only offspring. The comfort of loving someone that deeply. That completely. That forever.

"We just got him home again," she whispered, trusting James with her fear.

"But we can't make him stay, my love," he returned softly, unusually solemn. "He has to *want* to do that."

"If he thought we needed him—"

"Oh, no, my dear," James said. She could feel him shaking his head behind her. "You don't want him here out of guilt. Or duty. He wouldn't be happy."

"But what about that precious little girl, James? She needs us!"

"Yes, I believe she does. And I also believe Sam knows that. Your son is an intelligent man."

Carol turned, kissing James on the side of the mouth. "He gets that from his father," she said, tears brimming in her eyes as she worked up the courage to ask the one question no one had yet dared to raise.

"Do you think he and Cassie could ever—"

With one finger on her lips, James silenced her.

"Don't, Carol," he admonished. "You'll only torture yourself."

She didn't speak, but after almost forty years of marriage, she didn't need words to communicate with her husband. Her eyes pleaded with him to give her a little hope.

"The boy didn't leave himself any room for reparation," he said quietly. "The damage he did to Cassie was too great to be anything but permanent. There's nothing left for them to go back to."

Carol would still have hoped for a miracle, were it not for the truth she recognized in James's words. Cassie was not the woman she'd once been.

And her Sam was at fault for that.

Because of him, Cassie had been denied any second chances. She would never have a baby, never be pregnant again—because of what he'd done, and what he'd caused to happen, Sam didn't deserve a second chance, either.

An hour later, just before lunch, they were back. "How'd it go?" Carol Montford asked, before Sam and Mariah were even fully inside the house.

"Fine."

Sam wanted lunch. And some time with his drawing pad and pencil. Things were changing in Borough Bantam, confusing him. He needed a chance to think it all through, to work out these changes in a way that was beneficial to the village. And to the newcomer, as well.

He needed to find out the newcomer's purpose. His place in the Borough. His long-term intentions.

"How did the girls do?"

"Fine," Sam said again, wanting Mariah to know that she hadn't disappointed him. She'd refused to look at either Ben or Alex the entire awkward time he and his cousin had stood in the park and tried to talk without ever really saying anything. He couldn't let Mariah believe that there was anything wrong with her response. He had to assume it was the only response she was capable of right now.

"Isn't Alex a cutie?" Carol asked, trying valiantly to keep the concern from showing on her aged and still-lovely face.

"That she is."

"And you and Ben, you liked each other?"

"We just met, Mom. I hardly know him," Sam said, wishing he could reassure her. About so many things. The trouble was, he couldn't even reassure himself. He had no idea what the future held.

"But he's—"

"He seemed like a decent man," he allowed, when it became evident that she was going to push until she got some kind of commitment from him.

Carol ran gentle fingers down Mariah's back. "How'd our little one do?" she asked.

"I don't know," Sam said, releasing Mariah's hand and turning her to face her grandmother. "Did you have a good time, Mariah?"

The child stared at him blankly.

"Let me get her some chocolate milk," Carol said, moving away before the little girl saw the hint of tears in her eyes. "She likes chocolate milk."

She *drinks* chocolate milk, Sam amended silently. That doesn't mean she *likes* it.

There's no way of knowing what she likes and what she doesn't.

But for now, the fact that she would drink a glass of chocolate milk was enough.

Chapter 6

Armed with the advice of psychology professor Dr.
Phyllis Langford, and with the instincts that had been
serving her well, Cassie let Sammie off her leash in
the park Monday morning.

"Okay, girl," she said, squatting down, rubbing the
sheltie's ears, "you're on."

There were no rules here, no right ways, no answers. There were only bits and pieces of advice from
psychology professionals—not all of it consistent—
suppositions and a very few precedents to guide her.
And there was her absolute certainty that pet therapy could help where nothing else would. They were
breaking new ground. So far, with great success.

Because this was a Monday morning, a school day,
the park was deserted. Except for the man walking toward them with his daughter clinging to his hand and

staring up at him. Mariah's long black hair was in a French braid. She looked adorable—and fragile—in her yellow jumper and sandals.

"Go say hello, Sammie," Cassie said, her tone of voice changing as she gave the command.

Sammie's ears perked up, she barked once, and off she went, bounding across the park to the two figures drawing closer.

Concentrate on the job, Cassie told herself. *Don't watch the man.* Don't recognize that confident stride. Those long legs that had always looked sinfully good in denim. *Don't even look.*

He was an illusion. No matter how attractive he was, how kind he could be, how gentle and warm. Inside him lurked a man who could be carelessly cruel. A man who made promises he didn't keep.

He stopped in the shade of a palo verde tree—the only tree in this Arizona park—still holding Mariah's hand.

Sammie had reached them, and Cassie's full attention was riveted on the child. Though the sheltie was sniffing her hand, Mariah didn't seem to notice. She didn't look at the dog. Didn't look anywhere but at Sam. Cassie wondered if she was even aware of her surroundings.

The psychological reports had all agreed that Mariah was "in there" someplace. That the child's brain was fully functioning. Sam was certain of it, and Cassie was working under that assumption.

Mariah didn't seem to trust people at all. Apparently not even Sam—which was why she didn't dare take her eyes off him. So maybe she'd trust another creature, one who made no demands and required no

explanations; maybe she'd trust Sammie. But not unless they could get her focus away from Sam.

Standing there in her forest-green dress slacks and
white short-sleeved cotton shirt, Cassie continued to
watch, waiting for Sam to do as she'd instructed him,
when she'd called earlier that morning. He'd balked,
arguing that they'd been operating on the premise that
only by making Mariah feel totally secure were they
ever going to bring her back. Mariah's counselors
thought that maintaining her attachment to Sam was
so important, they weren't even trying to send her to
school yet; they felt she wasn't ready to be away from
him. Cassie knew that. Knew, too, that although Sam
left the child occasionally, Mariah would always sit
completely frozen, in the position he'd left her, until
he returned. And she wouldn't eat for hours afterward.
Cassie had spoken about these things with Mariah's
counselor in Phoenix. And at length with Phyllis.

Cassie's conversation with Sam had been all business. If he wanted her help, he was going to have to
trust her. And to do what she told him.

He'd eventually said he would.

A minute passed, and then another. Sammie went
on nudging Mariah's hand, sniffing at Sam's shoes.
She pranced around, waiting for someone to notice
her.

"Come on, Sam," she said softly. "I know it's hard,
but you can do this…."

Even standing several yards away, she could feel
the effort it cost him to disengage Mariah's fingers
from his. Could feel the doubt, the pain, even the fear,
as though she were experiencing it all herself.

But then, this was Sam. She'd always…felt him.

Holding her breath, she stood completely still, watching as he slowly left the child standing in the park alone. Tears welled in her eyes, but she ignored them. She was working. This was a job. Nothing more.

Ignoring everything but Sam, Mariah reached out her hand to him.

He hesitated, looked over at Cassie, then shook his head, face tense. "I'm just going to run back to the truck to get the picnic basket I forgot," he told Mariah.

Cassie barely heard the words, but she heard the very real compassion behind them.

"You stay here with Sammie," he said to the child. "Her name's just like mine. So you know you can trust her to keep you safe until I get back. I'll just be gone for a few minutes."

Mariah started toward him.

"No!" The sharpness of Sam's word cut into Cassie's heart. God, life was so hard! "I want you to stay here, Mariah," he said firmly. "I'll be back, okay? And if you need anything, my friend Cassie is over there."

Sam glanced at her, clenching the muscles in his jaw. Even across the distance of several yards, she could read the fierce look in his eyes. *She'd better be right about this.*

Cassie's tears fell when Sam turned abruptly and walked away from his needy daughter.

He trusted Cassie. Trusted her to help this damaged child.

Overwhelmed with sudden despair, she almost called him back. She couldn't handle this. Couldn't go through with it. Couldn't have Sam placing his trust in her so completely. Not when she didn't trust him. She brushed her tears away.

And focused on the child, who stood like a statue, staring at her father's retreating back.

Part of the idea was for Mariah to see that although Sam left, he always returned.

He wasn't going far. But he was going out of her sight. And he'd stay there until Mariah moved. Until she looked somewhere other than where he'd gone.

It might take all morning and into the afternoon.

But unless they taught Mariah that she wasn't as alone as she thought, the child wasn't going to recover. That was the conclusion Phyllis had drawn. One that the Phoenix counselor had eventually concurred with, though she'd believed they hadn't given Mariah enough time to come out of this on her own. She'd reiterated the list of known traumas Mariah had experienced—thankfully, none of them physical—the length of time it could take to recover from them.

Cassie didn't doubt the validity of the professional opinion. She just knew that sometimes animals could help speed up the process. There was scientific proof behind the theories. Though most psychology professionals only seemed willing to try pet therapy as a last resort, they almost all acknowledged that pets were sometimes responsible for lengthening the lives of their owners, for lowering blood pressure. Cassie believed it was just a matter of time until they universally acknowledged that animals could also be used to reach human beings who'd been so injured, so emotionally impaired that they couldn't be reached through normal person-to-person therapy sessions.

"Come on, Sammie, do your stuff," Cassie said, her stomach growing tenser with every passing minute.

The child was one stubborn little cuss. Which would serve her well.

Cassie knew.

It had been her own stubborn refusal to die that had brought her out of her dark pit all those years ago. At first, when her own physical health had been so precarious, she'd had her baby to think about. And then, later, when she'd finally admitted to herself that life did go on, she'd found a wellspring of determination she hadn't known she possessed.

Sammie nudged the little girl, but Mariah still didn't respond. She was staring so intently after Sam that Cassie wasn't sure the child knew the dog was there. Wasn't sure she'd notice if the always-blue Arizona sky suddenly clouded over and broke into thunderstorms. Everyone else in town would probably be running outside to gaze up at the heavens. And Mariah would continue to stand there, oblivious, watching for Sam.

Cassie, slowly approaching the child, got close enough to identify any small change of expression on that fixed little face. Was that a hint of fear in Mariah's startling blue eyes? Or was it just a reflection of the bright sun shining down through the tree?

So intent was she on the child's face, watching for any sign of reaction, Cassie didn't notice at first that Mariah's little brown hand had settled on top of Sammie's head. The fingers were moving back and forth from one of Sammie's ears to the other. It wasn't much. Most people would no doubt consider it unremarkable.

But Cassie knew better. She fell to her knees in the carefully manicured grass, not bothering to brush away the tears that rolled down her face. Mariah was taking comfort from the dog at her side.

Thank God.

It had been a long week. And a long day.

Sitting in a lounge chair so comfortable it could have been in the living room, Sam quietly sipped his bottle of beer, Muffy curled at his feet. He was part of the Saturday-night crowd on the back patio at Montford Mansion. But he was having difficulty concentrating on the conversation at hand, and found his thoughts regularly drifting to the ongoing plot of his comic strip.

Yes, it had been a long week, having that first breakthrough with Mariah on Monday and nothing else since. They'd had another session on Thursday. Sam had left Mariah for a little longer, but there had been no new results.

Harder than he'd ever thought possible was being here in town, close to Cassie and not seeing her. Not talking to her. Not sharing her life.

His mother had insisted on this get-together. A little gathering, she'd called it. But it didn't feel little to Sam. Ben and his wife, Tory, and little Alex. Ben's friend and Cassie's partner, Zack Foster, and his new wife, Randi used-to-be-Parsons, whom Sam and Cassie had gone to school with, grades one through twelve. James and Carol. And Sam and Mariah.

He couldn't remember one single family gathering in his whole life without Cassie. She'd always been there.

They'd just finished dinner—steaks out on the grill. A swim in the Olympic-sized pool—though Sam had spent the entire time with Mariah clutching his neck, so he could hardly call it a swim. He and Ben were supposed to be getting to know each other.

The girls were both asleep now—Mariah in a lounge chair on the other side of the patio, Alex in his mother's special guest room, the one he hoped would someday be Mariah's.

Everyone else was sipping drinks, relaxing, talking.

"We should play some canasta," James suggested.

Carol jumped up. "I'll get the cards." She was so obvious in her eagerness to make this whole thing work that Sam felt sorry for her. His mother had always been such a peaceful woman. Content. Secure.

Not this too-attentive mass of nerves, desperate to know that her world was righting itself.

He was completely aware that he was responsible for this, too.

Muffy followed Carol into the house, no doubt hoping for leftovers in the privacy of the kitchen. Sam hoped his mother wouldn't give in to those pleading eyes.

"So how long are you in town, Sam?" Randi asked, interrupting his thoughts. Although the question *sounded* innocent, Sam had a feeling it hadn't been. He was pretty sure Zack and Randi hated him. Couldn't see him gone fast enough.

He tried not to let that get to him. They weren't just his cousin's closest friends—they were Cassie's friends, too. They had a right to hate him.

"I have no plans to leave again," Sam said. He wasn't sure exactly what his plans were, but he knew that much.

Ben sat forward, hand entwined with his wife's.

"That's good to hear, cousin," Ben said. "I've been half afraid you were only here for a visit and that you'd be gone before we had a chance to spend any time together."

"Sure you wouldn't rather have the Montford crown all to yourself?" Sam couldn't help asking, though he kept his tone light. "After all, I was the heir apparent all my life. It's your turn."

Zack and Randi shared a glance. Sam suspected it conveyed nothing positive.

"I don't know about that," Ben answered. "But I've come home and I'm glad to be here. I'm also glad to have as much family in my life as there's family to have."

Carol returned, minus Muffy, bearing a deck of cards, and without a pause in the conversation, everyone, a reluctant Sam included, took seats around the big game table in the middle of the patio. Sam was a bit envious of the dog, who'd been allowed to stay inside.

"Sam seems to think there's some *distinction* attached to the Montford name," James said to Ben, as the cards were shuffled.

"A good distinction, right?" Tory asked. Of all the people visiting that night, Sam liked Tory the best. He knew a little about her story—from Cassie the evening he'd gone there. Tory had secrets, things she wasn't proud of. He could sense them. And yet, there was no mistaking the purity of her love for his cousin or for Alex.

"Not necessarily," Sam answered, before his father shared more of his past grievances than Sam was prepared to answer for. "Being a Montford comes with obvious advantages, but it also has its share of hardships."

"Oh, yeah," Zack said with a laugh. "I can see how it'd be a real hardship growing up in *this* house."

"You were always the prince in our fairy tales, Sam," Randi chimed in. "Your life was charmed."

She was right. But it had been a charm he'd never asked for—and in the end, it had come at a cost.

"It wasn't always that easy," Carol said, surprising Sam.

During the years he'd been fighting against a life he wasn't happy living, she'd been the last person to understand his discontent. To her, everything had always been so clear-cut and simple.

"People expected a lot of Sam. More than any of the other kids in town. He practically lived his life under a microscope."

"Let's get this game going, shall we?" Sam asked.

He might deserve to be the topic of uncomfortable conversation. Had been anticipating it. Figured everyone in town was entertaining thoughts that mirrored Zack and Randi's. But he could only handle the encounters in doses. And without Zack peering hatred at him from hooded eyes.

Because the teams were uneven, Carol was the self-appointed scorekeeper, and Sam conjured up next week's comic strip episode as he played out a few hands of canasta across from his father. The queen in Borough Bantam knew far more than she was revealing. She was on to the newcomer; he'd be wise to watch her, find out what she knew.

As he laid down a red canasta of kings, Sam's mind's eye saw the idiot magistrate, worming his way around his contained little circle, predictable as always. *I am. I am. I am.* And Sam was strangely comforted.

The next day, Sam was in his room working, his pencil flying across the page as the strip he'd envisioned the night before came to life. Mariah was napping on the bed across the room. His parents were in town having lunch with friends.

The bell rang downstairs.

His parents had a housekeeper during the week, but they were on their own on weekends. Which meant that it was up to him to get the door.

The last person he'd expected to see was Zack Foster.

"Hello, Zack." Politeness required that he step back, let the other man inside.

"I offered to stop by as a favor to Cassie," Zack said. "Your mother called about Muffy's allergies, and Cassie told her she'd bring over some Prednisone. Muffy should have one of these every twelve hours until they run out." Zack handed Sam a plastic bottle of pills.

"Thanks," he said. And then, in spite of the fact that he could have cut his tongue out for asking, he said, "Cassie was too busy to come herself?"

"No."

With no one else present, Zack didn't even pretend to like Sam.

"She just didn't want to see me," Sam said, sparing himself nothing.

"Right."

Sam stared at Zack. Cassie's partner was easily a

couple of inches taller than Sam. His large athletic frame and blond, blue-eyed good looks would be a definite plus where women were concerned.

Sam had to wonder if Zack and Cassie had been lovers.

Did Zack know about the patch of freckles sprinkled across Cassie's lower back? Did he know that she squirmed and begged when she was kissed there?

"Have you known Cassie long?"

"Ten years."

That long.

Much longer than Zack had known his own wife. They'd mentioned the night before that they'd just met this year.

"Do you know why she's never married?" Sam asked. He'd been so certain that Cassie would be happily ensconced in a huge family by the time he came home.

He'd been prepared to deal with the pain of seeing her living with another man. Loving another man.

He was totally unprepared for the sick feeling of regret he felt for her aloneness. If he really *was* in any way responsible...

"I know why," Zack said, his voice grim.

"But you aren't going to tell me," Sam guessed.

"I don't see that it's any business of yours."

No one in this town thought Cassie was any of his business. This was Shelter Valley, and they took care of their own. He'd deserted; he no longer qualified. Cassie had spent more time here than he had. They'd protect her—even against him. Especially against him. He'd been in town almost two weeks and knew absolutely nothing about Cassie's private life. Not even his own parents were talking.

He clenched his jaw in an effort to keep his mouth shut. Because Zack was right. Cassie's life, her decisions, were *not* his business.

He just couldn't find a way to convince his heart of that.

"Thanks for bringing the pills," Sam said.

Zack nodded, turned to go, then turned back. "I was actually hoping for this chance to get you alone," he told Sam. His belligerence was gone, but in its place was something that bothered Sam even more.

Sincerity.

"Cassie would kill me if she knew I was doing this, but I'm asking you, one man to another, to stay away from her."

A dozen smart-aleck responses sprang to Sam's lips. He uttered none of them.

"This is a small town," he said instead. "We're bound to run into each other. It might make things easier if we could be friends."

"You and Cassie will never be friends," Zack said with certainty. "If she'd been some other girl, from some other place, raised in some other way, she might have been able to get past your screwing around on her, but she isn't and she wasn't. What you did to her cut Cassie to her very core. You don't get second chances when you hurt someone that way."

"So, if she can't possibly forgive me, if she's always going to hate me, why are you so afraid for me to be around her?" Sam asked. "Surely she's immune."

"You remind her of things she's worked long and

hard to forget," Zack said, then strode out the door
and shut it quietly behind him.

With the truth of Zack's words heavy on his heart,
Sam walked slowly back up the stairs. Every time
Cassie saw him, she remembered the bad times. The
pain he'd caused her.

It was a pain so deep, so cruel, it wasn't ever going
to go away.

He and Mariah had another meeting with Sammie
that afternoon. He'd have to wake her up soon.

In the meantime, he had a script to write. A fic-
tional town to save.

And he had to figure out how to live in a real town
with his ex-wife. A woman who didn't want to see
him. A woman he'd never stopped loving...

Chapter 7

"Do you mind if I join you, sweetie?" Cassie asked the little girl standing stiffly under the palo verde tree in Shelter Valley Park. "I'm your dad's friend, Cassie. You met me at my work, remember?"

The child didn't even blink as Cassie sat down on the ground next to Sammie. Mariah's hand rested lightly on the dog's head, but she wasn't petting the animal or in any way acknowledging that she wasn't alone.

But they were making progress. Cassie had watched Mariah place her hand on Sammie's head almost the second Sam had left.

"If I'm bothering you or you don't want me here, just let me know," she continued. Sam had been gone for almost ten minutes, and the child's neck had to be getting sore from holding herself so stiffly, watching the exact spot where Sam had disappeared, waiting intently for his return.

Cassie wore denim shorts, a T-shirt with a road-runner on it, and tennis shoes with no socks. An outfit far more casual than she was used to, but perhaps one that would make the little girl more comfortable.

"I love your outfit," she said, her stomach knot-ting as she studied the child. She had an hour today. Longer than before. Long enough to force Mariah to focus on something aside from her missing father? Long enough, maybe, to force her to need someone else. "Those shorts are my favorite shade of green, and I really like how the shirt and socks match. You must have bought them all at the same time."

Keeping her head beneath the child's hand, as though understanding the significance of Mariah's gesture, Sammie looked over at Cassie. Cassie could swear Zack's dog was smiling at her. She'd long been impressed by Sammie's sensitivity to emotional un-dercurrents. Was certain that the sheltie understood much of what was going on around her.

"I think Sammie likes your outfit, too," Cassie con-fided. "She's listening to us."

Was that a little twitch of her fingers? Was Mariah responding to the conversation? It was impossible to tell if Mariah even listened when people spoke to her. Physically, she could hear just fine; medical tests had determined that. But no one knew for certain how complete her emotional death had been. How shut away she really was. Her catatonic state was most likely a case of the mind protecting itself from an in-tolerable reality. But how deep did that go? Would she ever be able to release herself from that protection, that silence?

Cassie, pulling her knees up to her chest, continued to chat softly with the child. Telling her about the park she had yet to look at, the children playing around her. Describing her surroundings for her, since she seemed unable, or unwilling, to look at them herself.

Five minutes later, with still no sign of Sam, Mariah's fingers began, almost indiscernibly, to move across Sammie's head. Cassie's stomach fluttered. Those tiny hands seemed so fragile. So helpless and vulnerable. Mariah was too young to have to deal with what life had already heaped on her. She'd seen things no one, let alone a child, should see.

Cassie desperately wanted more for her. Better. Wanted something to take away the anguish.

"I knew your dad back when I was your age," Cassie said suddenly. She shouldn't do this, shouldn't talk about Sam, shouldn't dredge up the memories. It was too risky.

But the words came, anyway.

"I had really long hair then, just like you do—though, of course, mine is red."

Mariah's fingers continued to move slowly across Sammie's head, stroking from ear to ear. Otherwise, there was no response from the girl.

The dog had been sitting still for more than fifteen minutes and would stay in that position until Cassie gave the command to move—even if it was two hours later.

"The boys at school used to tease me about my hair because no one else in our school had hair as bright as mine. And one day, a couple of them came up and pulled the ribbon off the end of my braid and wouldn't give it back to me."

Funny how clearly Cassie could remember that day. How angry and hurt she'd felt by their merciless teasing. And how helpless. They were boys. They were bigger, and there were more of them. There wasn't a damn thing she could do.

She hated that feeling.

"Sam came up behind them and told them that if they didn't give it back to me and leave me alone from then on, he'd make sure they never got served at the ice cream parlor again."

Wrapping her arms around her knees, Cassie smiled. "Of course, he couldn't possibly prevent them from having ice cream, but he believed he could. And because *he* did, so did they. Sam already knew, even that young, the role his family played in this town. He knew he had influence and how to use it…"

She broke off, thinking. Dwelling on a memory she hadn't visited in years.

"You know what was best about him?" she asked, willing the child to look at her. "Back then, he had an unshakable conviction that he could use his influence to the benefit of others." She realized she might be talking over the child's head, but she needed to think this through.

He'd really believed, she mused. So when had he stopped believing? It wasn't as though he hadn't accomplished good things after he'd left, but…

Mariah continued to stare off into the distance, where Sam had disappeared. "Anyway," Cassie said, shaking her head, "the boys never teased me again, and I thought your dad was the most wonderful boy I'd ever met."

It had taken almost fourteen years for her to find out differently.

Oh, Sam, why? Where did it all fall apart? And why didn't I know?

The fact that he'd never even given her a chance to make it right before he'd destroyed their whole marriage was something Cassie still struggled with. How could she trust her damaged heart to any other relationship, when she knew going in that it could all fall apart without any warning?

Cassie fell silent, watching the child, remembering. Remembering things she'd promised herself never to think about again. She'd lost so much. And what she'd lost could never be replaced.

So had this little girl, standing courageously in front of her.

"Mariah?" Cassie asked softly. "We don't know each other very well yet, but I just want you to know I loved your dad, Sam, very very much. For a long time. And when he went away from me, I felt just like I imagine you do now. Like I couldn't breathe. I couldn't imagine living without him...."

Maybe this was too complex for the child. Too disturbing. Maybe Mariah wasn't listening. But maybe she was. And maybe she needed to hear more than the simple assurances she'd been given to this point. Sam had told her that Mariah had been a precocious child. Maybe she could understand what Cassie was saying.

"But I did manage, honey. And life went on, and eventually I got happy again. And you know what else?"

The child continued to stare off in the distance, blinking only when absolutely necessary.

"Sam came back after all this time," Cassie said. There was no relief for her in that truth. And yet... there was. It meant no more waiting, no more wondering if she'd ever see him again.

Because now she had. It was done.

"So you see, sometimes people have to leave forever—not because they want to, but because it's their turn to go to God. That's what happened with your parents. And Mariah, they loved you *so much*. They still do. It's why they asked Sam to be your dad." Cassie had to stop for a moment as tears threatened. "Honey," she finally whispered. "Sam *will* come back. I promise."

She was watching the little girl, ready to be patient for a year if that was what it took to help her. Mariah was a real beauty. Her features were fine, her skin dusky, her eyebrows black above electric-blue eyes— that were looking straight at her!

Only for a second. A very brief second. But she had looked. For one heartbeat, the little girl had torn her eyes away from that spot in the distance where Sam would reappear and had looked at Cassie.

Yes!

She'd heard what Cassie had said. And she'd reacted!

Jumping up, Cassie had to wrap her arms around herself to keep from throwing them around Mariah. She couldn't wait to tell Sam. And Zack and Randi. And Phyllis, too. Mariah had *looked* at her. Cassie felt good all the way down to her toes.

Sammie was giving the lost, lonely child at least a

small measure of security. Without releasing Sammie from duty, Cassie praised the dog, silently promising her a game of Frisbee later.

Then, somehow, she found the means to sit calmly down again and resume her chatter, keeping up a steady stream of banter until she saw Sam heading toward them.

Mariah's hand stayed on the dog's head until Sam was standing right beside her. Her neck craned upward as her eyes followed him. And her hand stole into his.

His eyes met Cassie's and she couldn't help the great big grin she shared with him as she nodded *yes,* to his unspoken question. She'd have to wait until he called her later to tell him what had happened. But for now, at least he knew it had been something good.

Sam and Mariah waited with her while Sammie, off duty, took a turn around the park, squatting a time or two, barking at a bird, running circles around some kids over by the swings.

As she finally parted from them at the edge of the park, telling Mariah that they'd visit again soon, Cassie was still wearing the glow the afternoon had brought her.

For a moment, it had almost been as though Mariah were *their* child and they her loving parents, sharing the unending worry as well as the brief, transcendent joy.

Almost.

But almost didn't count.

And that was where she pulled herself up short. She could care about Mariah. She could help the child. But that was all. This was a job.

Nothing more.

* * *

She'd known Sam would call. Had been waiting for the phone to ring most of the evening and was prepared with a ready speech when he did. She was even braced for the warmth of his tone, the gratitude and relief he expressed when she told him what had happened. What she'd been saying when Mariah had responded to her.

What she hadn't been prepared for was his "wait a minute" when she said goodbye.

"What?" she asked, leery now.

"I think we should talk."

"We just did."

"I mean about us, Cass."

Standing there in her soft cotton pajamas, the television droning familiarly in the corner, Cassie curled her toes into the carpet. "We have nothing to talk about."

"We have plenty to talk about," he said firmly.

He'd obviously thought about this a lot. And wasn't going to give up easily. Even after all this time, she recognized the determination in his voice.

"I'm not asking for anything from you, Cassie," he went on. "I understand and respect the fact that you want nothing to do with me. But I still think it would be best for both of us if we could just...clear the air."

"I don't think so."

"How can either of us go on until we do?"

She sank down on the edge of the sofa. "I've been going on for ten years, Sam. You get used to it after a while."

"And you can honestly tell me that seeing each other again hasn't changed that?"

Of course it had. How could it not? She didn't answer him.

"I owe you some explanations, at least," he told her.

She heard the guilt in his voice. "You owe me nothing."

"Can you honestly tell me there aren't some questions you'd like answers to?"

Again, she didn't answer him.

"There are things I need to know, Cassie."

"You don't deserve anything from me."

"I know that, but Shelter Valley's a small place. We're going to run into each other from time to time. And we're going to hear about each other...."

He was giving her a chance to tell him what he was eventually going to learn from other people. He wanted to hear about the past ten years of her life from *her*. But there were some things she just wasn't ready to tell him. Things that—at the rate she was going—she might never be ready to tell him. Things he wouldn't hear from anyone else in Shelter Valley. Nobody ever spoke about that tiny grave. Or the tragedy that nearly took her life.

But there *were* things she could say to him. And he was right; there were things she wanted to know. Like, why he'd blown their lives all to hell without even telling her he was unhappy. Without giving her a chance to help, to fix whatever was wrong. Why he'd left town without a word of explanation.

If she had some answers, could she finally put the past to rest?

"When?" she asked him.

"Mariah's asleep. I can come now."

"No."

It was late. She wasn't dressed. She couldn't have him in her house.

"You name the time and place."

He was going to let her do this her way. Which made Cassie feel a little more in control. And able to acknowledge that she didn't want this hanging over her head for the rest of her life. Able to admit she wouldn't be getting any sleep that night, wondering what he had to tell her. Imagining his answers to questions she'd been asking for so many years.

There were very few occasions when he felt comfortable leaving Mariah. And if they did this at night, there'd be much less chance of anyone in town finding out about it—and making more of it than was warranted.

"Okay, now, but not here," she said. "I'll meet you at the park."

"I don't like the idea of you going down there by yourself so late at night."

"This is Shelter Valley, Sam," she reminded him. "And it's only ten o'clock."

"Will you at least promise you'll stay locked in your car until I get there?"

If it would get him off the phone and on his way to get this over and done with... "Yes."

Cassie's blue Taurus was the only car parked along Main Street when Sam got there. He pulled the truck in next to her, and met her at the hood of her car.

"Let's go sit on the bench by the sandbox," she said, leading the way without waiting for his answer. Or allowing conversation, either.

The sandbox was new since Sam had left. It didn't

hold any memories. He'd have preferred the bench by the palo verde tree.

They'd sat on that bench often during the years of their courtship. During their brief marriage...

The first time he'd taken her to sit there was after she'd fallen trying to beat him in a bicycle race. She'd gone too fast over the curb at the edge of the park. He'd been scared out of his wits when he'd seen her fly off that bike. And so relieved to find that she'd only skinned her knee that he'd made a total fool of himself. He'd told her then and there, sitting on that bench, that he liked her.

She'd laughed at him. "Of course you do, silly," she'd said. "We're friends."

"No," he'd brazened right on, his young heart too full to keep still. "I mean as in a boy liking a girl."

Astonished, she'd just sat there, staring at him, not knowing what to say. And because he'd been afraid she'd decide she didn't like him back, he'd leaned forward and kissed her.

Just a peck. They'd only been twelve or thirteen at the time. But there'd never been anyone else of consequence for either one of them after that. Certainly not for him. And, he suspected, not for her.

Cassie sat at one end of the bench. The park light across from them revealed the figure-hugging cotton top she was wearing, putting her breasts in a spotlight. God, he ached to touch them again. He'd once had the right to touch those breasts whenever—

Sam swallowed. He'd been wanting her too many years to allow his thoughts to travel that road. Especially when she'd already made perfectly clear that it would be a cold day in hell before Sam Montford ever had his hands on her again.

He sat on the opposite end of the bench. And wondered how to begin, now that they were both here. He'd had so many conversations with her in his mind, explained things over and over, looking for his own understanding by seeing the past through her eyes. Yet now he didn't know how to begin.

"First, I want you to know I've been paying for what I did to you, to us, every day of the past ten years," he finally said. "I'm so sorry, Cassie. More sorry than you'll ever know."

She nodded. That was all. No words.

Sam hadn't really expected absolution. His sins were too great for that. But God, he'd hoped for... something from her. Some sign of forgiveness.

"I wouldn't have been any good for you if I'd stayed in this town, Cass," he said next. It was a truth he'd come to realize over the years. "I was dying here, and I didn't even know it."

"Dying?" she repeated, staring straight ahead. He couldn't tell if she was really as numb as she appeared, as unaffected, or if she'd just learned to hide her emotions over the years.

"I'm not a lawyer. I never wanted to be a lawyer. Or the mayor of this town. Or a scholar."

"Then why did you say you did?"

Sam blinked. "I didn't ever say that. My parents did. The town assumed I did. No one ever asked me what I wanted."

"You were valedictorian of our class."

"Not because I tried."

"You have a brilliant mind, Sam. How could you not want to use it?"

The old trapped feeling climbed insidiously up his spine. Until he remembered that although he was back in Shelter Valley, back with Cassie, he wasn't the same man anymore. He knew who he was now. What he was about.

Sam watched her shadowed face, wishing he could see her eyes, her expression. "I do use it," he told her. "Just not in the way that was planned for me."

Cassie shook her head. "I don't understand."

"I know. You never did."

"Oh," she said, a trace of bitterness seeping into her voice. "So now it's all my fault?"

"No." The word was soft, filled with grief. "I know it's all mine. I'm just trying to explain, if I can, how everything went so wrong."

"Explain, if you can, why you screwed that…that bimbo."

The harsh words were so completely discordant with the peace of the quiet evening, with the Cassie he'd known. Sam flinched.

"She didn't mean anything, Cass," he said, sickened even thinking about that night. The things he'd done.

He'd never been so ashamed of anything in his life. And had never recovered, either.

"You're the only woman who's ever meant anything to me. You were then. And you still are."

"Don't give me that, Sam," she said. "It's not necessary now. It doesn't matter."

He'd known she felt that way—and he couldn't blame her. But the words cut him deeply.

"As much as I loved you," he continued, because

there was nothing else to do, "I knew things weren't good."

"Why?"

Ah. The first bit of emotion in her voice. So she *did* still feel something. Even if it was hate. She wasn't completely immune.

He was a bastard to take satisfaction from that.

"I was never going to be the man you expected me to be. The man you'd fallen in love with."

"And you couldn't tell me this? You had to go out and screw some other woman, instead?"

The verbal slap hit its mark. "I was only beginning to realize the truth myself," he told her. "It took me years to sort it all out."

"I don't understand," she said again.

"I didn't, either, Cass, not for a long time. All I can tell you is that I was ready to explode and I couldn't understand why. I didn't know how to fix it."

"Maybe if we'd talked about it..."

"Maybe." But he didn't think so. They'd both been so young. So set in the patterns their parents had created for them. He wasn't sure either one of them could have figured anything out at that stage.

"So you didn't want to be married?"

Sighing, Sam leaned forward, his elbows on his knees, his hands clasped in front of him. "I didn't know," he told her honestly. And felt a wave of pain when he heard her hissed-in breath. "I knew I loved you to distraction," he said, turning to look at her. "But I felt so *trapped....*"

"I can't believe you didn't tell me!"

"I didn't know what there was to tell. I didn't understand it myself. How could I love you and want out of our marriage at the same time?"

Chapter 8

Cassie's silence was revealing. She didn't believe he'd loved her.

And Sam couldn't just leave his question hanging.

"I can honestly tell you now," he said, willing her to look at him, and, when she didn't, continuing anyway. "I know with absolute certainty that it *wasn't* the marriage I wanted out of." He took a breath, then another. "But our being married was...connected to everything else. Back then, I couldn't distinguish one thing from another, so I escaped it all. But my problem wasn't the marriage, Cassie."

"What was it, then?" The question was soft, fragile, almost as though she was afraid to hear the answer.

"Shelter Valley. The Montford legacy. The life that had been planned for me. I'm not a desk man, Cass. I can't stand to be shut in all day. I have to be outside. Working with my hands."

She'd turned to look at him, and by the soft light from the street lamp he saw the disbelief in her eyes.

"You never did manual labor in your life."

"I picked up the bush trimmings when I was little."

"And that makes you a blue-collar worker?" she said incredulously.

"No, but stupid as it sounds, it's one of my fondest memories of being a little kid." He'd found his answers, and now he needed her to understand them, too. Because without her knowing, the outcome of his struggle didn't seem quite complete.

"I get satisfaction from working up a sweat," he went on. Whatever force had sent him running from this town, from her, ten years ago, pushed him now. "I'm good at making things, fixing things," he said urgently. "I look forward to going to work. In a classroom, all I ever felt was the need to get out."

Was she even listening to him? He couldn't tell.

"At night, sitting at our desk in the apartment working on papers for school, I would think about a lifetime of going to the office, reading investment reports. The most physical thing I'd do all day would be to pick up the telephone. And I wanted to jump out of my skin at the thought."

He thought about Borough Bantam, about telling Cassie what he did when he sat at a desk these days, but decided against it. The comic strip was a by-product of the understanding he'd finally, painfully, arrived at. Understanding of himself, of his life.

This wasn't about work. Or success. It was about spending his days doing something that fulfilled him. Manual labor did that.

Besides, Cassie—and the rest of the town—might

take offense at his animal portrayals of them. They might not see the compliment he'd intended....

"So our whole life together was a farce," Cassie was saying, her tone abrupt.

"No, it wasn't," he told her, because he couldn't bear the aching he heard in her voice. But in a sense, she was right.

And they both knew it.

On some level, Cassie wasn't ready to accept what Sam was telling her. Not because she wanted him to put on a suit tomorrow morning and get a corporate job. But because it changed everything.

Every memory she had—the good ones included—would be transformed by this. Would be made unnatural. Unfamiliar. *Different.*

He had to be wrong. He had to be rationalizing a life gone to waste. He was making the best of things, telling himself that he now had what he wanted out of life. To do otherwise was too painful, and there was no way to recover what he'd lost.

"Why didn't you ever remarry?" he asked, when the silence began to grow longer than their conversation had been.

Rubbing her hands along her thighs, Cassie braced herself. He wanted the truth. And she needed to give it to him. To be free of it. She'd been keeping things hidden inside for so long.

Measuring each word carefully, searching for total honesty within herself, she told him. "You destroyed my ability to trust, Sam." At that moment, there was no bitterness. Just a feeling of calm. "I can't open myself up to that kind of commitment again."

"I can't accept that."

The bench was hard beneath her, but the cool night air was refreshing against her skin. It was already blisteringly hot during the day, but the nights would be pleasant for a while longer. She wished she felt as numbly exhausted as she knew she must be.

"It's not up to you to accept or reject what I say, Sam," she said matter-of-factly. "This is how I feel. End of story."

"One person's untrustworthy, so you've sworn off all men?"

He still faced straight ahead, wasn't even looking at her, but she sensed the emotions churning inside him.

"It was more than that," she said, remembering, barely able to breathe, as she thought back to those first days and nights of their marriage. "You weren't just one person to me. You were my whole life."

Her voice faltered as she resisted her tears. For the first time, Cassie could really talk about the betrayal; for the first time, she was with the one person who would understand. The rush of pain that freedom brought was overwhelming.

A spouse being unfaithful was cruelty. But it wasn't just the sex that had killed her spirit. "You were the good honorable man, the eternal husband, the ultimate best friend." She had to stop. To take a deep breath. To blink away the tears welling in her eyes. "From the time we met, you were the one thing in life I could count on. And I fully believed, I *felt,* I was that for you as well."

"You were."

"No, I wasn't." The bitterness poured out now. She

hated it. And couldn't seem to stem its flow. "If I had been, you'd never have been able to do what you did."

"I was drunk."

Cassie shook her head. She'd been drunk often enough to know that excuse didn't fly. "No matter how drunk you were, if I'd meant to you what you meant to me, you would've thought of our marriage. Of us, of *me*. And that thought would have pulled you back."

"I don't agree."

"I'm not asking you to. We're talking about what I know and what I believe."

"But you might be wrong, Cass—have you ever considered that? I was there. I know what I was feeling. And what I wasn't feeling. I know how much you meant to me. Have meant to me all the years I've been away. I *know*." He banged a fist against his chest. "I'm the one who has to live with the emptiness, the regrets, every day of my life."

Her heart started to pound, her blood racing in a way only Sam had ever made it race.

"I know how I felt coming home to you the next day, driving up our street, seeing the front door of our apartment building, remembering the night I'd taken you there for the first time and known it was our home. I carry with me the complete and utter misery I felt the morning after my...disgrace in Phoenix, when I contemplated walking in that door and telling you what I'd done, what I'd destroyed."

He spoke so vividly, his words brought it all back to her. The look on his face when he'd walked in and found her crying on the couch, disheveled, having stayed up all night worried sick about him. She could still feel the shock, the nausea, the dark despair when she'd found out where he'd been. The possibility of another woman had never once crossed her mind. A car accident, some kind of fall, a car-jacking, robbery—she'd even imagined him being bitten by a scorpion or hit by a bolt of lightning. All kinds of crazy possibilities had tormented her that night. But never another woman.

She'd felt a complete and utter fool. Worthless as a woman. As a *person*. She'd given her very soul to another person, thinking they shared everything, and she'd been the only one doing the sharing.

And that day hadn't been the worst of it.

"You have no idea what you lost," she said now, her stomach knotted with bitterness, with remembered despair.

He hadn't just lost *her* that morning. Ultimately, he'd lost their daughter, too.

Not that Cassie didn't blame herself, as well. Her overwhelming desperation, her resulting depression and inability to look after herself, had contributed to the baby's death.

For a moment she considered telling him, but knew she couldn't. Wasn't ready. Didn't have the emotional wherewithal to relive that part of her life. To deal with the emotional reaction that would trigger, the guilt and agony she'd feel.

"I have an idea of what I lost," Sam said after a lengthy pause.

Oh, no, you don't. She shook her head.

Hands on either side of her, Cassie resettled herself on the bench.

He glanced at her. She didn't look at him. But she

could feel him watching her, each of them lost in thought.

"You say you lost the ability to trust, Cass, but did you ever try to trust anyone else?" he asked softly. "Another man? Did you even try to see if you *could,* if you could marry and have the life, the family and kids, you always wanted?"

"What I always wanted was you."

"Me and the predetermined life that came with being the wife of Samuel Montford the fourth."

"No, Sam." She shook her head, adamant. "Sure, I was happy with our plans, but they weren't what brought me real joy. That came from the security of knowing that no matter what the world did to us, no matter what happened, we were in it together. I wasn't *alone,* and neither were you. That's what marriage meant to me."

"I felt that way, too."

"Apparently not." She heard her tone of voice and told herself to calm down. "If you'd really felt that way, you'd have come to me that night instead of having sex with another woman. And you'd have stayed around afterward."

Sam sighed. "It's all so confused, Cass. I needed you desperately, yet I knew that if I stayed, I was going to damage the very heart of who you were. I was too messed up to protect you from myself."

Oh. God. Don't do this to me. Don't make me feel you. Don't make any sort of sense. Not now. I can't bear to walk that road again.

"I know we can't go back, Cass, but I'd like to see if we could find something new."

She stood. "No. And this conversation is over, if

that's what it's about. I have absolutely nothing to give you, Sam. Nor do I want anything from you ever again."

The earnest look in his green eyes tore at her, and she tried to steel herself against him. "Have you listened to us tonight, Cass?" he asked before she could take a step. "What we have between us is a once-in-a-lifetime chance very few people get. How can we just walk away from that?"

She turned to leave, and he grabbed her wrist.

"Let go of me," she snapped, staring down at his hand.

His grip softened, his thumb almost caressing the sensitive skin on the underside of her wrist. "You just finished saying that what you always wanted was me. For the first time in my life, I have a *me* to give you, Cass."

"That was then, this is now. And if you don't agree to stop talking about this right now, I'm leaving."

He still didn't release her wrist.

"I mean it, Sam."

Sighing, he dropped his hand. "You win." And then, a silent moment later, he said, "I just can't stand the thought of you living your life all alone. Especially since I seem to be responsible."

Though she wasn't sure why, Cassie sat back down.

"It's who I am now."

He turned, pulling up one knee, resting it on the bench between them. Cassie was a little uncomfortable with the closeness, but decided that learning how to ignore him would be the best course. The healthiest course. The course most likely to prepare her for a future of living in the same small town.

"It doesn't have to be who you are, Cassie," he murmured. "You have so much love inside you, so much to give a relationship. It's criminal to let that all die just because I acted like an idiot."

What he said was logical. Unfortunately, logic didn't help.

He tapped her thigh, once, lightly. "The world is full of good, trustworthy people."

Cassie squirmed. "I know."

Silence hung between them again. She took deep calming breaths, trying to rein in the emotions he was unleashing. She couldn't believe, after all this time, that she was actually sitting here in Shelter Valley with Sam. Couldn't believe that any of this still mattered.

And yet...it did.

"It's kind of ironic, you know?" he said suddenly.

She swung her head around to meet his half-smiling gaze. "What?"

"You want to teach Mariah to trust again, when you don't believe in it yourself."

There is a big difference, dammit!

"Don't you see a pattern here?" he asked. "You've dedicated your life to a new therapy whose entire purpose is to reach damaged people and teach them to do something *you* can't do."

"I work with victims."

"And you weren't one?"

Coming from him, from the man who'd caused her the lifetime of heartache and grief, the statement had a debilitating impact.

She *felt* like a victim.

"It's not other people I'm afraid to trust, Sam," she blurted.

"You said it was."

She shook her head, looked out into the darkness in front of them. "No, I said you destroyed my ability to trust."

"Same thing."

"No. It isn't." She needed air. And the deep breath she took didn't give her nearly enough. "It's myself I don't trust."

The words, spoken aloud, were frightening. She'd never said them before. Never really allowed herself to think them. But she'd known.

"I don't understand."

"I let myself down. I was partly responsible for what happened to me and…" Her words trailed off.

Elbows on his knees again, hands clasped, Sam contemplated her for a moment, then asked, "How? And what's that got to do with trust?"

"Because I chose to love you, to give you every single part of me. I held nothing back, had nothing in reserve to see me through without you. I had nothing left because I'd given it all to you." She exhaled shakily. "That's why I can't trust myself in another relationship. I can't trust my judgment, can't trust myself to see when something isn't right. I can't trust myself not to give away everything I have—again. I just can't risk it. That's what I mean by letting myself down."

Sam straightened immediately, his back rigid. "That's *not* letting yourself down!" His voice was loud. "That's the purest form of love, Cassie, the kind God must have intended for all of us to share. And by offering that, you opened yourself up to the purest form of joy."

"I must've missed that part," she said wryly.

"No." He shook his head. "I missed it. Or rather, I let my own inadequacies get in the way. It's not your fault, Cassie. I blew it."

"Of course you did." She glanced at him, and then away. He was too damn close. "But before then, I blew it, too. I made the choice. I turned myself over to you lock, stock and barrel. I made a bad judgment call." She paused, wet her dry lips. "My instincts told me I could trust you completely, Sam. They were wrong, and it cost me dearly. I can't afford to give them a second chance."

They sat silently for a while, each looking out into the night. Some detached part of Cassie wondered which of them would get up first. Wondered why she wasn't already home, getting some much-needed rest. She had a long day tomorrow.

Church. Which would be hard with all the tongues wagging due to Sam's return. People were going to be watching her. Wondering. Some good-hearted souls who still believed in happily-ever-after would be looking for signs that she and Sam had found their way back to each other.

Others would be waiting to help if it looked as if she was going to fall apart again.

With her family on their extended trip, she'd been sitting with the Montfords at church. She'd have to sit alone tomorrow.

And then, after church, she'd have a full day at the clinic, still playing catch-up because of her time away. This next week she was supposed to submit an article to a worldwide professional journal, and she couldn't afford to pass up the opportunity. It wasn't a veterinary journal, but a psychology one. She'd been invited to write an analysis of pet therapy as an accepted form of trauma counseling.

Sam broke the silence. "You know, after I left Shelter Valley, I wandered around the country for a little while, doing odd jobs."

She didn't want to know.

"When I first started out, I was determined to make it on my own, not to use one dime of Montford money. But that was too easy. It didn't take me long to figure out that life had to be about more than I'd realized. Somehow, I was missing the big picture, but I had no idea where or how to find it. Soon after that, I signed up for the Peace Corps. And that's where things started to become clear to me."

In spite of herself, Cassie listened, hearing far more than his words were telling her. She could feel his struggle. Was there, struggling with him.

"Some of the things I saw would make you physically ill.

"The deprivation, the filth and disease, the atrocities. The children whose bones protruded due to malnutrition. The barbaric medical practices."

He paused, rubbing his hands together as though washing them.

Washing away disturbing visions?

"Those things taught me very quickly to measure life on a different scale. When you're standing in the middle of a town that's little more than dirt paths and falling-down shacks and you're among people clothed in things we wouldn't consider good enough for rags, and you watch the joy on their faces as they witness a marriage between two of their own, you know that all the wealth in the world can't buy what matters most."

His voice slid across the cool night air. Touched her. This was her friend. The man she'd grown up with, the man she'd once known as well as she knew herself. She was nineteen again, soaking up his every word.

Every time Sam had talked to her like this, she'd felt more complete. Right with her world. She couldn't let herself feel that now. She just *couldn't*.

"But according to you, we had that kind of love," Cassie said. She had to freeze up inside. It was either that, or crumple.

She started to cry, and looked away.

"That was only the beginning of my journey," he told her slowly. "I helped rebuild that village before I left. And although I missed you constantly, for the first time I went to bed at night feeling *good* inside. I'd done something worthwhile."

"You did worthwhile things here."

He shook his head. "I ran for student council, fought for better food in our high-school cafeteria. I visited a few nursing homes, participated in fund-raisers like that leukemia foundation thing, and got good grades. None of that compares to saving lives. To providing a decent way of life where there is none—digging proper wells for clean water, building a school or medical clinic, planting crops. It was *real,* Cassie. Not like what I did at home."

"You were just a kid here, Sam," she said. She had no idea why it was so important to fight him on this. "Had you lived in Shelter Valley as an adult, you'd have accomplished a lot more than cafeteria food and fundraising."

"But I wouldn't have gone to bed at night bone-weary from a day's labor. I never would have experienced the feeling of lying down, knowing I'd done what I was meant to do. Knowing, for that one day, I'd done all I could."

Threatened but not sure why, Cassie didn't argue with him anymore.

"Anyway," he continued after a few minutes, "when I got back to the States with Moira and Brian, we signed up as volunteers for a national disaster relief organization. Any time of the day or night, any time of the year, we'd get calls, and within hours we'd be on a plane to someplace where a tragedy or disaster had occurred. We'd attempt to fix things. To save people. To clean up. To put lives back together. Years of that teaches you many things, Cass—and one of them is that as long as there's breath, there's hope for a second chance."

He'd caught her, and she hadn't even seen it coming.

"I'm leaving." Rigid, frightened, crying, she walked quickly away.

But she wasn't quick enough. His "I can't give up on us, Cass" hit her before she made it to the safety of her car.

And stayed with her all the way home.

Mariah watched Sam as they drove to church on Sunday morning, but she wasn't thinking about breathing right then. Sam had said the church was God's house. She'd never been there before. Sam said he didn't go much, either, but that if they went, it would make Grandma and Grandpa happy.

She didn't know about that. Seemed kind of mean to make them happy because that would make the sadness worse. The way she figured it, if you didn't know happy, you couldn't know sad. Seemed kind of dumb of Sam not to have figured that out yet. But he would. He was a smart man.

As smart as her daddy had been. And her daddy hadn't been able to make the bad men stop. Hadn't been able to keep the sad things from happening. He couldn't tell Mariah to be quiet so they wouldn't hurt him anymore, or hurt her mommy. She hadn't meant to cry out loud like that....

She wasn't too sure about going to this house that belonged to God. Except that the lady Sam called Grandma said it was a place to talk to God, who lived in heaven. Mommy lived in heaven, too, and she really, really wanted to talk to Mommy again. To see if she was breathing and...and if her throat had stopped bleeding. It was okay if Mommy didn't want to live with Mariah anymore. Heaven must be very nice, and someone would want to stay there. Mariah understood about that. She just wanted to see Mommy breathing.

And Daddy, too.

Everyone kept saying Sam was her daddy now. Even Sam. And that her name was Montford, not Glory.

She liked Sam a lot—but he was Sam. And her daddy wasn't breathing. And she didn't want Sam to stop breathing, either.

"Why are you frowning, honey?"

Mariah waited. Okay. It was all right. He'd breathed again. She hated it when Sam talked. She couldn't see breaths when he talked, and that scared her. If Sam ever quit breathing, if he went away...

For just a second, she thought about Sammie. The dog. Could he be at God's house, too?

Sammie was the best dog Mariah had ever known.

She thought about Sam's friend, Cassie, who had a nice voice. And told a story about Sam that Mariah was still guessing about.

Maybe Sammie would be at God's house and would sit next to Mariah. That wouldn't be bad.

Sam was still breathing....

Chapter 9

"Hey, you two mind the interruption?" Sam asked his parents Sunday night. They were in bed, reading, as they'd done every Sunday night of his boyhood.

It was reassuring to find them still doing so.

"No, son, come on in." James laid down the book he'd been reading. *Standing For Something.* Sam read the title as he settled on the end of their four-poster bed, pulling his foot underneath him.

"Good book?"

"So far," James said. "I picked it up because the forward's by Mike Wallace from *Sixty Minutes*. I figured anything he was endorsing had to be interesting reading."

His mother closed her book of poetry, setting it on the nightstand along with her reading glasses. "What's on your mind, Sam?"

Sam shrugged. He'd rather talk about his father's

book another minute or two. "Did you read on Sunday nights all the time you were in Europe, too?"

"You can't have come in here just to ask us that," Carol said.

And James followed with, "Of course we did. Anytime we were in for the evening."

Sam nodded, tracing the quilted pattern on the white bedspread with his index finger. They were both watching him, waiting. Carol was frowning, James withholding obvious concern until he'd heard what Sam had to say.

He looked up at them. "I've been starting to make some plans and I wanted to keep you apprised."

Burrowing out from under the covers, Muffy shook her head, tags jangling. Her entire body quivered, and Carol pulled the dog onto her lap.

"So what are they?" James asked.

It had been so easy when he'd tried out this conversation in the shower that morning. He'd come home ready to be the man he really was. So why did he suddenly feel like a little boy again? A Montford boy, with all the responsibilities and expectations the name entailed.

"I have to be here pretty constantly right now, for Mariah's sake, but I can't just sit around and do nothing all day."

Tears sprang to Carol's eyes. "You aren't leaving."

"No." Sam wished he could ease the fears he'd planted so deeply inside her. "Not unless you're kicking us out," he said.

James quietly took his wife's hand. "The house may be ours to live in as long as we're alive, but you know darn well it's yours, Sam. Yours and Ben's. We couldn't kick you out if we wanted to."

"Not that we ever would," Carol assured him swiftly, wrapping her fingers around James's.

Envy of their closeness, their intimacy, coursed through Sam. But so did contentment. It felt good to come home from a world gone crazy, to find his parents still very much a team. Very much in love.

"You want to start going down to the office?" James asked. "I turned everything over to Lyle Simmons before your mother and I left for Europe, but I'm sure he'd be glad to have you taking an active interest in the business."

Lyle had been his father's righthand man for most of Sam's growing-up years. He ran Montford, Inc., one of the nation's most prestigious investment firms, and he probably ran it better than Sam could ever have done. That was partly because Lyle loved doing it, and Sam never would.

The old trapped feeling started to emerge, but Sam shoved it away. "I'm not joining the business and I'm not going back to school, Dad," he said firmly. There wouldn't be any discussion about this.

"Okay." James nodded. Carol looked from one to the other. With her free hand she was slowly petting Muffy.

"I have no intention of being a lawyer." Even though two previous generations of Montfords had gone into the legal profession. Including his father, who hadn't even wanted to practice law. He'd opened Montford, Inc. shortly after passing the bar exam.

"I think, after all that's happened, your mother and

I have already figured that out," James said, a hint of a grin on his lips.

Okay, so maybe he was coming on a little strong. Rather like the know-it-all fifteen-year-old he was trying not to be.

"What *do* you want to do?" Carol asked softly, her eyes filled with concern.

He looked closely, but didn't see any disappointment there. Maybe the years had changed them, too. Or shown them alternatives that hadn't been clear all those years ago.

He could tell them about Borough Bantam. Perhaps he should. Only that morning, he'd seen his mother reading the strip in the Sunday edition of the Phoenix paper. But it was too important that they accept the man he'd found himself to be. The man who would rather fix cars in a garage than count money in a bank. The success of Borough Bantam was a fluke. It was great. But he'd been just as happy building roads in Illinois before he'd ever begun to even think about marketing the comic strip.

That, actually, had been Moira's idea.

And once the strip had become successful, she'd urged him to take advantage of all the attention the press wanted to give its creator. Sam had adamantly refused. He'd carefully avoided any mention of himself at all. His publisher, accepting that he wasn't going to budge, had decided to play on the mystery element, instead. No one knew who S.N.C. was.

"I'd like to open a business renovating homes," he said. "It would have to be on a part-time basis to begin with, until Mariah recovers, but I'd like to start with some of those old homes down by the cactus jelly plant. They've become awfully rundown in the time I've been away."

"People started moving closer to town," James said. "The value of the houses dropped, but that allowed some of the farm workers in the area—cotton-pickers and field laborers—to buy them. Gives these people a solid base from which to raise their kids, send them to school."

"But they can't afford to keep the places up as well as they'd like," Carol said.

"So I'll help them."

"They can't afford to renovate, Sam."

"I'll work cheap," he said. "I wouldn't charge them anything if I thought they'd let me get away with that."

"They've got their pride."

"So let's give them something else to be proud of." Sam was eager to get started. And delighted to see that his parents weren't falling all over themselves to talk him out of his new venture.

Or into a different one.

"I can set them up on payment plans, ten dollars a month if need be. And I'll enlist their help as much as possible—work *with* them, not for them." There would be real satisfaction in that, as there'd been in his Peace Corps assignments and in disaster relief. He didn't need these people's money. What would he do with it, anyway? Except donate it someplace.

His share of the ever-growing Montford fortune aside, he made enough off the now nationally syndicated Borough Bantam to keep them all quite comfortably.

"You know how to do all this?" James asked. "The plumbing, electrical, woodworking, everything?"

His dad sounded impressed. Sam had never even considered that possibility.

"I do." He nodded, almost embarrassed. "I told you about renovating those homes in New Jersey, but I also spent a winter learning the plumbing trade. Another eighteen months with an electrician. Another eighteen months in total doing mechanic's jobs. I've got certification in all of those trades. Oh, and I built roads, too."

Carol still seemed bemused. "Why, Sam?"

He met her gaze. "Because it felt right."

They talked a while longer, his parents asking questions that Sam was happy to answer. He'd liked the renovating work best of all—finding the perfect fixtures to match the time period of whatever house he was working on. Discovering the exact trim for an old wooden farmhouse, or a claw-foot tub to fit a Victorian-era bathroom. It had been like putting together a big puzzle full of history and family memories.

"So you're really home to stay?" Carol asked, when the conversation finally wound down.

"Yes." Sam had never been more sure of anything.

The pattern in the bedspread interested him again. A lot. "I have something else to tell you," he said.

"About Mariah? Or her poor parents?" Carol had already put pictures of Moira and Brian in the Montford family photo album. She'd tried to get Mariah to help her, and when the child had simply sat, staring at Sam, she'd kept up a steady monologue, describing every photo so Mariah could share in the event, anyway. Assuming Mariah was listening....

Sam shook his head. "About Cassie."

"What about her?" Carol's voice was suddenly sharper.

"You haven't done anything to her, have you?" James asked gruffly.

"Hey." Sam held up both hands. "I surrender!"

"We're sorry, Sam," James said, sharing a sideways glance with his wife. "That girl's had some pretty rough times. She doesn't need any more."

Sam's parents felt responsible for what he'd done. He had no idea why that fact hadn't occurred to him before. He'd always known he'd hurt them, disappointed them. He hadn't realized he'd also shamed them.

But he *should* have known. He knew them.

"I have no intention of hurting her," Sam assured them.

Carol leaned forward, touching his face with one gentle hand. "Your presence here has got to hurt her, Sam. But she's a strong woman, and she'll be able to deal with that. All I'm asking is that you be sensitive and stay out of her way as much as you can. Make things easy on her."

Sam felt the muscle in his jaw twitch. "I told her last night that I intend to try to get her back."

Carol gasped.

"No!" James said immediately.

Carol glanced over at him, and though Sam couldn't translate the quick conversation that took place, he had a feeling his mother was begging his father for a chance to hope.

He felt better already, knowing he'd have her on his side.

"Promise me you'll stay away from her, Sam," James said. He looked older as he leaned back against the headboard. Old and tired. As though he'd aged in the past five minutes.

Sam swallowed. How did a man forgive himself for all the damage he'd done? The anguish he'd caused to those he loved?

How did he ever make restitution? Was it even possible?

"I can't do that, Dad."

Carol wrapped both arms around Muffy, watching Sam and his father.

"You owe it to her, to all of us—"

"I owe it to her to try to bring back the person I know is still living inside of her," Sam said fiercely. He'd felt their connection last night. Only briefly. But it had been there.

And Cassie had felt it, too.

Carol's eyes were wide. Worried.

Swinging his feet to the floor, James sat on the edge of the bed, a hand on either side of him. He was staring at the wall. "There are things you don't know, Sam. Things that make it impossible for you and Cassie to ever go back."

"I know she's sworn off relationships," Sam told him. "We had a long talk last night, and she told me about her inability to trust. I believe trust is something we can reestablish."

"Sam…" Carol began.

"It's okay, Mom," he said, standing, one hand on the cherry-wood post at the end of their bed. "I know I have my work cut out for me, but who better than the person who betrayed her trust, to give it back?"

"There are some things you can't give back, Sam. Some things that can't be fixed." James stood, too.

"Maybe, but this isn't one of them."

"You don't know everything."

"I know what I have to know."

"Did she tell you anything else, Sam?" Carol asked softly, both hands buried in Muffy's fur. "Anything about that time after you left?"

"I know it was really hard for a while."

"Specifically," Carol said. "Did she say anything specific?"

Sam thought back to the night before, trying to remember exactly what Cassie had said. And realized that it had been relatively little.

It was what she *hadn't* said that had spoken to him the most. He'd sensed that the only way she'd ever be healed was to find what she'd lost. And he was the only one who could help her do that.

No matter where life took them, no matter what they suffered, they needed each other. They always had.

"I guess not," he finally admitted. "Nothing specific."

"Well, there are things you don't know," James said again. His eyes were sad, almost…pitying.

Sam's heart beat faster. "What things?"

James shook his head. "They aren't for us to tell you, Sam. If and when she wants you to know, she'll tell you herself."

His head swung toward his mother. He couldn't accept that. She had to tell him.

"I'm sorry, Sam." Carol shook her head, too. "It has to come from Cassie."

"Is she ill?" he asked, his voice tense. "Has she got some kind of disease?" She couldn't have. She looked healthy and fit. But tired. Alarm shot through him. Was there a reason for that fatigue other than overwork?

"No disease," James said, dispelling that particular fear. "And we're not saying anything more. Just forget about the two of you ever getting back together. It's no longer possible."

His father's warning came too late. Sam had already made up his mind.

Cassie and Sammie saw Mariah in the park twice more that next week. Although there was no new progress—and that in itself was a step backward—Cassie still believed they were on the right track. That they had a chance of reaching the child. Mariah always stood beneath the palo verde tree and stared after Sam. She didn't speak or show any sign that she was listening to Cassie.

But Cassie couldn't give up hope. She continued to talk to the child. Telling her about Sam when he was a boy. About some of the escapades the two of them had gotten into. Like the time they'd ditched school to dig for gold, and she'd fallen in the stream and caught a cold, which turned into pneumonia. They'd only been about ten. Sam had gotten his hide tanned.

She probably would have, too, if she hadn't been so sick. Instead, she got spoiled.

Each day with Mariah, she ended her monologue

with the statement that there were some things in life you could count on. Like Shelter Valley. It was always there. For more than a hundred years, Shelter Valley had survived one crisis after another. Lack of water. Too much rain. Mountain lions. Marauding javelinas. A tornado. And always her people were steadfast. Helping each other in whatever way was needed.

As long as Mariah was in Shelter Valley, Cassie told her, she'd have friends.

Mariah's position, facing the direction Sam had left, never changed. Cassie wondered how the child had the self-control to be so still; most seven-year-olds couldn't sit still for two minutes.

Mariah's lack of response didn't change, either. No matter how much Cassie spoke to her, how many times she tried to get the child to look at Sammie—or a bird or other children or a tree—it was as though Mariah didn't hear her.

But what did change, finally, was Mariah's body language. The child wasn't so rigid the following Thursday afternoon. Her spine was more relaxed, her shoulders not quite so stiff. And the fingers tangled in Sammie's fur were moving constantly.

There was nothing tentative or noncommittal about the child's communication with the dog. Mariah didn't look at the dog, but caressed her from ear to ear, back and forth, burying her fingers in Sammie's fur. She was using her sense of touch to connect with the world.

Sammie sat grinning, her tongue hanging out of her mouth, basking in the attention.

Cassie wanted so badly to hug the child, she crammed

her hands into the pockets of her navy slacks, her elbows pushed against her sides.

Sam noticed right away that there was a change, when he came to collect Mariah. Even before he got close enough to take the child's hand, Cassie saw him watching Mariah's fingers. Then he looked at Cassie, brows raised, mouth stretched wide in a smile.

"I'm making the old apartment over the garage into an office," he told Cassie as he followed her to her car that afternoon. He'd told her on Tuesday afternoon about his venture in the house-renovating business.

Cassie tried to busy herself with Sammie, getting the dog to the car and then inside. But Sammie was too damn good to need any prompting. The dog would probably find a way to open the car door herself if Cassie forgot to do it.

"I've already got a couple of suppliers lined up, referrals from some of the folks I worked with back east. I figure it'll only be a couple of weeks before I'm ready to find my first project."

She didn't want to know this. Confused by him, by herself, she shut the door behind Sammie and walked around to her side of the car. "We can come here again on Saturday?" she asked Sam.

"Of course."

Their eyes met, held, until Cassie looked away. She focused on her charge, on the only thing that mattered. "It was great seeing you, Mariah," she said. "On Saturday, maybe we can get Sammie to play Frisbee with us. She looks really funny running around with that thing in her mouth."

Mariah was staring at Sam's shirt. She didn't blink.

* * *

After dropping Sammie off, feeling guilty for being glad that Zack and Randi weren't there to ask questions, Cassie drove straight to Phyllis Langford's house. Her new associate—and friend, Cassie thought—had told her to stop by anytime. Cassie was hoping she'd meant it. Hoping the psychology professor was at home.

Phyllis *was* home and seemed glad to see her. Cassie found herself sitting at the kitchen table, a glass of iced tea in front of her, before she had a chance to change her mind about being there.

"I need some advice," she said, as soon as Phyllis, dressed casually in cotton shorts and a knit top that showed off her trim waist, was seated across from her.

"I kind of thought so," Phyllis said, grinning. "Shoot."

Cassie frowned. "I'm that obvious?" She'd taken great comfort in her ability to hide from the world. Hated to think she was really so transparent.

Hell, the whole town would be pitying her if they had any idea how messed up she felt right now.

"Not at all," Phyllis said. "I've just had enough experience to recognize the look. So what's up? Mariah?"

"Partly." Cassie told Phyllis about the five visits they'd had so far. The slow progress. "I didn't want to call her counselor in Phoenix yet," she confided. "She wasn't all that convinced there was any point in doing this, and I don't want her to pull the rug out from under us, especially when I still think we have a chance to make this work."

"There's no reason to call her unless you notice

some worsening in the child's behavior," Phyllis assured her. "Mariah's having her biweekly meetings with the woman, right? If there's a problem, the doctor will catch it."

Cassie took a sip of tea. "Am I kidding myself, here?" she asked Phyllis.

"In what way?"

"I don't know." Cassie pushed a strand of hair out of her eyes. Her twist had come loose while she was in the park with Mariah. "Maybe I'm looking for something that isn't there, taking hope where there really isn't any." She gazed across at Phyllis. "I mean, she's moving her fingers, and that's it."

"It's a step, and when you're dealing with something like this, every step counts."

"You don't think I'm getting too personal to be objective?"

Covering Cassie's hand with her own, Phyllis shook her head. "There's no such thing as 'too personal' with what you're doing, Cassie. Your work with Mariah is all about getting personal."

Sighing, Cassie looked down. "You'd think I'd know all of this by now. Anyone might have the impression, that this was the first case I'd ever worked on."

"I think there's more going on here than a case," Phyllis said gently. "You're not losing your objectivity where Mariah's concerned. What you *are* losing is trust in your own professional judgment."

Phyllis's words hit her hard. Were the insecurities going to infiltrate her work now, too? It was the one thing she'd always been able to feel completely confident about. She was a pioneer in her field. She knew the value of her skills.

"So, you want to talk about what might be getting in your way?" Phyllis asked gently. She gave a great deal of attention to her glass of tea, stirring methodically, adding sugar, stirring again.

"I'm not certain that full recovery is imminent, but I feel convinced that we're helping Mariah," Cassie said slowly, stirring her own glass of tea. "What I'm not sure about is *my* ability to survive her therapy."

Chapter 10

Cassie sat in Phyllis's kitchen, an educated professional, world-renowned in her field, feeling like a kid who needed her mommy.

"I'm losing control," she told Phyllis. "Having Sam around is undoing everything I've done to get myself grounded over the past ten years. So much for being an emotionally stable woman, in charge of my own destiny."

"You *are* stable," Phyllis said firmly, leaning her forearms on the table. "The fact that you're here, talking to me, means you're in charge. You aren't helpless. You haven't buried yourself in the past, or forgotten the lessons you've learned. Yes, you're having a tough time. You're feeling off balance and that's a natural and appropriate response under the circumstances. But instead of giving in to despair or bitterness, you're fighting back."

Cassie shrugged, a bit embarrassed. "You make me sound…impressive."

"If you could step outside yourself, see what I've seen in the short time I've known you, heard what I've heard from people who love you, I think you'd be surprised at what you'd find." Phyllis held Cassie's gaze. "You're helping Sam's daughter in spite of your past history, and that alone says what a remarkable woman you are."

Looking over at the other woman, a redhead like herself, Cassie smiled tremulously. And tried to let herself believe what Phyllis was saying.

"I've been telling Mariah stories about Sam, incidents from when we were younger, trying to build a sense of continuity for her in Shelter Valley," she said after a while.

"And also a bonding tool for the two of you," Phyllis added.

It was something Phyllis had suggested to her in the first place. To find such a tool.

"Yeah, well, it may or may not be helping her bond with me, but it's sure making it hard to keep my distance from Sam. I've got him coming at me from one side every time I see Mariah, telling me about his plans, giving me updates on his activities. And I've got the past coming at me from the other side as I relive it all for Mariah."

"What do you think you should do?"

"Move." Cassie attempted a grin.

"It's your turn to run away, huh?" Phyllis asked.

"Of course not. But I'm human. You've got to admit, from my point of view it's a tempting proposition."

"I can see that it would be."

"So what do I do?" Throat dry, she sipped her tea.

"What do you *want* to do?"

It wasn't a question Cassie asked herself very often. "I want to quit hurting," Cassie answered.

"I know," Phyllis replied, her eyes filled with compassion. "Believe me, I know."

Cassie studied the woman, the tremors around her mouth, the pain in her eyes. "It sounds as if you really do."

"My ex-husband was unfaithful to me, too." Phyllis's eyes were shadowed.

"Oh." And then she added, "Did you just want to die?" It had taken Cassie a long time to get over that feeling.

"At first," Phyllis said. "And then I wanted him to."

Running a finger along the rim of her glass, Cassie blinked back tears. "Me, too."

"We'd been married for four years, and we both had successful careers. I thought we were on the right track...."

"What happened?"

Eyes moist, too, Phyllis shrugged apologetically. "He was intimidated by my intelligence. He hated when I analyzed things. And he was threatened by the fact that I understood him so well."

Cassie and Sam hadn't had any of those problems. "He told you all this?"

"No." Phyllis shook her head. "He just salved his ego with a leggy brunette from the PR department. I figured out a lot of it afterward. At the time, I knew something wasn't right, but I assumed it was because of our job demands, that sort of thing. And then, one weekend when he was supposedly out of town on business, I ran into him and his brunette at a restaurant in downtown Boston—which is where we're from."

"What did you do?"

"Gained almost fifty pounds." She smiled sadly. "Not that night, of course, but over the next year."

Cassie leaned over to look up and down Phyllis's trim frame. "What were you before, anorexic?" she asked.

"No." Phyllis laughed. "Since I came to Shelter Valley last summer, I've been working on a weight-loss program with Tory Evans. You know her, I think— she's married to Sam's cousin Ben."

"We've met several times," Cassie said.

"Tory's older sister, Christine, was my best friend. She was killed last year in a car accident that wasn't an accident."

"And Tory, who was the intended victim of the accident, posed as her sister here, in Shelter Valley," Cassie said, remembering. "She took Christine's new job in the English department at Montford as a way to hide out."

"Right." Phyllis took a sip of tea. "She lived with me before she met and married Ben. She thought I was doing all the helping in our relationship but she helped *me* realize that I was hating myself, blaming myself, for something the jerk I'd married had done. It wasn't my fault he was intimidated by me. It was his. There was nothing wrong with me. And plenty wrong with him. I was being a masochist, feeding my body stuff I didn't even want as a way to punish myself for not being woman enough to keep my man."

Cassie couldn't believe how well Phyllis had just

explained Cassie's own feelings of inadequacy. "So what do I do?" she asked softly. "I don't have any weight to lose."

"Search your heart," Phyllis said. "Listen to what it tells you."

"Sam wants us to try again, to find out if there's anything left of what we had."

"Is that what you want?"

Cassie shook her head. She didn't need to listen to her heart. She already knew what it had to say. "I can't trust him." *Or myself...*

"Maybe he had a reason for doing what he did. Something that would allow you to see things differently. Maybe the infidelity was a one-time thing. A horrible mistake."

"It was that, all right," Cassie said, a trace of bitterness slipping through. "But it wouldn't matter, even if there was some acceptable way to explain it." She rose to pour the rest of her tea down the sink and rinse her glass. "We can't ever go back to the life we'd planned. Things have changed for me, major things. Taking up where we left off is impossible."

"Maybe you can create a new plan."

Wiping her hands on the towel by the sink, Cassie thought about that. There was no new plan for her and Sam. Talking to Phyllis was only confirming that. "I can't forgive him."

"And that's the basis of your problem," Phyllis said. "I don't blame you. I'm having a hard time in that area myself. But this I do know—you don't have to open your heart to him again, you don't have to trust him, but if you don't find a way to forgive him, you're never going to heal. You'll have allowed him to rob you not only of your past, but of your future, too."

The words were hard to take. More so because Cassie knew that Phyllis was right. But forgiving was an agonizing business. It required thinking about things she'd promised herself she'd never think about again.

It required feeling things she was afraid to let herself feel.

In Harmon's Hardware store on Saturday afternoon—doing a bit of work while he waited for enough time to pass before he could go back to get Mariah from the park—Sam perused a binder of suppliers' information that Hank Harmon had just given him.

He'd need everything, from nails and hammers and wood glue to power tools and scaffolding. And buying wholesale in bulk, at least for the supplies he'd be replacing often, was much more cost-effective than buying over the counter. No matter how much money Sam had, he didn't believe in wasting it. Not after the want he'd seen all over the world.

"I suppose you've heard that Junior's trying to pull the plug on Becca Parsons's Save the Youth program," Hank said, an elbow on the counter, watching Sam. His overalls looked as though he'd worn them one day too many without washing.

"Mmm-hmm," Sam said, trying to focus on payment and delivery terms rather than the rock that was taking form in his gut. Junior, as most people dismissively called him, was the current mayor, and derided for his lack of initiative and leadership. But he was a Smith, the "other" branch of the Montfords. They'd been brought into the family by the original Smith's marriage to the original Sam Montford's daughter. On the whole, the Smiths were more self-centered than the Montfords, less civic-minded and more mercenary. But they were of Montford descent. And as the second-wealthiest family in town, they had power in their own right.

Junior wasn't all bad. He wasn't evil, didn't have unethical business dealings. He just wasn't a doer. Or a thinker, either.

Now, Becca Parsons—that was another matter. Older than Sam by a decade, Becca was on the town council and married to the president of Montford University. No one loved Shelter Valley more than Becca did; no one served the town better.

"Your folks told you all about the play the youth program produced last summer, I'm sure." Hank tried again when it was obvious Sam wasn't going to bite. "It was the story of your great-great-grandfather's life."

"Yeah." Sam nodded. "I understand they performed it the day the statue was dedicated."

"That's right. It was great, too. Could rival anything you'd see in children's theater in Phoenix. And besides the theater division, the program's got a sports division, arts and crafts, drug and alcohol awareness, all kinds of things. They were planning to hold biweekly dances this summer, too, to let the kids get together in a controlled environment." Hank went on and on, as was his way, cheerfully imparting every bit of information he had. "The dances are one of Becca's newest projects. She wants to bring in DJs from Phoenix, do it up right so the kids'll not only want to come, but will feel like they can get everything in Shelter Valley that they'd get in the big city. She says it'll keep them from wandering, always thinking they have to run off to Phoenix for the real fun."

Sam nodded a second time. He'd heard all about the project. Four times in the past week—though only once from his parents. He was in full support of it.

He just couldn't be responsible for it—or any of the other projects that were stalled or threatened by the spineless Junior Smith.

"You got a piece of paper, Hank?" he asked, grabbing a pen from the counter.

With stained and callused fingers, Hank slid a pad of notepaper bearing the Harmon Hardware logo across the bottom toward him, and said, "You know why Becca started the program, don't you?"

Sam nodded yet again, though he didn't look up from the names, numbers and figures he was copying. "My folks had her and Will over for dinner last Monday night."

It was the night after Sam had had his conversation with his parents about what his future plans did and did not entail. But to be fair, they'd already invited the Parsonses. It hadn't been a deliberate slap in Sam's face—or a refusal to accept the place he chose to occupy in Shelter Valley. Or more to the point, the place he chose *not* to occupy.

Regardless, he'd enjoyed renewing his acquaintance with Will and Becca. And he'd been charmed by little Bethany, who'd entertained them by rolling all over his mother's handwoven wool carpet.

"They tell you about Becca's niece being killed by

that teenage drunk driver a couple years back?" Hank asked, his gaze intent.

Looking up from the page, Sam met Hank's eyes. "I think the program's great, Hank. I'm all for it."

With Mariah growing up in this town, he'd fight for that program, just as any other conscientious citizen would. He'd offer financial support, as well.

But that was all he could do.

"You know elections are coming up this next fall." Henry Crane, an optometrist who'd moved to Shelter Valley when Sam was just a kid, came up behind Sam. He'd obviously been eavesdropping.

The rock in Sam's stomach was getting bigger by the second. He owed this town; he knew that. He was a Montford—had been born to privilege. And responsibility.

But he had to pay in his own way. Didn't he?

Ron Christie, his ex-Little League baseball coach, now gray and walking with a cane, joined the threesome at the counter. "Yeah, and with you back in town, Sam…"

"Wait a minute, guys." Sam held up his hand. He couldn't let them go any further. "I'm a construction worker."

"You're a Montford," Chuck Taylor said. Chuck had been the quarterback of Sam's high-school football team. He'd gone on to play for Montford U, and then a couple of pro teams, before a knee injury forced his early retirement. Sam had heard that Chuck now owned a portion of the Shelter Valley Cactus Jelly Plant.

"Can't argue with you, there," Sam said. "I am a

Montford." He tried to keep things light. Tried not to let the pressure of their hopes get to him.

The last time he'd done that—let the expectations of other people unsettle him—he'd made the biggest mistake of his life. He'd hightailed it to Phoenix. Gotten drunk. Slept with a woman whose name he couldn't remember. He'd betrayed Cassie. Run out on their marriage...

"What do you say," Chuck said. "You were always the guy leading the crusades."

Closing the binder, Sam slid it back across the counter to Hank. He turned to face the men—Chuck with his balding head and potbelly, Henry whose glasses had gotten much thicker over the years, and Ron who was far too skinny and frail for Sam's liking. He cared for them all. They represented what was best about Shelter Valley. Love. Loyalty. Home. You could count on all three of these guys for anything.

Sam hated to let any of them down.

"I appreciate your faith in me, gentlemen, but I don't even have a college degree. I'm not qualified to run this town."

Chuck lifted a booted foot up onto the barrel of electrical tape by the counter, leaning an elbow on his upraised knee. "Hell, Sam, you're the smartest guy I know. You could run this town in your sleep."

The thing was, there was probably truth in Chuck's assessment. While Sam might need to stay awake to sign checks, he *could* run Shelter Valley. He just didn't want to.

He'd promised himself before he came back here, that he wouldn't allow them to influence him. He would ignore their persuasions and compliments. At one time he couldn't handle the pressure this town put on him, and that had caused him to betray his wife, to hurt those he loved most, to destroy his life.

But he was stronger now. And armed with his hard-won self-knowledge, he wasn't going to fall into the trap of other people's desires.

On Monday, after work, Cassie went straight home, changed into an old pair of cut-off shorts and a cropped T-shirt, and pulled her hair back into a ponytail. She had a mission.

She was going to tile the alcove in her guest bathroom.

Leaving on the television in her bedroom, she went to the kitchen, flipped on that set, and helped herself to a large glass of soda with lots of ice. She'd eat later if she got hungry enough to quit work. Next stop was the garage for the supplies she'd bought the day before—the plastic floor protector, two-by-two, yellow-and-green ceramic tiles, paste and putty knife, and the hammer she was going to use to break the square shower tiles into smaller pieces.

She loved to decorate. Had studied interior decorating in the evenings a few years ago and still avidly read the magazines she received each month. After her talk with Phyllis, she'd decided to concentrate on something she loved, something other than her work. An activity that would take up her time, consume her.

With the set on in the bathroom, as well, she waited for her evening companions to appear and keep her company. She felt as though she knew Pat Sajak and Alex Trebek personally.

Jeopardy came on first. Cassie was on her knees

cracking tile, angling the hammer to get varied shapes. Later she'd lay them out in designs that let the different colors and shapes complement each other, before applying them to the wall.

"What are Lisbon and Madrid?" she mumbled between cracks of the hammer. The two Iberian cities the Lusitania Express ran between.

As Diane, the thirty-something contestant with the stylish navy suit and short fly-away hair, asked the correct question, Cassie picked up the piece of tile she'd just broken. Round on one end, it was jagged on the other. She really liked that one. She set it aside to become a focal point in the finished design.

The television droned on. Tuning out the five minutes of commercials, Cassie continued to break up tiles, allowing her artistic eye freedom and refusing to let her mind roam. Sam had taken Mariah into Phoenix for an appointment with her counselor that afternoon. And he hadn't called with a report.

She didn't want to place too much importance on that.

Mariah hadn't made any more progress on Saturday. Had not, in fact, seemed as interested in Sammie. She hadn't looked at all while Cassie laughed and made a big production out of playing Frisbee with Zack's dog. And her little hand had merely rested on Sammie's head when Cassie brought the dog back to her. There was no burying of fingers in Sammie's fur.

But it could have been that she was simply taking comfort from the dog with less effort.

Or maybe she'd been paying more attention to Cassie. Cassie had been telling her about their senior prom, when she and Sam were crowned king and queen. She'd described the crown in great detail. And remembering back, she'd described Sam as she'd seen him that night. A true king—not just at the dance, but always.

"What is Nevada?" she said aloud. The show was back on. She had something to focus her thoughts on. The U.S. state that had sagebrush as its state flower.

She and Diane both got it right.

Diane chose "Feather Fun" for two hundred dollars. "The reptilian feature that evolved into feathers." Alex read.

"What are scales?" Cassie looked up, willing Diane, the person she was rooting for, to get it right. "Scales," she said again.

Before she found out if Diane knew the answer, the doorbell rang.

It was Sam.

"Where's Mariah?" she asked, opening the door, forgetting what she must look like. Forgetting she didn't want Sam there, alone with her, in her house. He was still wearing the slacks and polo shirt he must've worn for the trip in to Phoenix. His longish dark hair was mussed, his green eyes troubled. His face was grim.

"Home," he said, lips tight. "The trip into town tired her out. She fell asleep right after dinner."

"Your mother's with her?" Cassie asked. They didn't want Mariah waking up alone, being frightened, just when they'd begun to make a little progress.

Sam nodded. "I'm interrupting something?" he asked, pointing to the hammer still clutched in her fist.

Glancing down at herself, Cassie brushed self-consciously at the tile dust on her knees. Though why it should matter what she looked like for this man, she didn't know. It didn't matter. Not at all. *He* didn't matter.

But his daughter did.

"I was just working in the guest bathroom," she explained.

He frowned. "Did you need help fixing something?"

Cassie shook her head. "I'm creating." Because his presence in her house was bothering her, making her too aware—uncomfortably aware—of her own confused feelings, she headed back to her project. She needed something other than Sam, other than her own emotions, to focus on.

Sam followed her, leaning against the sink as she showed him what she was doing. She felt like a nervous teenager.

"I'm impressed," he said, kneeling to put together a couple of odd-shaped pieces of tile. They complemented each other perfectly. "What kind of grout are you planning to use?"

Before she knew it, she and Sam were discussing the project in detail, with him giving construction pointers as she showed him her plans. Until that moment, she'd completely forgotten he was in the renovation business. That projects like this were the kind of work he did.

She found herself kneeling in her bathroom beside him, sharing ideas, approving of what she heard. Laughing at small jokes.

Almost like old friends.

Sam seemed more relaxed than when he'd first come in, and Cassie was glad. It was good to see the Sam she used to spend hours with, working on some project for school or planning a dinner party. He laughed, and her stomach melted.

When he reached over her for a piece of tile and his hand grazed her arm, Cassie stood up, moved away from him.

Things were suddenly far too intimate. Too dangerous.

"I imagine you had a reason for stopping by," she said, hammer in hand.

He placed a couple more tile shards in the mosaic they'd been building on the floor, brushed his hands and stood up.

The party was over.

"They want to institutionalize Mariah."

"No!" She took a step toward him, forgetting everything but the little girl who'd already grown to mean so much to her. "They can't *do* that to her! She shouldn't be with strangers, in a place where they're constantly testing her, monitoring her, studying her," Cassie said passionately. "She needs to be with family, with people who love her."

"I know."

"You're not going to let them do that, are you?" she asked. *Jeopardy* ended. *Wheel of Fortune* came on, and Cassie didn't even notice.

Sam frowned. "I have to consider what's best for her. Her counselor believes that if putting her someplace where they can work with her every day, where they'll have several doctors assessing her, is going to help her—" He broke off. "I don't know."

"We're making progress, here, Sam. Taking her away from you now might just lock her away—emotionally—forever." Cassie might not have all the education that psychiatrist in Phoenix had, but she had a fair amount of training. Some relevant experience. And instincts that hadn't led her wrong yet.

"I know," Sam said. "Dr. Abrams mentioned that possibility. Cassie, she's already lost so much."

The pain in his eyes broke through the ice that had to surround Cassie whenever she was with Sam. Making her heart bleed for him. For the decision he had to make.

And for the little girl whose future lay in the balance.

"What do your parents think?"

Sam shrugged, and she watched his solid shoulders move. He was leaning against the sink, facing her. And his back was reflected in the mirror behind him.

"They don't want to send her anywhere. At least, not yet," he said. "But we've lost six months of her life, Cassie. She's going to be a year behind in school if we can't get her back soon, help her catch up before next fall."

But to send that lonely, frightened little girl away? To an institution? No matter how they tried to fix those places up, they were still cold.

Because an institution wasn't home.

Cassie acknowledged that they were right for some people, with certain kinds of problems. But not Mariah.

The child would just die there. Or learn to cope— but in the process lose the person she really was. Both the love and the hatred in her past would be difficult to think about, painful to remember, but it had to happen if Mariah was to return to herself. And to them...

"She's in there, Sam," Cassie said urgently. "The

fact that she watches you so intently has got to be a sign that you mean the world to her. If not, why doesn't she just stare at whatever happens to be around? It seems quite deliberate that she won't look at things—as though she's afraid to take them in, get too involved with her environment. But she takes *you* in. That has to mean something."

The muscles in his jaw were working as he gazed at her, his eyes bright, emotions in check.

Cassie wanted so desperately to help him. *Needed* to help him. It was as if they were teenagers again, feeling each other's pain.

"Give me a little more time. I'll move more quickly, take her out of the park this week. Perhaps she'll participate more with the world if she's exposed to unfamiliar stimuli without you to focus on."

"Sending her away seems so wrong," Sam said, the intense struggle he was experiencing evident in his voice. "But what if I make a mistake? What if this *is* what she really needs? How can I rob her of that chance?"

Without conscious thought, Cassie reached out to Sam, grabbing his hand between both of hers so naturally that she didn't even notice what she'd done until the warmth of his skin sent shocks right through her. Abruptly, Cassie let go. "Listen to your heart, Sam. It'll tell you what to do."

Phyllis had given her the same advice a few days before. And recalling why, Cassie turned away.

"Cassie…" He stretched out his hand, taking hers again.

Her skin burned, her body remembering other

times those fingers had touched her, and she found herself reacting automatically.

She jerked her hand away. "I'm here if you decide to continue," she said, turning from him. "Just let me know."

"Cassie," he said again.

Cassie didn't face him. She couldn't. She faced the bathtub, instead, and listened to Pat Sajak congratulate a winner as he started the next round.

Sam didn't try to talk to her anymore, but he was taking a long time leaving. She didn't know how much more she could stand.

"Can you still do tomorrow afternoon?" His voice sounded weary when he eventually spoke.

"Of course." Cassie looked over her shoulder at him, but only briefly. "We can meet in the park as usual." *Go now,* she silently begged.

"Thanks," he said, and it sounded as if he'd turned to go.

Cassie waited.

"And thanks for listening," he added. "You have no idea how badly I needed to see you tonight...."

She waited until she heard the front door click quietly behind him before she turned around.

And then, with her three televisions droning in the background, she fell to the floor, buried her face in the tile dust and sobbed until her ribs ached.

Chapter 11

Things at Borough Bantam were running amuck. The king and queen had adopted a little mouse that had crawled into their town. They were preoccupied, scurrying around, trying to please the little creature. Their usual pursuits were being neglected.

Leaning over his desk, Sam concentrated on the page coming to life beneath his rapidly moving pencil. Without the king and queen's watchful eye, the kingdom was falling into chaos and disrepair, and the magistrate was too busy worming around his empty little circle to see anything wrong. *I am. I am. I am.*

Without forethought, Sam moved to the last frame of this week's episode, a figure of the newcomer—the wild stallion—forming quite naturally. He was sitting under a ledge, gnawing on a piece of straw, a cowboy hat on his head while he watched. And waited.

The king and queen glanced at him from time to time. They weren't opposed to his being there. But they were withholding judgment.

Could be that they were too involved with their new addition to give him their complete attention. Or that he'd never be fully welcome here.

So, did he have a role in Borough Bantam? A purpose? Or was this just a stopping place on his way somewhere else?

Eager to find out, Sam was looking forward to next week's episode.

"Phyllis? It's Cassie. Am I interrupting something?"

"I'm grading papers, so interrupt away."

Cassie grinned. It'd been so long since she'd allowed herself friends. "I have a question for you."

"What's up?"

"Sam came by last night and said that Mariah's doctor in Phoenix has suggested the possibility of institutionalizing her. Sam doesn't want to do it. And I don't think he should." Cassie glanced at the television playing softly in the background in her office. "At least, not yet. We're making progress with Sammie. We just need a little more time."

"Reaching her in a normal life environment, if it's possible, is certainly better than trying to do it in the controlled environment of a hospital," Phyllis said slowly, as though choosing her words carefully.

"Then you think I was right to encourage Sam not to rush into anything?"

"As long as he's comfortable with continuing the way you are."

"He says his instincts are telling him to hang on to her."

"Then he probably should."

"That's what I thought, too."

"They *might* get quicker results in an institution. Forcing her to respond within a very predictable, structured situation, having her live around other traumatized kids, surrounded by caring staff—it could work," Phyllis said. "But not necessarily. And not necessarily with the best results."

"What do you mean by that?" Cassie had another fifteen minutes before her first appointment of the day. And she'd been worrying about Sam and Mariah for most of the night.

"Just that Mariah might come out of herself a little sooner that way, but she may not emerge as completely."

"She might be emotionally alienated," Cassie said. "Disaffected. Able to function adequately on a surface, everyday level but lacking emotional depth."

"Right." Phyllis gave Cassie a rundown of several cases in which recovery had been complete after the patient had been allowed to recuperate from a tragedy in her own time, in the safe environment of a loving home. "It takes longer sometimes, but the result could be a perfectly normal, well-adjusted life."

"Rather than one with dysfunctional relationships due to an inability to feel, to open oneself to others."

Thinking of the little girl who'd stolen her heart, a heart that had been empty since she'd lost her own little girl, Cassie knew which scenario she'd rather have. It was up to her and Sammie to make sure Mariah got that chance.

* * *

Sam, dressed in cutoffs and an equally revealing tank top, brought Mariah to the park right on time the next afternoon. Cassie's breath caught in her throat. He was so gorgeous.

A couple of mothers with strollers watched him cross the park. Sam seemed completely oblivious.

Cassie wished *she* was oblivious to *him*.

How was it possible, after all he'd done, that she could still feel such attraction?

The women followed him with their eyes, one leaning toward the other to say something. They both nodded; the second woman said something. They both laughed.

Probably fantasizing, Cassie thought. About how good that body would look stepping out of the shower, slick and wet. The chest would be contoured to perfection, firm to a woman's touch. The hair would be dripping over his forehead and into his eyes, large drops of clear, warm water...

He strode with such confidence, yet was the epitome of tenderness as he leaned toward his daughter, giving the unresponsive child his entire attention. He spoke to her as though they were both involved in the conversation.

The woman across the park actually turned around to stare once he'd left their line of vision. His tight backside wouldn't disappoint them.

Cassie could practically see them drooling.

He's mine, she wanted to tell those women. *He's always been mine.*

But the moment wasn't real. It was like a scene from a movie she was watching. Or a particularly good

book she was reading to pass the time on this warm
April afternoon. She was just a witness. It wasn't happening to her.

Until Sam and Mariah reached her and Cassie
couldn't find the breath to say hello.

Oh, God. What was happening to her? She was losing control of her world.

Sammie greeted Mariah, butting her head up under
the little girl's free hand.

"Is an hour long enough?" Sam asked, looking at
her strangely.

Cassie nodded.

"Right here?"

"Yeah." She found her voice. And hoped her composure wasn't far behind.

He lowered himself to Mariah's eye level as he let
go of her hand. "You stay with Cassie and Sammie,
okay, honey?" he said. "Daddy has some work to do
in town, and then I'll be right back to get you."

Mariah stared at him, making no response, her little
face lifting as he rose.

Good luck, Sam mouthed to Cassie. With one last,
concerned look in her direction, he turned his back
and walked away.

As intent as Mariah, Cassie stared after him until
he was out of sight. Something would have to give
soon. Before Cassie's sanity did.

Maybe it was time to go to Phoenix and find herself a man. But after ten years of celibacy, she wasn't
sure she'd know what to do with one if she had him.

She couldn't imagine *wanting* one. Not if he wasn't
Sam.

And she didn't want Sam at all.

* * *

Cassie decided to take Mariah to the ice-cream shop. Close to the park, the shop was fairly safe, she thought, since she could get the child back to her usual spot if it appeared that the outing was going to upset her too much. And all kids loved ice cream. Didn't they?

"You like chocolate ice cream?" Cassie asked the little girl, as soon as Sam had been gone long enough for her heart to slow down to its normal speed.

Mariah didn't answer. Nor did she react when Cassie took the small hand Sam had dropped. Mariah didn't pull back, and she didn't grab hold. The limp little fingers just lay in Cassie's grasp.

"Have you been to the Shelter Valley ice-cream shop yet?" Cassie asked, starting down the sidewalk as though there was no doubt that Mariah would walk beside her. "Come on, Sammie."

As Sammie moved, so did Mariah, although the little girl looked neither left nor right. Or straight in front of her, for that matter. Her stare was almost vacant, focused—if you could call it that—on some point between her waist and the ground.

Cassie refused to be daunted; the possibility that Mariah might be placed in an institution kept her going. She chatted all the way to the ice-cream shop, trying to engage Mariah's interest. The child had a difficult moment when she had to leave Sammie to wait outside as they reached the door, but when Cassie turned and walked inside, Mariah followed, her hand sliding from the dog's head.

Cassie ordered them each a scoop of ice cream in a paper cup. "You'll have to hold this one, honey, until we get outside." When Mariah made no move to accept it, Cassie lifted the child's hand, placed her fingers around the cup, then carefully let go. Mariah held on to the cup.

Without another word, Cassie took Mariah's free hand and ushered the child outside and back to Sammie.

Sammie started off walking at Cassie's side, between her and the street, and Mariah did an amazing thing. She dropped Cassie's hand and switched to the other side, between Cassie and Sammie. She couldn't touch the dog, not if she was holding Cassie's hand and a cup of ice cream, too. But she'd made her point. She and Sammie stuck together.

Cassie blinked back tears as she silently applauded the little girl.

Zack didn't want to do it, but Randi made him. She and Ben had set up a little game of basketball at the university on Friday afternoon, making use of the vacant gym, and Randi thought he should call Sam and invite him to join them.

Zack, who saw no point in encouraging the man to hang around, argued with her until she reminded him he could bring Sammie, Sam could bring Mariah, and the two could have a little session of pet therapy without involving Cassie.

That was incentive enough. He'd seen Cassie through the worst of times, but he'd never seen her quite the way she'd been this past week. Focused and determined one minute; lost the next.

Keeping her away from Sam, even for one session, was a good enough reason to ruin a game he'd been looking forward to. Though, he had to admit, he was a little surprised by how readily Sam agreed to join them. Either the man was stupid—Zack's personal opinion—or he didn't care that he'd be hanging out with people who came pretty close to hating him.

When Ben heard that Mariah was coming, he decided to bring Alex along, as well, giving Tory a few hours to herself to catch up on the study time she'd missed the night before, when she'd had to comfort a crying Alex and rock her to sleep. The girl's natural mother had called that day, catching Alex before Tory or Ben knew who was on the phone, and had brought back memories that were still recent enough to disturb the child.

Ben had told Zack this morning that Alex's mother wanted him not to testify in the child abuse trial Alex's natural father was facing. Ben refused to consider such an option. He expected to be subpoenaed but even he wasn't, he intended to represent his daughter's interests. Zack couldn't help wondering if it might be best to let it go and get that white trash out of Alex's life, once and for all.

But that was a conversation he'd have with his friend on another day.

Zack had been watching from center court as Sam arrived with his daughter; the other man immediately spotted Sammie and walked Mariah over to her.

"You sit right here, honey."

Zack's heart lurched when, without taking her eyes from her father, Mariah sat down, inched as close to Sammie as she could, and laid her hand on the dog's head.

Damn. Cassie was right. Sam's little girl could be reached. At least, by Zack's dog.

She was right about something else, too. Sam Montford was devoted to his adopted daughter; the look on his face made that abundantly clear.

But as far as Zack was concerned, the man still had a lot to answer for.

"So, we doing two on two?" Randi asked, as soon as Ben had joined them on the court.

Zack sized up his three opponents. Ben and Sam, both dressed in gym shorts and tank-style T-shirts, had a lot of muscle. Zack knew he could take Ben at least half the time. Which left Sam the unknown entity.

"Since I want a friendly bed-partner tonight, I'm not playing against you, Zachary," Randi said, grinning. She looked at Sam and Ben. "He hates it when I win."

"Because you cheat," Zack said, grinning back at her.

"I do not." Her chin jutted out sexily. "It's merely a case of brain over brawn."

She was going to pay for her sassiness when he got her home—probably even before dinner—and she knew it. That was why she egged him on. They both loved the payback.

"Brain, my a—"

"Zack!" Randi said, as the men laughed. "There are children present."

"Yeah, Zack, I'm present!" Alex called from the corner of the gym. She was sitting on Sammie's other side, coloring.

"Did you ask Mariah if she wanted to color, squirt?" Ben asked.

"Yeah, but I don't think she does."

Randi bounced the basketball at her feet. "Okay, Sam and Ben against me and Zack. Jump ball!"

She waited while Zack and Sam got into position, then tossed the ball up.

Zack came down with the ball. Barely. And he had the most uncomfortable feeling that Sam had let him have it.

The game was grueling, but Zack had to admit that it felt damn good to pound Sam Montford on the basketball court. Or at least to attempt it. He was on the man full court, never letting up. Trying to steal the ball every time Sam had possession, blocking every shot or pass he tried to make.

The score reflected his aggression. But not as much as he would've expected. He and Randi were barely ahead. Not only that, but Randi seemed a little annoyed when she met Zack under their basket about ten minutes into the game. Sam and Ben were inbounding the ball.

"Cool it," she wheezed, slightly out of breath.

Zack glanced down at her, loving her so much it hurt. "I can't," he said simply. The cousins made their way down the court. "He deserves it."

Zack couldn't wait for her reply; he ran up-court, guarding Sam.

With some impressive footwork, Sam got around him and scored. Zack moved to the sideline to take the ball that Randi was going to throw him.

"I know he deserves it," she whispered, pretending to talk strategy with him. "But you're a better man than this. And he's getting his comeuppance. He's not happy. My guess is he's still in love with Cassie. What better punishment than to live this close to her, see her all the time, and know he can never have her?"

Imagining himself living in the same town as Randi without the right to take her home to bed every night, to wake beside her every morning, to listen to her fears and laugh at her jokes, Zack agreed with her. Sam Montford was getting the punishment he truly deserved.

He just hoped Cassie didn't end up suffering, too. She was the sister he'd never had, and Zack was going to protect her. Come hell or high water.

A little while later, Ben said he needed some water. Sam was looking a little thirsty himself. But Zack wasn't finished with him.

Zack didn't have any choice. The other three walked off the court and left him standing there. Sam and Ben saw to their daughters, showing them to the bathroom, then Ben gave both of them juice boxes from Alex's miniature backpack. Afterward, the two men retrieved water bottles from the bags they'd brought with them and stood at the end of the court, dripping sweat and squirting water into their mouths.

Randi had disappeared into her office for something. Zack stood off to the side, figuring he'd much rather be in Randi's office with her than on the court with these two. Even though Ben was just about the best friend he'd ever had.

"So what're you studying at the university?" Sam asked Ben, as they leaned against the gym wall. Sam was watching Mariah, who hadn't touched the box of juice Ben had placed on the floor in front of her. Zack wasn't even sure she knew it was there. She'd been staring at Sam the entire game, her little head moving back and forth as Sam ran up and down the court.

But her eyes, as far as Zack had been able to tell, had not followed the play at all. They'd only followed Sam.

"I'm starting out with a business degree." Ben was answering Sam. "I thought about law, but that'll have to wait a while."

"Ben's spent the past eight years supporting Alex and her mother so he's getting a late start on his education," Zack chimed in. "But he's carrying a 4.0. As soon as he graduates, there'll be no stopping him."

Zack rather enjoyed bragging about Sam's cousin's accomplishments in the face of Sam's failures.

"Business, huh?" Sam asked, eyes narrowing as he took them off Mariah long enough to look at Ben. "Life at a desk appeals to you?"

Ben shrugged. "Don't know about that. Manipulating money appeals to me. Especially when I'm manipulating it in my direction." He grinned an all-male grin.

Sam, doing a damn fine job of dividing his attention between his daughter and the conversation at hand, smiled at Mariah. At the same time he asked Ben, "You working now?"

Ben shook his head. "I saved enough to get through this first year. It's been so long since I was in school, I wasn't sure what I was signing on for, but I'm going to look for something this summer." He glanced over at Alex. "To be honest, I didn't count on supporting a wife and daughter, when I made my plans."

"Have you talked to my father?" Sam asked. "You're entitled to Montford money."

Silently sipping his own bottle of water, Zack searched for the malice, the jealousy or selfishness behind Sam's offer. Even a little bitterness would have been a welcome confirmation of his opinion. He wasn't all that happy when he heard none of them. He didn't want to find anything impressive about the man who'd damn near destroyed one of his dearest friends.

Ben pushed away from the wall, tossing his empty water bottle in the big plastic can at the end of the court. "I don't take handouts," he said. "When I'm rich, it's going to be because I made myself that way through honest hard work."

Sam jogged onto the court beside Ben. Zack followed, but hung back just a little, waiting for Randi.

"There's a job available at Montford, Inc., if you're interested," Sam said, grabbing the ball from Ben to make a hook shot. "But I gotta tell you, if you take it, you might have to be mayor of Shelter Valley someday, too. It all comes with the Montford territory."

Sam made the job sound like a death sentence.

And if he felt that way about it, Zack wondered, how had he handled growing up in this town, where half the people still thought he was their savior come back to rescue them. That would've been one hell of a lot of pressure for a young guy.

It gave Zack an insight into the man, one he wasn't ready to accept. He was on Cassie's side. That meant he needed to hate Sam Montford, not sympathize with him.

They were all tired, but too damn stubborn to quit without a win, when a couple of Montford's senior basketball players came barreling into the gym for a little one on one. Zack recognized them immediately. At the U on scholarship, both men were destined for the pros as soon as they graduated the following month. They'd both already signed with well-known agents.

"Hey, Bo, Glen," Randi called out to them. "Come to let us old folks show you how it's done?"

"Hell no, Coach," Bo called back across the court, whipping a basketball at Randi's middle. "Come to give you few lessons."

The boys made a couple of spirited runs up and down the court with the four of them, everyone enjoying a healthy bout of physical competition. No one noticed the little girl sitting on the sidelines, her hand gripping the dog crouched next to her.

Not until Bo got a little too rough with Sam, knocking him flat when Sam came down with a rebound. Sam was still on the floor, his nose dripping blood, when Sammie's pain-filled yelp resounded through the gym, deafening them all, turning seven pairs of alarmed eyes in her direction. Mariah was shaking so hard that she was almost convulsing, her eyes unfocused as she stared vacantly somewhere in the distance. In her little hand was a hank of Sammie's fur. Pulled from the dog's neck.

"Oh, my God!" Zack heard Randi's cry, as he and Sam raced to the little girl's side. Running, Sam wiped his nose on a towel Glen had thrown him.

"Mariah?" His voice was filled with love. And overflowing with fear. "What's wrong, honey? Daddy's right here." He dabbed at his nose again.

Even though he'd been down on the floor, he reached her first, lifting her gently into his arms, cradling her against him.

"Daddy's right here, honey," he said, over and over, attempting to calm the child.

Zack had never seen such terror in another man's eyes, as the little girl continued to shake.

"She's scared to death," Sam said.

"Sammie's just fine, honey," Zack said, with no idea what to do. "She just makes noises like that sometimes. It's nothing to be afraid of."

His eyes met Sam's. Something more than the dog's yelp had done this. Something that had made Mariah react convulsively, yanking out Sammie's fur. "Randi's gone for her blood pressure cuff. Should I have her call an ambulance?"

"I don't know," Sam said. "I'm afraid having strangers fussing over her would only scare her more." He rubbed the little girl's back, tried to see the face she had hidden in his chest. "What do you think?"

Ben, with Alex in his arms, came up behind them. "Is there anything I can do?"

Sam shook his head. "Why don't you take Alex home?" he suggested. The other little girl looked scared to death.

"You'll call me later, let me know she's okay?" Ben asked anxiously.

Nodding, Sam turned his attention back to his daughter, trying to persuade her to release him long enough for him to see her face, to assess the situation.

The two boys, after making sure there was nothing they could do, had disappeared, leaving Zack and Sam alone in the gym with Mariah.

"Should we call her doctor?" Zack asked. He'd never felt so helpless in his life. Never seen another man look that way.

Mariah was still shaking.

"I've got her psychiatrist's number in my wallet over in my bag. Would you mind?" Sam asked.

Without another word, Zack ran off, grabbed Sam's wallet, and was at a phone by the time he'd found the number.

One thing was certain. Sam Montford's love for his daughter was very real and as deep as it gets. And no man who cared that much for a child who wasn't even his own could be all bad.

Chapter 12

An old Andy Griffith rerun was on after the late news on Friday night. It was the one in which a very young Opie was in love with Barney Fyfe's girl, Thelma Lou. Cassie had seen it often enough that she didn't need to look at the screen to know what was happening as she listened. And grouted.

All the tile was now applied to the wall. It had dried sufficiently that she could smear the grout on. And then begin the painstaking job of rubbing off the excess. It was a lot of work, but she was going to be very happy with the result. The guest bath might turn out to be her best room yet.

This time, when her doorbell rang, she knew instinctively who it was. She'd been letting the machine get the phone all night, as Zack was on call at the clinic and she was elbow-deep in sticky white stuff.

Not that Sam should be calling *or* visiting her. They'd already confirmed her Saturday-afternoon session with Mariah.

Wiping her hands on the towel slung over her shoulder, Cassie made her way slowly toward the front door. Wearing the same cutoffs and T-shirt she'd had on the night before, she wasn't even wearing a bra. She was barefoot and had tied her hair back with an elastic. She was not prepared to receive anyone. Especially not her ex-husband.

Sam was getting into the very bad habit of stopping by unannounced. She was going to have to cure him of that.

The bell pealed a second time.

"I'm coming," Cassie called. Whatever he wanted, he was just going to have to tell her while they stood on her front porch. He wasn't coming in her house again.

Flicking on the porch light, she pulled open the door.

Sam's face was ashen, his lips tight. The blood drained from Cassie's cheeks as she stepped back, allowing him room to come in. "What's wrong?"

"Mariah had an attack today."

"An attack?" Cassie asked, frowning, following him into her living room. He looked freshly showered, was wearing a pair of khaki shorts and a black polo shirt with black sandals. "What kind of attack? Where? When?"

"We were playing basketball," Sam said, shaking his head. "Zack and Randi, Ben and I. Mariah was sitting on the side of the court with Sammie and Alex, staring as usual. I never noticed anything amiss."

Cassie slid down beside him on the couch, her fingers itching to hold his hand, to smooth the still-damp tendrils of hair back from his eyes. She knew so naturally how to comfort him.

"Suddenly Sammie lets out this horrendous yelp, and Mariah's practically convulsing."

Oh, God. This was bad. "She had a seizure?" Did that mean there was brain damage, after all?

"No, thank God." He shook his head, his shoulders slumped forward, hands between his knees. "She was severely traumatized by something and couldn't seem to stop shaking."

"Where is she now?" They hadn't institutionalized her, had they? Not that quickly.

"Home. She's been given a sedative. She'll be out the rest of the night."

Home. Cassie started to breathe again. "You've seen her psychiatrist, then?"

"No." He looked over at her, his green eyes filled with agony. And doubt. "I spoke to her briefly this afternoon. She had me go to the urgent-care clinic here in town to make sure there wasn't anything physically wrong."

"Which there isn't."

"Right."

Cassie's relief was tangible and so overwhelming, she forgot she had to draw a circle around herself to keep Sam out.

"We have an appointment with the psychiatrist on Monday." His eyes were clouded.

"You're thinking they might want to keep her."

"Her doctor said as much."

"Shit."

He shook his head, glanced over his shoulder at her. "Maybe it's for the best, Cassie. Maybe this is what she needs."

"Do you truly think so?"

"No." His expression was fierce. Then he looked away, his hands clasped. "But what do I know?"

"You know that you love her, that you'll do whatever it takes to help her."

"Which certainly doesn't qualify me to make this decision."

"I think," Cassie said slowly, "that perhaps, when it comes to parenting, you're supposed to trust your instincts."

She was actually sitting there, advising Sam on how to be a good parent. She, who could never be one herself. At some point, this memory was going to hurt.

"Doctors aren't always right, Sam."

His mouth a grim line, Sam didn't look convinced.

"At least, promise me you'll get a second opinion before you do anything."

"She's already with the best doctors available."

Her head shot up, her eyes searching his face. "So, you're just going to send her away?"

"No." He shook his head. "How can I desert her like that?"

He couldn't. She'd known that.

"But I'm not sure I'm making the decision that's best for Mariah," he added. "Maybe, because of my own need to keep her close, I'm merely deferring the inevitable."

"I've seen some miraculous things over the past couple of years, Sam—things that even the best psychologists in the nation didn't expect. I don't think you're wrong to give her this chance. The hospital will always be there."

He nodded. "She's already lost six months. It seems like an awfully long time to lose...."

Not compared to a lifetime. Cassie swallowed. Their own daughter had lost a lifetime. Sometime, she'd have to tell him about that.

But not now. She wasn't strong enough to get through that. Not yet. Not until she could trust herself to talk about her baby girl and remain immune to her baby's father.

"These past six months haven't been lost," Cassie finally said. "You've been loving that little girl, building a new sense of security for her, a new life, that will be there for her when she's ready to come out of hiding. I'm not pushing this because of the pet therapy, Sam. I don't have an agenda, and I don't need another test case. It's just that I've seen situations like this before. The slow building of trust. The successes. I know we're reaching her...."

Sam's eyes filled with worry. And hope.

Mariah was luckier then she knew. Cassie would've given anything to have Sam's steady, gentle caring during the months after their baby had died. To have the security of his love, while she came to grips with the fact that she wasn't ever going to have other children.

"Mariah's got a better chance with you, Sam." She couldn't fight for the daughter she'd lost, but she could fight for this child who'd lost her parents. "I really believe that withdrawing your constant love and support right now could interfere with her ability to become emotionally whole."

"You really care, don't you?" he asked softly.

"Of course I care. I've spent a lot of time with that kid. She's a special little girl." It couldn't be any more than that.

He turned to face her. "And do you exact promises concerning the welfare of all your patients?"

Cassie held his gaze as long as she could. And then looked down. "I care about them all," she prevaricated. "I couldn't expend so much emotional energy on them *without* caring."

He watched her silently, and Cassie brushed at some tile dust on her knee. Fiddled with a strand of hair that had come loose.

"Do you ever wear it down anymore?"

The soft question took her by surprise. "Not usually. It gets in the way when I'm working."

"Pity."

He'd always loved her hair. Had often begged her never to cut it. That thought had come to mind a couple of times over the years when she'd been tempted just to chop off the whole fiery mess.

"So you don't have any idea what set Mariah off?" Cassie asked, squeezing her hands between her knees.

"Not for sure." Sam's expression lost the intensely personal look. "We weren't doing anything any different than we'd been doing for the hour or so we'd been playing."

"You said Sammie yelped. She didn't do anything to frighten Mariah, did she?" Cassie could hardly imagine such a thing. Sammie was too smart, too well-trained, to slip up. Cassie was convinced the dog cared for her charges as much as Cassie did.

"She yelped because Mariah had just yanked out a fistful of her fur."

Cassie frowned. "So something upset her *before* Sammie made any noise."

Leaning his elbows on his knees, Sam said, "Obviously."

"And you noticed nothing different in the room?"

"Nope." He frowned slightly as he apparently tried to picture the gym in the moments before Sammie yelped. "I'd just gone up for a rebound and landed on the floor, but it wasn't the first time that happened."

Cassie's mind raced. There had to be something there. Something that might help them understand what Mariah was hiding behind those beautiful blue eyes. "Maybe she thought you were hurt."

"Actually, my nose was bleeding a little," he said. "Do you think, considering what she saw the day her parents died…?"

"It *has* to be connected, Sam," Cassie insisted. "And if we know that much, we can help her. She reacted because she was remembering and—"

"What if we're wrong, Cass?" He voiced his darkest fear. "What if I decide to keep her with me and she never gets better?"

"The same could happen if you send her away."

Her tone reminded him they'd been through all that. But Sam just couldn't seem to shake the feeling that he was going to let Mariah down somehow.

"Now tell me again about the game," Cassie continued. "Zack was guarding you, you said."

"Like a killer whale on a hunk of meat."

"So he was the one who knocked you down?"

"No." Sam shook his head. "A couple of basketball players had joined us by that point, and I think it was one of them who caught me on the way down from the rebound."

Cassie sat up straighter. It took everything Sam had not to pull her up against him. Her warmth would do so much to dissipate the cold that had infiltrated his body.

"I thought you said it was just the four of you."

He shrugged. "It was, right up until the last few minutes when a couple of guys joined us."

"Who were the guys? What did they look like?"

Sam threw up his hands, let them fall again. "I don't know. They were a couple of students, Cassie. There was nothing harmful about them, if that's what you're thinking."

She frowned. "I don't know what I'm thinking, but it seems more than coincidence that she was fine right up until the end. And it was only then that the boys were there."

Wishing he could smooth that frown from her brow, Sam said, "They did nothing to her. I don't even think they noticed her."

"What did they look like?"

"I don't know, not threatening." Sam tried to remember them, but since Mariah's bout, the rest of the afternoon had become a blur to him. "They were pretty tall, I guess. One of them skinnier than the other, but neither one was all that big." He shook his head again. "I'd never seen them before."

A spark lit Cassie's eye. "They were strangers. And in her view, they attacked you. They hurt you, made your nose bleed."

"You may be right," he said thoughtfully. "The way

Zack had been guarding me, it was the first time anyone else got close." He glanced at Cassie. "And there
was blood on my face."

Cassie leaned forward, touching Sam's hand. "That
has to be it. She saw the blood. And didn't you say she
watched the terrorists hit her father?"

"You really think she was remembering?"

"I'm almost certain of it."

"So she hasn't blocked the horror," Sam said aloud,
feeling sick. "She's living with it, day in and day out."

"Who's to say?" Cassie asked, leaving her hand
on top of his. "Maybe she was blocking it until today,
and now it's all going to come back to her. Maybe she
needs to remember in order to heal."

"Maybe."

He stared at her. "Do you really think that's it?"

"It's possible, Sam." Cassie's look was sympathetic.
"But it's just as possible that she's been remembering
all along, torturing herself for some reason. Until she
can talk to us, we just won't know."

As Sam digested her words, anger, frustration and
hopeless despair built inside him. He was solely responsible for another human life, a little girl who was
struggling and hurt, and there didn't seem to be a
damn thing he could do to help her. What was it with
him? Why did he always let down the people he loved?

"Hey." Cassie's hand traveled up his arm and back
again, grabbing his right hand. "She's going to be
okay. I really believe that."

Sam covered her hand with his left. With the excep-
tion of the one time he'd done something so reprehen-
sible that he'd had to cut himself off from her, Cassie

had always been able to rescue him from the darkness. From the void fashioned within his own mind.

He'd never needed rescuing more than he did that night.

"It's just going to take time. And a lot of love," Cassie continued through his silence. "We'll reach her, Sam. I know we will."

He tried to smile, but his jaw was too tight; he squeezed her hand again, instead. He had so many questions and not a single answer. No set course. No right way. He'd never felt so lost.

They sat together, connected, silent, for several minutes. Cassie's warmth seeped into him, reminding him so vividly of how it used to be for them. Every disappointment, every worry, had been diminished by their sharing. With Cassie he'd been completely unguarded. With her he'd felt safe. Until it all started closing in on him...

Sam didn't know when his hold on her changed from seeking comfort to seeking more. The decision was not a conscious one, but rather a progression that was so natural he didn't even see it coming. One minute he was holding her hand, and the next he was caressing the underside of it.

Rather than fighting him, as an hour ago he'd have predicted she would, Cassie leaned into Sam, resting her head on his shoulder. And suddenly it dawned on him that he might not be the only one in need of rescuing.

His strong, valiant, beautiful ex-wife was fighting battles, too. Was she searching for a way out of her private agonies? Just like he was?

Peering around him at her attractive, well-ordered

house, at the furnishings that looked as if they were straight out of a decorating magazine, Sam had a tough time matching Cassie's surroundings with the vivacious young woman he'd known her to be.

Where was that woman? Behind the career she seemed to live by? Underneath the showcase rooms? Hidden by the television shows that were so much a part of her life?

Could Sam help her find her way out?

Once, he would've been sure of it. "Cass?"

"Shh." She slowly moved her head against his arm as if saying no. But she didn't back away.

He pulled her hand between both of his. Her fingers were cold. "Are you okay?"

"Just give me a minute."

Glancing down, all he could see was the top of her head. Because, after ten years away from her, he wasn't sure what she needed, he did the only thing he could. He listened to his instincts.

His arm stole around her shoulders, and he settled her against his chest, in a position so natural to them, it was as though they'd never been separated. Still holding her hand, he brought it close to his body, running two fingers up and down her forearm.

The minute she showed any resistance, he'd let her go. But if she needed this connection—this intimacy—anywhere near as badly as he did, there was no way he could deny her.

"Remember the night Jamie Littleton died?" he asked a few moments later.

"Yeah."

It had been terrible for both of them. Jamie was the youngest son of some friends of Sam's parents'.

The two of them had baby-sat Jamie practically since he was born. As teenagers, they'd pretended a time or two that Jamie's house was their own, that he was their son, that they were raising him together. They'd been practicing for the day they both knew was coming, when they really would have a home and children of their own.

And then one morning Jamie's mother had called to say she'd just come from the doctor. Jamie had leukemia.

The day he'd died had been the darkest either Sam or Cassie had ever known. It had been their first experience with life's harder realities. The fragility of it all. Their first realization that they weren't invincible. That there were things they couldn't control. Things they couldn't prevent, no matter how zealous they were.

Over the two years of Jamie's illness, they'd managed to raise a lot of money for the leukemia foundation. They just hadn't managed to save Jamie's life.

"I was feeling pretty hopeless the night he died, and scared to death," Sam admitted, remembering back. "And then you came over...."

"You held me, just like this."

"And, although I was still just as sad, I felt so much better..."

"...like even though there were horrible things in life, there'd always be good things to help you through."

Sam had other memories of that night. Some of the most beautiful memories. "We made love for the first time...."

Cassie was silent, but he knew she was remembering, too. Her palm was still against his stomach, her fingers moving lightly against his shirt.

There was so much more he needed to say to her, to explain. He needed her to know how much he'd loved her that night. He needed her to know that the feeling had never stopped.

"Is it too late for us, Cass?" he whispered, tilting her face up to his. "Does it have to be too late?"

He couldn't read the expression in her eyes as clearly as he'd once been able to. She'd learned how to hide her thoughts. Or perhaps they weren't clear even to her.

She didn't answer him, just continued to look up at him, pleading.

"What?" he asked. "What can I do to make you happy again?"

Her lips trembling, she opened her mouth, but didn't say anything.

"I'll do anything to make you happy again," he whispered, knowing in his heart that even if it meant leaving her forever, he would do so. His years away had taught him the value of what Cassie had once given him so openly.

Tears sprang to her eyes and she tried to blink them away. They spilled down her cheeks, and Sam lowered his head, gently kissing her face, kissing away her tears.

Cassie's moan was filled with need. With regret. And pain.

Sam's body throbbed, responding automatically to the cry it recognized. Her head turned, and her lips met his in a kiss that stopped his world from spinning so crazily out of control.

And spun *him* out of control, instead.

She tasted so perfectly right. So familiar. And so, so hungry. Hardening instantly, Sam welcomed her kiss. "Cass, are you sure?" he asked throatily, barely able to get the words past his own hunger.

"Don't talk, Sam," she begged. "Please, don't talk. Just love me."

He wanted to talk. He needed to know that being there, doing this, was as right for her as it was for him. He'd told her he thought they had a second chance.

Had she decided they did, too?

Her hands, roaming freely over his body, were telling him with unmistakable clarity what she wanted. Her words had told him the same thing. Sam could deny her nothing.

With a heavy groan, he rolled her over, down to the floor, and kissed her as he'd never kissed her before. Like a mature man kisses the woman he loves.

For the first time in ten years, his life felt right again.

Chapter 13

Cassie couldn't slow down. Couldn't slow her rapidly beating heart, her panting, the blood racing through her veins or the heat burning in her belly. Her body was trembling, groping. She'd been starved for so long.

She was strong. Had been strong all these years, battling emotions that threatened to overwhelm her. And Sam's familiar hands holding her, his lips on hers, felt—right.

It was so long since she'd been touched. Forever. A lifetime ago.

"You are beautiful," Sam whispered against her neck. His lips trailed downward, leaving little kisses in their wake. Along her neck, pushing against the ribbed top of her T-shirt to reach her collarbone.

He pulled the elastic out of her hair, spreading the long strands around her.

"Mmm." Cassie hardly recognized the sounds she

was making. She wasn't herself. Wasn't in control. No thought. No conscience. Just instinct.

She explored Sam's body eagerly, the solid masculine shoulders a delight. And so much larger than she remembered. His ears were the same as she recalled them, though. Cassie's tongue flicked across the lobe. He liked that. He'd always liked that.

She was a sensual woman, with a woman's desires. And no man but Sam had ever touched her.

He lifted the bottom of her T-shirt, and Cassie raised herself from the floor long enough for him to pull it up. She couldn't let him do this. Had to stop him.

Sometime.

She was so tired of fighting. Of being strong. Of being lonely.

His hands slid along her belly and up, until he found her unfettered breasts.

Cassie gasped as his hands took possession of her, squeezing gently, molding, stroking.

"You have no idea how many dreams I've had about these," Sam growled, lowering his head to suckle her nipple.

Sensation shot through Cassie, making her wild with need. For more. She spread her legs, lifted her hips, whimpering.

They'd first made love when they were seventeen, and after they were married it was often twice a day. The hunger had never lessened. Cassie had known, from the very first time, that it was her destiny to be sexually connected with Sam. It was as though their bodies instinctively recognized each other.

"You've grown a little," Sam muttered as his mouth

moved to her other breast. "But your shape is still as perfect as ever."

He cupped both breasts, looking at them with hungry eyes. "God, I've missed this...."

Afraid of what else he might say, afraid she might have to think, Cassie lifted her hips again.

"I'm getting there, my love," Sam said, grinning. "I'm just enjoying the journey."

His grin melted her all over again. "You're overdressed."

Sam slid her T-shirt up and over her head as he stood up. The air was cool on her exposed skin, and Cassie suddenly felt naked, half sitting there on her living-room floor with her breasts in full view.

Very naked, and very, very much alive.

Watching as Sam tore his own shirt over his head, she sucked in a tight breath. He'd always been sculpted like a work of art, but because of the years of manual labor, his upper body now brought art to a whole new level.

"You've got chest hair," she said, her voice thick. He'd had only a little the last time she'd seen him naked.

He ran one hand over his chest. "It happens," he said.

"I like it." Her fingers were itching to run through it, her breasts already tingling as she thought about that wiry roughness rubbing against her.

His hands moved to the button on his fly, and Cassie's hands began to shake. Her body grew moist in ways it hadn't been in years. She'd forgotten how incredible sexual desire could be. How all-consuming.

She'd never forgotten how great sex with Sam could be.

The rasp of his zipper increased her anticipation, and Cassie almost wept with the wanting. She'd never known such powerful need. Never even imagined she could feel so aroused.

He could ask her to do anything at that moment— run naked in the street, climb a tree topless—and if he'd appease the desire burning inside her, she'd definitely do it.

"Please, Sam," she whispered, watching his hands as he slowly drew his pants down over the bulge under his fly.

Sam had been a mere twenty years old when he'd left town. He'd come back a full-grown man.

Tears sprang to Cassie's eyes as he revealed his erection—hard and proud. Kicking off his sandals, he dropped his pants and came back to her, completely naked. Completely man. Completely perfect.

He started to say something, but Cassie couldn't bear any more words, any more fear. She had to have this tension abated, to find the release that only Sam could give her. To know again the excitement—and the peace—his body brought hers. Lifting her head, she kissed him hotly, opening her mouth, searching his tongue with her own.

"God, Cassie, slow down..." he said.

He slid down her body, kissing her all over—her neck, her breasts, her belly, stopping where her shorts still covered her hips. Her legs, shamelessly open, tensed as she felt his hand cup her most private place.

"Ohhhh," she breathed out, then took in a couple of short, gulping breaths.

Sam moved again, frustrating Cassie. He'd been so close. Had he no idea that she was dying for him?

With one finger he flipped open her shorts, then yanked softly, pulling them slowly down her legs. For an instant she panicked, knowing almost subconsciously that this was dangerous. That she was muddying waters that were already so murky she could hardly pass through them. But on a conscious level, she just needed him to hurry. Before she lost her mind with want. Before she had to *think*.

And besides, the scar was craftily hidden in her pubic hair line. Her doctor had been quick to assure her of that. There was no need to bring any of that history here, tonight.

He sat between her legs, looking down at her, and started to gently, reverently fondle her, using both hands to bring her to the brink.

Because he was Sam, because her body recognized him, she felt no shyness, no embarrassment in having him sit there, having him see her. Instead, it felt natural. And free.

"Please, Sam," she finally begged, lifting her hips against his fingers. "Please, now."

She couldn't hold on any longer. She was going to burst into tears if he didn't relieve the agony he'd created. Her arms and legs were trembling, her lower belly quivering with need. She could hardly breathe.

With a hand on either side of her, Sam rose to his knees and then lowered himself, finding her instantly. He pushed. Hard.

And Cassie exploded.

There was pain—it would have been impossible not to experience some discomfort after ten years of celibacy—but the ecstasy was so encompassing that Cassie almost welcomed the discomfort as a way to measure the boundless pleasure.

Sam pulled out and pushed again. And again. Moving faster as his breathing quickened. His body slick with sweat, he hovered over her, and Cassie met him thrust for thrust, building to a crescendo a second time.

When they reached it together, the glory was unfathomable. Cassie floated almost to a state of unconsciousness as wave after wave of pleasure washed over her. Through her. She could feel Sam's body flooding her, could feel his heart pounding above her. Wondered how one ever recovered from such a moment.

Even they had never done anything so incredible before.

And most assuredly never would again.

Because it wasn't real.

Sam was still drifting on a sea of blissful sensation, when Cassie moved beneath him, pushing him away.

"Sorry, honey," he said, instantly contrite. He knew he must be crushing her. He rolled to one side, only briefly aware of the rug burns on his knees, taking her with him. He hoped her backside had fared better.

His arms enfolded her, but Cassie didn't relax against him. Her body was tense, nothing like the limp, satiated woman she used to be after they made love. She pushed against him again until he had to let her go.

"What's wrong?" he asked, his stomach knotting.

She reached for her shirt. "Nothing." The word was

muffled as she pulled the T-shirt over her head. In record time, she had her shorts on, too.

Frowning, Sam sat there, naked, watching her. Something was not right. "Talk to me, Cass," he said.

She shook her head. "I think you should go."

Staring at her, he continued to sit on her floor. "I don't believe this."

Her back to him, Cassie didn't answer. She was struggling, he knew that much; he just didn't know why.

"What was this?" he asked, emotions on overload as the peace of moments ago was shattered. "A quick screw for old times' sake?"

If this reversal of hers hadn't been so ironically cruel, to both of them, he never would have said such a thing. He hated hearing the words roll off his tongue. But he was falling apart, here.

He'd thought he and Cassie—the only woman to whom he'd ever given his heart and soul—had recommitted themselves to a love that had never died. She'd been...

What? What had she been doing?

Cassie stood a few feet away, her back still turned, her shoulders slumped beneath the tangled red hair. He couldn't tell if she was crying or not, but he had a feeling she was. He had a feeling he was, too.

"I'm sorry," he said softly. "I didn't mean that."

Though she didn't turn around, Cassie nodded. "Please go." The words were whispered, and hinted of tears.

Sam stood, pulled on his pants. "I can't, Cassie. Not like this. Not until we talk."

She turned then. He'd been right about the tears.

"There's nothing to say, Sam," she said. The certainty behind those words cut him badly.

"Of course there is! We just made incredible love, Cassie."

"It changes nothing." At least she hadn't tried to deny his assertion.

"It changes everything."

Cassie shook her head, sniffling. "It doesn't, Sam. It can't."

He reached for a tissue from the table beside the couch, crossed over to gently wipe away her tears. "Of course it can, honey. We have a gift, you and I, a tangible connection that can't be broken."

She backed away from him. "It *was* broken, Sam," she said firmly. "You broke it."

Frustrated, frightened, Sam stared at her, not knowing what to do. But knowing he had to do something. He couldn't let her confine them to a life of emptiness because of one mistake he'd made when he was little more than a kid.

"Can we talk about it, Cass? Can we talk about that night?"

Her beautiful brown eyes filled with tears as she sat down on the couch, gazing up at him. "What's there to say?" she asked. "While I waited at home, worried sick about you, you were in bed with another woman. End of story."

Sam swallowed. He'd hurt her beyond measure. He'd known that. But to be face to face with that fact made him feel that raw pain all over again.

"We weren't in bed." He regretted the stupid words the second they left his mouth. He had no idea what to say. How to atone for what he'd done. And yet, he was a good man. A faithful man. If she could only give him a second chance. Give *them* a second chance. After the way they'd just made love, the things her body and heart had told him, he knew he wasn't the only one who was going to lose one of life's greatest gifts if she couldn't move beyond the past.

"I don't care where you were." She enunciated carefully, bitterness in her voice, in the wet eyes that tortured him. "You had sex with her."

He'd give his life to be able to deny that statement. But he couldn't.

"I was drunk, Cassie, and strangling on the expectations here. I knew that if we continued as we were, I was going to disappoint you. There was just no way I could be the man you—and everyone else in this town—wanted."

"Was she worth it, Sam?"

"Worth *what,* dammit?" He strode over to haul her into his arms, to remind her of what they'd just shared, what they had—but when she shrank back, he stopped short of the couch. "She was nothing, Cassie, nothing. A stupid attempt to find mindlessness. To convince myself that I could act outside all those expectations."

Cassie wouldn't meet his eyes.

"I don't even remember what she looked like," he added.

But he'd remembered every inch of Cassie's body. Every touch. Every scent. He'd noticed changes, too. A little more shape. A line or two that hadn't been there before.

"Was she good?" The question was so softly uttered, Sam barely heard it.

"How would I know, Cassie? I was too drunk to

care. I don't even remember her. How 'good' could it have been?"

But he'd remembered the feel of Cassie's long legs against the sides of his hips, her tender flesh wrapped intimately around him. He'd remembered the look in her eyes when she came, the sensual smile on her lips. He'd remembered how she'd said his name with that breathless throaty growl.

Sam kneeled in front of her, wanting so desperately to touch her, to take both her hands in his. "Please, Cass," he whispered, "can you please try to forgive me? I'll do anything, promise you anything, call you every time I leave the house, carry a pager and a cell phone and be accountable to you every single second, if that's what it takes to win back your trust."

She still wouldn't look at him, but she seemed to be listening. "That night wasn't about sex, Cass," he said. "I don't really know what it *was* about..." He paused. "Maybe it was about freedom," he said quietly.

Her eyes instantly clouded again. "You needed to be free from me?"

"Not from you," Sam said. "Never from you. But from *here,* maybe. And from the things you needed me to be."

She digested the words silently.

"It was about my life, Cass. About finding answers. It was never about sex." He inhaled a deep breath, knowing this might be his one and only chance to reach her. "I've found my answers, know who I am and where I'm going. And I know that you're the only woman who's ever turned me on to the point of forgetfulness." He was giving her everything, laying it all at her feet. She deserved that from him. "I swear to you I will never, ever need another woman the way I need you. I will never again make love to another woman as long as I'm with you."

Cassie turned away from him, but not before he'd seen the fresh tears come to her eyes.

"But you've been with other women, haven't you?" she asked. "In your years away."

"Not for a long time, honey. Not since I knew there was no point. You were always the woman in my heart."

Her shoulders held stiffly, she didn't respond.

"Can you honestly tell me the love is gone, Cass?" he asked, risking everything. Was he just kidding himself about the connection between them? The spiritual and physical communion they'd just shared?

"It's too late, Sam," she said.

"I can't believe that."

She hadn't denied her love for him. Intuitively, Sam understood that she couldn't.

During his years away, he hadn't always been sure of the bond they shared, but now that he was back, now that he'd seen her again, he knew for certain that what he and Cassie had was stronger than life. Stronger than death.

"Please, just go."

Sam kneeled there a while longer, watching her. In all that time, she didn't speak another word, but her rigid shoulders told him that what she'd said was true: she needed him to go. His presence here was only causing her more heartache.

He'd promised himself he wouldn't do that.

"Okay, I'm going," he said, standing, pulling on his shirt, slipping his feet into his sandals. "But I'm not deserting you again, Cass. I love you. And someday, somehow, I'm going to prove that to you."

Cassie waited until she heard Sam's truck drive away before she dared to move. Almost immediately, panic set in, taking her breath, her ability to think. She had to get help.

Phyllis would have been a likely candidate, but right now Cassie needed someone who'd already seen her at her worst. Someone she'd trusted for years with her deepest secrets. Someone who wouldn't make her talk about things she couldn't face.

Barefoot and braless, she scrambled frantically around her house, until she remembered that she'd left her purse in the bedroom. She grabbed it, fumbled inside, spilling stuff on the floor until she pulled out her keys.

Thank God, Randi and Zack lived so close. She could make it the couple of blocks from her house to theirs. It was the middle of the night. Shelter Valley streets would be deserted.

She had to get to Zack.

Sometime after two in the morning, a very disheveled but partially dressed Zack Foster answered his door, still too sleepy to wonder who was there. Sammie was barking beside him. Bear, sleeping in the corner of the foyer, opened one lazy eye. Brat was barking from her kennel in the laundry room, which was right where the dalmatian puppy was going to stay.

He was instantly wide awake when he saw his partner standing barefoot on his porch, her hair a mess.

"Cass?" He flipped on the porch light as he swung

the door open. "What's happened?" he asked, his arm around her before the door had even shut.

"Cassie?" Randi met them in the hallway, pulling on a pair of gym shorts. "What's wrong?"

When Cassie burst into tears, Zack's alarm grew.

"I slept with him."

His eyes met Randi's over Cassie's bent head. Hers said *I told you so.* Zack's heart sank.

"You're a grown woman, Cass," Randi said, running one hand lightly along Cassie's arm. "You're allowed to do those things."

Zack's look told Randi in no uncertain terms to shut up.

"Not with Sam," she said, trying to regain control but not succeeding. Her hair was hanging in her face. Her makeup had long since worn away. Her face was tear-streaked, her expression anguished.

The way she looked brought back memories of old times. Old and very difficult times. Zack was going to kill Sam Montford.

He guided Cassie to the couch in the living room, and he and Randi sat on either side of her. Randi handed her a tissue. Sammie settled at Cassie's feet.

"How'd it happen?" he asked her softly.

"Do you really need to ask?" Randi frowned. "Surely you've figured that out by now."

Zack knew that Randi didn't think Sam and Cassie together was bad news. She'd been predicting this exact outcome for more than a week. Had a bet with Zack, as a matter of fact, a bet he'd just lost. But he didn't care about any bet with his wife at the moment. What he did care about was his partner's emotional health.

She'd fought a long, hard fight to achieve calm and contentment—and then her ex-husband showed up.

"He came over to tell me about Mariah's attack," Cassie finally said.

Zack nodded. Sam had been distraught, and Zack should've have guessed where the man would go for solace. Zack had sought Cassie's strength himself, back when he'd been struggling with the break-up of his first marriage—struggling with his own sense of identity upon discovering that his first wife was leaving him for another woman.

Cassie had kept him sane back then. It was up to him to keep her sane now.

"How is Mariah?" he asked. One thing at a time. She was calmer. That was the first step.

"Okay." Cassie nodded her head once, still looking down at her lap. "There's nothing physically wrong with her. She's sedated for the night and has an appointment in Phoenix on Monday."

"Poor thing," Randi said. "Her little heart was beating faster than a bird's."

Zack still felt sick every time he thought about the debilitating fear he'd seen in Sam's daughter that afternoon. He'd felt so helpless, so powerless to do anything. By the look of things, Sam Montford had been feeling the same, but on a bigger scale.

"So how did you get from Mariah's attack to sleeping with him?" Zack asked. No matter how much Sam might be suffering, Zack couldn't feel any real softening toward the guy. His job was to protect Cassie.

Cassie shrugged. "I don't know." She started to cry softly again. Jumping off the couch, she paced around the living room. Sammie sat at attention, watching her. "I guess because I'm a weak fool."

Randi shook her head. "Or in love."

"How can she love him?" Zack asked his wife. "He ran out on her, left her alone to deal with—"

"And now he's back," Randi interrupted. "I have no idea why Sam did what he did," she said to Zack, but she was watching Cassie, too. "I do know that up until the point where he screwed up, he was the most reliable kid any of us knew. And it was also obvious that he adored Cassie. You don't just walk away from that if you have a chance to make it right."

"I think you'd just like to see everyone as happy as we are," Zack said quietly.

"He said the town put too many expectations on him," Cassie told them suddenly, frowning as she looked at Randi. Cassie was tearing a tissue apart, stuffing the pieces into her palm. "He didn't want to go into law or politics. The thought of working at Montford, Inc. all day, every day for the rest of his life was killing him. He tried to talk about it—I remember him saying things to me, to his parents, but they just thought he was blowing off steam. I guess I took my cues from them. We all thought he *wanted* the life that had been planned for him. He fit into that mold so perfectly."

Randi nodded. "It must've been tough growing up the way he did, with everyone deciding who he was going to be the day he was born. The poor guy never had a chance."

Didn't sound like a whole lot of fun to Zack. What man wouldn't have to fight back?

"He should've gone to Cassie. Not to the arms of another woman," Zack insisted.

"But weren't you encouraging him to go to law school, just like everyone else?" Randi asked Cassie. "Maybe even expecting it?"

Cassie shrugged, her expression confused. "Maybe. Because that seemed to be the plan. But it never dawned on me that he wouldn't want to."

"He was young, too, Cassie," Randi said softly. "Maybe he didn't feel you were really hearing him. Maybe he didn't trust you enough to love him for what he *was,* not for what everyone thought he was going to be. Or maybe he just didn't want to subject you to an entirely different life than the one you wanted— the one you signed on for."

They were silent for a couple of minutes. Zack was looking for a solution, but the whole thing appeared to be one big screw-up. A lose-lose situation, if he ever saw one. Sam had loved Cassie back then. Cassie had loved Sam. In one way they'd been so close; but in another, their lives were careering in different directions.

And so much had happened since then. So many irrevocable hurts.

"Now what?" he asked.

Cassie tried to smile. "Life goes on."

Randi threw up her hands. "That's it? You sleep with him…and nothing?"

"What else is there?"

"I don't know. Love, maybe."

"Don't you see," Cassie asked, her eyes beseeching as she gazed from one to the other.

For the first time, Zack understood what Randi

had seen all along. Cassie still loved her ex-husband. Desperately.

"It doesn't matter if I love him or not. I can't trust him. And I can't forgive him, either."

"For sleeping with another woman?" Randi asked.

Cassie shook her head, and Zack knew what was coming.

"For deserting me when I needed him most." The words choked her. "I was a little over two months pregnant when Sam left town."

Randi sat stock-still. "I'd heard something about a baby," she whispered.

"Largely due to the stress of Sam's betrayal and desertion, I had a lot of problems with the pregnancy." She stopped. Took a deep breath. "My daughter died," Cassie said, her voice breaking.

Zack waited for the rest. The worst part of all.

"And after it was all over, they told me I can't have any more children."

"Does Sam know?" Randi asked.

Shaking her head, Cassie sniffled, reached for a fresh tissue.

"So you tell him," Randi said, exasperating Zack with her optimism. And captivating him, as well. "And then you adopt!"

Even as Zack tried to catch Randi's eye, to tell her to shut up, Cassie said, "I can't be with Sam."

"Why not?" Randi's brows drew together.

"Because although I know logically that Sam's not to blame for Emily's death, my heart still says he is. And I can't forgive him for that."

Chapter 14

Sam was up all night. The newcomer to Borough Bantam had a plan now. But as was the case with all worthy undertakings, the way was not yet clear. The creatures in the kingdom scurried around as they'd done for years, each week bringing some new crisis that seemed so huge to them and so small to the reader.

To them, all of life was right there in the Borough, their little problems and triumphs of utmost importance. The stories were satirical, and yet the residents of Borough Bantam somehow managed to teach Sam every single week. Essential truths. Life lessons that Sam had learned in Shelter Valley. Lessons he'd taken with him without even realizing it.

He figured his readers must see the value in them, too, since the comic strip was unbelievably successful.

I am. I am. I am. And then in the bottom corner,

S.N.C. Sam dropped his pencil. There was something so reassuring about that damn worm.

If he could only figure why, Sam knew he'd have a major problem solved. But as always, the answer eluded him. He folded up the drawings, put them in their envelope and cleaned up, slipping his satchel on the back of the closet shelf.

Borough Bantam was just one more thing the people of Shelter Valley would never understand.

They'd think he was poking fun at them. When in reality he was giving the rest of the world what everyone here in this small town had already discovered. The secrets to a happy life.

Two weeks passed, and Cassie managed to keep up such an effective semblance of normalcy, she almost convinced herself that she'd survived her weak moment with Sam unscathed.

If only she didn't have to go to bed at night. To sleep. That was where the memories, the desires, and especially the unending regrets attacked her. If she slept, she dreamed. If she was awake, she thought of nothing else. Round and round. How could something be so right and so completely impossible at the same time? How could the same man make her feel so wonderful, so right inside—and so endlessly distraught?

And more to the point, what did she do about it? He'd been patient with her, bringing Mariah for her sessions four times now without any pressure. Not asking anything of her other than that she help his little girl. There'd been no more surprise visits to her house. And when she'd run into him at the diner last week, he'd been congenial. And had left her alone.

She missed him like crazy.

And yet she was relieved.

She was going to have to tell him about their baby. About Emily. There was just no other way to get beyond this whole mess. To find a peaceful place to exist for the rest of her life. She had to get it all out. And she needed him to know.

But not yet. Not until she could at least think about going through that without falling apart. Without accusing him of killing their daughter and destroying any chance she'd ever have of having another child.

Logically, she knew he wasn't really responsible. Any more than she'd been. But in her heart, she also knew that if Sam hadn't deserted her, Emily's chances would have been so much better....

Now, a tiny, almost imperceptible tug on her hand brought Cassie back to the present. Dressed in navy shorts and a white button-up blouse with the sleeves rolled up, her hair in its usual twist, she was walking down Main Street with Mariah. They were on their way to Weber's Department Store, where she was going to buy the little girl a new dress.

She glanced down at her charge. "Did you want something, Mariah?" The little girl slowed as Cassie slowed, stopped as Cassie stopped, but there was no response.

Thinking the child must have tripped, Cassie started to walk again. "You hot, Sammie girl?" Cassie asked.

Panting, the dog looked up at her, but continued trotting beside Mariah. If Sammie was uncomfortable, she didn't seem aware of it.

"What color dress do you want, sweetie?" Cassie

asked the little girl. She might as well have been talking to herself. There was no way to be sure the child listened, or comprehended much of what was said to her.

Cassie wondered if the shopping spree was such a great idea. Mariah didn't need any new clothes. She always looked very cute. Today her long black hair hung in two braids down her back, and the little brightly flowered sundress matched her sandals perfectly. They probably wouldn't find anything that fashionable at Weber's. But Cassie was hoping Mariah might enjoy their expedition. Or, at least, find a different environment interesting.

There hadn't been any reaction from Mariah since her "episode," but the child didn't seem to have gone backward, either. There'd been no resistance to their outings. No more shaking.

The one thing Mariah did seem to respond to was Sammie. If you watched closely enough to tell.

"Wouldn't you hate to be wearing all that fur Sammie's got on?" Cassie asked Mariah. The child walked steadily, but she wasn't staring as vacantly as usual. She seemed almost to be sneaking peeks sideways.

Cassie walked a little faster. And felt another little squeeze on her hand.

Heart beating rapidly, she stopped again, certain now that Mariah was trying to tell her something. "What is it, honey?" she asked, kneeling in front the child.

Mariah's stare instantly became vacant again. But her hand was rubbing Sammie's fur agitatedly. The dog looked over at Cassie, as though expecting some kind of action from her.

Cassie wished the dog could talk. Could tell her what to do. There was no visible sign of distress on the little girl's face, and Cassie straightened. "You just tell me if you need something, Mariah," she said. "Now, how about we go find some new clothes?" With the child's hand still in hers, Cassie started to walk.

The child refused to move.

Cassie knelt down again. "Sweetie, you can trust me," she said. "We've been together a lot. I bring Sammie to you every time, and you like Sammie, don't you?"

Mariah didn't even blink.

"Whatever's bothering you, try to let me know. I'll help you."

Still no response. A couple of people walked by, smiled at Cassie, glanced curiously at the child, and moved on. Mariah didn't even appear to notice them.

"Do you have to go to the potty?" Cassie asked. That had never happened on Cassie's outings with the little girl. Sam always made sure she'd gone just before he brought her.

"Come on," Cassie said. "We can pop into the ice-cream shop and use the bathroom there." Mariah liked chocolate ice cream—as long as she could wait until Sam was back before she ate it. "And then we'll have to stop for a scoop of ice cream on our way out."

Mariah still refused to budge.

Elated, Cassie tried not to smile. Mariah was responding! Cassie could hardly contain her excitement.

Now, if she could just figure out what the hell Mariah was being so adamant about.

"Everything okay?" Liz Meiers, the church choir director, stopped to ask.

"Fine." *Please go away,* she begged silently. She didn't want anyone scaring the child back into her shell.

Liz moved on, and Cassie put her face close to Mariah's, trying to get the child to focus on her.

"Is it that you don't want to buy new clothes?" she asked next. "We could skip that and settle for a soda at the diner. Or stop at the dime store for some candy. We could even look at the toys."

They could go back to the park, too, but the idea was to keep Mariah out and among the bustle of strangers. As much of a bustle as they could find in Shelter Valley, anyway.

Cassie had already tried taking the child to the clinic, but Mariah had shown no interest in being there. She'd curled up in the fetal position in a chair, one hand on Sammie, and had laid her head on her knees, waiting for Cassie to say they could go.

"You want to look at the toys?" Cassie asked a second time, starting toward the dime store.

Again, Mariah held her ground.

Cassie was thrilled Mariah was trying to communicate with her. And she felt a terrible sense of urgency, a need to figure out exactly what the child was trying to say.

"Sammie, *you* know what she wants, don't you?" Cassie said.

Mariah's hand stilled on Sammie's head, and her eyes turned to the side again.

"Sammie and I are both here, willing to help, honey. I just don't know what the problem is. Can't you please tell me?"

The child didn't respond. Didn't even blink.

They were attracting a bit of a crowd. Cassie had to get rid of these people. She had to find out what Mariah was telling her before the child escaped inside herself again.

With Mariah's hand still firmly in hers, she turned away from the little girl, addressing the small concerned gathering quietly. "She's going to be fine, Mrs. Morten," she said to the seventyish woman, a client of Cassie's who had three cats at home. "All of you, she's going to be fine. We just need to be alone for a couple of min—"

The sound behind her was so foreign that Cassie stopped mid-sentence, frozen. Afraid to turn around.

"Sam." It came again. Very clear. And tinged with anxiety. "My daddy Sam."

Spinning, Cassie stared. Mariah was leaning over, her small lips barely moving as she addressed the dog at her side. She wanted Sam—her father—and she was trying to get word to Sammie without alerting anyone around her.

Tears flooded Cassie's eyes. She grabbed the child in her arms, holding her, hugging her. Whirling in a circle, while the crowd around them grew. Everyone was smiling. A few had tears in their eyes, though they probably weren't all aware of what they'd just witnessed.

"Welcome home, little Mariah," Cassie said, tears dripping unashamedly down her face. "Welcome home."

The little girl's stare was vacant again. She held herself stiffly against Cassie. But Cassie knew they'd broken through. Mariah was coming back to them.

"You want Sam?" Cassie asked, setting the little girl down. "Then let's go find him."

Smiling at the congratulatory people around them, Cassie took Mariah's hand and started off toward the park.

The little girl jerked on Cassie's hand, pulling her around the other way.

Sharing a puzzled glance with Mrs. Morten, who waved Cassie on, Cassie allowed the child to lead her back the way they'd come, to an alley that ran between the hardware store and the dentist's office.

And there, just around the corner, where the child had probably seen him from her peripheral vision as they walked by, sat Sam on a stoop, his head in his hands. Looking like he didn't have a friend in the world.

Hearing them approach, he raised his head. The instant terror in his face as his eyes darted from Mariah to Cassie's tear-stained face tore at Cassie's heart, but all she could do was smile at him.

This was his daughter's show.

Mariah walked up to Sam, slid her tiny hand into his. And that was all. She'd obviously done what she needed to do.

Sammie sat beside Cassie, tongue hanging out of her mouth, obviously proud of her day's work.

Which left Cassie to explain.

"She said your name, Sam!" Cassie said. "She saw you sitting here! She just led me back to you! She must have thought you were in trouble, needed help. She never came after you for herself, when you left her in the park and she wanted you, but she insisted that we come for you when she thought you were in trouble!" Cassie's words tumbled out, one on top of the other.

Sam's eyes widened as he glanced quickly from her to his daughter and back again. "You're certain?"

"I heard her, Sam. She said your name twice."

Looking dazed, as though he didn't dare believe that the nightmare could be coming to an end, Sam knelt beside the child, taking both of her shoulders in his hands. "Mariah Glory Montford, if you've got words in your head, I expect to hear them," he said sternly, though his voice wobbled just a bit with emotions barely held in check.

Cassie didn't even try to wipe away the tears still dripping slowly down her cheeks. "Don't expect too much too soon," she warned him.

"When I wasn't sure she *could* talk to me, there was nothing I could do," Sam said, still watching Mariah intently, his eyes bright. "If my little girl's in there, listening to me, then I want her out here where I can have some of the fun, too."

Mariah didn't move, her face expressionless, her eyes trained on Sam's chest.

Sammie stood up, not quite at attention, but watching Mariah and Sam closely. Again, Cassie wondered how much the dog sensed.

Just when Cassie thought Mariah had given them all she had, all she could give them that day, the child's head lifted. Her eyes focused on Sam's. She didn't say anything, but there was no doubt that she was connecting.

Sam's lips trembled. And his eyes filled with tears. "Welcome back, squirt," he said, breaking into a huge smile. "I've missed you."

Gathering Mariah into his arms, he hugged her fiercely, lifting her so her legs dangled in front of him. "I've missed you *so* much." His eyes were shut tight as he buried his face against her hair.

Mariah's bony little arms stole up Sam's chest and locked themselves around his neck.

Cassie stood there watching them, and started to sob.

At home that night, sitting in the living room with his parents, Sam was still grinning inside. Mariah was upstairs, in bed asleep. Sam had placed the receiver to the monitor system he'd bought months ago on the end table next to him. The base was upstairs right beside his sleeping daughter. He used to listen for Mariah's breathing, or any sounds of distress. Tonight, he was wondering if she just might talk in her sleep.

The three of them had yet to hear her say a word.

But you wouldn't know that, judging by the celebration held that evening. Carol, with occasional bouts of happy tears, had prepared Mariah's favorite foods—or what Sam could remember of them. Hot dogs. Mashed potatoes. Canned peaches. And for dessert, she'd made the chocolate chip cookies Sam had been telling Mariah about for months.

The child had still focused mainly on Sam's shirt. She'd sat where he put her, making no moves on her own. Except to eat. Sam hadn't had to coax her at all. With her eyes trained on him as usual, she'd dug into the food in front of her and finished every bite. It was a small thing, but to the three adults sitting at the table, who'd been holding their collective breath over every bite of every meal, it seemed a miracle.

"What did the doctor have to say?" Carol asked, her feet tucked under her violet silk lounging gown. Muffy was curled up next to her on the sofa.

Slouching in the overstuffed velvet chair across from his mother, Sam thought back to the conversation he'd had just before dinner. He'd been dying to share it with Cassie. And his parents.

"She said this is the breakthrough we've been waiting for," he told them. "She used lots of medical jargon, but the gist of it was that once Mariah starts to emerge from this catatonic state, it should be only a matter of time until she's back to normal."

Sipping from the cup of cocoa she'd made, his mother nodded. Carol Montford, a millionaire many times over, could afford an army of household help, but—other than cleaning and laundry—insisted on doing everything herself. The shopping. The cooking. The dishes. The decorating. And making cocoa. She was addicted to her nightly cup of homemade cocoa.

"She expects full recovery, then?" James asked Sam. He wore his reading glasses, feet up on the footrest of his tipped-back easy chair, but he hadn't opened the book on his lap. He sucked on the pipe he hadn't lit in years.

Sam slid his hand down the leg of his khaki shorts. "According to her, it's very hopeful. But until we know the extent of what Mariah saw—and heard—and the extent of what she might have suffered herself at the hands of those bastards…"

"We've got her now, Sam," Carol reminded him. "And she's young. In time, those memories will fade."

Taking a deep breath, trying to rid himself of the

sudden tension, Sam sent his mother a grateful smile. "I know."

Once again he realized that the people of Shelter Valley knew what really mattered in life. While Sam sat there, consumed by the need to murder the men who had tortured and killed his best friends, while he focused on the past and the things he could do nothing to change, his mother homed right in on what was most important—the future. His daughter had been given back her life.

That was what mattered.

"Oh." Carol set down her cup. "I almost forgot in all the excitement, but this has truly been a day of happy news."

"What else happened?" Sam and his father asked together, both relaxing in their chairs, letting the day's events wash over them.

"Ben called this afternoon. He and Tory were just back from the doctor. Tory's pregnant!"

"I'll be damned," James said, sitting up a little straighter.

Sam grinned, happy for his new cousin. Now that he'd spent a little time with Ben, his cousin was growing on him. Ben had a rough time growing up, from the sound of it, sacrificed a lot. Sam wished him and Tory the best.

"Another Montford," James said, his pipe in his raised hand as he pondered the good news. "How do you like that, Carol?" He smiled at his wife. "A year ago, we were two lonely old coots thinking we might've seen everything life had to offer—and look at us now. Two sons—" he glanced at Sam "—or damn close to it, two grandkids and another on the way.

Goes to show that you can't give up. As long as you're kicking, there could be a surprise waiting around the corner. A surprise of the pleasant variety."

The intimate look his parents shared could have seemed exclusive, but somehow it didn't make Sam feel shut out. He just felt damn lucky to be sitting there, part of this family. Loved.

"You're right, of course," Carol said. "As always. Gets a bit hard to take now and then, you know?" she teased, her expression changing to an impish grin. "You always being right, I mean."

Nearly seventy years old, and looking impish. Sam filed that away. Borough Bantam needed that grin.

"Now, if only I could convince the rest of the world…" James said, pretending to frown as he slipped his pipe back between his teeth.

"You ready for more news?" Carol asked.

"There's more?" Sam asked. James raised his eyebrows.

"There is." Carol nodded, grinning as she drew out the suspense. "Ben was telling me that Zack and Randi just found out that they're expecting, too."

"No kidding," James said contentedly. "Life is good, isn't it, Carol."

Sam probably would have filed away that reaction, too. But he was trying too hard to keep himself from darting out of his chair and into the night. His mother's last piece of news had made him wonder what was in the air. If babies were contagious.

That fanciful thought led to another—this one much more alarming. He knew how babies were made. And he and Cassie had done a fine job of illustrating that process a couple of weeks before. Without protection of any kind.

He'd been so caught up in all the emotional intensity surrounding that night. And he'd been used to making love to her without thoughts of birth control—after all, ten years ago they'd been hoping for a large family, the sooner the better—that the possibility of a baby hadn't dawned on him until this very moment.

Cassie was as regular as clockwork. Surely she'd have said something if it was the fertile part of her cycle. But there were always other factors to consider. Emotional upsets that changed timing.

He had to get over to her. Talk about that night. About possible repercussions. He had to take full responsibility. Giving her time was no longer an option.

"Think I'll go for a drive, if you two don't mind." He tried to keep the words casual. He certainly didn't need his parents suspecting anything—not until he'd spoken to Cassie.

He wondered if they could see his heart pounding in his chest.

"Don't hurt her, son."

James's warning followed him out into the night.

Chapter 15

"You want to come in and see a movie?" Phyllis asked as Cassie dropped her off after dinner in Phoenix on Friday night.

Cassie shook her head. "Thanks, but I'm in the middle of a dried-flower découpage on my kitchen wall. I want to get the first coat done tonight so it has time to dry before tomorrow."

Opening the passenger door of Cassie's Taurus, Phyllis said, "Well, dinner was a great idea. Thanks for asking me."

"Thanks for coming," Cassie replied. "I really needed to talk."

Climbing out, Phyllis turned and leaned against the door frame. "Yeah, well, you're also a good listener, Cassie. Do you want to do this again?"

"Are you kidding?" Cassie asked. "I was wondering if next week would be too soon for a repeat performance. There's that new Greek place we passed on the north side of Phoenix."

"How's Friday night?"

"Great!"

"I'll call you later in the week to set a time," Phyllis said. Then she added, "You take care, okay?"

Cassie put the car in gear. "I will."

"Call if you need me...."

Feeling more in control than she had in a long time, Cassie drove home, a Supertramp CD blaring on her stereo. *"Know who you are,"* she sang along.

It was advice she was working on. But not something she was certain she'd ever fully achieve. There were so many facets to life, so many roles to play, so many changes to adjust to—could anyone ever know who he or she really was?

And what about Phyllis? She seemed content with her life, had a meaningful career, was a good friend to so many people in this town. Yet when she'd talked tonight there'd been an underlying emptiness. She might assert that she was happy without a man in her life. But Cassie believed Phyllis wanted to be in a relationship and was scared to death to try again.

And who could blame her? She'd had her heart broken, not because of something she'd done but because of who she *was*.

As she considered this, Cassie suddenly frowned. Somebody was sitting on her front steps; she saw him when she passed her house on the way to her driveway. She didn't need to spot Sam's truck out by her garage to know it was him.

She wasn't really surprised. After the breakthrough they'd had with Mariah that afternoon, she'd been half expecting him to show up. Sam never seemed to just pick up a phone.

Now that she thought about it, he'd rarely called her when they were young. He'd always just appeared on her doorstep. Or at her locker, or her softball game, or her pew at church, or the grocery store where she'd worked for a while as a kid…

And she'd always been thrilled to see him.

But as she'd said before, *that was then*. This was now.

"How is she?" she asked in lieu of hello. She walked around to her front porch, joining him on the steps.

He was still wearing the shorts and white polo shirt he'd had on that afternoon. Cassie, having changed for her trip to Phoenix, felt overdressed by comparison in her form-fitting, short navy dress.

"She's asleep," Sam said. "But she ate every bite of her dinner."

"Did you talk to her doctor?"

Sam nodded, then gave Cassie a full report. Although he remained noticeably happy about the day's events, he seemed to have something else on his mind. He wasn't really meeting her eyes, was spending more time looking at the palm leaf between his fingers than at her.

He was making Cassie nervous.

"Did Mariah say any more?"

Sam shook his head. "Not yet, but it'll come."

Gazing out over her yard, Cassie said softly, "Be prepared. When she does start talking, I suspect she'll have some pretty horrible stories to tell."

"She may not remember them." But his protest was half-hearted.

"She remembers, Sam. You just have to look at that solemn little face to know."

He didn't argue.

The night air was hot—hotter than usual for May. Cassie felt a drop of sweat trickle between her breasts. Why was Sam just sitting here?

She wasn't going to invite him in. She couldn't.

"We need to talk, Cassie," he finally said, his voice firm.

"Okay." She wasn't sure what he thought they had to talk about. They'd already been over things. Gotten nowhere.

"Zack and Randi are expecting a baby."

"I know." The two of them had been like kids when they'd come in to tell Cassie the day before. She'd been the first to know.

And she'd been so happy for them, she'd worn a smile for the rest of the day. Right up until she'd come home last night…and remembered that she would never again know the joy of having a life growing inside her. Would never again experience that sweet anticipation Zack and Randi were now sharing. Never know the wonder of—

"Ben and Tory are expecting, too."

"No kidding!" She hadn't heard that. But she was happy for them, too. If anyone deserved a miracle, it was Tory Sanders. Cassie really admired the woman. Coming from an abusive past involving both her stepfather and her first husband, she'd managed to retain a sense of self—and an ability to love.

"We have to talk, Cassie."

He'd already said that.

She waited. And suddenly wished she hadn't eaten that order of honey chicken for dinner.

"When's your next period?"

Cassie choked on the breath she'd been sucking in. "Excuse me?"

"Have you had one since I was here last?"

"Nooo." Like it was any of his business anymore. Then it dawned on her where he was going.

"I didn't even think to use protection that night, Cass. Did you?" He turned his head, trying to meet her eyes in the glow from the streetlight.

Cassie looked away. "I didn't think at all that night."

"So we could be expecting, too."

"We aren't." Staring into the night, she had a sudden urge to run. To lose herself in the darkness. "If that's why you're worried, don't be."

Dropping the palm leaf, Sam threaded his fingers, elbows on his knees. "You just said you haven't had a period yet."

"I haven't, but…" Cassie searched for something to convince him. "The timing's not right." Something aside from the truth. She wasn't ready for that.

"So you'll be starting some time this next week?"

Okay, sure. "I guess." Since Emily, she hadn't been regular.

"And what if you don't?"

Cassie pulled her knees up to her chest, hugging them. She could think of only one conversation that could be worse. The one where he found out what he'd really left behind ten years ago.

"Then I'll have it the week after that," she snapped. Discussing her personal functions with him was far too intimate.

But more frightening was the direction in which they were heading. She had to tell him sometime. Not because he had a right to know; he'd lost that right when he'd abandoned her.

She needed him to know for *her*. So *she* could leave it all behind and move on for good. Her talks with Phyllis—and with Zack—had helped her see that. But she needed more time—

"And what if you don't?" Sam's voice broke into her thoughts.

"Don't what?"

"Have your period the week after that."

"Don't worry, I'll have it."

His hands still clasped in front of him, staring out at the street, Sam said, "I think we should get married."

"What?" Her voice was much louder than she'd intended.

"You might be pregnant, Cassie. I think we should get married."

He'd lost his mind.

Or she had.

"We've already done that. It's not something I care to repeat."

And yet…she did. Marriage to Sam was all she'd ever wanted. The Sam she'd seen these past weeks, loving his daughter, his parents. Doing little things to make her life easier. Appreciating the people of Shelter Valley. Playing basketball with his cousin, and her best friends.

It was the other parts of him that she couldn't bring herself to love again. He'd been unfaithful to her. Left her alone to deal with the birth—and death—of their child. How did a woman ever forget that? Or forgive it?

"We still love each other, Cassie," he said now. She could hear the frustration creeping into his voice.

She opened her mouth to deny what he'd said. Except that she couldn't. The night they'd made love again had made it impossible to deny that Sam still had power over her heart.

And he knew that, dammit.

"I'm not marrying you again."

"I'm not giving up on us."

Stalemate.

"Go home, Sam," Cassie said wearily. "You've got Mariah to concentrate on right now. She needs you."

"She needs you, too."

Cassie wasn't so sure about that. "It was Sammie she spoke to," she reminded him. "Which is something I've been meaning to talk to you about. Now that she's beginning to recover, you really should get her a dog of her own. One she knows is hers, part of her family, sharing her daily life. The sooner the better. Before she gets too attached to Sammie."

"Mightn't it already be too late?" Sam asked. She could see his brow crease in the dim light.

Cassie shook her head. "I don't think so. She's hardly even looked at Sammie. Right now, Sammie's just a dog. I don't think the particulars mattered. But they probably will from now on."

He turned his head toward her again. "You know anyone who might have a puppy for us, Doc?"

"I just might." Cassie folded her hands, clenching them to stop their trembling. "The litter my puppy's coming from is just being weaned. The puppies should be ready to leave their mother by next week. Last I heard, there was still one available. I can get you the owner's number on Monday, if you'd like."

"Thanks." And then he added, "You think Muffy'll be okay with another dog around?"

"Her nose might be out of joint for the first while, but as long as she still gets lots of attention, she'll probably just take the little one under her wing."

Silence fell, each of them staring out at the empty street. The family in the house across from hers went to bed. Cassie watched their upstairs lights go out, one by one.

Would Sam leave now?

"If you're pregnant, we should get married right away." Sam's low voice was startling in the silence.

Cassie swallowed. If he kept this up forever, could she keep fighting him forever? Did she have any other choice?

"I'm not going to marry you again."

"If you're pregnant—"

"I'm not pregnant," she interrupted sharply.

He turned to face her, his hand brushing her cheek briefly before dropping against his knee. "You don't know that for sure, Cass. If—"

"I do know for sure, Sam." She bit the words out. Whether she was ready or not, she couldn't keep this in anymore. "In fact, I couldn't be more sure."

He frowned, his head tilted as he tried to read the expression she was trying just as hard to hide. "What do you mean by that?"

"I can't have children, Sam," she said through gritted teeth. "Ever." All the agony she'd been struggling to subdue rose up to choke her. Telling Sam made it…final.

Because Sam was the only man she wanted to have a baby with.

Bitter tears spilled down her cheeks, and as Sam reached over to wipe them away with the pad of his thumb, Cassie bowed her head. She couldn't share even her tears with him. Couldn't have him trying to make it better.

He was ten years too late.

Sam froze, his hand suspended above Cassie's bent head, staring at her. She wasn't making any sense.

"Run that by me again?" He hadn't meant to whisper, but that was how the words came out.

"I can't have children."

Oh, God. Cassie infertile? That news must have killed her. Cassie had always wanted babies of her own. Sam ached for her.

"Why not?" His throat was dry.

"Scarring."

She was still crying. He could hear the tears in her voice. And felt so helpless. How could he fix this one?

"Scarring where? From what?" Maybe there was a specialist somewhere. They had the money; there had to be some way to help her.

But if this horrible thing was true, he now understood the emptiness he'd sensed in Cassie's life. In her heart. It wasn't just a matter of regaining her trust. This was much bigger. Much worse. She might still love him, but would that be enough? Marriage without the children she'd always wanted. Was this why she couldn't contemplate marrying again? Couldn't marry him—or anyone.

Were they destined to a life apart, after all, no matter how deeply they loved each other? Sam didn't want to believe that.

He'd asked about the scarring. She hadn't answered his question.

"Scarring from what, Cassie? How long ago? With all of today's new technologies—laser surgery and so on—maybe there's something that can be done."

Cassie's head shot up, her gaze locking with his, and Sam felt the shock of that look deep inside him. They weren't in this together. He was the enemy.

"It was ten years ago," she said, her voice hard, accusing. "And the scarring…was caused by…the problems I had when I—" She stopped, took a breath shuddering with sobs. "When I gave birth to our daughter."

Sam's heart stopped beating. He stared at her, numb. Her blunt words slammed into him over and over again.

This wasn't happening. This whole nightmare just wasn't happening.

He was vaguely aware of Cassie crying beside him, could feel her body next to him, shaking with sobs. Instinctively, he reached out to put his arm around her. To pull her close while they figured out what to do.

She shrugged him off.

"We had a daughter," he said woodenly. It didn't make sense. Wasn't real.

Cassie nodded. Her head bowed as she cried softly.

"Where is she?"

Cassie looked up then, and the agony in her eyes reverberated inside him. Somehow, he was responsible for this.

"Shall I take you to her, Sam?" she asked, tears pouring freely down her face.

Not in all his years of dealing with tragedies had he felt such utter despair.

"Please," he said slowly. Wherever his daughter was, he wanted to be with her. Wanted to share her with Cassie.

Shoulders slumped, Cassie walked slowly back to her car, climbed in and turned on the ignition, waiting only until Sam had shut the passenger door before shooting off down the drive.

Where was she, this child of his? Was she in a hospital, an institution? Where was she that, without any warning, they could go and see her after ten o'clock at night?

A horrible, logical possibility lodged itself in the back of his mind, but Sam couldn't acknowledge it.

"What's her name?" he asked, staring out the windshield, not blinking.

"Emily."

He could tell that talking was difficult for her, so he just let her drive, his mind scrambling furiously to work out what might lie ahead. And how he could somehow help them both through this. How he might make up to Cassie for whatever hell he had left her to deal with all alone.

When she made the second turn on a country road he recognized, Sam's throat closed up. His chest was so tight, he couldn't breathe. But that was okay. He wasn't sure he wanted to.

He knew, before she turned, where they were going. He watched her take the curves of the cemetery road without slowing.

The car stopped suddenly, and Cassie got out, stumbling as she approached the tiny headstone. Sam was beside her without even realizing he'd gotten out of the vehicle.

He read the small stone. *Emily Carol Montford.* After Cassie's mother. And his. Emily was born five months after Sam left home. And died a month later.

Pain seared through him.

"After you left, I couldn't eat, couldn't sleep." Cassie started to talk, each word laced with a despair so deep he knew she'd never be free of it. And with each word, Sam wished he was dead, too.

"Nobody suspected I was pregnant, at first. Including me. I'd lost track of days and weeks. Upset as I was, missing a period was to be expected. But then I started getting sick to my stomach every time I ate. For a long time the doctor thought it was stress, but when it got to the point where I couldn't keep anything down, she did a pregnancy test. I was almost four months along by then. I'd had no real nutrition for two months. No rest. No vitamins..."

She was trembling, her arms wrapped around her middle. Sam wanted to haul her into his own arms and shelter her.

He was afraid to touch her.

"I tried to take better care of myself after that. Quit school, made myself stay in bed as much as possible—but that just gave me more time to think. And I still couldn't keep much food down. For a while, they had me on an I.V. at home. That seemed to help, and I gradually gained back a little of the weight I'd lost...."

Bile rose in Sam's throat. While he'd been out finding himself, his wife had been home fighting death.

Jaw clenched, he felt as though he'd been carried off in a sea of anguish so treacherous, he knew he was never going to be the same again.

"I was seven-and-a-half months along when I started to hemorrhage." She stopped, swallowed. Wiped her nose and eyes with a tissue she'd brought from the car.

She handed one to Sam. Until that moment he hadn't known he was crying.

"It all happened very quickly after that. They did a cesarean, took Emily. She was beautiful...." Her voice broke completely, and Sam had to touch her, pull her into his arms, cradle her against his heart.

"I'm so sorry," he choked. "God, Cassie, I'd rather be dead myself...."

She lifted her head, but didn't draw away. "Her lungs weren't fully developed, but they thought she had a fighting chance," Cassie told him. "She had a strong heart."

She had to stop again. Took a couple of gulps of air. "I was in bed for the first few days because of the C-section—"

"I didn't notice any scarring." Sam hung everything on that point. Surely he'd have noticed a C-section scar on Cassie's smooth belly.

"It's right in the bikini line," she told him. "They made a big deal of telling me at the time that it wouldn't show. As if I cared..."

The anguish just kept growing. His young, beautiful wife, barely beyond childhood herself, having to face such a tragedy.

Alone.

Because of him.

Turning back to the headstone, Cassie bowed her head, crying harder. But she stayed close to Sam. He didn't deserve that sweet torture. He deserved to be as utterly alone as she had been.

"By the third day, they couldn't keep me away from her," she whispered hoarsely. "I was with her every minute after that. They tried to get me to go home, but I wouldn't leave the hospital. Not once that entire month."

"How big was she?" Sam asked, remembering Mariah's birth. The squalling, kicking seven-pound bundle of health and joy that she'd been.

"Just under five pounds."

Small enough to fit in his palm. Less than a bag of sugar. A tear dripped off Sam's chin.

He stared at the headstone, as if he could somehow picture the child who'd lived for such a short time. The child he would now never see.

"Could you hold her?"

Cassie nodded. "Every day. I fed her, helped bathe her, changed the pad under her little bottom…"

Cassie broke down completely then, her legs going limp as she fell against Sam, sobbing out ten years' worth of grief. Somehow Sam supported her weight, his gaze locked on that tiny tombstone.

Cassie was right. They couldn't ever go back.

He could never, in a million years, make this one up to her.

Or to himself.

Chapter 16

Cassie went one better than getting Sam the phone number of her client, the collie breeder. Mrs. Stonethaler had had a cancellation on one of the puppies and was delighted to have Cassie bring a potential buyer out to her home. So, late Tuesday morning, after Cassie had seen to her morning appointments at the clinic, she, Sam and Mariah were in Sam's truck on their way to the Stonethaler ranch. Although the air conditioning was on full blast, it hardly seemed to help. Cassie had taken off the white lab coat she often wore at the clinic, but she still felt hot in her linen slacks and sleeveless silk blouse. Sam didn't look any more comfortable in his denim cutoffs.

Cassie couldn't tell if Mariah was comfortable or not. Her sweet face showed no sign of distress at the nearly one-hundred-degree heat. In her cute pink sundress, with its bows tied at the shoulders, she certainly *looked* cool and composed.

"Are you excited about having a puppy of your own?" Cassie asked the child. When Mariah didn't reply, Cassie continued, infusing her voice with a cheer she was trying very hard to feel. "Mrs. Stonethaler is the owner of the puppies' mommy, and she's a very nice lady. She'd be happy if you could give one of her puppies a home."

Mrs. Stonethaler raised collies, she told Mariah. Mr. Stonethaler raised Arabian horses. Cassie told Sam he ought to be glad Mariah was only in need of a puppy. An Arabian horse would have cost him thousands of dollars.

Sam nodded, brushed his free hand down Mariah's French-braided hair, and continued to drive.

Cassie fell back into the uneasy silence that had marked their relationship since they'd returned from the cemetery the other night. They'd seen each other in church the next morning, when Cassie had made a point of speaking to an unresponsive Mariah. Sam, his eyes filled with shadows, had merely nodded at her and disappeared.

Today he hadn't once met her eyes. Twice she'd started to speak to him about Emily, then stopped. He'd created such an effective wall between them, it was almost as if he wasn't there.

She should be happy about that. She was finally getting her wish—Sam Montford out of her life.

Except that she didn't feel happy.

Telling him about Emily had brought it all back. The helplessness. The fear. The anger. The guilt.

Unexpectedly, sharing it with Sam had brought her

closer to him, reawakening needs, reminded her that Sam was the other half of her heart. With him she'd been able to reason out the ways of the world, make sense of them. Find a way to be peaceful with them.

But when it came to Emily's brief life, her death, there was no peace to find.

Cassie was worried about Sam. After they'd left Emily's grave, he'd shut himself off. It was the first time in her life that Cassie had been with him and completely unable to *feel* him.

It was unsettling. Frightening. As if she'd looked in the mirror and seen a face that didn't belong to her.

Mrs. Stonethaler, after showing them to the nursery, as she called it, in the sun room of her huge home, left them alone with one of the puppies that was, as yet, unclaimed. The mother and other puppies were in a large crate at the other end of the room.

"What do you think, Mariah?" Cassie asked, holding the puppy. "She looks just like Sammie, only smaller."

Mariah, clutching Sam's hand, was engrossed in the three buttons on the collar of his short-sleeved shirt.

"Has she said anything since Friday?" Cassie asked Sam. She'd wanted to ask him yesterday on the phone, when they'd made today's arrangements, but he'd had to go before she had a chance.

Glancing down at his daughter, Sam shook his head. And then said, "Mariah, don't you want to look at the puppy?" With his hands on her shoulders, he turned the child to face Cassie. "If you like her, you can have her."

Mariah stared vacantly in front of her, eyes slightly lowered.

Cassie knelt down, until the puppy was at Mariah's eye level. "You have to see if you like her, honey, before we can buy her for you. She needs to know that she's going to a home where she's wanted, or she'll be afraid."

The child blinked. Her tiny hands squeezed into fists.

Cassie tried to catch Sam's gaze, to see if he'd caught Mariah's response, but he didn't meet her eye.

"Let's sit down and see if the puppy likes us," Cassie said, pulling Mariah onto the ground with her.

Sam stood back, his expression brooding as he watched them. For a second, Cassie couldn't take her eyes off him. He looked so good to her, standing there. Fit. Sexy. Strong. His legs were defined, his stomach lean and trim at the waist, his chest straining against his polo shirt. Manual labor sure hadn't done anything to hurt Sam in the looks department.

The puppy squirmed in her arms. She'd been gnawing on Cassie's finger—not that Cassie had even noticed.

"You're so cute!" Cassie said, raising the puppy to her face. "Look, Mariah, she has a white spot on her nose."

Mariah blinked again. Not once had she turned around to look at Sam.

Putting the puppy down, Cassie pushed the wriggling bundle over to Mariah, and then moved back. Again she tried to meet Sam's eyes. Again his focus was solely on Mariah.

With her little butt up in the air, the puppy danced around the child, smelling her hands, tasting her sandal. Then, apparently finding the child acceptable for further inspection, she climbed onto Mariah's lap. Her hands on the floor, the little girl didn't move. The puppy did enough moving for both of them. She licked Mariah's arm. Turned around several times in her lap. Jumped off. And back on.

Mariah blinked again, but sat completely still. The puppy, apparently not offended by Mariah's unresponsiveness, put her front paws on her chest, sniffing her chin. And then she lunged up, grabbing one of the ties to Mariah's dress and tugging hard.

Cassie and Sam both started forward at the same time, intending to rescue the little girl, but before either one of them could reach her, they stopped, shocked by the sound they heard.

Mariah was laughing.

She ceased abruptly, as soon as she heard herself— but it had happened. She'd taken a step forward. There was no going back now.

Cassie's gaze collided with Sam's over the child's head. His were filled with tentative hope. Gratitude. And sorrow, too.

They'd deal with that later. For now, Cassie's stomach relaxed simply because she'd connected with him again.

She'd deal with that later, too.

Motioning to Sam to stay put, Cassie left the puppy on Mariah's lap, until the puppy's exuberant attempt to untie the bows at her shoulders began to succeed and the child finally reached up with one hand to push the puppy down.

She didn't, however, push the dog away.

Cassie had an idea. "Do you want the puppy, Mariah?" she asked.

Mariah froze, as though she'd been caught doing something she shouldn't.

Moving a little closer on the ceramic-tiled floor, she lifted the little girl's chin. "If you want that puppy, she's all yours, but you have to *tell* me you do," she said seriously. "I need to know she's going to be loved, or I can't ask Mrs. Stonethaler to sell her to us."

Mariah's hand slid quickly up and down the puppy's back. The child wanted that dog. Cassie's instincts were telling her so.

Which meant it was time to help Mariah help herself. The child had given them enough signs to let them know she was ready. Praying she wasn't pushing too hard too fast, Cassie sat back, letting go.

"I mean it, Mariah. I can't let you have that puppy unless you promise me that you really, really want her."

Sam stepped a little closer, standing protectively behind the little girl. Cassie couldn't look at him, couldn't be distracted. She had a feeling Mariah was really struggling, that she had things to tell them.

"You don't want to hurt Cassie's feelings, do you, squirt?" he asked, and Cassie breathed a little easier. He was on her side.

The child didn't say anything, but she continued to stroke the puppy's fur. And when the puppy started to squirm away, she reached out her other hand to keep her in place.

Mariah wanted that dog.

Cassie swallowed. Took a deep breath. And plunged in. "Mariah, I know you understand what we're saying to you. I know you can answer us. And I know you want that dog. What I *don't* know is why you won't talk to us. Please, sweetie. Sam and I are the only ones here. We both love you very much and we'll do anything to help, but you've got to talk to us, sweetie. You've got to tell us what's going on so we know what to do."

When Mariah shook her head, every nerve in Cassie's body tensed. She felt Sam settle beside her, and was a little afraid to have him there.

"Why?" Cassie asked, her throat raw with the effort it took to control her emotions. "Why won't you talk to us, sweetie?"

The child's head moved slowly as she looked up at Cassie. Her eyes were clear, focused. And filled with tears. And then she lowered her head again.

"When I talked, it killed my mommy."

She'd spoken! Such beautiful sounds. Such unthinkable sentiments. Cassie felt Sam tense beside her, but didn't dare look at him. She had a job to do. Swallowing the lump in her throat, Cassie forged ahead.

"No, honey, don't ever think that," she said. "Bad men killed your mother. You had nothing to do with it."

She felt like such a fraud. She hadn't been there. Had only vague reports to go by. God only knows what images the child might be seeing as she stared at the floor.

"Are you remembering things, honey? Things you thought you'd forgotten?"

Mariah shrugged. A tear trickled off her chin.

Sam moved then, pulling his daughter onto his lap, cradling her against him. "I know with all my heart that your mommy and daddy would want you to talk to me. You know that, don't you, Mariah?"

The little girl stared up at him, her big blue eyes filled with tears. She nodded—and then she opened that rosebud mouth and the vile stories started pouring out.

Mrs. Stonethaler, probably wondering what was taking so long, had come back to check on them, but with one look at the situation, merely whispered that they should take all the time they needed. She quietly closed the door as she left them alone.

"They had a big knife, Sam," Mariah was saying, the words once released coming so quickly that Cassie could hardly understand them. It seemed that now Mariah had decided to break her vow of silence, she couldn't get rid of her thoughts fast enough.

Cassie, stayed in the background, an outsider now. On the one hand, she could hardly believe the miracle of hearing that sweet childish voice; on the other, she was hurting with each word the child uttered. *Precious, precious little girl, you should never have seen such things.*

"They cut Daddy and made him bleed, and they hit him and made his eye all puffy and then his mouth was bleeding and he told Mommy and me how much he loved us and he told me to be brave and mind my mommy and they took him away. He couldn't walk good because they kicked his leg and he kept falling..."

Through it all, Sam's expression of warmth and love never changed. He slowly rocked the child, smoothing the hair back from her forehead. Cassie, tears streaming down her face, could only imagine what that control was costing him.

"They took some other people, too, and they went

away for a while, and Mommy and me just cried and said how much we loved each other, and Mommy told me we'd see Daddy again real soon, that the men just took him out so I wouldn't see him bleeding while they got a big Band-Aid..."

Mariah's blue eyes were focused on Sam's mouth, her little finger reaching up to touch it. "I knew they weren't going to help him, Sam. They were bad men. But I didn't know about the not-breathing part. When you stop breathing, you *die,* Sam. The bad men hurt Mommy and Daddy because I talked and cried when they told me to shut up and they made them stop breathing, and I'm scared you're going to stop breathing, too...."

Her tirade ended as abruptly as it had begun. Mariah clutched Sam's shirt in her fists and buried her face against his chest.

"No, Mariah," he said soothingly. "I'm not going to stop breathing."

"I watch you, Sam. And every time you talk, I can't see your chest go up and down so I don't know if you're going to stop breathing...."

"And that scares you, huh?" Cassie asked, understanding so much now.

Sobbing, the little girl nodded.

Cassie reached over, rubbing Mariah's arm. "Sometimes people you care about die, honey. But then there are other people who love you who'll still be around to help you when you're lonely. They'll go on loving you and living with you and taking care of you. That's how God makes it when someone goes to live with Him."

Mariah shook her head. "Mommy wasn't there." The words were muffled against Sam's shirt.

"Wasn't where?" Sam asked, frowning.

"God's house."

Cassie could hardly make out the words, meeting Sam's look over Mariah's head. What was Mariah talking about?

"People said Mommy went to live with God, but when you took me to God's house to make Grandma happy, Mommy wasn't there."

Sam's frown cleared suddenly, and he pulled Mariah away so he could look into her eyes. "Church is called 'God's house' because that's where people go to talk to him, but He doesn't *live* there, honey. He lives up in heaven, and that's where your mommy and daddy are."

"Are…are they better now? Did they stop bleeding? They don't hurt anymore, do they?"

Sam swallowed hard.

Cassie sensed how urgently Mariah needed to know that her parents were no longer in pain. And she got her first real glimpse of the precocious child Mariah must have been before tragedy shattered her life.

"They don't hurt anymore, honey," Sam said with obvious difficulty. "They're all better. And they're looking down at you now, glad that you're better, too."

"Are you sure, Sam?" the child whispered.

"Absolutely sure."

Cassie knew there were some grueling counseling sessions ahead for the little girl, and for Sam, too. But Mariah could resume her life now.

And Cassie could finally get on with the rest of *her* life.

Whatever that was going to be.

* * *

Two weeks later, Cassie was reading her favorite section of the Sunday morning paper—the comics—when she stopped short, chills spreading through her body.

The folks at Borough Bantam had been in a furor for weeks now, with the newcomer in their midst, and the little mouse appearing from nowhere, being adopted by the king and queen. Cassie followed her favorite comic strip religiously, had since its inception, though she couldn't explain, even to herself, what made it so special. She just knew that her week wasn't complete without it.

And now, here she was, sitting alone at her kitchen table in her pajamas on a Sunday morning, wondering, once again, where she was going to find the strength to be happy. With Mariah no longer needing her help, Cassie had only seen her and Sam twice. Once when they picked up "Teddy" from the clinic, and the second time when they brought her back in to be wormed.

Mariah was thriving. Though there were still shadows in her eyes, times when she was very quiet, she was well on the way to recovery. She was certainly thrilled to have her new puppy, and held her very tenderly. And she obviously adored Sam.

Cassie wasn't surprised. He'd be a wonderful father. She'd always known that about him.

He barely spoke to her. And never met her eyes. At first she thought it was because of her, because he was angry with her, but as soon as she'd had time to think—and talk to Phyllis—she'd figured out that it was himself he couldn't forgive.

For something he could never change.

Cassie understood that. She'd been hating him for a long time. And hating herself, as well.

And, oddly enough, this little comic strip had expressed not only the feelings she'd been struggling with, but the resolution she'd finally arrived at.

Ripping it out, Cassie hurried back to her bedroom, and quickly got dressed in a pair of shorts and a white T-shirt. She brushed her teeth and ran a comb through her hair, though she didn't take the time to pull her hair back or put it up. Then she went to find Sam before he left for church.

Sam was sitting out front in cutoff shorts, waiting for his mom and dad and Mariah to leave for church, before he headed up to his office above the garage. The only remedy he knew for what ailed him, the only way to cope with the unending regret, was to work.

He recognized Cassie's Taurus, as she pulled into his parents' drive. His heart going into overdrive, he strolled down to meet her. Something must be wrong for her to come roaring up here like that.

"We have to talk," she said, her door open before she'd even put the car in park.

"Sure," Sam said, forgetting for the moment that he'd taken himself out of her life—because the only way to lessen her pain was to stay away. Not to be a constant reminder of everything she'd lost.

She got out and shut the door. "In private."

"My office is over the garage," Sam said, leading the way. "We'll be alone there."

When they reached the office, she took a cursory look around, seeming to approve of the big metal desk, the bookshelves covering one whole wall, the easels and tools stacked neatly in a corner. "I'm also taking over the fourth stall in the garage downstairs," he told her, "as a supply house and storeroom for the renovation business."

Cassie nodded, took a seat on the leather couch he'd brought over from his parents' attic, and slapped his comic strip down on the wood-slatted coffee table. *Borough Bantam*.

"Have you read this?" she demanded.

Things were coming at him so fast, Sam's heart was about to beat out of his chest. He hadn't seen Cassie like this since before he'd betrayed her all those years ago. So full of spunk and confidence.

What was going on?

"Yeah, I've read it," he said warily, circling the table. Did she know? Was she angry with him?

"Well, read it again," she told him. "Especially that last frame."

Sam didn't need to read it. He knew it by heart. He'd written the damn thing. But because he wasn't sure what she knew or where she was going with any of this, he picked it up and read it, anyway.

He'd written the strip shortly after Mariah's near-seizure in the gym. The king and queen had just discovered that the newcomer was the knight who'd run out on them years ago, leaving them undefended and defenseless when the kingdom, for the first time in its 600-year history, came under attack. The newcomer had returned to the Borough, to his home, to protect its inhabitants. In his years of wandering, he'd learned much. And he'd realized that there was nothing to be had worth having that he couldn't find at home. The king and queen, upon identifying him, didn't scorn

him as he'd expected. They welcomed him home, like
the prodigal son. They saw into his heart and knew
that he'd never have left them if he'd thought the Borough would ever be at risk. He'd have given his life
for them, if he had to. At the end of the strip, the
stupid magistrate still didn't seem to realize that the
newcomer was in the Borough—had no idea that his
position was being usurped. That he was going to be
replaced by someone relatively new to the Borough, a
long-lost brother of the king. And he'd managed, with
carefully chosen words and pictures, to convey all of
that in one week's episode.

The ending was, as always, the magistrate in his
little circle, a worm going round and round. *I am. I
am. I am.*

"Don't you see?" Cassie said, when he looked up.
"It's us, Sam. Not *exactly,* of course, but this is like
you and me. You left, Sam, but you wouldn't have if
you'd realized how much I needed you. You'd have
given everything to be here with Emily and me. Just
like that wild kingdom would have—to protect the
kingdom."

His breath caught in his throat. Did she know? Or
didn't she?

He wasn't sure what to say. Wasn't sure what *she*
was saying.

"We have to forgive ourselves," Cassie said. "Both
of us—we have to forgive ourselves and each other."

Sam frowned. What did she have to forgive herself
for? And there couldn't possibly be anything *he* had
to forgive *her* for.

"We've made some pretty serious mistakes," she
said, looking up at him, her beautiful brown eyes be-

seeching. "I know you're hating yourself for what happened after you left town, and part of me has been hating you all these years, too. Or at least trying to."

He'd figured that out at the cemetery; hearing her give voice to the words were a knife to his heart. Cassie's hatred was the worst form of torture. But one he deserved.

"Mostly, I was so badly hurt, I couldn't do anything but try to cope with that—not to care—but when you came back, I was scared to find out that I *did* still care. And that all the hate I thought I'd stored up wasn't really there. I couldn't understand that. Until today."

She'd definitely lost him now. As her eyes reiterated what her words had just told him, his heart gave a hopeful lurch—but he knew there was no hope. Not for him. Not with her.

"What happened today?" he asked.

"I read this." She picked up the comic strip. "I wasn't just hating you, Sam. I was hating me, too. I should've known I was pregnant. I'd always been so regular, I should've suspected—"

"How could you be expected to keep track of *anything* after what I'd done to you?"

Cassie shrugged. "I should have been stronger, more…more my own person, able to handle having you gone. If I'd realized sooner, who knows what might have happened differently? Maybe if I'd taken vitamins sooner, gotten more sleep, better nutrition…"

Sam couldn't let her go on. "Cass, don't do this to yourself. You did the best you could." He sat down beside her, took both her hands in his. "Look inside yourself, honey. Listen to the truth. You know you would never have put our baby in danger, would have given your life to save her."

"I know," Cassie said, grinning through a sudden spurt of tears. "Just like in this strip," she said, waving it in front of him. "The knight would have stayed, given his life, if he'd known how badly he was needed."

Sam sat back, stunned, as he started to suspect what she was trying to say.

"You would never have left if you'd known I was pregnant, Sam. You'd have stayed, gone to law school, become the mayor of Shelter Valley in a heartbeat, if you'd known the cost of your leaving."

Of course he would have. But Borough Bantam was just a damn comic strip. Emily Carol Montford was his *daughter,* for God's sake.

Cassie stroked a finger across the back of his hand. "You know, I've been doing a lot of thinking, and I can see now that I was to blame, too, long before you left town."

"No!" Sam said sharply. "You were the best wife a man could ask for, Cassie. So loving. Unselfish. Doing special little things every day to let me know you loved me."

"But I stopped listening to you with my *heart,*" she whispered, her eyes shadowed. "I promised to love and cherish you forever, and then, after we were married, I—I didn't hear you, Sam, because I wasn't listening. You tried to give me clues, I can see that now. That time when you asked me to look at model homes in Phoenix. You said for decorating ideas, but then you went on and on about the community center there. You were looking for a way out, and I never even gave it another thought."

He had really liked that community center. It'd had a full-scale basketball court. An entire floor of exercise equipment. An Olympic-size swimming pool. And acres and acres of parkland.

"I should've tried harder to explain."

"Maybe you didn't come right out and tell me what was wrong," Cassie continued. "But you didn't *know* what was wrong, so how could you make it clear to me?" Sam was moved by how much thought she'd given all of this. Moved, but not surprised. This was his Cassie—the woman he'd been loving for as long as he'd known what love was.

"You needed my help to figure things out, but I'd been too busy living the life we'd already chosen, the life people expected us to live."

"You're being very generous—you know that, don't you?" Sam asked, a wry grin on his face.

He was afraid to hope, but it felt damn good to be able to talk to her again. To really talk. With no battle-scarred walls between them.

Cassie shook her head. "I'm not, Sam," she said. "I'm being honest. With you, and with myself. I've been blaming you all these years, because without you here, it was easier to do that. But I've known, deep inside, that it was my fault, too."

Perhaps, although most of the blame was still his, he told himself. Yet she might have found a way to set him free. Because she was right. He would never have left this town if he'd thought, for one second, that tragedy would follow in his wake.

He'd left for Cassie. Because he'd been afraid, after

his betrayal, after sleeping with another woman, that his staying would destroy her. He couldn't trust himself not to hurt her.

Acting purely on instinct now, Sam leaned forward, placed his lips against hers and, in the best way he knew how, begged for her forgiveness. Her lips opened to him and welcomed him home.

When the kiss turned into more, when Sam knew that if he continued he was going to have her naked on this old leather couch, he stopped. But he couldn't make himself pull away. He sat back on the sofa, pulling her close to him, instead.

If they were going to find a second chance—and he was completely determined that they were—there had to be a little more honesty. Another revelation.

"Cass? About Borough Bantam—"

"Oh, Sam, have you ever read that strip?" she interrupted.

Sam nodded, looking for the right words to tell her that he'd read every single episode that had ever been printed. Would she lose some of her faith in him if she knew he'd been using Shelter Valley all these years?

"Did it mean to you what it meant to me?" she asked him, almost eagerly.

Sam hesitated. "I don't know. What did it mean to you?"

She laughed a little self-consciously. "You're going to think I'm crazy, but I almost feel as if that strip saved my life, Sam. You have no idea how many times I was at the end of my rope, and then I'd read that thing and some simple little truth would pop out—as though it was written just for me. It always seemed to be what I needed to hear."

His throat tight, Sam fought back the overwhelming emotion that threatened to overcome him. The true freedom she'd just given him.

He hadn't deserted her, after all.

"You do think I'm crazy," she said, her shoulders settling back against the couch.

"No—" Sam started, and when his voice broke, had to start again. "I'm thanking God there was a way for us to be together even when we were worlds apart," Sam said. "If ever I needed confirmation that you and I were ordained to find each other, confirmation that what we have is stronger then either of us, this was it."

Cassie turned, frowning as she looked at him. "What are you talking about? The strip helped you, too?"

"I wrote that strip, Cass. I am S.N.C."

She jumped up. "No way!" And sank back down, her hand on his chest as she stared at him. Then, grabbing up the comic strip, she stared at it. "You're S.N.C. What does S.N.C. stand for?"

"Sam 'n' Cassie."

Epilogue

Sam and Cassie Montford were remarried the last weekend in May of that year. Until they found a house they just *had* to have, they were going to live with Carol and James, who weren't too proud to beg them to stay. Nor too proud to pull out all the stops, either. Mariah needed them, they said.

They sold Cassie's house to Tory and Ben, who were delighted with all the space. And the decorating. Ben was already working at Montford, Inc., and James had started to groom him for the mayoralty campaign, expecting him to take over the mayor's seat from Junior Smith in the November elections. Ben thought he was going to finish college first; Sam didn't think so.

Ben would get his college degree—Sam had no doubt of that—but he'd be reaching his other goals a lot sooner than that. Sam knew how Shelter Valley worked, and Ben would figure it out soon enough.

With a little brown bag in his hand, Sam approached the suite he was going to be sharing with Cassie at Montford Mansion. It was his wedding night. And what a night it was going to be.

But there was something that had to be done first.

"Sam?" Cassie called from the open bathroom door. He heard the sound of water, telling him she was in the double-wide garden tub.

"Yeah?" he asked. He shouldn't be feeling relieved by the brief reprieve her bath was giving him. But he was. A little weak in the knees, he sat down on the side of the bed.

He was probably wrong. Putting himself through this for nothing. Would be putting *her* through it in a couple of minutes, too. But if there was one thing Sam did well, it was to learn from his mistakes.

"Can I ask you something?" she called out.

"Sure." Dropping the bag on his dresser as he passed, Sam stood in the bathroom doorway. And almost talked himself out of the test he was planning. Cassie looked stunning, lounging back against the side of the tub, bubbles caressing her milky skin, her breasts and nipples provocatively revealed.

"Why did every episode end with *I am, I am, I am?*"

So far, Borough Bantam was still his and Cassie's secret, but she was nagging him to share it. She was sure everyone in Shelter Valley would be proud as hell. He figured, eventually, that she was going to win this one.

"I wondered that for a long time myself," Sam admitted now, thinking about her question. "He was a worm, something most people think of as slimy and disgusting."

"Which is how you saw yourself."

"Maybe."

She arched her brow at him.

"Okay, yes. But he also represented the never-changing values of Shelter Valley. It took me a while to figure all this out. Regardless of what happens in the world, we can always count on the people here to continue, to be who they are. Family and community are the things that matter to us. It's been that way for over a hundred years.

"It was how I reminded myself that Shelter Valley, and my place here—whatever that turned out to be—were waiting."

Cassie smiled at him. "I thought you'd say you were trying to send me a message."

Sam shrugged, a little embarrassed. "I think I was. I just didn't dare hope you'd ever get that message."

Cassie's eyes brimmed with tears. "I got it, Sam. How could I not? It was from you."

Sam turned, reaching for the bag on the other side of the doorway. If he didn't do this now, it wouldn't get done.

"Hey, mister." She called him back. "You wanna join me?"

Taking a deep breath, Sam turned again. "I want you to get out, Cass," he said. "At least for a minute."

Frowning, probably at his tone of voice, Cassie sat up, holding a washcloth over her breasts. "What's wrong?" And then she saw the bag. "What's in there?"

Sam pulled out the box he'd bought earlier that day, when he'd gone into town to pick up Cassie's flowers for the simple ceremony they'd had in the living room at Montford Mansion.

"No," Cassie said as soon as she saw the box.

"Yes."

"Don't do this, Sam." Her eyes were full of tears. "We're so lucky to have Mariah. And we can adopt others if we want to. But don't keep hoping. I can't bear to hope with you—"

Her voice broke, and she stood, reached for a towel, began drying herself.

"You haven't had a period in almost two months, Cassie."

He'd asked again the day she'd come to his office, and she'd told him she hadn't had one yet but had assured him she would soon. They'd been making love ever since, and Sam knew for a fact that it hadn't happened yet.

"I've been irregular ever since Emily." She said the words softly but firmly. She wanted no part of this.

But he wasn't giving up. "Please, Cass, just humor me here? It's not even that I'm hoping, because I'm not. I've got you, and that's enough to keep me happy for twenty lifetimes." He turned her to face him, his eyes earnest as he looked into hers. "You had problems before because you didn't find out you were pregnant in time. Every day that your period isn't here, I'm more afraid of what might be happening, what could go wrong. Please, won't you take a couple of minutes to set my mind at ease?"

Cassie held his gaze for another couple of minutes, then grabbed the box from him. "Give me a little privacy, will you?" she grumbled.

His wife was not happy with him.

Sam left the room, but didn't close the door. He didn't want her feeling trapped in there, all alone.

As soon as he could tell she was finished, he went back in.

"How about we get back in that tub now?" he asked.

"Don't you want to wait for the results? It'll only be a minute."

Sam shook his head. He'd check later, just to make sure she was right. And then the worry would be behind him.

Dropping her towel, Cassie climbed back into the tub, but she was distracted. Sam undressed and joined her. She didn't even seem to notice he was there.

She finally just got out. Dripping water all over the bathroom, she headed for the little vial with the stick. "Damn it, why did you have to do this?" she cried. "I was just fine until you—"

Her voice stopped, and the stick in her hand fell to the floor.

"What?" Sam asked, flooding the floor as he leaped out of the tub.

Cassie looked up at him, tears streaming down her face, a joy that he'd never seen before in her luminous brown eyes. A spiritual joy, a connection, that he felt clear to the depths of his heart.

"I am," she said. *"I am. I am."*

* * * * *

We hope you enjoyed reading

STRANGERS IN PARADISE

by *New York Times* bestselling author

HEATHER GRAHAM and

SHELTERED IN HIS ARMS

by *USA TODAY* bestselling author

TARA TAYLOR QUINN

Both were originally Harlequin® Silhouette
Intimate Moments and HQN stories!

Discover more compelling tales of heart-racing
romance and high-stakes suspense from the
Harlequin® Romantic Suspense series.
Featuring strong, adventurous women and brave
men, **Harlequin® Romantic Suspense** stories
are filled with powerful relationships and life-and-
death situations that deliver a strong emotional
punch and a guaranteed happily-ever-after.

(H) HARLEQUIN®

ROMANTIC suspense

Heart-racing romance, high-stakes suspense!

Look for four *new* romances every month
from **Harlequin Romantic Suspense!**

Available wherever books are sold.

www.Harlequin.com

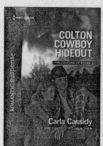

HARLEQUIN®

ROMANTIC suspense

Heart-racing romance, high-stakes suspense!

Save $1.00

on the purchase of

COLTON COWBOY HIDEOUT

by Carla Cassidy, available July 5, 2016, or on any other Harlequin® Romantic Suspense book.

Available wherever books are sold, including most bookstores, supermarkets, drugstores and discount stores.

Save $1.00

on the purchase of any Harlequin Romantic Suspense book.

52614095

5 65373 00076 2   (8100)0 12200

NYTCOUP0716

Her voice sounded oddly hollow. "Something wrong?" he asked, doubling back.

Mirabella turned the monitor so he could see the screen more readily. The anonymous email sender was back. He glanced at the time stamp and saw the email had been sent out early this morning. It was the first thing she had seen when she'd opened her computer.

"What new bridegroom is getting away with murder?" the first line read. "Better be careful and watch your back, Mirabella, or you might be next on his list."

Anger spiked within him. Zane bit back a number of choice words. Cursing at the sender, or at her computer, would accomplish exactly nothing. He needed to take some kind of effective action, not merely rail impotently at shadows.

Zane put his hand on her shoulder in a protective gesture.

"Don't be afraid, Belle. I'm going to track this infantile scum down. I won't let him get to you."

He meant physically, but she took it to mean mentally. "He's already gotten to me, but I'm not afraid," she fired back. "I'm angry. This jerk has no right to try to say what he's saying, to try to poison people's minds against us." Her eyes flashed as she turned toward Zane. "What the hell is his game?"

Her normally porcelain cheeks were flushed with suppressed fury. He'd never seen her look so angry—nor so desirable. Instead of becoming incensed, which he knew was what this anonymous vermin was after, Zane felt himself becoming aroused. By Mirabella.

Now wasn't the time, he upbraided himself.

It was *never* going to be the time, he reminded himself in the next moment. He'd married her to save her reputation, to squelch the hurtful, damaging rumors. Stringing up the person saying all those caustic things about them, about *her*, did not lead to the "and they all lived happily ever after" ending he was after—even if it might prove to be immensely satisfying on a very primal level.

Nothing wrong with a little primal once in a while, Zane caught himself thinking as his thoughts returned to last night.

Don't miss
THE PREGNANT COLTON BRIDE
by USA TODAY *bestselling author Marie Ferrarella,*
available August 2016 wherever
Harlequin® Romantic Suspense
books and ebooks are sold.

www.Harlequin.com